MURDER AMONG THE RUBBLE

TAM MAY

Murder Among The Rubble

Adele Gossling Mysteries: Book 7

Tam May

Published by Dreambook Press.

Click or visit:
https://www.tammayauthor.com

Cover Design © 2024 by Aries/100 Covers

ISBN: 9781734671469

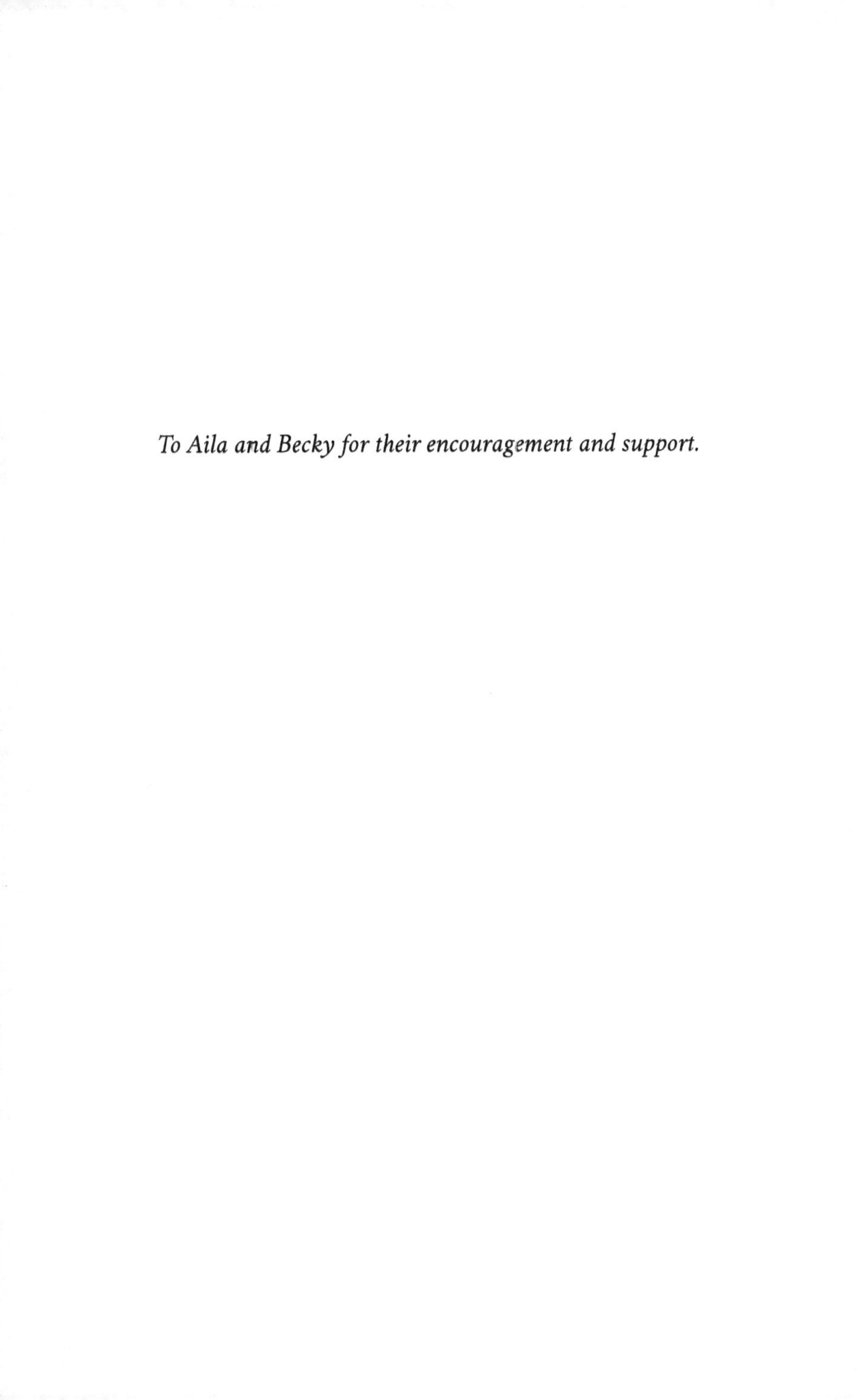

To Aila and Becky for their encouragement and support.

AUTHOR'S NOTE

<u>Screaming Horses Tell No Lies: The Great 1906 San Francisco Earthquake</u>

While no one could predict an earthquake of massive proportions would shake San Francisco to its core, they could have predicted the damage and destruction such an earthquake would cause.

The 1906 San Francisco earthquake is still considered the biggest natural disaster in California. Indeed, it's high on the list of the deadliest natural disasters in American history, right up there with Hurricane Katrina in 2005. The earthquake exposed the corrupt politics, vice, and racism running rampant in what was then the greatest city in the Far West. At the same time, it also showed the deep resilience of the people of San Francisco in its aftermath and brought the city together in a way that was much needed at that time. San Franciscans are no angels, but they come together with a "roll up your sleeves and get it done" attitude when necessary. From the beginning, the plan was to get rid of the weak structures that were a result of political corruption and build a stronger, better, and more modern city.

The details of the earthquake and the fires that followed are well documented. At 5:12 a.m. on April 18, 1906, a large-scale earthquake hit the Bay Area. It began in the ocean rather than on land, and rolled its way to shore, damaging about 300 miles of Northern California. The most affected cities were those on the coastline: Santa Rosa, San Mateo, Santa Cruz, and, of course, San Francisco. Reports of how strong the earthquake was vary, but the consensus is that it was around the 7.7-7.9 range. In contrast, the Loma Prieta earthquake, which struck the Bay Area on October 17, 1989, was in the 6.9 range.

The only ones who knew the earthquake was coming were the animals. Morgan Thomas and Max Morgan-Wittis describe in their book, *The San Francisco Earthquake: A Minute-by-Minute Account of the 1906 Disaster*, the extreme agitation and nervousness of the city's horses, screeching and fidgeting only hours before the disaster happened.

When the earthquake hit the city, the forty-five-to-sixty seconds it lasted caused eighty percent of the city to lie in ruins. Part of this wasn't due to the earthquake itself but to the fires that burned for four days afterward.

The cause of the fires is a little vague, but historians believe many were a result of human error. Some say the fires were started by an unsuspecting housewife living in the South of Market area (then known as South of the Slot). Intent on making breakfast for her family, she lit the gas stove, unaware the gas lines had burst, and this caused a domino effect of fires burning through the downtown area. Another source cites the earthquake as upsetting wood-burning stoves that then toppled and lit buildings aflame. There was no doubt that the inexperience of firefighters and the military left to deal with such a disaster may have been responsible as well. They chose to dynamite buildings to avoid their being burned down once the fires reached them, but it was said their clumsy use of dynamite caused more fires to ignite.

The death toll was over 3,000, all told, with about 900 of those in the city alone, though one source I read estimates that, due to lost records, it was probably higher.

When I first conceived of this book in the Adele Gossling Mysteries series, I knew it was going to take place around the time of the earthquake. Because Adele's roots lie in San Francisco, I didn't want to ignore this life-changing event. But as I researched the tragedy, what fascinated me more than the quake and fires themselves was the rebuilding that took place in San Francisco after all the fires had burned out and the city was a mass of rubble, ruin, and black smoke.

How does a major city on the West Coast recover after a natural disaster that leaves a quarter of a million people homeless with nothing more than the clothes on their backs and what they can carry on them?

In this case, the political entities of the city, who were so steeped in graft and corruption that a movement to investigate them was already underway before the earthquake occurred, formed a committee that took charge of the rebuilding. The military, already mobilized by General Fredrick Funston, initially without approval from San Francisco mayor Eugene E. Schmitz, created camps around the city, the largest of those located at their headquarters, the Presidio. Supplies and provisions brought into the city by train (once they were up and running) and ferries from Oakland were organized and rationed to citizens. People lived in tents, ate in dining room tents that resembled army mess halls, washed themselves in abandoned train cars converted into washrooms, and sent telegrams and letters to their loved ones assuring them of their safety from makeshift post offices. Later on, shanties and cabins were built, but these massive city camping grounds lasted for several years until houses and buildings were restored.

How did the citizens of San Francisco handle living in tents and temporary shacks for the good part of two years? According to Thomas and Morgan-Wittis, after the initial shock, they adjusted like the pioneer troopers they were. Eyewitnesses and survivors of the quake describe it as almost one big camping trip with many going about good-naturedly, accepting the situation without a murmur.

The difficult task of rebuilding the city began once the camps were set up. Clearing away the rubble for a city that was mostly leveled to the ground was the first order of business. Citizens helped clear the bricks, wood, and stone, dumping them into the bay, until skilled workers could be brought in to continue the job. Every vehicle (whatever few there were at that time) that hadn't fled the city with refugees was seized as was every wagon and every horse. Old cable car tracks had to be cleared to make room for new, more modern electric streetcars since transportation was essential for the city to get back on its feet. This proved more challenging than you might think. The intense heat of the fires that had raged in the city for four days melted the iron tracks into the ground and they needed heavy machinery, including the then innovative steam tractor. The city pulled together and every able-bodied man helped. This is the main order of business when Adele and her friends arrive in the city.

Later on, there was the task of actually planning and building new buildings, using more stable materials such as concrete and steel rather than wood. There was also the task of making sure people who had lost everything would get what was due them. While many homeowners had insurance, their policies, then as now, did not cover earthquake damage. However, their policies did cover fire damage and most were insured with Lloyds of London, who stepped up to fulfill their commitments to their policyholders. Lloyds ended up paying out over fifty million dollars in damages, which would translate to about one billion dollars today—not a common thing at the turn of the century.

Religious leaders claimed the earthquake and fires were an act of God, a sign that the sin and vice San Francisco had been living under for so long needed to be cleansed to make room for a more morally upright city. Whether the city that came out of the ashes was indeed more moral is hard to say. But it was certainly more modern and tidier. Even the local city government was cleaned up.

The earthquake and rebuilding that followed delayed things a bit, but a year later, indictments against government officials, including the mayor and Abe Ruef, who was known to be the puppet master of the whole political organization in the city, were issued. Both Mayor Schmitz and Ruef were convicted, though only Ruef served jail time.

We can't mention the Great Earthquake of San Francisco without talking about the Chinese community who play a role in this book. On the West Coast, vicious racial prejudice raged against the Chinese and all people of Asian descent. Nowhere was it more prominent than in San Francisco. Chinatown was seen as a ghetto of squalor and poverty, the root of the city's evil, with its opium dens and prostitution houses. Citizens of San Francisco blamed the Chinese for the city's unsavory reputation, lack of jobs, pestilence, and even everything that went on in the city's most notorious neighborhood — the Barbary Coast.

But the earthquake and fires affected the Chinese just as much as the rest of the city. Chinatown was in total ruins and the 40,000 Chinese living there were displaced. Many fled to Oakland, but about 400 remained in the city. These people were housed in the Presidio along with everyone else, but complaints forced the army to set the Chinese camp apart from the main area. The Chinese community was placed near Fort Point, a cold and windy section of the Presidio, isolated from the rest of the camp. Food, clothing, and medical supplies were scant compared to those offered to the white population.

Not only were the Chinese displaced as unwanted city refugees, but there was also talk of abolishing Chinatown altogether when the rebuilding began. City officials lobbied to move the Chinese community from the prime real estate location of the downtown to Hunter's Point. However, the community was not without its defenders. The Chinese government, which did a lot of business with the city, as well as men from the Six Companies (representatives from six large Chinese businesses whose goal was to better the conditions of Chinatown and help Chinese refugees and citizens in the U.S.), threatened to boycott trade. They won in the end, and Chinatown returned to its original location. This time, it was rebuilt to reflect Asian culture, complete with the colors, decorations, and arches we associate with this community.

Considering the rack and ruin San Francisco faced with five hundred city blocks destroyed, it's pretty amazing to think that not only was the city completely rebuilt by 1915, but was able to host the Panama-Pacific Exposition that same year. Not only were San Franciscans living full lives in their city by the bay nine years after it was leveled, they were showing it off to the rest of the world.

There are two more things I should mention about this book. The story differs from others in the series so far because it includes much more background about the tragic events that draw Adele and her friends to San Francisco. The murder plot is still central but so are the social and psychological ramifications of such a catastrophe on the survivors. Also, I've mixed fact with fiction in some places. For example, one character, George Wu, tells Adele and Nin he's a representative of the Younger Six, sons and friends of men from the Six Companies. The Six Companies existed in San Francisco at that time, but the Younger Six is fictional.

To keep consistent with the way the Chinese were treated at the time, I've included some expressions that might be considered politically incorrect and even a little offensive today. Mostly, I tried to use neutral terms. For example, Adele and others often refer to the Chinese as "Orientals," which was very common at the time but is now a term we consider outdated and distasteful. You will also see the word "miscegenation" used, which is the old-fashioned term for what we now call interracial or multiracial marriage but was used widely at the time.

In addition, though I've stayed away from highly derogatory references, some of the characters in the book are racist and would have used these terms freely. I've tried to keep them to the bare minimum and made clear from the context that it is NOT OKAY to use these terms. It's always a struggle when writing historical fiction about social and/or political issues to remain accurate when accuracy includes terms we know are wrong and unacceptable today. But I have done my best.

Tam May
June, 2024

CHAPTER 1

If you're interested in reading more early 20th century mysteries, my free offer at the end of this book is for you! So don't forget to check that out when you get to the end. Happy reading!

Mrs. Faderman and the prominent ladies in town had always held the opinion that Arrojo was the cream of the crop as far as towns in the Bay Area were concerned. They boasted about how, in spite of some of its more unsavory corners in Quarry Lane, Arrojo had dignity and gumption without the vice and corruption that plagued the reputation of the Far West . When Adele came to town three years ago, her San Francisco roots were a subject of gossip among the ladies and, indeed, they viewed her suffragism and progressivism as nothing short of "the consequences of living in a city of sin and greed." Adele had always tried to defend San Francisco as a vibrant, dynamic city filled with culture and good people. Sometimes she won the arguments, but often times she didn't.

Adele's pride in her birthplace took a fall when, on April eighteenth, the earth shattered underneath the city's feet, and fires consumed many of its buildings and houses. She read about it in the newspapers with the horror of someone who had known a fallen city in its celebratory days. Her hand trembled as she wrote telegrams to her San Francisco friends, knowing she was unlikely to receive an answer, perhaps for some time, perhaps not ever.

Arrojo itself felt the tremors, though not to any horrendous magnitude. Although the ground shook with some vigor, most of the houses and businesses experienced little more than upset shelves, toppling furniture, and swinging lamps. Mrs. Faderman came to Adele's shop the morning after the earthquake, waving the *Arrojo Courier* with a smirk on her face, as if to say *What have I been telling you all this time?*

But Adele hardly gave her a thought as she scrambled to get word to her friends and survey the damage to her shop in the week that followed. She was lucky, and most of her wares had come out of the tremors in a chaotic mess scattered all over the floor. Her assistant Beatrice declared they looked "artistic" until she realized she would be responsible for cleaning up the chaos.

Only a few months before, Adele unveiled the typewriter room in her shop, which had impressed the Sacramento papers enough to write about them. The typewriters, with their heavy iron keys and platen rollers, fared the worst in the tremors. Many crashed to the ground and, because the floor in that room was of wood, some had even made sizable splinters in the floor panels. Two in particular, a Smith Premier and an Underwood, proved themselves to be less than what their salesmen had promised and broke to pieces.

Three years as a businesswoman had taught Adele to be resourceful and persistent. The first thing she did was wire the Zimbro Insurance Company, with whom she and Nin had a policy, and requested that someone come out to assess the damage. She then convinced Vera Mead, owner of Mead Building & Contract, who had built the typewriter room for her, to replace the broken floor panels, much to the chagrin of Vera's partner and brother. She also hounded the Smith and Underwood company salesmen and cajoled them into agreeing to replace the broken typewriters.

Her business acumen was not, unfortunately, reflected in Nin Branch, the only person in Arrojo who had befriended her. Even though Nin had her own income from her wealthy mother's inheritance, which meant she didn't have to depend on the sales of her curioso and herb shop to survive, she would have more to do to rebuild her place after the earthquake.

Earlier that year, Adele finally persuaded Nin to give her shop a name, and Atha's (named after Nin's beloved mother) began to look more like a business. She placed shelves of herbs neatly labeled with little cards explaining what they did on one side of the room, and the curiosos Atha collected over the years on the other. Adele found out a long time ago Nin had a head for business when she put her mind to it, and it looked like Nin was destined to make a profit from her shop for the first time within the first few months of 1906.

But when Adele walked into Nin's shop the morning after the quake, she saw the tremors had taken their revenge on the place. Unlike her own shop, which had only scattered items, the baskets and jars Nin carefully compiled were spilled or broken and herbs mixed together to concoct a strong scent that made Adele's eyes water. Several of the curiosos were destroyed beyond repair, and others had fallen and cracked into the crevices of the shop.

Nin sat on the floor staring at the ruin, her face showing more irony than dismay. "Sister Earth has been very unhappy."

"I should say so," Adele said dryly, surveying the place.

"She doesn't like it when her folds are weighed with coins," Nin continued in an almost dreamy tone.

"Nonsense," Adele snapped. "You've earned your living fairly, just like all of us."

Her friend's cat-like eyes were round like a confused child. "What do we do now?"

"I've already wired Zimbro to send someone," Adele said. "We might at least get something for the damages."

"And then?"

Adele pressed her shoulder. "We go to work, dear. That's what women do after a crisis."

Nin seemed to take this to heart. "I think I can salvage most of the herbs, if I can separate them out."

"After they've been on the dusty floor?" Adele eyed her. "I wouldn't advise it."

"A little dust hardly matters." Her friend sniffed.

Adele laughed. "Your waywardness will be the death of me, Nin."

"I'll wait until the insurance man comes, then," her friend said with determination. "Let him see this mess. I won't tell him I could easily wash some of the herbs, dry them out and resell them."

Adele saluted her. "Now you're talking like a businesswoman." She could tell by the look on her face that Nin hardly saw this as a compliment.

Beatrice, who had always had a nagging curiosity about Nin's shop, tried to convince Adele to let her help, but Adele sent her home. "I'll need you to clear ours once the insurance man comes."

"Golly, me do all that?" She looked distastefully at the messy floor.

"A woman survives on her wits," Adele said.

"A *lady* cajoles others into helping her," Beatrice said with the airs of her Wrigley School education.

"You keep insisting you'll be hanged before you'd let people call you a lady," Nin observed.

"I'll bet I could get some of the boys around town to help me," Beatrice said with a gleam in her eye.

"That's your only interest in them, isn't it?" Nin glared at her.

The girl grinned. "I like to make them look like dogs."

"Poor John and Steven Lynn," Adele said. "You're going to bring those two brothers to blows one of these days, Bea."

"If they come to blows over a woman, they deserve what they get," snarled Beatrice, and Adele couldn't help but laugh.

She kept away from Adele's Stationery for a few days, waiting for the telegram from Zimbro to come. It finally arrived at the breakfast table with a curt message: *Expect Mr. Malone to arrive nine a.m. sharp.*

"Nine a.m. *sharp!*" Adele threw the telegram on the table. It slid to the floor, and Maria, the eldest of the Cordoba children, bounded from the discreet corner her father usually occupied when he served the meals. Imitating her father, she picked it up, dusted it off, and put it with the stack of telegrams for filing on the desk in the parlor.

"He's going to be a businesswoman hater, I can tell already," Adele continued.

"Nonsense." Her brother, Jackson, unfolded the *Arrojo Courier.* "I'm sure the man's just harried from running around the county making estimates and payouts." He peered at her. "How badly are you out, Del?"

"A hundred or so should do it for me," she said. "It's Nin I'm worried about."

"How much could those herbs cost her?" He shrugged.

"She spent hours collecting them in the woods, Jack," she said. "As to the powders, she got those from people with whom she had to bargain hard. I don't think she has more than ten percent of her stock intact. And some of those valuable curiosos her mother got from the Orient are ruined."

"It's a good thing you persuaded your friend to take out insurance," he remarked. "I'm sure Mr. Malone will be very fair."

"And I'm sure he won't," Adele grumbled.

He looked at her from the top of the newspaper. "May I

remind you, Del, the insurance companies aren't liable for damages in an earthquake?"

"And how would you know that, dear brother?" She glared at him.

"Because I read the insurance documents they sent you," he said.

"So did I," Adele said. "I saw nothing there about not covering damages from earthquakes."

"Precisely." He folded up his paper. "You saw nothing. If they were liable, they would have included it."

Adele's annoyance subsided. "I see what you mean."

"The papers have been saying the insurance companies are paying for fire damages but not for earthquake damages," he added. "I hope you keep your temper with Mr. Malone, or you'll get nothing and neither will Miss Branch."

Adele went to Nin's shop first. "Hopefully Mr. Malone's check will pay for a good cleaning of this place." She looked around.

"I don't think Mr. Malone will give me any money." Nin sighed.

"Nonsense, dear," Adele said. "He's being paid to by the insurance company. They want to look good for the papers by paying out claims. Fire damage or no fire damage." She added the last in a mumble, thinking of what her brother had said.

"What has fire to do with it?" Nin questioned.

Adele patted her hand. "Never mind. He'll be here at nine sharp."

"He better have just as sharp a signature on that check as he has on his timetable," Nin growled.

Beatrice came in to tell her that Mr. Malone was waiting.

"It's not nine sharp." Nin smirked. "It's only eight fifty-five. Let him wait."

"I think we ought to make a favorable impression, Nin," Adele said. "Jack reminded me this morning that the company isn't liable to pay us for earthquake damages."

"So we must be sweet and silky toward him?" Nin frowned.

"He could use some sweetening up," Beatrice said, pulling her shawl around her shoulders. "He looks like a turnip."

Though Adele chuckled at this, she was a little dismayed to find Beatrice was right. Mr. Malone had a round head, and had styled his hair with pomade, leaving a small tuff at the top. He was one of those young men who looked older than his age and spoke in a wary tone.

"Miss Gossling?" He gave them both a questioning look.

"That's her." Nin pointed to her friend.

"We appreciate your speedy response to this occasion, Mr. Malone." Adele held out her hand.

The man did not take it. "Best to get these things over with as soon as possible."

"Where were you when the earthquake hit?" Beatrice questioned with narrow eyes.

"I'm not from California, young lady." He didn't even glance at her. "I'm from the New York office."

"Lucky you," Beatrice mumbled as she retreated to the back of the shop.

"It's very kind of you to take the time to help business owners like us," Adele continued, trying to sound "sweet and silky." "I'm sure you realize we've been hit as badly as San Francisco."

"Considering the papers are saying nearly eighty percent of the city was leveled, Miss Gossling, I doubt that very much." The young man glanced out the window. "I don't see your little town has fared too badly."

"Little towns still have to do business, Mr. Malone," Adele mumbled, trying to keep her nerves calm.

He shrugged. "Why don't you tell me a little bit about what sort of work you do, and then we can go around and see what this unholy tremble did to it."

As Adele spoke, she noticed the look on his face changed from wariness to steel. She realized the assessment she had made about him being a businesswoman hater was all too true.

"You do a fair amount of business with paper and things?" he inquired as he scratched on his yellow pad.

"I don't sell paper, Mr. Malone," Adele said. "I sell stationery."

"She has a whole room in the back with some of the latest innovations," Nin insisted.

"Indeed?" He raised a brow.

"That's primarily where the damage is." Adele led him to the typewriter room.

He examined the floor boards and the typewriters that had broken or been misaligned. "How many of these have you sold so far? Before the quake, of course."

"I haven't really sold any yet," she admitted. "I only opened it a month ago."

"I don't see how we can be liable —"

"No one said you were liable for anything," Nin snarled.

"If you had been selling them for a year, six months even, and showing a good profit with them, that would be different," he continued. "But at this point, it's really a gamble."

"I'm not a bookie, Mr. Malone," Adele said in a cold voice. "I know what will sell in my shop and what won't."

"Nevertheless," Mr. Malone said, "we can't afford to overestimate right now. We have many other clients who have been through much worse damage, and our funds are as limited as anyone else's."

"How much are you going to give her?" Nin shot out in her blunt way.

The man scratched at his pad for a few moments, which Adele felt was more for show than for anything else. "I suppose I could give you twenty dollars for the damages."

"Twenty dollars!" Adele stared at him.

"That won't even pay for the broken floor," Nin snapped.

"Maybe twenty-five," the man said.

Adele leaned against the wall. "And if this sort of damage had occurred at the general store next door, you would no doubt have found it in your iron heart to give Mr. Raleigh a generous amount because a businessman deserves more than a businesswoman?"

"Businessmen usually have families to feed," the young man said in a snippy tone. "I don't imagine you're the sole support of an aging mother and father now, are you?"

"What the devil does that have to do with anything?" Nin growled.

The man closed his yellow pad. "I was hoping I wouldn't have to remind you, Miss Gossling, but your policy includes no protection against earthquakes."

"How terribly convenient of you to exclude it," Nin said.

"Neither does yours, Miss — Branch." He consulted a list. "We're paying out damages for fire, but fire hasn't touched this town as it has San Francisco. Our company knows full well what to expect from this land, and we can't be liable —"

"My friend already told you no one is accusing you of being liable for anything, Mr. Malone," Adele interrupted.

"We can't be *responsible* for the whims of Mother Nature."

"It's nice you admit nature is a mother," Nin mumbled.

"We're paying out because we want to contribute something to the relief efforts of your state in this unfortunate tragedy." He folded his hands.

"Why unfortunate when you just admitted California could be swallowed up by the San Andreas Fault at any moment?" Adele eyed him.

"The point is, Miss Gossling, we don't have to pay you anything." His voice was now steely again. "We're doing so out of the goodness of our hearts."

"Goodness!" Nin snarled. "You're doing it so your company gets its name in the papers for being benevolent."

The man's lips were white, but when he spoke, his voice was

contained. "I'm authorized to write checks for modest amounts on the spot. Will you take the twenty dollars I offered you?"

"I'll take the twenty-five you offered me," Adele said pointedly. "I'm sorry I lost my temper, Mr. Malone. I realize you've no obligation to pay me a cent, and this has all been very trying." She was feeling less than apologetic, but she realized the young man was the kind to be more considerate to women who supplicated. And, indeed, Mr. Malone softened a little as he wrote the check and handed it to her.

While Adele was willing to be complacent for her share of the insurance money, she fought more heartily for Nin's shop. Although she could see Mr. Malone recognized the damage to her wares was more extensive than Adele's, he kept the same rigid economy, offering her forty dollars for the damages.

"Not a penny less than seventy!" Adele insisted.

"That Chinese vase is worth three times that much, and it's completely shattered," Beatrice, who had been standing in the doorway, argued.

"And so covered with dust it must have sat on the shelf for years." His voice was snide. "I don't see anything of great value that would make a profitable business here."

"Do you know what my friend does for a living, Mr. Malone?" Adele asked.

The man almost shuddered, as if he'd rather not know, as he shook his head.

"She helps people heal. She's like a doctor but works with auras, not medicine."

"Auras?" The man backed away slightly.

"I'm a witch," Nin said in a harsh tone. "Ask anyone in town. I put hexes on people who try to cheat other people." She looked him in the eyes.

"Really, I don't think —" He pulled his coat tight around his shoulders.

Nin advanced with such a vicious look on her face that even

Adele was a little frightened. "You'd better write me that check for seventy dollars, or I can't answer for the consequences."

"You mean you would really put a hex on me?" He stared at her.

"Not I, Mr. Malone," she said. "I only do Sister Earth's bidding. You've already seen Sister Earth is not exactly in a good mood these days."

"I don't believe it!" he said, still wide-eyed. "That sort of mesmerizer's trick — it's all hogwash."

"Oh, but I'm not a mesmerizer." Nin advanced even further toward him. "I told you, I'm a witch."

"She really is, Mr. Malone," Beatrice said. "Why, you ought to see what she did to the husband of a friend of mine when he took a whip to her. The man's in an asylum, and they say he won't ever get out."

Adele raised her eyebrows at this bald-faced lie, but it seemed to do the trick. Mr. Malone scribbled out the check and put it on one of the empty shelves as if he were afraid to hand it to Nin.

Adele smiled. "Thank you, Mr. Malone. We'll be sure to tell everyone just how generous the Zimbro Insurance Company has been in the face of this unfortunate tragedy."

He glared at her as he scurried out of the shop.

"Bea, really!" Adele turned to her. "What tall tales you tell."

"It's not so tall," Beatrice argued. "You weren't at Rachel's wedding. She had to go and marry one of those hawk-faced aspiring priests. He looks like he'll go crazy in another three or four years."

Adele laughed and pinched Beatrice's cheek. "Well, it got Nin some of the money she needs to rebuild her place."

Beatrice clasped both of them on the shoulder. "And rebuild we will! If an entire city can do it, so can we!"

CHAPTER 2

The next morning, when Adele told Jackson about the insurance man, he was furious. "You ought to have called the sheriff. Hatfield would have made him give you a fair amount."

"The man did have a point, Jack," she said. "As you said yourself, there was no earthquake clause in our policy. They didn't have to pay out anything. Most companies aren't."

"Then it's poor business on their part," he said. "The millions they'll get when people around the nation hear about their contribution to those left destitute from the quake should more than make up for whatever loss they'll suffer now."

Adele sighed as she cradled her coffee cup. "I don't think we ought to be grumbling about anything now. We just have to be thankful for what we have."

"And thankful we weren't in the city," he declared. Then, seeing the look on her face, he pressed her hand. "I'm sorry, Del. I shouldn't have said that."

"Nin was talking about taking all the lucky herbs from her shop and sending them to San Francisco," Adele said wryly. "They need all the luck they can get.

"Our friends aren't exactly weak." Jackson gave her a tender look. "I'm sure the moment Elsie gets settled in one of the refugee camps, she'll telegraph you."

"They've been up for a week," she said in a hollow voice. "Why hasn't she telegraphed already?"

"Because it's not easy with hundreds of others doing the same thing," Jackson insisted. "Hatfield said he's checking with his police friends. They'll know better than anybody how to find people."

"It's all so awful, Jack." She buried her face in his arm.

"Well, at least you got Miss Branch most of what's owed her from the insurance man." Jackson patted her shoulder. "What would she have done if she hadn't gotten that check?"

"We would have taken her in," Adele insisted.

"She would run Tomas and Ruth out of the house if she ever came here," Jackson said with a grin.

"Well, they're not here now," Adele reminded him.

"True." He rose. "I don't think Maria or Consuela would have much interest in Miss Branch's visions."

Adele watched as he carefully put on his coat. "Back to Quarry Lane?" She felt the butterflies fluttering in her stomach.

"It's not as bad as all that," he assured her. "I think it's more hue and cry than anything. After all, it's not like we're dealing with the sort of looting they're reporting in the papers that is going on in the city right now."

"Still, I don't like it that you and Hatfield are patroling down there," she said.

"We have no choice, Del," he said. "The place is practically in ruins. Seems the fault line is closer to them than to us."

"And their buildings are like sandcastles," Adele said. "I suppose it can't be helped."

Maria growled in Spanish toward the hallway, and her younger sister Consuela appeared. Together, they started to clear away the dishes, mumbling disapproval at the half-eaten plates.

"It won't be for long." He said. "Hatfield asked Sheriff Hill to send down some of his men so they could help us patrol the area."

"I'm sure he has his own streets to worry about," Adele said.

"Sacramento didn't sustain much damage," he said. "He's sending them down within the next few days."

They first went to the post office, but there were no letters or telegrams from any of their friends. With a heavy heart, Adele watched Jackson make his way toward the train station where he would meet Hatfield and Assistant Deputy Edison so they could walk down Quarry Lane together.

The morning gave a brighter color to the days they had seen with coats of dust and chaos on Bridge Street. Other businesses had rushed to clean their shops and several looked as if nothing had happened when Adele walked by. Others had finished cleaning up early and gone to their neighbors to help them. But they stayed away from Nin's shop, as, even after so many years, they still were a little edgy about the strange and wonderful gifts nature had given her.

"Maybe we should take Beatrice up on her offer," Adele remarked as she placed a brick against the door to keep it open. "We could use some help here."

"I wouldn't let those bumbling boys touch a leaf of basil," Nin insisted. "They'd probably make a disagreeable brew that would set off another earthquake." Suddenly, her friend grew pale and pressed her hands into the floor where she was bent down with the dust brush. "Maybe. Maybe."

"Maybe what?" Adele knew the look on her friend's face meant she had seen something.

"It's — begetting."

"Begetting?" Adele stared.

"One thing begets another," she said. "Good and bad."

"You mean like the earthquake beget the fires?" Adele asked.

"I suppose so." Her voice was dull.

"We're bound to feel some aftershocks," Adele said. "Don't let it worry you, dear."

"You're worrying enough for both of us." Nin eyed her. "No word from Elsie?"

Adele tried to sound cheerful. "I imagine sending a telegram right now is almost impossible with the chaos going on there."

"She could still send word," Nin grumbled. "She must know you're worried."

"She thinks I've become completely detached from the city." Adele began to survey the darkened shop. "But you never really leave behind a place like San Francisco. Never in your heart, that is."

"You'll get back there," Nin said in her vague tone. "A little while, but you'll get back."

Adele studied her, but she couldn't tell if Nin was speaking from an aura or from regret. "I hope all my friends won't be moving out of the city once it gets on its feet." She looked out the dusty window where Bridge Street was moving slower than usual. "I want to help, Nin."

"Then let me find a broom, and we'll get to work," said her friend simply.

"I mean in San Francisco," she said.

Nin shrugged. "What can you do?"

"What any single person can do," Adele said. "Right now, people are going from single effort to contributing to the entire effort, one person at a time. They need me."

"They need us," Nin corrected. "If you go, I go."

Adele smiled. "Let's wait and see if we hear from Elsie first. Perhaps the situation there isn't as bad as the newspapers make it out to be."

Through the doorway appeared a bundled face with wide cheeks and a flash of iron-gray hair. "Why, Miss Branch, you do look a sight sitting there on the floor."

Adele couldn't help but notice Mrs. Faderman, though still

with all her usual energy, looked frayed. It made her feel almost sorry for the woman.

"I find it restful," Nin said. "I always have."

"Yes, well, it's time to get rid of that nasty habit," Mrs. Faderman said. "You're not a child anymore, after all." She stepped gingerly around the debris and held out her hand. "Come, I'll help you up."

"I can do it, Mrs. Faderman," Adele said, hoping this would get rid of the woman.

Mrs. Faderman looked around the shop with distaste. "This will never do. We're going to have people flocking into Arrojo soon enough after this abominable calamity, and they simply can't see our commercial district looking like this!"

"Then they won't see mine," Nin said in a savage tone. "I don't care to see anyone now anyway."

"We were just waiting for the insurance man to arrive before we cleaned up," Adele said. "After all, he had to see the damages, didn't he?"

"You mean you and Miss Branch took out insurance?" The woman's face was aghast.

"Just like Mr. Raleigh and Mr. Pringle and all the rest of the businesses here, Mrs. Faderman." Adele smiled sweetly. "It's what business people do."

"Well, I hope you got a fairer settlement than they did." Mrs. Faderman sniffed.

"Adele got cheated, and I told him I was a witch so he gave me more, but I still got cheated," Nin said.

The woman grunted. "It's impossible to rebuild this town without their giving *something*."

"But we didn't suffer much damage," Adele reminded her.

Mrs. Faderman patted her shoulder. "Never mind, dear, the council is meeting later this week to discuss relief funds, and I'll see to it that you get your share."

"Give it to the poor people in San Francisco," Adele said in a somber tone.

"But *this* is our town, not San Francisco," the woman pointed out. "Now, both of you, come out and join our tea. You both look peaked."

"You're having one of your tea parties *now?*" Adele stared. "Amid the shock that ruined the state's greatest city?"

"Really, Miss Gossling, you do think a little too highly of your birthplace." Mrs. Faderman took her arm and Nin's.

"It isn't right." Nin agreed. "It's like Marie Antoinette telling the poor to eat cake."

"Well, if she said it, she had a reason." Mrs. Faderman's voice was vague as she pulled them out to the street.

In spite of Adele's protest, there was something about the people strolling down the sidewalks glancing at shop windows that comforted her. She let herself be taken to the table Mrs. Faderman always laid out with tea, cakes and toast when she gave one of her movable tea parties. Nin followed her lead.

"Miss Gossling." Mrs. Lynn smiled at her with her bird-like figure hunched inside the brown dress she wore. "Have you heard anything from your friends?"

Of all the ladies, Mrs. Lynn was the kindest, though it seemed as if her constitution had been weakening in the last several months. Adele held her hand, though it seemed as fragile as a leaf. "Nothing yet."

"Oh, terrible, terrible!" the woman bellowed.

"Well, Carolyn, you can hardly expect them to be thinking of her living all the way in Arrojo when they have more important matters to attend to," Mrs. Atherton insisted, patting the curls at the back of her neck.

"Survival does rather take up one's thoughts," Adele said dryly.

"You can't deny, Miss Gossling, it was their own fault." Mrs.

Cricket carefully chose a thick slice of vanilla pound cake from the second tier of the cake platter.

"What on earth do you mean?" Nin glared at her.

"Everyone knows what's been going on in that city." The woman shrugged.

"Sin and corruption." Mrs. Fourier's eyes sparkled like two stones.

"You sound like the signs for the melodramas." Nin threw a glance at the Arrojo Theater further up the street. The woman flinched.

"Well, why not?" Mrs. Jessel objected. "That's what the big city is for, isn't it?"

"Ever since you went there last spring, you've been praising it." Mrs. Abberton sniffed.

"The papers say they plan on making it clean and modern," Mrs. Jessel insisted.

"Clean and modern!" Mrs. Abberton snorted. "I told Albert if we ever went there, it would be over my dead body."

"Whatever works," Nin mumbled.

"I hope they do make it cleaner," Mrs. Faderman said with a surprising defensiveness.

"I wouldn't have thought to hear that from you, ma'am." Adele eyed her.

"It's a matter of practicality, Miss Gossling," said the woman. "This part of the state needs a large city. If there is no big city, there will be no people coming to Arrojo to get away from it. That affects us all, including you."

Adele couldn't help but laugh. "I give you credit, Mrs. Faderman. You're nothing if not practical."

The woman seemed unsure of whether to take that as a compliment. "As for more modern, that's questionable. To be modern, a city must have a steady foundation."

"They can hardly help it if they're on the fault line," Mrs. Leighton pointed out.

"I didn't mean that foundation." Mrs. Faderman poured Mrs. Cricket more tea. "I meant the houses and buildings. Everything was ready to crumble at the slightest tremor and everybody knew it."

"You can't build a big city without cheap materials," Mrs. Cricket agreed.

"Now, when my grandfather first came to Arrojo," Mrs. Faderman said, "he insisted the buildings on Bridge Street be built with solid materials. He knew there might be problems down the line." She nodded knowingly.

"That was rather shrewd of him," Adele admitted.

"That's why Arrojo is *not* San Francisco, dear," the woman said.

"Oh, but there were rumors of those men vying for materials in a, well, not-so-nice way." Mrs. Lynn looked down at the ground.

"Those were just rumors, Carolyn," Mrs. Faderman snapped. "That's the only reason the insurance company was willing to pay out." She shook a finger at Adele. "They aren't so keen on giving compensation for poorly made structures after a tragedy for fear they'll be built just as badly all over again."

"They're very careful about their pockets," Adele agreed, her anger rising at the thought of Mr. Malone's steely eyes.

"Oh, I don't know." Mrs. Leighton shrugged. "Mrs. Raleigh told me they were quite generous when the man came to the store and saw the damages."

"I'm sure Mr. Malone was very benevolent to Mr. Raleigh." She glanced at Nin with a knowing look.

"She said the man praised them for being the 'pinnacle' of the town with their 'country store' and that such places were so rare these days, even in the country," the woman continued. "It seems like every town these days is replacing family-owned businesses with all these wretched department stores."

"Never in this town!" Mrs. Faderman proclaimed. "When

there was talk of bringing a Taylor & Main store here last year, I told them it would take a cyclone to allow them to build on Bridge Street."

"Maybe it takes an earthquake," Adele murmured.

The woman set the cup down in the saucer with a small crash. "I don't find that amusing, Miss Gossling."

"I wasn't trying to be amusing." The bread-and-butter Adele had been persuaded to take was now churning in her stomach. "You can't keep big stores out of small towns anymore, Mrs. Faderman."

"Nor their big ideas, I daresay?" The woman eyed her through her pince-nez.

Adele stiffened. "I'm sure I don't know what you mean, ma'am."

"She's going to start in on you again about being a lady detective," Nin grumbled.

"Well, it had occurred to me — to us —" Mrs. Faderman cleared her throat as she glanced at the ladies who always stood at her beck and call. "It had occurred to us you might be getting notions in that direction."

"I always have notions, Mrs. Faderman," Adele said in a cheerful tone, knowing full well what was coming. "Why, just this morning, I had the idea for my shop to —"

"Not your shop," Mrs. Abberton interrupted.

"A much more sinister notion." Mrs. Cricket narrowed her eyes.

"Oh, I wouldn't say sinister, dear," Mrs. Lynn objected. "Why, Miss Gossling isn't that way in the least."

"It's not Miss Gossling we're talking about, Carolyn," said Mrs. Faderman. "It's her notions."

"Well, what is this notion you're all so afraid I'll get?" Adele held on to her empty cup and saucer.

"Now, don't get upset, dear." Mrs. Jessel patted her shoulder.

Adele felt a little dizzy. "I'm sorry. This has all been so unnerving."

"Precisely," Mrs. Faderman said. "Which is exactly why we wanted to speak to you."

"Here it comes," Nin mumbled.

Adele looked from one to the other. "In other words, this invitation to your tea wasn't just a friendly community gesture."

"Certainly it was," the woman insisted. "But we were all wondering —"

"You always wonder too much," Nin snarled.

"We were wondering what your plans are now after this calamity."

"I've no plans except to rebuild my shop," Adele said. "Just like everyone on Bridge Street."

Chests heaved a sigh from one to the other like a wave. Mrs. Lynn blinked at her. "Then you're not thinking of becoming a policewoman?"

"Policewoman!" Adele stared at her.

"Irene told us you were headed in that direction." Mrs. Cricket's mouth twisted. "The idea!"

"You mean the 'sinister notion,' don't you?" Nin raised her eyebrows.

"Well, you must admit, Miss Gossling, you readily jump in to help your brother and the sheriff." Mrs. Fourier held her chin up a little. "Why, I saw you myself at the station not long ago."

"And you couldn't wait to blab about it to everyone else," Nin shot out.

"I never had any such idea, Mrs. Fourier," Adele assured her.

"Why not?" Mrs. Abberton asked. "You've done it often enough.

"That's not the same thing as being a policewoman," Nin argued.

"But a police consultant is nearly the same thing," Mrs.

Cricket said. "We know you persuaded the sheriff to ask Mayor Willett to make you one."

"She didn't persuade anyone!" Nin's anger rose with black fury. "You're talking more nonsense than usual, Mrs. Cricket."

"I don't propose to stay here and be insulted by this witch, Irene!" Mrs. Cricket flared as she snatched up the last of the lemon cake and stalked down the street.

"Old bat!" Nin snarled. But Adele pressed her hand to quiet her.

In a calm tone, she said, "It's true Sheriff Hatfield put in a request but of his own free will. And you'll be happy to hear it was refused."

"Yes, we know," said Mrs. Jessel.

"Do you?" Nin eyed her.

"Irene intervened," said Mrs. Fourier. "And it's a lucky thing for you she did. If word had gotten out that the Arrojo police force had a woman advising them —"

"And why not a woman?" Mrs. Jessel immediately jumped up, as she had always had some sympathy for women making their own way.

"Oh, a coarse lady who had been raised in the dirty alleyways of the city would perhaps have been a different story," Mrs. Faderman said. "But Miss Gossling comes from a good family. It would hardly be fitting for her to work with the police. Officially or unofficially." She said the last with a pointed look toward Adele.

Adele grabbed her friend's arm. "You'll be happy to know, Mrs. Faderman, my energies right now are going toward rebuilding my business and helping Nin rebuild hers. I'm sorry, but we're far too busy to linger here any longer."

She had no need to drag her friend away from the ladies. Nin practically leapt ahead of her as they crossed the street back to her shop.

"I should have known she would interfere!" Adele snapped as she shut the door with a bang.

"Now we know what was behind the mayor's rejection," Nin agreed.

"I wonder how she found out."

"She has floating ears all over town," Nin growled. The image of Mrs. Faderman's rather flat ears floating through Bridge Street made Adele laugh and eased her annoyance.

CHAPTER 3

Though she and Nin managed to get a good deal done by the time the sun began to set, the shop was still dusted with powders and broken glass. Adele could see her friend was discouraged as she glanced at the broken vases and artifacts they hadn't even gotten to yet.

"Don't worry, dear." Adele pressed her arm. "We'll get it all done."

"Perhaps Sister Earth didn't intend for me to go on with this place," Nin murmured.

"If that were the case, Sister Earth wouldn't have left the most important herbs and curiosos intact," Adele argued as she climbed the narrow stairs to Nin's abode above the shop. "Didn't you tell me the bowls on the top shelf are the most potent?"

"That's true," Nin admitted as she stuck the key in the lock.

"And that marble Muses statuette is still in place — Nin!" Adele stood in the doorway of her friend's flat.

"The window is a little crooked, isn't it?" her friend remarked, a little ironically.

The left side of the living room was damaged from the quake. In addition to the crooked window in the corner, the others were either broken or unhinged and there was a space in between two of the windows where wooden panels were loose, letting in the breeze from the early evening.

"Nin, you can't stay here," Adele insisted.

"Why not?" the woman blinked.

As much as Adele revered her friend, she marveled sometimes at the primitive way she had of thinking of her environment.

"Dear, why don't you come stay with us?" Adele pressed her hand. "I don't like to think of you being here with the windows broken and those boards falling off."

"I don't mind." Nin shrugged. "I've nothing to steal anyway."

"But people go crazy after such a tragedy." Adele led her outside and took the key to lock the door. "I saw more than one person lose their minds when a tenement burned down."

"I suppose there are a few people in town who don't like me and might go crazy after an earthquake," Nin admitted.

Adele took her arm. "Jack would appreciate the company too."

Nin grimaced. "I doubt that very much."

"You're wrong, dear. He's become very fond of you." Adele smiled. "Tomorrow, I'll call Vera Mead and see what her company can do about the damage. I was going to call her anyway about the typewriter room now that I have some money to pay for the floor." She peered at her friend. "You'll come?"

"All right," said Nin. "As long as your brother keeps his pipe in his pocket after dinner."

Adele laughed as they started down the street. "I didn't even think to call. Jack's going to be annoyed."

"Let him," Nin growled. "I'll take the blame."

As it turned out, Jackson was in a jovial mood when they arrived. It was obvious why when Adele heard Hatfield's soothing tones and Lady Augusta's deep laughter.

Hatfield's mother greeted them with warmth and even Rowena, the Hatfield housekeeper and Lady Augusta's companion, smiled. "I brought a bottle of Napoleon brandy with me," said the elderly woman. "Horatio promises to break it open after dinner."

"As long as you keep to one or two glasses, Ma," said Sheriff Hatfield with a grin. Adele felt a pinch as she saw how there were crinkles around his eyes that weren't there a few months before. She knew how close he was to his mother, and the earthquake had provoked worry for her health.

As if sensing this, Nin ran to the woman and knelt down, putting her head in her lap like a child. "You oughtn't to be here at all!"

"You're here, aren't you?" the woman countered.

"I think Miss Branch means here in California," Jackson poured another cocktail for Adele and a glass of soda water for Nin.

"Oh, nonsense!"

"It's not nonsense, Ma," the sheriff said. "We still don't know what to expect with the aftershocks. They could go on for days, even years, and there's no telling how bad some of them will be."

"Pfff!" The woman waved him away as she drank the rest of her cocktail. "Jackson, another glass, please."

"The sheriff's right, ma'am," Jackson said. "And, as your house suffered some damage, it's not safe for you to stay there."

"Two broken shutters and a few collapsed shelves are not damage, young man." Lady Augusta was adamant. "The lord and his friends caused more damage after a hunt. Lucky thing Horatio was a baby then."

"There might be more damage to come, Ma," her son argued.

"I'm staying put," Lady Augusta said in a stubborn tone. "I can bear it better than any of you can. After all, I was in the malaria epidemic of thirty-three." She raised her glass to her own resilience and drank.

"You were barely seven, Ma," her son reminded her. "Young people take things differently."

"And you're no spring chicken yourself, Horatio," she said. "Perhaps you ought to remember that."

He cringed a little at the reprimand but took it in his usual good humor. "I wish you'd let me call John and Mary, Ma. I'm sure they'd have plenty of room for you and Rowena."

Lady Augusta shot him a look as if he were crazy. "Me go to those people? The Lord would turn in his grave!"

"Who are John and Mary?" Adele started to feel the warmth of the cocktail.

"John and Mary Strimple," Hatfield said. "Relatives of ours."

"*Distant* relatives of the lord's," the elderly woman corrected. "No relatives of ours and, I daresay, the lord would have disowned them had he known why they left England."

Hatfield leaned toward Adele and said in a low voice, "Mormons."

"Oh, I see," Adele said.

"He probably has three more wives at this point," said his mother.

"I believed their church outlawed polygamy several years ago, Lady Augusta." Jackson tried to hide his smile.

"John always had that English arrogance that no rule applied to him," said the elderly woman. "He has them, mark my words."

"At least you would be safe in Utah," her son mumbled.

"You think so, do you?" She eyed him. "And what makes you think Utah won't have its share of disasters? Utah gets earthquakes too, you know."

Hatfield held up his hands as if he wasn't going to even try to argue with that logic.

Nin pressed the old woman's hand. "I suppose you're right, Lady Augusta. You're as safe here as anywhere."

"Exactly!" The woman was triumphant. "And it has the added benefit of being amongst friends." She patted her cheek, then threw her head back. "What do you say, Rowena, do you fancy a trek to Utah just to avoid a few tremors?"

"If you'll pardon my saying so, ma'am, I'd rather be eaten by a crocodile," said the woman in her usual colorful manner.

They all laughed as Consuela came in and announced that dinner was served.

"How are your parents down in San Jose, my dear?" Lady Augusta asked kindly as Maria cleared a space for her in her wheelchair at the table.

"Papa writes things aren't so bad," Maria said.

"They've already built two houses," said Consuela with pride.

"It's wonderful they went down there to help." Adele smiled.

"And if either of you need any help, let us know," Jackson insisted. "We'll hire anyone at any time."

"Señor is good," Maria said with a shy smile.

But her younger sister seemed offended. "We have Pilar and Ana," she insisted. "Even Marco can carry the wood now."

"Soon he'll be chopping it too," Adele said.

"He wants to now," Consuela said. "But Papa won't allow it."

"A seven-year-old boy might easily slip with the ax," Jackson agreed. "I'll chop the wood when you need it. Just let me know."

Consuela curtsied as she and her sister retreated to the corner.

Jackson turned to Hatfield. "Have you heard from your police friends in the city, sir?"

Hatfield took a generous portion of potatoes. "Things are settling down now that the army and the Red Cross are there. But they're having a difficult time scattering men around the city."

"Is it true what they say — they're shooting anyone who has so much as a candlestick in his hand?" Nin questioned, her dark eyes wide.

Hatfield laughed. "I don't think it's quite that bad, Miss Branch."

"It soon will be if the militia doesn't get out of there," Lady

Augusta said in a rough tone. "I don't approve of the army over-stepping its authority."

"What else was Funston to do?" Jackson asked. "No one was taking charge. They were too busy arguing in city hall about who was in charge."

"That Schmitz!" The elderly woman nearly spit out the name. "He couldn't take charge of a horse."

"The Committee of Fifty will do what's necessary," Jackson said firmly. He was quiet for a moment, staring down at the roast duck in front of him. "Perhaps we ought to go there and help, sir."

"Could you get through, Jack?" Adele asked.

"There are trains to the Oakland pier," he said. "From there, we could take the ferry across the bay. Or we could drive up in the police car. They're in dire need of vehicles."

"And who would watch over law and order in Arrojo County?" Hatfield glanced at him. "We still have our duty to perform here, Deputy."

"You said Edison has become a fine policeman," Adele pointed out. "Why not leave him in charge?"

Jackson made a face at this idea and Nin giggled.

"He's a good boy, Horatio," the sheriff's mother pointed out.

"Good doesn't make for an effective policeman, Ma," her son reminded her. "We still have that mess down on Quarry Lane to deal with."

"You told me that's all settled," Lady Augusta insisted.

"It's nearly settled," he said. "The men Sheriff Hill sent down are good men, but young and inexperienced. There's no telling what aftershocks might erupt in the next few weeks and what chaos that might cause."

"There will be no more aftershocks for now." Nin's words were sure.

"Is that a message from the spirits?" Jackson asked with rolling eyes.

"I should think you would know by now that I don't talk to spirits, Mr. Gossling," she sneered. "I tell the truth."

"If Nin says there will be no more, there will be no more," Adele snapped. "Nin is a guest in our house, Jack, and you'll treat her gifts with the respect they deserve."

As they retreated to the parlor for coffee, her friend took her arm and said softly, "Thank you."

"Jack needs to be reminded your gifts have helped solve more than one crime in this town," Adele answered.

Maria came in carrying the coffee tray, which Hatfield graciously took from her hands. Consuela followed, leading in Missy Grace, the editor of the *Arrojo Courier*.

Lady Augusta greeted her. "You're just in time for a slice of Rowena's fudge cake."

Missy flicked the usual springy curls over her forehead out of the way and smiled. "It's always good to see you, ma'am."

"To what do we owe this pleasure, as they say?" Jackson bowed, handing her the first cup of coffee Maria had poured.

She sat down next to Adele. "I bring good news, I hope?"

"You hope?" Nin glanced at her.

"I was just at the post office, and Mr. Duncan was sorting through the telegrams. I saw these." She took two small envelopes out of the pockets of her linen suit. "I told him I would deliver them to you."

Adele's heart nearly stopped. "How kind."

"Kind nothing!" Nin snorted. "She thinks she's going to get a story out of it because they're from your city friends."

"That's not true, Miss Branch." Missy looked hurt. "I've my own connections in Oakland. They give me the latest news on the situation."

Adele's hands trembled a little as she took the telegrams. "One is for you, Jack."

"Me?" He blinked. "I didn't wire anyone in the city."

"Some young fawn hasn't forgotten the heartbreaking lawyer's son," Lady Augusta teased.

Jackson took the telegram with a grim look on his face. Adele knew the grimness came from the mention of their father, now four years dead, who had been one of the most prominent criminal lawyers in San Francisco.

It seemed everything was suspended in silence for a moment. Even the Cordoba girls seemed to be holding their breaths.

Nin finally broke the silence. "Well, aren't you going to read them?"

Adele peered at her friend. "Is it bad news, Nin?"

She felt her friend's hurt feelings pierce through her cat-shaped eyes. "You know I don't work that way, Adele."

Hatfield, who was sitting in the stuffed chair beside her, leaned forward and laid his hand on hers. "You're braver than you think, Adele."

"Thank you, Sheriff." She smiled. "I can always count on you to say a good word about me."

His face reddened a little as he cleared his throat, taking another slice of cake.

"Oh, for heaven's sake." Jackson ripped open his telegram. "I'll go first."

Only the soft clamor of cups and saucers filled the room for a moment. Adele realized Nin was right about Missy as she noticed the newspaper woman leaning forward as if trying to get a glimpse of the telegram in Jackson's hands.

He turned it over once, and then read it again.

"Well?" Adele demanded.

"It's not from one of *our* friends," he said.

"Our friends," she repeated. "But a friend of yours?"

"A man I knew." He stuffed the telegram in his pocket.

"Well, what does it say?" Lady Augusta asked. "It can't be that private if you didn't expect it."

"It's from a Lieutenant Edwards," he said.

"A lawman you knew in Chicago?" Adele asked.

"A man I worked with when I was in the Anspatches."

"I see." She was quiet.

"He's in the army now. He's been dispatched to the Presidio to help with the rebuilding."

"Not surprising," Hatfield said. "There's been a call to send troops to the city from all over the country."

"He wants me to come out." His tone was quiet.

"To San Francisco?" Adele stared.

"They need help keeping law and order," he said. "I suppose he's trying to recruit old buddies he knows in this area."

"But you're not going?" Adele asked.

"I have a job here, Del." He poured himself another cup of coffee.

"Nonsense!" Lady Augusta said. "Horatio!" She tapped the side of her son's shoe. "Tell the man you can spare him."

"You took the words right out of my mouth, Ma," he said. "You can go if you like, Jackson. I can get along without you for a while."

"Jack, you have to go." Adele clutched his arm. "Think of all our friends and the people all over the city."

"I'm sure the army is doing its job," her brother mumbled.

"But they don't know the city like you do," she insisted.

"My newspaper friends told me the mayor put up orders to shoot looters on sight," Missy chimed in. "They also said the militia is taking those orders at their word. Some are shooting people down like turkeys at a turkey shoot."

"And your friends just couldn't just be exaggerating, could they?" Nin eyed her.

"As a matter of fact, they could have, but in this case, they didn't," Missy retorted. "Not much, anyway."

"At least consider it, Jack," Adele begged.

"I'll consider it," he promised.

"And your telegram, my dear?" Lady Augusta patted her hand. "Isn't it time you opened it?"

Adele carefully undid the envelope. "It's from Elsie." She read it aloud:

City recovering. We are all right. With Valda at The Presidio. Destitute women and children's aid. We need you. Bring country mouse. Love, Elsie.

"'Bring country mouse'!" Nin snorted.

"Well, dear, it looks like we're going to San Francisco even if Jack isn't." Adele smiled at her friend.

"What for?" Nin asked.

"To help them with their destitute women's aid, of course." Adele shook the telegram. "I know how Elsie thinks, and that's what she means. They've no doubt set up some sort of aid for women, and they need all the help they can get."

"So we're going to San Francisco." The prospect clearly did not please Nin.

"You mean *we're* going to San Francisco," Missy said in a firm voice.

"Haven't you a paper to run?" Nin asked.

"Carla can take over while I'm gone," she said. "She's become quite a little reporter. A little too colorful in spots, perhaps, but she'll learn."

"Just a minute!" Jackson put down his cup. "Nobody said you were going anywhere."

Adele glared at him. "You're not trying to forbid me, are you, Jack?"

"You know I wouldn't dare forbid you anything," he said. "I know where it would get me if I tried." Hatfield laughed and Lady Augusta chuckled. "But we're not talking about a leisurely visit to San Francisco to see friends for the day. We're talking about a city that's all smoke and ashes."

"What has that to do with it?" Adele asked.

"Everything!" He took her hand. "Del, it's not going to be

pleasant. The whole city is in ruins. People don't even have homes anymore. The army is everywhere with their bayonets ready to shoot."

"The camps are safe," Adele argued. "They said so in the papers."

"It's not going to be pleasant," he repeated.

"Since when have Nin and I ever shrunk away from anything unpleasant?" she snapped.

"It seems to me we've braved unpleasantness more than you have, Mr. Gossling," said Nin. "An attack from a golden tiger, for instance." She gave him a sly grin.

"As I recall, Miss Branch, that tiger was in a cage," he said.

"I don't like it much either, Adele." Hatfield held the coffee cup with both hands. "If the army and police have orders to shoot to kill anyone suspected of looting or stealing, just as Miss Grace says, I know for sure the police won't hesitate to do so."

"We don't plan on walking the streets among the rubble, Sheriff," Adele said.

"We're going to help," Missy agreed.

"You mean Adele and I are going to help and you're going to get a story," Nin said. "You'll get the firsthand experience ever country newspaper is dying for."

"And why not?" Lady Augusta insisted. "Maybe what people need right now is firsthand experience."

"I won't deny I'm going for my newspaper too," Missy said. "But it's the human side I'm interested in. I want to see the people and talk to them myself."

"You know Missy isn't a yellow journalist, Nin," Adele protested.

"Maybe she isn't but her paper gets just a little more pallid every day," Nin grumbled.

"We're going, Jack." She looked at him. "With or without you."

"I don't think Miss Branch wants to go." He glanced at her.

It was true. Nin had her knees and her hands pressed tightly together and there was a tightness around her mouth that Adele had never seen before.

She slipped beside her friend and put her arm around her shoulders. "In spite of Elsie's rather thoughtless remark, she wouldn't ask you to come if she didn't think you could help."

"It isn't that," said her friend.

"Is it the aura this afternoon?" Adele asked.

"What aura?" asked Lady Augusta

"Nin had one of her visions," she said. "What was it you said? One thing begets another."

"What is all this about begetting?" Jackson sniffed.

Nin glared at him. "You wouldn't understand, Mr. Gossling." This seemed to revive her. "Of course I'll go."

"That's the spirit!" Lady Augusta raised the glass of brandy her son had just given her. "If I weren't so chained to this damned chair, I would go myself." She glanced over her shoulder. "Maybe you ought to go, Rowena."

"Heaven bless me, ma'am!" The woman looked horrified.

"She's not going anywhere, Ma," said Hatfield. "It's out of the question. Who's going to look after you while I'm doing my work?"

His mother chuckled and pressed her son's large hands. "I wasn't serious, dear."

"Well, if you're going, I suppose I can't stop you." Jackson sighed.

"Have you ever stopped me from doing what I thought was right?" she challenged him.

"What you think is right, dear sister, is sometimes a little reckless!"

Later that night, after everyone had gone and she had gotten Nin settled in one of the guest rooms, she sat brushing her hair in front of the mirror and thinking. She heard heavy footsteps coming up the stairs.

"Jack?"

He appeared at the doorway.

She turned to him. "We can't abandon the city we were born in when it needs us the most."

He gave her a half smile. "You were the one who wanted to leave, remember?"

"Peace and small pleasures," she recalled. "And I was right, wasn't I?"

"Except for a few murders and thefts here and there, it's been peaceful," he agreed.

She reached out her hand and he came into the room and took it.

"I'm not saying we should go back," she said. "I'm only saying we owe San Francisco a debt of gratitude. We were born and raised there, after all."

"Don't tell me you're getting sentimental in your old age," he said ruefully.

"I don't consider twenty-nine old!"

He laughed. "You're almost thirty, Del."

"It's not sentiment, Jack," she said. "It's — I don't know. When a place gets ingrained in your experience—in your soul even—you just can't bear to think of it destroyed."

"That's hardly our fault," he pointed out.

"We have a chance to help rebuild the city," she insisted. "Don't you want to take that chance?"

He sighed, looking at the glass lamp she had on the vanity table as it threw patterns on the wall. "Maybe I do."

"I knew it!" She threw her arms around him. "We'll check the train schedule and send off the telegrams tomorrow."

"Telegrams?"

"So Elsie and this lieutenant friend of yours will know we're coming."

"I have to let Hatfield know," he said.

"I think you ought to convince him to come with you," Adele

said. "He's as much of the experience and soul of San Francisco as we are."

"You have more persuasive powers than I have," he said with a gleam in his eye. "It might not be a bad idea at that. I think things have calmed down here enough for Edison to take over."

"Take over what?" Nin appeared in the doorway in her nightgown, her hair falling over her shoulders.

"Law and order in Arrojo," Adele said. "Jack is coming with us, and maybe the sheriff will too. That would leave Edison to run the sheriff's office here."

"One shouldn't tempt the fate of pandemonium," her friend advised as she toddled back to her room. Jackson burst out laughing.

CHAPTER 4

The next morning, true to his word, Jackson came with her to the post office. They scribbled off telegrams to both Elsie and Lieutenant Edwards to meet them at the Ferry Building tomorrow evening. As Mr. Duncan reviewed the telegrams, his face grew a little sour.

"I thought you had nothing more to do with that city." He sniffed as he rang up the charges.

"We still have friends there, Mr. Duncan," Adele said. "One doesn't forget one's friends."

"You have friends here," he said. "The entire town is trying to recover, and you two go off to San Francisco as if —"

"As if?" Jackson questioned in a rough tone.

"Well, it ain't like you got roots there anymore," the man grumbled.

"I should think the fact that I'm the town deputy is proof enough of that," Jackson said dryly.

"Then why this rush back there?"

"We want to help with the relief effort," Adele explained. "As I said, Mr. Duncan, one never forgets one's friends."

"Seems to me the town deputy ought to stay in town," Mr.

Duncan said as he gave Jackson back his change. "How long you plan on being away?"

"A few weeks, maybe," Jackson said. "I really don't think there's going to be an outbreak of crime in Arrojo County while I'm gone."

"Never can tell, Deputy," said the man with a knowing look. "Read somewhere that when the ground cracks like this after an earthquake, all kinds of bad things come up."

"You sound like Nin." Adele couldn't help smiling at the man's obvious displeasure at this comparison.

They left and started toward the police station. "Now the entire town will know we're going and for how long by the time the day is out," Jackson remarked.

"By the time the day is out?" Adele snorted. "They'll know by lunchtime!"

He laughed. "So now we're town traitors again, just like we were when we first came."

She took his hand and swung his arm like she used to do when they were children. "And they'll get over it just like they did after we solved our first case."

"*Our* first case?" He eyed her. "It wasn't ours to solve then."

"It is now," Adele insisted. "You're the deputy, and I'm as good as a police consultant."

"Don't get ahead of yourself, Del," he said. "The mayor rejected the application, remember."

"No thanks to Mrs. Faderman," Adele grumbled.

"You didn't expect it to come from Willett's own mind, did you?" Jackson asked. "He hasn't had an original thought since he learned his ABCs."

Adele laughed. "I think Mayor Willett is going to find he has one persistent sheriff on his hands. Hatfield said he would apply again."

"The same thing will happen," Jackson insisted.

"Not necessarily," she said. "Women will be making strides in law enforcement all over the country before long. The sheriff says he plans on including a pamphlet of case studies where women helped to solve criminal cases. Maybe it won't seem like such a ridiculous thing once the mayor sees that."

"I think Willett finds the idea more terrifying than ridiculous," Jackson said with a smile as they entered the station. "Women out on the street carrying guns and a license to use them."

Edison, who was sitting at his desk, looked up. "I think Miss Gossling would be bully with a gun, if you want my opinion, sir."

"No one asked for your opinion!" Jackson snapped.

"Miss Oakley says ever girl ought to know how to shoot a gun," Edison insisted. "Why, my two sisters —"

"Edison!" the sheriff's voice rang out, making the small station shake. "What nonsense are you filling Miss Gossling's head with now? Didn't I tell you and Curd to go through those boxes?"

"But the earthquake didn't upset anything in the file room, sir," Edison said.

"We can't be sure of that unless we check them, can we?" Sheriff Hatfield threw the keys to the file room on the assistant deputy's table. "Where is Curd, by the way?"

"He went to help Mr. Gardner and Mr. Pringle," said the young man. "It seems they just got a box of lobsters for the mayor's party. The lobsters ran all over the place and he's helping to catch them."

The sheriff threw his head back and his deep laugh lent an air of comfort to the otherwise colorless station. Adele was equally amused, though more at Edison's serious expression and sincere words.

"Well, you get started back there, and when Curd returns, I'll send him in," said the sheriff. "Provided his fingers aren't too pinched from those lobsters to hold the files!"

"If you'll excuse me, sir, I don't see why Dooland and Scott are on patrol in Quarry Lane with the Sacramento men while Curd and I are here going through files," Edison complained.

"Are you questioning the sheriff's judgment, Assistant Deputy?" Jackson asked in a severe tone.

"No, sir, no indeed!" The young man twiddled his thumbs. "I just thought — with you off to San Francisco to help out, and maybe the sheriff too — well, we need all able-bodied men down there."

"Who said anything about my going to San Francisco?" Jackson stiffened. "You seem very anxious for us to be out of the station, Edison."

"Oh, no, Deputy, not saying that at all. Why, I —"

Adele couldn't help but laugh. "Leave him alone, Jack. Don't pay any attention, Assistant Deputy. Jack loves to torture people when they annoy him."

Sheriff Hatfield laughed too. "The boxes are more important at the moment. They're the only records we have of our cases. I'd rather trust them to you than to Dooland."

Edison grinned and saluted the sheriff as he trotted off to the file room.

"You always know the right thing to say, Sheriff," Adele said in a warm voice.

"Not to mention if you left Curd to do it, he'd misplace every piece of evidence and every file we have," Jackson remarked. "The boy's a scatterbrain, to say the least."

"He tries, Jack," Adele protested.

"He does indeed," Sheriff Hatfield said. "And you know I'm not averse to getting all the help I can, especially during this tragedy. Speaking of help," he glanced at Jackson, "I don't fancy Edison as a mind-reader, but he's right, isn't he? You've decided to go down to the city to help your friend?"

Adele threaded her arm through her brother's. "Don't blame Jack, Sheriff. It was my doing."

"If you object, sir, I'll send off another telegram canceling my trip right away." Jackson looked anxiously at his superior. "I only sent it on the strength of what you said yesterday."

Sheriff Hatfield leaned back, glancing out the window. "I meant what I said, Jackson. I think it's good that you go. They need a lot of help out there."

"Exactly why you should join us." Adele exchanged a glance with her brother.

"I'm sure they need lawmen with your kind of skill and knowledge, sir," Jackson said. "More than they need someone like me."

"You ought to, sir!" This excited call came from Edison, who was now standing in the file room doorway. "What an exciting thing to be right in the thick of it!"

"This isn't an adventure story, Assistant Deputy," Jackson snapped. "Nor is it a western at the moving picture theater. We're not going because we want to. We're going because it's necessary."

"Oh, I didn't mean —"

"You never mean," Jackson said. "You just open your mouth without using your head about what comes out of it!"

"Don't be harsh on him, Jack." Adele smiled at Edison. "It is a sort of adventure, but Jack's right. We want to help those thousands of people who have lost their homes and loved ones."

Hatfield had been quiet for a time, twirling the letter opener from the set Adele had given him as a gift earlier that year.

She sat at the edge of his desk. "You've been thinking about it, haven't you, Sheriff?"

"Ma wants me to," he said. "I had a telegram waiting for me too when we got home last night. My friend on the police force sent it. They're having a mighty hard time."

"And he asked you to come?" Adele guessed.

Hatfield chuckled. "You should know lawmen well enough by now to know that most don't ask for help even when they need it. They like to stick to their territory."

"Maybe he won't appreciate your coming, then," Jackson said.

"Walker isn't the kind," he said. "I just don't like leaving Ma alone."

"With Rowena there?" Adele asked. "She's as good as a mother grizzly bear."

"Her health has been better since the spring set in," Jackson reminded him. "You told me so yourself, sir."

"I know," he said. "But this whole calamity has affected her more than she's willing to admit."

Adele laid her hand on his. "How would it be if I asked Maria and Consuela to visit her every day and make sure she has everything she needs?"

"They're fine girls," Jackson agreed.

"They're fine young ladies," Adele corrected. "And they like Lady Augusta very much."

Hatfield smiled. "I'm not sure how Rowena would like that."

"Maria and Consuela have youth on their side," Adele said. "They also have intelligence. They'll know how to get around Rowena when she gets too crotchety."

Hatfield laughed. "Well, I suppose it's my duty to go."

"That's just your spirit, Sheriff," Adele said. "Always jumping in to lend a helping hand. You don't just accept help, you give it unconditionally."

The sheriff's countenance, surprisingly boyish for his middle age, glowed with the compliment. "Well, after all, it *was* my department once."

"That's just what I was saying to Jack yesterday," said Adele. "When a place is in your history and in your soul, you can't get away from it entirely."

Hatfield whirled his chair around to catch Edison, who was still listening at the doorway. "Well, what do you say, Edison? You think you can take command here while the deputy and I are in San Francisco?"

"Yes, sir!" The young man's enthusiastic wail filled the small station.

"You be fair to the lads now," the sheriff warned. "And I don't want to hear about you and Dooland sniggering at one another while I've been gone."

"Oh, no, Sheriff," said the young man with a salute. "Not if he knows *I'm* in charge." A sly look appeared on his face that made Jackson roll his eyes.

~

In spite of the tragic reasons for their departure, the group from Arrojo boarded the train in good spirits. Adele was surprised to see the cars were filled with people, many of them carrying picnic baskets and heavy suitcases.

"It looks like other people had the same idea as we did," she remarked as she squeezed past the straight skirts and linen trousers of people standing in the corridor. She peered into the compartments, looking for three vacant seats.

"Where are they all coming from?" Nin's tone was nervous. Adele knew the confinement of the train car was bad enough for Nin but crowds made it ten times worse for her.

"Sacramento, most likely," Missy said.

They found a compartment with two seats vacant and a gentleman rose, tipping his hat, and offering Missy his seat. As she thanked him and settled in, his eye examined her with approval. Though Missy wasn't exactly pretty, she had a vivacity to her face that men found equally attractive.

The forth passenger in the car, a woman who looked to be in her early forties with bright red hair tucked under a green hat, gave him an arch look. "Well, sir, if you'll kindly vacate, I'm sure we could find a breath of fresh air in here."

The man pursed his lips, tipped his hat again to Missy, and went out of the compartment, shutting the door behind him.

"Thank you." Missy bowed to the woman.

"Wolves looking for sheep," the woman mumbled.

Adele laughed. "I hardly relish the idea of being thought of as 'sheep.'" She held out her hand. "Adele Gossling."

The woman shook it with a vigorous smile. "Felicia Burne. Vice-President of the San Francisco City Beautification League."

"So you're going to San Francisco to help beautify the city?" Nin asked. When the woman gave her a questionable glance, she introduced herself without holding out her hand. "Miss Branch."

"Missy Grace, owner and editor of the *Arrojo Courier*," Missy put in, taking out her pad and pencil.

"You're going to help with the rebuilding, then," Adele said with a nod of approval.

"We're doing what we can to ensure the city gets back on its feet better than it was," Mrs. Burne declared.

"We all want that," Missy said.

"But you don't live there, do you?" She looked at each woman in turn.

"I used to," Adele said. "I grew up there."

"Then you know what a cesspool it's become," said Miss Burne in a hard tone. "Poor construction, graft, corruption."

"My friends regret the day Mayor Schmitz was elected in office." Adele's face set in annoyance.

"Oh, Schmitz is just a mouthpiece." Nin waved her hand.

"Mr. Ruef is the devil behind Lucifer," Miss Burne agreed.

"At least they're doing their duty now by modernizing the city," Missy said. "My reporter friends say they've heard the cable transportation will be replaced by electric."

"They might even rebuild to protect people in case of earthquakes now," Nin said with a sniff. "Not that they'll spend a penny more than they have to in order to do it."

"Everything is going to change." Miss Burne looked out the window. "Sewage, water, gas, electricity. Everything."

"I doubt the Barbary Coast will change," Adele remarked. "Too lucrative for the city politicians."

"Sin always brings a profit," Nin agreed with a flinch.

"I don't think so, Miss Gossling," said Miss Burne. "Everyone in the city is tired of the dirt, noise and vice. Especially those isolated in their mansions just up the hill." She chuckled. "It won't happen in a day or even a year, I grant you. But the Barbary Coast *will* shut down."

"As will the Chinatown's opium dens and brothels," Missy chimed in. "There's even talk of moving Chinatown outside the city."

"I hope not," Miss Burne said fiercely. "They've been pushed into the gutter enough. Now they want to push them into the bay."

"I don't think the Chinese will allow it," Adele argued. "The Orientals are not a weak people, and they don't wish for the vice in their backyards any more than the rest of the city. They were forced into it under vile circumstances."

"They say tragedy is the great leveler," Miss Burne said. "Perhaps people will see that, rich or poor, Chinese, Mexican, or Caucasian, we are all the same, and we all need purity and beauty." She sighed as her head turned toward the window again.

"'Out of the ashes will rise peace and goodness,'" Missy said in a misty tone. Then she wrote this down on her pad.

CHAPTER 5

They arrived at the Oakland pier already exhausted from the train ride and anxious to get to the city. The terminal was like a large tube that fed into the edge of the bay with train tracks paralleling one another. People scurried between puffs of steam, and Adele feared losing sight of her brother and the sheriff who had found room in a car farther down the tracks. But the men quickly located them, and they all boarded the ferry after bidding Miss Burne goodbye and good luck.

The women were the only ones willing to brave the crisp, whipping wind on deck. They stood in a corner with many others, also mostly women, with one hand pressing down their hats, trying to keep them from flying away, while the other grasping the edge of their skirts so they wouldn't flounce out.

"Where are all the men?" Missy lamented.

"They're too afraid of the cold!" Nin snorted as the loose pins in her thick dark hair made tendrils swing back and forth around her face.

"I don't think it's the wind they're afraid of," Adele murmured as her eyes caught a glimpse of the gray, flat surface of the city some distance away. "It's the city."

"Why should the city frighten them?" Missy looked at her.

"They don't want to see what the city looks like now," Adele said. "They know they're not going to see magnificent buildings and people hurrying along the streets."

"They don't know what the city is like now, so they'd rather not find out before they have to," Nin agreed.

Missy looked at her admiringly. "Why, Miss Branch, that's a very keen observation. Do you mind if I quote you in my paper?"

"I can't stop you, can I?" Nin challenged.

Adele laughed. "Just don't mention her by name, Missy."

The newspaper woman nodded, gathering her skirt and hat between her legs so she could write in her pad.

"Don't you want to interview people about their experience seeing the city from the bay?" Adele inquired.

Missy hestiated. "Do you think I ought to? I don't want to — well, it might be an emotional moment for some of them."

"City people are more resilient than that, Missy." Adele smiled. "I think they'd be delighted to talk to you."

"Everyone wants to be in the papers," Nin pointed out.

"Well, if you think I should," Missy ventured.

"Will you be able to get the story out of the city once we're there?" Adele asked.

She nodded. "My reporter friends told me they have devious means of telegraphing their papers without the military knowing using all kinds of code words. Carla and I already devised our own code."

"Aren't you giving her an awful lot of responsiblity?" Nin asked.

"I told you she fancies herself a junior reporter now," Missy said with a grin. "I'm simply taking advantage of the fact." She waved and began circulating around the deck.

Adele sighed as she watched her. "Women are so much braver than men, aren't they?"

"We're more practical," Nin said. "If a place is in ruins, we don't whimper about it. We simply roll up our sleeves and get to work."

Adele began to feel queasy as the ferry turned and headed toward the wharf. She could already see the clock tower of the ferry building and the flat surface of land on either side. She began to realize the crushing blow she would receive when they emerged from the building and viewed what was left of San Francisco.

They reached the ferry building and filed out with the crowds. The inside was as chaotic as the one in Oakland, but here, there was a nervous kind of chatter, as if the people darting from place to place had little idea of what was going to happen next.

A young man about Jackson's age with a handlebar mustache, wearing an army uniform, came toward them. Jackson introduced him as Lieutenant Monte Edwards.

"The years have been good to you, Jackson." The young man smoothed down the top of his cap. "You look like a gentleman with purpose now."

Jackson blushed a little. "I think my superior here would find that a contradiction in terms."

Hatfield roared with laughter. "I'll confess I knocked some of the gentle manners out of my deputy, but he's had a much better influence on me than I've had on him." He clamped Jackson on the back. "I don't mind telling you, Lieutenant, that he's the best lawman I've ever worked with."

Jackson blushed again but Adele knew he was pleased by the compliment.

"So you're Jackson's lovely sister." Edwards regarded her with an approving eye. "And you've brought some lovely friends with you." He cast the same eye on Nin and Missy, letting it linger on the former.

"That's an awful lot of loveliness in one place." Nin smirked.

"Miss Grace is a reporter," Jackson said.

The eyes immediately became guarded. "You'll have to be careful what you print, Miss Grace. We're very strict about what goes in the papers."

"I'm sure you are," Missy said dryly.

"Miss Grace is very respectful," Hatfield insisted. "If you ask her to withhold information, she will without argument."

"I'm glad to hear it." Edwards relaxed a little. "And you and Miss Branch, Miss Gossling? Have you come to keep your brother company?"

"Hardly," Nin snapped. "He came with us, not us with him."

Adele hid a smile. "Nin and I are here to help some friends with the refugee aid work."

"We could use it," Edwards said.

Just then, Adele saw Elsie's tall head bobbing up in the crowd and waved at her. Her heart sank as the woman came forward. Contrary to Elsie's usual polished appearance, she looked rumpled and frayed. Her dress was wrinkled and her hair poorly made up under the hat. She clutched her handbag as if it were the last thing she had on earth. Adele had no doubt that it probably was.

She rushed to her friend and threw her arms around her. Elsie, though she usually disliked public displays, held her tightly. The tears Adele had been holding back for days now gushed forward, and she sobbed loudly as she buried her face in Elsie's shoulder.

"Now, now, none of that." Elsie's vigor reassured her. "We learned a long time ago that tears are useless, didn't we?" She brushed Adele's face with her long fingers and Adele noticed she wore no gloves.

"I'm sorry." Adele could hardly speak but she managed to get her handkerchief out of her purse and compose herself.

"You have nothing to apologize for." This came from Nin. Missy regarded her with a tender look.

"I'm touched by the sentiment," Elsie said with a smile. "But where would women be if all we did was sob into our handkerchiefs, eh? There's too much work to be done."

"That's the spirit, Miss Blessings," Missy said with a salute.

"As you see, the country mouse is here to help too," Nin said in a wry tone, but she shook Elsie's hand with warmth.

"And very glad I am to see you, Miss Branch." She eyed Missy. "Is this another country mouse?"

"I'm a reporter," Missy said with dignity.

"Good!" Elsie gave her a pat on the back. "We need more lady reporters to stand up for us. All those men have been doing is showing the plight of the poor mother with her five children in the face of destruction brought on by San Francisco's corrupt politics, et cetera, et cetera."

"Well, isn't it true?" Missy asked.

"Of course it's true," Elsie scoffed as Adele put her arm around her and led her to the men. "But they need to know we're not completely helpless. They need to know we're here for destitute women, and we need all the resources we can get."

"I'll be glad to report whatever I see," Missy promised.

"Good to see you, Elsie." Jackson held out his hand with some trepidation. "I see you're looking fit."

"And I see you've got useless compliments hanging from your tongue as usual, Jackson," she said in a brisk tone. "I don't look fit. I look like I've been digging through the rubble, which is more or less what I've been doing."

"Speaking of tongues, I'm happy to see you haven't lost yours," Jackson said with a dignified smile.

"Don't start, Jack." Adele took his arm. "Elsie's doing a lot of good work for the women and children who have been left with nothing."

"Valda and I have called a temporary truce," she said.

"I wasn't aware you were at war," Adele said dryly.

Ignoring this, Elsie continued, "We managed to cajole the army into giving us a small tent —" she glanced with authority at Lieutenant Edwards, "— so we could give them somewhere to go for whatever they needed."

"That is indeed good work, Miss Blessings," Hatfield said.

Elsie examined him. "So you're the infamous Sheriff of Notthingham, shall we say? I've heard so much about you from Adele."

In spite of the sheriff's tall and broad build, his boyish face looked meager as he nodded.

"My father speaks highly of you as well." Elsie's severe face relaxed. "Papa rarely praises any man, so consider that a compliment."

"How is Dr. Blessings?" Nin asked, her anxiety genuine.

Elsie patted her shoulder. "You needn't worry, Miss Branch. Right after the earthquake, Papa managed to get a spot in a wagon heading for Los Angeles. We have relatives there. I received a wire this morning that he's doing just fine and wishing he had been able to take more books with him before the fires —" Here, a lump caught in her throat and she pressed her hands together. "Before the fires devoured them."

"I'm sorry," Jackson said with genuine regret.

"It was an old house anyway." She brushed aside her dismay. "My mother used to say it's sometimes good to be forced to start fresh in life."

"It is indeed," Missy agreed.

Just then, a heavyset man with dark red hair and bloodhound eyes appeared. He shook Hatfield's hand with the certainty of an old friend. Hatfield introduced him as Sergeant Harold Walker.

"Sir!" Lieutenant Edwards saluted him.

"You needn't stand on ceremony, young man," said Walker, chuckling. "I'm from the police, not the army."

"Aren't the police wearing uniforms?" Nin asked.

The man laughed. "Some of us are, Miss Branch and some of us aren't. It rather depends on who was wearing them when the fires started."

"You mean it ate up everything?" Adele's voice quivered.

"When you walk out this building, you'll see for yourself," Elsie said.

"You won't have to walk far," Edwards said. "Captain Best allowed me to take one of the wagons when he found out there would be several people about." He looked at Walker. "You're staying at the Presidio, Sergeant?"

"I am, Lieutenant," he said.

"You'll permit me to extend the army's hospitality by inviting you to ride with us?" the young man asked.

The sergeant gave a smile. "Only if there's enough room. The ladies and our guests come first."

"We'll make enough room," Adele said kindly as she took the man's arm.

He patted her hand. "Horatio said he'd found a lady who was both intelligent and charming and as good as any policeman on the force. I see he wasn't wrong."

Adele felt humbled by this shower of compliments and smiled at the sheriff.

As they walked out into the street, Adele tried not to gasp. She now knew what Elsie meant by "digging through the rubble." Rocks, granite, wood, and piles of unidentified materials were pushed to the sides of the dirt road. Tents were strung up where women, men, and children loitered about, some dressed as fine as if they had just been to a ball while others were in rags. A cable car stood as if frozen in time without tracks on which to run.

The sight of the city where she had spent many joyful times and had once been beloved to her reduced to rocks, wood, soot, and dirt was too much for her. She turned away, ducking her head, and when a nearby horse that seemed sympathetic to her feelings let out a string of neighing, she allowed herself to break into sobs. She fell behind the others who were making their way to the wagon, but Nin was at her side. She felt her friend's strong arms around her shoulders, and she remained silent while the tears rolled down her cheeks.

As Adele began to calm down, she wiped her face with a handkerchief. Then she realized it was bordered in black and had the initials O.G. Seeing her father's handkerchief made her want to burst into tears again.

"Thank God he wasn't alive to see this," she choked out as Nin lay her head on her shoulder.

"He couldn't have endured it," her friend agreed.

This brought Adele back to reality. She finished wiping her face, patted it with a little powder, and took a few deep breaths. "I'm sorry. I shouldn't have broken down like that. We've come here to do a job, haven't we?"

"And damned if we're not going to do it!" Nin's voice was so fierce that Adele laughed and took her friend's arm.

When they got to the wagon, Adele could see that her brother was also affected by the ruined city. As Edwards arranged everyone in the wagon, Jackson couldn't take his eyes off Market Street's crumbled buildings. The scent of smoke still hung in the air, and a gray haze shielded the blue sky.

"Armageddon, isn't it, Jack?" she lamented, grasping her brother's arm.

Jackson whispered, "Don't worry, Del. In a year it will be like nothing ever happened."

"A year," she echoed.

"Maybe two," he admitted.

"I see the rebuilding has already started," Hatfield said as he helped them into the back seat of the wagon. The hearty tone in his voice told Adele that, although his connection with the city was more remote than hers and Jackson's, its ruin had touched him too.

"You could say that, sir." Edwards took the reins in his hands. "They've been mostly clearing away the marble, wood, and other materials so they can start the actual rebuilding."

"They have to get the rubble out and the cracks filled first," Elsie agreed. "Don't want people or horses falling into the ground, do we?" Edwards glared at her, clearly not appreciating this gruesome image. "But you can see why we need every able-bodied man and woman," the young lieutenant continued as he nodded toward the people they passed, many of whom looked bewildered and a little envious at the horse-drawn wagon.

"It's good we all came, then," Adele said.

"I ought to have given you more notice," Hatfield said to Walker.

"Not at all!" Walker patted him on the back. "We're glad to have any good man we can find."

"Is it as bad as the papers say?" Jackson turned to Edwards. "Maintaining law and order, that is?"

"I think the army has managed quite well," Edwards said, not without a little pride in his voice. "There have been accidents, it's true —"

"You mean like the private who shot the Italian dry-goods man in North Beach who allowed people to take what they liked from his store?" Missy eyed him.

The man stiffened in true soldier fashion. "That was one of the many tales the press told in the days after the quake, Miss Grace."

"So you deny the military have been too free with their bayo-nets?" Missy probed.

"If they have been, the guilty ones aren't Funston's men," Edwards declared as he carefully turned a corner.

"Some say Funston was a little too eager to take hold of the city." Walker eyed the young man.

Edwards was quiet for a moment. "I expect the police would have done the same if they had had the authority."

"I don't judge, Lieutenant," said Walker in a firm tone. "I only relate what I hear."

"General Funston did what he had to do," Edwards insisted. "The mayor and the rest of the committee certainly weren't doing anything quick enough."

"They were too busy trying to decide who would be in charge," Nin agreed with a snort.

"When a city is on the brink of pandemonium, someone must take action," Jackson agreed. "I think the General ought to be commended rather than condemned."

"That's not for us to say, Jackson," Hatfield reminded him. "We're here to do a job, and we'll do it."

"Just as *we're* here to do a job." Adele smiled at Elsie.

"And ours is much more peaceful than the military's," Elsie agreed.

They entered the Presidio. Adele was relieved to see that here, at least, people had benefitted from army organization and precision. Rows of tents were arranged neatly with wide pathways in between. There were tents labeled as the dining room and the hospital. People looked calmer and less bewildered.

Edwards brought the horses to a halt in front of the stable. "I reserved a tent for you, Jackson." He jumped off the wagon. "It's one of the smaller ones, but it's all yours at least. It's what comes with army privileges." He grinned.

"I hope it's close to the ladies." Jackson pulled his bag over his shoulder. "I don't like the idea of Del and Miss Branch being alone at night."

"They won't be alone," Elsie insisted. "Valda and I are staying in the same tent."

"And you, sir?" Edwards glanced at Hatfield.

"I'm afraid I haven't your connections, young man," said

Walker in a jovial tone. "I haven't yet been able to find a place for you, Horatio."

"I can sleep outside." Hatfield grinned. "It wouldn't be the first time."

"I imagine a Wells Fargo detective must make his bed where he can out in the open," Adele said with amusement. The sheriff blushed.

"Ah, but Horatio were a much younger man then," Walker said which made Hatfield wrinkle his nose. "The old bones don't adjust to the ground so well now."

"If you'll excuse me, sir, Jackson's tent has an extra cot," said Edwards. "As I said, it isn't very big, but it can fit two."

"I'd prefer you stay with me, sir," said Jackson.

"Then I accept." Hatfield smiled. "I'd like to send a telegram to Ma to let her know we arrived safely, if I may."

"You can use the civilian telegraph line." Edwards took Missy and Adele's small bags. Nin held her purse tightly. "It's a little way down in the other direction."

"That's all right," said Hatfield. "We'll get settled first. Time enough."

They all trudged through the camp. Rows of tents pitched between pathways. Adele was surprised to see the overall congenial tone of the place. People smiled and chatted with one another. Women hung clothes out to dry on cords strung between poles and men sat outside smoking pipes. Children of all ages and races played together.

"It's as if the entire city has gone on one long camping trip," she observed.

"Everyone has been very cooperative," Edwards agreed. "Before the professionals came in, we had most of the men from the camps clearing of rubble. We hardly had any trouble with anyone, wouldn't you say, sir?" He turned to Walker.

"You can't keep the spirit of San Francisco down," Walker agreed. "It's that spirit we're trying to maintain now."

"It's not the evil spirit but the restless one that gets into trouble," Nin agreed.

The lawman grinned at her. "Well put, Miss Branch."

She turned away, as she always did when someone complimented her.

"Still," said Missy. "I can't help thinking someone could easily commit a murder here and no one would notice."

"I disagree, Miss Grace," Walker said. "If one wanted to commit a crime, he would have several thousand eyes watching. Someone would be bound to see something. Even the shrubbery here wouldn't hide a dead body."

"At any rate, people are far too practical at the moment to think about committing murders," Elsie said. "When you're grasping for food and water and wondering how you're going to live and work, you haven't time to think of killing anyone."

"Let's hope you're right, Miss Blessings," Hatfield said.

"Even if Elsie is wrong, it won't be your problem," Nin pointed out. "Not here."

"Nor yours or Del's, Miss Branch," Jackson said. "At least we have that off our minds."

Nin grimaced, knowing how Jackson felt about his sister involving herself in crime.

CHAPTER 6

That night, they all met at the dining room which was really a large tent with long tables set with army dishes and utensils. The ladies had arranged themselves in the roomy tent with Elsie and Valda and had even been able to freshen up with a basin of water one of the neighboring women used for washing and some army towels. The men had made themselves comfortable in the smaller tent.

As they settled in, Adele noticed people pushing suitcases and bags under the table at their feet.

"Everyone looks as if they want to camp out here," she said wryly.

"They're afraid of looters," said Walker.

"As if the army would allow such a thing," Edwards said with some indignation. "We have men patrolling all the time."

"Don't worry, Lieutenant," Adele said with a laugh. "We trust the army."

"There isn't much they could steal from us anyway," Nin added.

Adele noticed Missy scribbling furiously in her notepad as several enlisted men and women who had volunteered to help in the kitchen laid plates of food between them. Edwards, who had gotten permission to sit with them, saw this too and his handsome face contorted with a frown.

"I hope you're right about this woman's discretion," he said to her brother.

"Don't you want people to know how the army is taking great care to feed the refugees?" Adele asked.

"It's not for me to decide, Miss Gossling," he said. "I've no connection with the people in charge of communications." He started on the soup. "I would highly recommend, Miss Grace, that you seek permission from our Signal Corps before you wire your stories to your office."

"Permission!" Missy glared at him. "Even when I was working with my brothers, who were as subtle as you are about their opinion of woman reporters, I never asked permission to print anything."

"Monte said nothing about you being a woman, Miss Grace," Jackson pointed out.

"I know what he was implying," she said. "Lots of men think women don't belong in the press room."

"Lots of people think women don't belong anywhere," Adele said. "That doesn't stop us from ignoring them and doing what we like."

Hatfield laughed. "And where is the good Miss Blessings tonight?"

"She and Valda have a table in the other tent," said Adele. "She wanted to join us, of course."

"Adele thought it might be too crowded," Nin put in. "There doesn't seem to be much logic in the way things are run here." She eyed Edwards.

"It's difficult to establish order when we have hundreds of people to accommodate," Walker said. "I think the army is doing its best, Miss Branch."

"And the police force?" Jackson asked.

"We're working with as many good men as we can," Walker said. "With no money to pay them, there are those who prefer to take a leave of absence."

"Dinan should make them stay and do their duty," Hatfield said with a growl.

"Dinan can only do so much, Horatio," said Walker. "He's getting criticism from all sides because of the looting."

"I've heard they fear even worse crimes will occur once houses go up and people return from Oakland," Missy said.

"Perhaps that's to be expected," Walker said with a sigh. "We'll deal with that when we come to it."

"We're in a better position now than we were during the fires," Edwards pointed out. "We had too many outsiders using bad judgment to make decisions. Now we're all under the same orders."

"Including orders to shoot to kill if anyone looks suspicious or argues with authority?" Nin raised her eyebrows.

"I told you, Miss Branch, those are not our men," he insisted.

"And it's not the police either," Walker said, equally as firm.

"The devil of it — oh, pardon me —" Edwards nodded to the ladies. "The problem is we're taking orders from the committee and, if you'll forgive me, Sergeant, the police, rather than military personnel. Situations like this need people who are used to dealing with mob panic and violence."

"I'll admit the police don't have the kind of experience the army has with dire situations." Walker fished for another chicken leg on the platter near him.

"Precisely," said Edwards.

"That's why the mayor had no choice but to issue the 'shoot to kill' order," said Walker. "Oh, here, we're all conducting ourselves in an orderly manner. You saw, Horatio. It's almost like a picnic."

"I wouldn't say that, sir," said Edwards.

"Nonetheless, the army is doing its job," said the man. Edwards looked proud. "But outside the camps, our men aren't having an easy time of it. They have to guard relief supplies, keep fights from breaking out, and make sure the bars stay closed, and talk civilians out of leaving the camps and settling near their destroyed homes."

"Why shouldn't they if they want to?" Nin asked.

"It's very dangerous, Miss Branch," said Walker. "We still don't know the extent of the damages until we examine every half-crumbled building. There might be a loose gas line or electric cable. One careless move could start the fires all over again."

"Well, there wouldn't be much left to burn," Jackson pointed out.

"But there's people," Walker reminded him. "If a fire can't consume wood, that's what it will look for next."

"Horrible thought." Adele shuddered as Missy wrote it down on her pad.

"I can't blame them for wanting to return to their homes," Jackson admitted. "Even if only to salvage what they can of their personal belongings."

"Everyone wants that," Edwards said. "We had a hard time getting the Chinese to abandon their neighborhood to come here."

"You've set up camp for them?" Adele asked.

"Well, they had to go *somewhere*, Miss Gossling," Edwards said. "Of course, we're keeping them distanced from everyone else."

"So we don't catch their diseases, heaven forbid?" She eyed him.

The lieutenant sniffed. "Well, Miss Gossling, you can't deny the plague in '04 came from Chinatown."

"And never went beyond it," she reminded him. "I had friends who worked with the Chinese and told me all about it."

"Perhaps it's not the plague the army is afraid of but their wisdom," Nin added slyly. "They say the Chinese philosophers are the wisest in the world."

Edwards shrugged. "I don't know about that, Miss Branch. But we made sure they were all checked when they came here."

"A newspaper friend told me most of the people from Chinatown crossed the bay to Oakland," Missy said.

"They did," said Walker. "I believe only a few hundred remained in the city."

"Stubborn lot," the lieutenant remarked.

"And city residents," Walker insisted. "They deserve to receive aid just like the rest of the people."

Hatfield looked down at the banana cream pie in front of him. Adele wondered if he missed Rowena's desserts, which were known all over Arrojo as the best.

Adele found it easier to get to sleep that night than she thought she would. The events of the day had made her as limp as a rag doll in spite of the cot's boniness. There was a quiet lull in the camp early on, as if everyone had retired to their tents. Edwards warned them the army enforced a strict ten o'clock curfew. Adele fell asleep well before that.

The next morning Elsie took them to the small tent she and Valda had set up with the sign "Destitute Women's Aid Society." There was already a line when they got there. Adele's hear went out to these women, some with small children or holding babies in their arms. Some were dressed in ill-fitting mourning clothes, which, she guessed, had been donated from other cities.

"Poor ladies," Nin breathed.

Missy surveyed the line. "I'll tell Carla to get in touch with women's organizations around Arrojo county and ask them to urgently send over what they can now that the trains are running."

"That's kind of you, Miss Grace." Elsie was clearly touched.

"Call me Missy." The newspaper woman smiled.

Valda greeted Adele warmly, her lovely heart-shaped face showing the same kind of fatigue she had seen on Elsie's. "You see what all this shaking and rumbling has brought us." She glanced her more radical friend.

"I don't think Elsie has politics on her mind just now." Adele pressed her hand. "She hasn't had for a long time because of her father."

"We all have survival on our minds," Elsie agreed. "The city's red tape is making even getting bread and shoes slow. Women are suffering the most, especially those of us without families."

"Priority is being given to wives and mothers," Valda said.

"Isn't that natural?" Nin asked.

"It may be natural, but where does it leave women with children but no husbands or women like us?" Elsie asked fiercely. "Ill-clothed and ill-fed."

"Relief is the right of everyone," Adele agreed as she looked around. "I see you've tapped into all your resources."

"Don't be fooled, Adele," Valda said. "We're very limited, and she almost gave it all away to the ladies who came yesterday."

"Then we get more," Elsie said with vigor. "I have a few friends in Sacramento who can talk anybody into giving anything, including society ladies."

"You mean Oda?" Nin asked.

"Oda?" Valda questioned.

"A lovely woman who helped us solve the case of a dead schoolteacher several years ago," Adele supplied.

"She now has rather a high position in the Women's Freedom Society down there." Elsie arranged herself on a crate that served as a chair in front of two crates with a board stretched over them to make a table.

"The supplies will run out at some point, Elsie," Valda warned, moving a cot close to the table so the ladies could sit. Nin sat down on the ground.

"So they'll run out!" Elsie motioned for the first woman in line to come forward.

They spent the day working like an assembly line. Elsie and Valda managed the ladies while the three visitors doled out the supplies. The process was slow because the women seemed determined to tell their stories before they got around to asking for what they needed. Many had not only lost their homes but their husbands and loved ones. The women in mourning clothes knew for certain their relatives were dead under the rubble. Valda was more adept at easing their sorrow, and her connections made it possible for her to promise them some kind of work once the city was up and running.

Elsie had less patience for the stories but more practicality, and she was good at coming up with solutions for the ladies' immediate problems, assuring them that, at least for now, they and their children would be taken care of. Adele could tell as the hours went by that even Nin was impressed by Elsie's vigorous determination to see to it that every woman got her share of supplies or a promise of a job. Missy, too, was thriving with her pencil constantly moving against her pad during the story time, and she almost despaired when she realized she had run out of paper until Elsie found a children's notebook for her. They were so caught up in their work that a compatriot brought them sandwiches and coffee at lunch so they wouldn't have to leave the tent.

"Jack's going to be looking for us all over the camp," Adele said with amusement.

"Let him," Elsie growled. "He's got to learn sometime that he's not your father."

"Lord knows he tries to be," Nin mumbled.

Adele laughed. "I think even Jack has realized by now that I can take care of myself."

"If you weren't here, he might have reason to be nervous," Valda said. "There have been stories —" She shuddered.

"Don't tell me you're getting lily-livered." Elsie glared at her. "I'm not surprised."

"We don't all know how to use a gun, Elsie," Valda retorted.

"Neither do I," Elsie retorted back. "I'd probably shoot a poor duck if I tried." They all laughed.

Adele was tired by the late afternoon when the line had dwindled. Elsie sat back with a sigh, and Valda rose and stretched her arms. Missy had gone out with a few of the ladies to interview them for her paper.

"Valda was right, Elsie." Adele glanced at the scant pile of clothes and toiletries. "You gave everything away."

"Susanna is on the train from San Mateo right now. She'll be here tomorrow morning with four other ladies." Elsie grinned. "They're bringing trunks full of things."

"Why didn't you tell me?" Valda's gentle features looked tortured for a moment.

"Now, now, dear." Elsie patted her cheek. "Wwearing doesn't become those aristocratic lips of yours."

Adele laughed, and even Nin smiled. "Trust Elsie to get the work done." She became thoughtful. "What about the Chinese?"

"What about them?" Elsie asked.

"We were just talking about them this morning," said Adele.

"Nobody's giving the Chinese anything," Nin said.

"We're here to help the destitute women and children, Adele," Valda said. "We can't start giving away our supplies to everyone."

"I *was* thinking of the women and children," Adele said. "There are destitute Chinese women too and many have children."

"Not as many," Valda argued.

"Can't we find room on our list for those women also?"

"Adele." Valda's voice was low. "It isn't done."

"What do you mean, 'it isn't done'?" Elsie snapped. "You mean *you* don't do it. Wasn't your group one of the first to go down to Chinatown during the plague when no one else would?"

"That was different, dear," said Valda. "That was their territory."

"Right now, the city is everybody's territory," Nin insisted. "Everybody is in the same boat."

"Nonetheless," Valda said in the same low tone, "we have benevolent societies who have generously given us things and promised more. If they should get wind that some of it is going to the Celestials —"

"It's none of their damn business!" Elsie barked as she rose. "I think we ought to at least try. They may not even accept our help."

"That's right. They probably won't," Valda agreed. "They have their own way of doing things."

Adele rose and held out her hand to help Nin up. "Since we have a shipment coming in tomorrow, we may as well try now."

"What do you mean, Adele?" Elsie blinked.

"She means go to the Chinese camp and offer our help," Nin said.

"Good heavens!" Valda turned white. "You don't mean it!"

"What did you expect her to do, send them a telegram?" Elsie demanded as she put on her hat and threw Adele's hers. Nin had refused to wear a hat once they reached the camp.

"But you can't, dear." Valda jumped up. "It's — it's dangerous."

"Nonsense," Adele said. "No one is going to hurt me. The Chinese are as destitute as the rest of you."

"I meant the soldiers," said her friend. "They're patrolling all over the place. They won't let you in."

"This isn't a prison, Valda." Elsie opened the tent flap.

"I'm sure they'll be generous when we tell them why we've come," said Adele. Beside her, Nin snortted.

They seemed to walk for miles as Elsie led them away from the main camp into the bowels of the Presidio. The sun was now beginning to dim though it was still daylight, and the vast overgrowth made the light look even dimmer.

"Where have they put them, in the bay?" Nin asked in a dry tone.

"They may as well have," Elsie said. "Their camp is near Fort Point."

"Good Lord!" Adele glanced into the distance. "That's clear on the other side of the Presidio!"

Elsie grimaced. "Apparently, some of our fine citizens complained they were too close so they moved them there."

"The gall!" Nin growled.

"Where are the hospital and supply tents for them?" asked Adele.

"They have some," said Elsie. "You can imagine how precious little, though, being way out here."

"I'm glad we're going then." Adele felt more secure.

They finally reached the Chinese camp. There were candles lying in the narrow path they had followed, and Elsie had thought to take a few from their own tent which they now lit. In the pale sun, Adele could see four or five soldiers standing around, their bayonets poised. The anxious faces of Chinese men, women, and even children regarded the newcomers with curiosity. It was almost like a silent signal, as many began to come out of their tents to peer at them. The Chinese people had been given small, triangular tents rather than the large circus-type ones housing those in the main camp.

"Halt! Identify yourself!" one of the soldiers demanded.

"Speak to us with respect, and maybe we'll answer you," Elsie snarled.

The young man took off his cap. "I apologize, ma'am. I didn't realize —"

"You also didn't realize I'm a miss, not a ma'am," she answered.

"Miss." He bowed.

"Now we'll identify ourselves." She gave her name, and Adele's and Nin's. "We're from the Destitute Women's Aid Society."

"Ladies aren't allowed this far away from main camp, miss," the young man mumbled.

"Unless you plan to chain our ankles to our cots, we can go where we like," Nin snapped.

"It's for your own safety, miss," he said.

Adele saw the hostile approaches of both her friends would hardly get them what they wanted. She gave him a congenial smile. "What's your name, Sergeant?"

The young man pressed his hands on his hat. "I'm only a private, ma'am — I mean miss."

"Well, what's your name, Private?"

"Private Dobson, miss."

"Well, Private Dobson, I congratulate you and your men —" This earned a chuckle from his fellow soldiers who, Adele guessed, were all privates. "— for your diligent watch during this difficult time."

"I'm only doing my duty, miss." But he seemed pleased.

"And we need soldiers like you," said Adele. "None of us have had an easy time of it. And these people —" she swept her arm toward the Chinese camp, " — have had it even worse than we have."

"Oh, I wouldn't say that, miss." The soldier slung his bayonet across his back. "Their Tongs will take care of 'em. They'll probably be set up before we can get the first houses built."

Nin growled, and Adele bit her lip to keep back a retort. She continued in her pleasant voice, "We've come to offer our help to the Chinese women and their children."

The young man stared at her. "Help *them?*"

At the word "help," the people standing near the border of the camp started to murmur in Chinese and look at one another.

"Why the blazes not?" Nin snarled.

"Women and children need the most help during this tragedy," Elsie preached. "It doesn't make any difference who they are."

"Well, that's nice of you, I'm sure," Private Dobson said. "But it's out of the question."

"On whose authority do you speak?" Elsie demanded.

"On my authority." The voice rang out strong as an older man approached, saluting the women, "I'm Sergeant Kerry."

"I was just telling them, Sergeant —" Private Dodson began.

"No one is allowed in this camp," The sergeant interrupted. "Now, what's this all about?"

Adele explained their mission. As she spoke, she glanced at the Chinese. The people seemed more bewildered than anything else, staring as if they were waiting to see what would happen. She quickly finished her explanation, hoping the sergeant was more amiable than the young private, though he looked decidedly less pleasant.

The man was brisk. "Any aid given to these people must go through the proper channels."

"They're not 'these people,'" Nin said. "They're Chinese people."

"Our group has been authorized to provide aid for women and children," Elsie insisted. "We've signed a document with the army to that effect."

"You've been authorized to offer aid to *white* women and children," the man said evenly. "Not 'Chinese people.'" He gave Nin a pointed look.

"I don't recall the document implied any special favors to one group of people or another," Elsie said.

"It would have been implied, miss."

"Implied!" Elsie snarled. "You mean interpreted by narrow-minded men like you!"

"Miss, I've no patience for goody-goodies!" His temper was clearly rising. "The mayor and his committee have authorized the army to give the orders during this time, and our rules are meant to protect everyone."

"Everyone except the Chinese." Adele raised her eyebrows.

"Don't you think they're also starving and in need of medical attention?"

"We're giving the Orientals as much as we can," Sergeant Kerry said.

Adele heard from a distance one of the privates say, "Ungrateful beggars!"

"I hope, Sergeant, you encourage your men to speak respectfully about the Chinese and remind them every citizen in San Francisco is under their care," she said in an icy tone.

"I don't want to hear that kind of language from you again, Private!" the sergeant thundered in such a way that Adele guessed he was making a show for the benefit of civilian ladies. Returning to her, he said in a lighter tone, "You're welcome to submit a request to the Captain Best, miss, and if he approves it, you can leave whatever provisions you have with him, and he'll send a few men with it here."

"More likely they'll take them for their own women and children!" Nin snarled.

"Captain Best is the man you want to speak to," the sergeant repeated. "Private Dobson, Private Polburn! Escort these ladies back to their tents."

"Don't bother," Elsie snapped. "We made it here without a scratch, and we'll make it back without a scratch on our own."

"I can't let you do that, miss." Sergeant Kerry's voice was stern. "The army is responsible for everyone's well-being while you're our guests."

"Guests!" Nin snorted.

Out of the corner of her eye, Adele saw a flashing of candlelight. A face showed in the last dregs of daylight. It belonged to a woman framed with lovely curls, deep eyes, and lips that were very red, even in the dim candlelight. The features disappeared as the woman lowered the candle and in a swirl of movement disappeared into the dark blue. Adele had seen enough of her face to know she was not Chinese.

"That's very kind of you, Sergeant," she said in a steady tone. "We'll be glad for Private Dobson and Private Polburn's assistance."

Away from their superior, the two young men seemed eager to chat and told them about the small Chinese camp as they walked, pushing the wild shrubbery out of the women's way.

"They're talking now 'bout putting them in Hunter's Point," said Dobson.

"Then the rumors we heard are true?" Adele asked.

"Looks like it, miss," said Polburn.

"Why would they want to do that?" Nin asked.

"The old Chinatown's on prime land, miss," said the young man. "City wants it back."

"And push them all the way to Hunter's Point?" Elsie growled "That's practically in the sticks."

"Well, miss, might be the best place for 'em," said Private Polburn. "Keep the opium dens and such out of the city.

"I don't think the Orientals are going to let that happen," Dobson insisted.

"Why is that, Private?" Adele asked.

"I heard them talking in the camp last night," he said.

"They?"

"Some of 'em from the Six Companies."

"Oh, but that's just talk," said Polburn.

"It was the young ones," said Dobson. "The merchants' sons. They're not going to let the city bully them."

"Good for them," said Adele.

"They've no right to interfere with what the city wants," insisted Polburn. "They don't own the property, after all."

"But they can get building permits," Dobson objected. "They can rebuild Chinatown just like we're rebuilding the rest of the city."

"I'd like to see 'em try and get permits!" scoffed Polburn.

"They'll get them," Elsie said in an assured tone. "They're resourceful people, these Chinese."

They had no time to seek out Captain Best's office to put in their request, as dinner had already started when they arrived. Jackson gave Adele and Nin a good verbal beating about wandering off "under such circumstances." Adele barely listened to him as she picked at the stew, thinking about the grave, intelligent faces of the people she had seen under the candlelight and the figure of the Caucasian woman stealing behind them

*L*ater that evening, Missy, who had not been with them at dinner, appeared just as Elsie was setting a coffee pot on the small stove she had borrowed from another tent.

"What a day!" Missy sighed as she flopped on her cot.

"So many stories?" Adele asked with a smile. She noticed Missy now had three children's notebooks with her.

"Not the stories, but trying to send them to Carla," she said. "Those ninnies at the Signal Corps would only allow me to send two. They're being mighty cagey about the press." She raised her eyebrow.

"I don't see why when your stories could bring more help," Nin said.

"It makes you wonder what the army is hiding, doesn't it?" There was a gleam in Missy's eye. "Papa always used to say people aren't antsy about the press unless they have something they don't want the press to find out."

"I wouldn't be surprised," Elsie said.

"Thank goodness Adam convinced his editor to let me use their telegraph," said Missy.

"Who's Adam?" Adele glanced at Nin. This was the first time they had ever heard Missy mention a man's name.

"I told you I took a few courses in journalism at the University of Missouri," Missy said. "He was there. Then he went to work for the *San Francisco Humanist.*"

"The socialist newspaper?" Elsie groaned.

"That's all bunk," Missy said. "They simply believe everyone has a voice."

"And they make it heard loud and clear all over the city," Elsie remarked.

"They managed to set up a communication line to Sacramento," Missy continued. "No mean feat considering the *Chronicle, Call,* and *Examiner* are all operating from across the bay at the *Oakland Tribune* office and won't let anyone else in." Her face became subdued. "You ought to see their office, Adele. Half the building is in ruins, and they have to keep the telegraph lines hidden so the army won't yank them out."

"The army can't control everything!" Nin grumbled.

"They're certainly trying." Adele slipped into her nightgown. "You saw that sergeant today."

Missy raised her head. "What sergeant?"

Adele related their experience with the less-than-charming Sergeant Kerry and his men.

Missy's fatigue disappeared as she sprang up. "You went to the Chinese camp and you didn't call me?"

"Why should she call you?" Nin asked.

"Adam said they've been trying to get to a story about them since they came here."

"Oh, for heaven's sake." Elsie poured out three coffee cups, handing one to Adele and Nin.

"For heaven's sake nothing!" Missy looked Adele in the eye. "Remember our bargain, Adele."

Adele remembered all too well: *You tell me what you know and I'll tell you what I know.* It was a bargain she and Missy had made long ago to help with cases in Arrojo. But she was starting to feel the burden of that bargain.

"Haven't those poor people suffered enough at the hands of the press?" Nin growled.

"What do you mean, suffer?" Missy glared at her. "I told you, I'm writing human interest stories. I'm as interested in their story as in anyone else's."

"You would have exploited the story by showing it as the result of the mayor's corruptive regime," Adele said. "Just like you would have made a romantic love story out of the poor girl —" She stopped.

"What poor girl?" Missy sat on the cot next to her.

"Nothing."

"What poor girl?" Now even Elsie was curious.

"The poor girl who was sneaking around the Chinese camp," Nin answered. Adele glanced at her.

"A Chinese girl?" Missy's eyes widened.

"No, a Caucasian one," Adele said quietly.

Elsie sighed. "Slipping away to see her lover in secret, no doubt."

"I don't know that she was slipping away," Adele said thoughtfully. "She was more interested in looking at the Chinese."

"Maybe she has as much compassion for their plight as we do," Elsie offered.

"I don't know," Adele said. "I think she was looking for someone."

"Among the Celestials?" Elsie chuckled. "Maybe her lover is hiding among them. They say the Chinese will do that for a fee, of course."

"Nonsense," Missy scoffed. "It is rather curious, though." She looked at Adele. "Now I really wish you had called me."

Nin narrowed her eyes. "Why can't you let people be?"

"And why can't *you* stop being so disengaged from everyone?"

Missy shot back. "You care for nothing but those potions of yours!"

Adele could see this hurt her friend deeply as her face became troubled.

"It isn't doing us any good to fight amongst ourselves," she said.

"Adele's right," Elsie said. "If we squabble, the work we're doing here is going to go to pot. There are more important things for us to think about right now."

Missy gnawed on her fingernail for a moment. Then she went to Nin and put out her hand. "I'm sorry, Miss Branch."

Nin accepted the handshake and mumbled an apology.

"I think we should all get to bed." Elsie put the empty coffee cups in a basin of water. "We've got to battle Captain Best tomorrow. I've a feeling he's going to be like it's going to be the Civil War all over again trying to reason with him."

But after Elsie had blown out the candle, Adele found herself restless. She slipped on a coat and stepped out of the tent, sitting near the entrance. The camp was quiet but many people were still up, as it was barely past eight. In the distance, voices floated over the chirping birds getting ready for the night.

She heard the canvas move behind her and Nin came out.

"Don't take any notice of what Missy said," Adele said. "You know she didn't mean it."

"Perhaps she's right," Nin said. "Even when the world is falling apart, I can't seem to — I wish I were back home with my plants."

Adele smiled and put her arm around her friend's shoulders. "We all do, dear. It only means we hold compassion in our hearts because we don't like to see suffering."

She heard her name being called in a gentle tone. Turning around, she was startled to see the figure of a young man. Nin was immediately on the alert. She jumped up, grabbing a rock near the tent, and growled, "Don't come any closer, or I'll bash your head in."

"I won't hurt you, miss." The young man came into the circle of light. Adele could see his face had a strange shape. The features were calm but the eyes were watchful and a little pear-shaped. The young man's smile was kind but cautious.

"He means it, Nin," Adele said. "May we help you with something?"

Nin sat down again, but kept the rock in her lap.

He bowed his head. "My name is George Wu."

"Are you Chinese?" Nin asked in a brutal tone.

"My father is Chinese," said Mr. Wu. "My mother was of Irish descent."

Adele understood now why the young man's eyes were so arresting. "Please sit down, Mr. Wu."

He sat a little distance away from them. "I'm very sorry if I frightened you."

Adele looked at Nin. She could see her friend had calmed down, her features relaxed into the wax-like beauty that astounded so many men. She put the rock back in its place.

"Anything is liable to happen under such strange circumstances, Mr. Wu," she said. "We would have been startled if a rabbit had come up behind us."

He nodded. "We're all on edge right now, aren't we?"

"But we're all making the best of it," Adele said kindly.

"Shouldn't you be —" Nin glanced toward the path they had taken earlier that evening.

"I suppose I should be," said the young man, amused. "But I came here to thank you."

"Thank us?" Adele blinked.

"I should explain," he said. "My father owns an antique shop —"

"In Chinatown?" Nin interrupted.

"In Chinatown." The young man bowed. "He's been ill recently, so I left the university to come back to San Francisco and help him. I work with the Younger Six."

"The Younger Six?" Nin asked.

"You know the Six Companies?" Both women nodded. "We're the sons of some of the Six Companies merchants and professional men. We formed our own group after the earthquake so we could help our people."

"Are your parents safe?" Nin's face gathered a little.

"Mother's been dead for three years," he said in a regretful tone. "I sent my father to Oakland with the others."

"And you stayed behind to help?" Adele began to like the young man. "That was very good of you."

"And it was very good of *you* and your friends to want to help us," he said. "I wasn't at the camp when you came, but I heard about it."

"How did you know it was us?" Adele asked.

"You gave the soldier your names," he said. "There were many ears listening."

Adele laughed. "Everyone was so quiet!"

"We're used to being quiet," he said. "One can say more with silence than any incessant chatter could say."

"Very true, Mr. Wu, very true," Adele said.

"We know of more than a few ladies who could apply that rule to themselves," Nin said with a sly look. Adele knew she was thinking about Mrs. Faderman and her brood.

"It was very brave of you to venture out to our camp," he said. "We — the Younger Six — were told the soldiers had their bayonets poised the entire time."

"You don't know my friends," Adele said with a smile. "They would scarcely let a bayonet scare them away."

"And you also, I imagine," he said with admiration. "I know of another woman like you." He was quiet for a moment. "In my culture, women are thought to be the inferior of men. My mother taught me this isn't true."

"Strength depends on character, not sex," Nin said boldly.

"I couldn't agree more, Miss —"

"Miss Branch," said Nin.

"Miss Branch." He smiled.

Adele wrapped her arms around her knees. "Tell me, Mr. Wu, is it true the city is going to move Chinatown to Hunter's Point?"

"They may try." His tone became serious. "We're protesting it. There's already been a delegation to see the governor."

"It's sickening," Nin growled. "Moving people from the homes they've always known."

"I'm glad you feel that way, Miss Branch," said the young man. "Some have resented us being there from the beginning. Reporters call us a blight on the city landscape."

"I'm sure you can get them to change their minds once they're reminded that they could lose valuable trade relations with China," Adele remarked.

He smiled. "I see you know something of our position in San Francisco."

"It stands to reason," Adele said.

"For what it's worth, I don't think they'll succeed in moving Chinatown," said Mr. Wu as he picked up a thin branch lying on the ground beside him and began to bend it back and forth. "Too much opposition and not just from our standpoint."

"I hope you can all get back to your homes as much as anyone," Adele said kindly.

The clap of footsteps in the dirt made the candle flames dance. Jackson appeared, followed by Hatfield. Her brother's eyes immediately narrowed at the sight of Mr. Wu sitting beside her.

"This is Mr. George Wu, Jack," Adele said before her brother could speak. "He's been kind enough to call on Nin and me in gratitude for what we tried to do for his community today."

"His community?" Each word sounded like a wooden coin dropping into a waste paper basket.

"Your sister and her friends offered to help Chinese women and children," Mr. Wu explained. "I'm afraid they didn't get very far."

"I'm not surprised at that," Hatfield's boyish features looked more stoic than usual.

"You shouldn't have come here, sir," Jackson said in a sharp tone. "My sister is inclined to be — indiscriminate — in her efforts to help others, but you look like a gentleman who would know better than —"

"Jack!" Adele shrieked.

Her brother advanced, his hand on his hip as if he were going to reach for his gun. "I think you'd better return to your camp."

Mr. Wu looked at him for a moment and then at Hatfield, whose pose was a little less threatening but still determined. "Perhaps I'd better." Rising, he bowed to the ladies. "A thousand thanks again for your efforts."

The moment the young man retreated into the darkness, Adele pounced on her brother. "How dare you threaten Mr. Wu, Jack!"

"I wasn't threatening anyone, Del," he insisted. "I merely asked him to leave."

"Your brother's right, Adele." Hatfield sat on the ground beside her, his large figure somewhat awkward in the cross-legged position. "He shouldn't have come here."

"You mean he should have stayed on the other side of the camp out of sight and out of mind?" Adele eyed him.

"I didn't mean that," said the sheriff. "It could have been dangerous for him if he had been caught."

"He was polite and respectful," Nin insisted.

Jack said warily, "If *you* say that, Miss Branch, I'm bound to take your word for it."

Nin sniffed and turned away.

"Perhaps we were a little severe," Hatfield admitted with a sigh. "If you had seen what we saw today, you'd be suspicious of anyone."

"I wouldn't have been with my hand on my gun." Adele glared at her brother.

Jackson dropped to the ground beside her. "It's a good thing we bought them."

"I hope you didn't need to use it," Adele said.

Her brother looked into the distance toward the bay. "We almost did."

"What happened?" Forgetting her annoyance, she laid her hand on his arm.

"Sergeant Walker took us on patrol today," said Hatfield. "We went to South of the Slot. It wasn't a pretty sight. So many piles of rock, wood, and ashes."

"They're still digging for survivors," Jackson said sadly.

Adele stared. "Surely, the police can't think there are survivors after almost two weeks!"

"Not the police," said Jackson. "Or the army either. The residents."

"Oh my God," Adele mumbled.

"We came across one mam tearing through the rubble, half crazed," Hatfield said. "He insisted he heard the cries of his wife and newborn child underneath the tumbled bricks. He's been hearing their cries in the night, he said, and he finally had to come and dig them out." He picked up the stick Mr. Wu had abandoned and began drawing circles in the dirt.

"He's at camp in Portsmouth Square. When we brought him back, his neighbor told us the camp doctor was arranging for him to be kept with some of the insane. Seems they have several people who have gone out of their minds after their families disappeared in the tragedy."

"Poor man," Nin said in a sad tone.

"I wouldn't feel too sorry for him, Miss Branch," Jackson said. "He pulled a gun on us, and we had to wrestle it from him. Where he got it, heaven only knows."

"Probably beat some private's head in to get it," Hatfield said. "Desperate men will do anything in desperate times."

"The army has everything under control, sir," Jackson pointed out. "Monte showed us that this morning."

"Human nature defies order sometimes, Jack," Adele reminded him.

He grimaced. "And I suppose Miss Branch will say Mother Nature has her own order."

"Mother Nature has chaos," Nin said. "We've no right to try and bring order to her. We can only pick up the pieces she leaves us."

"Which is exactly what we're here for," Hatfield agreed. "You both had better get to bed. The curfew whistle will be blowing in another few minutes."

"See you at breakfast," Adele said with a salute.

"We haven't yet asked you what you've been doing all day." Jackson eyed his sister. "Though from what we've seen from this Chinaman, I'm not sure I want to know."

"He's not a Chinaman," Adele snapped. "Mr. Wu is as American as we are."

"His mother was Irish," Nin added.

"And he was born here," Adele said. "That makes him an American citizen."

"Just don't get yourself mixed up in anything illegal, Del," her brother cautioned. "All supplies have to go through the army."

"So we were told by a very insistent sergeant today," she said in a dry tone.

Hatfield laughed. "I gather your sister and her friends will find a way around any insistent sergeant or even a harsh general."

"Elsie can get her way around Atilla the Hun himself," Adele declared.

CHAPTER 8

In spite of the somber finish to the day, the next morning was Saturday and found them cheerful at breakfast. Edwards joined them, more relaxed than he had been the day before. Someone at camp had managed to get hold of flour and milk and maple syrup and the cooks had made hotcakes. The sweet scents filled the dining room tent with warmth.

"It almost smells like our house on Sunday mornings, doesn't it, Jack?" Adele remarked.

"It's a kind smell," Nin said as she nibbled on a pancake.

"You mean it's an inviting smell, Miss Branch," Jackson corrected. "Like inviting one to the table."

"I mean what I say, Mr. Gossling," she said stiffly.

"I imagine you do, Miss Branch." Edwards feasted his eyes on her. She glared back.

"Ma makes hers with buttermilk," said Hatfield. "Once Rowena put milk in them, thinking Ma wouldn't notice, and Ma had a fit." He laughed.

"Have you heard from Lady Augusta?" Missy asked.

"She sent a telegram yesterday," he said. "You were true to

your word about making sure anything with our names on it went through quickly, Lieutenant." He nodded at Edwards. "I'm much obliged to you."

"The army does what it can for the civilians," said the young man. "You're under our care, after all."

"I think the police have a hand in the care of the civilian population as well, Lieutenant," said Walker in a dry tone. Turning to Hatfield, he asked, "I trust your mother is well, Horatio?"

"She and Rowena are doing fine," Hatfield assured him. "They say Consuela — she's the daughter of the people who work for the Gosslings — is a little devil, insisting on helping to clean the house. But Ma says she polishes the lamps better than Rowena does." His eyes sparkled.

"I don't imagine Rowena would be happy to hear that," Adele said with a laugh.

"Ma says the council is meeting next week to discuss compensation for Arrojo businesses," the sheriff continued. "Mrs. Faderman is in an uproar."

"I imagine she is," Adele said.

"She loves something she can sink her teeth into," Nin agreed.

"She's determined to see that every business on Bridge Street receives funds to rebuild," Hatfield said.

"That's good news," Jackson said. "That means you and Miss Branch ought to get what's coming to you, Del."

"Better than the paltry sums Mr. Malone gave us," Adele snarled.

"If a little town like Arrojo can strain its pockets to help people, the insurance companies could too," Nin said fiercely.

Walker laughed. "I'd like to visit your little town one of these days, Horatio. It sounds a lot like the little place in Texas where I grew up."

"Oh, were you a rancher?" Adele asked.

"I'm afraid I was never much interested in ranching, Miss

Gossling." The man laughed. "I was more apt to roam town with the sheriff and his men or join a posse to catch cattle thieves!"

They all laughed, sending a pleasant song into the air. Adele noticed a commotion near the dining room entrance as a soldier with a dreary look on his face argued with another. Finally, the soldier was let in. He came straight to Edwards and pulled him aside.

"I wonder what's going on." Missy's reporter eyes watched the two military men.

"Whatever it is, I'm sure we'll hear about it soon enough," Adele said.

This proved true, as the young man saluted Edwards, and the lieutenant returned to the table. His features were grave and troubled.

"Anything wrong, Lieutenant?" Missy asked eagerly.

"I'm afraid there is." He turned to Walker. "I'd like to elicit your help, sir."

"Anything I can do," said the sergeant.

"It seems there's been —" He glanced at the ladies as if hesitant to go on, but then continued, "It seems a young woman has been discovered."

"Discovered in the camp?" asked Hatfield.

"Yes, sir."

"What do you mean by discovered?" asked Adele.

"For heaven's sake, man, don't shilly-shally," Nin said in a distracted way. Adele bit back a smile, thinking of how much she sounded like Mrs. Faderman.

"Well, it isn't very pleasant, Miss Branch," he said.

Adele's hands suddenly felt stiff with the fork and knife. "She's dead. That's what you're trying to say, isn't it, Lieutenant?"

"Yes, Miss Gossling, I'm afraid that's it."

"Oh, we've seen lots of dead bodies." Nin waved her hand.

"I'm happy you're not alarmed," he said in a wry tone.

"Where was she found, Lieutenant?" Walker became official.

The young man paused for a moment before he answered, "The other side of the camp, sir. Not far from the Chinese tents."

"Good gracious!" Missy stared.

"That doesn't mean they are responsible," Adele said quickly.

"That's what we need to investigate," said Edwards.

"*We*, sir?" Walker eyed him.

"Captain Best asked me to look into the matter, sir," he said.

"Has he?" Walker's arched eyebrows showed a flicker of temper. "Perhaps Captain Best doesn't realize that murder is a police matter."

"Don't get into a huff, Harry," Sheriff Hatfield warned him.

"I'm sorry, Horatio, but murder is serious business!"

"I realize that, sir, and so does Captain Best," Edward said. "He's not questioning the authority of the police. But this crime happened in army territory."

"What has that got to do with it?" Sergeant Walker demanded.

"We are responsible for everyone here," Edwards said. "If a criminal gets away, we're the ones who will have to answer to the mayor, not the police!"

"I hasten to remind you, Sergeant, that Monte worked with the Anspatches before he enlisted," Jackson put in. "I can vouch for the fact that he's no stranger to crime."

"Thank you, Jackson." The young man bowed. "It's why Captain Best asked for my help."

"With all due respect, Lieutenant, private detection and police work are two very different things," Walker insisted. "I'm sure Mr. Gossling, in his work with the Arrojo police, can attest to that."

"Crime is crime, wherever you find it!" Edwards scoffed.

"And do you propose to use the same vigilante methods here as you did with the Anspatch agency, Lieutenant?" Walker retorted. "The committee has put the police in charge of law and order in the city and the military are under our orders."

"Gentlemen!" Hatfield rose. "It does no good to fight when every moment counts."

"You're right, sir." Edwards took a breath. "The murderer might be escaping into the bowels of the city right now."

"With men patrolling everywhere, I doubt that very much," Walker said. "We have that on our side at least."

"I'm sorry for losing my temper, sir." Edwards put out his hand, which Walker pumped. "I'm not suggesting the police yield to the army. I'm well aware we're under the orders of Chief of Police Dinan and his men and so is Captain Best."

"And I'm one of his men," Walker said. "Don't forget that."

"I'd like to suggest a solution," Hatfield said. Adele admired how his mild-mannered ways and fairness allowed him to take hold of the situation.

"Please do, Sheriff," she said.

"I'm not sheriff here, Adele," he said with a half-smile.

"If you were, no one would be fighting," Nin said.

"Thank you, Miss Branch, for that compliment." He bowed. "Now then, Lieutenant. You agree the army is under orders from the police. And I'm sure you agree Sergeant Walker's experience solving crimes far surpasses anything the military has encountered?"

"I do." The young man nodded.

Hatfield turned to his friend. "And you, Harry, you agree, as short-staffed as the police force is right now, Lieutenant Edwards could supply the men to help with the investigation that would be vital in solving this case?"

"Of that I have no doubt," said Walker.

"Then it would make sense to put Sergeant Walker in charge of the investigation with Lieutenant Edwards as his aid," Hatfield said, "provided Chief of Police Dinan decides to put it in your hands."

"I'm sure he will do that." Walker nodded. "I heard he'll be here in the camp this morning so I can seek his authority."

Hatfield smiled. "And now, I suggest you proceed with the case without further argument. Harry needs to know the basics so he can present them to Dinan. Everyone agreed?" His commanding way made it clear he expected them to comply.

"Agreed," said Edwards.

"Agreed," echoed the sergeant. "And I'll let the chief of police know I have two more very able lawmen to assist me. As you say, Horatio, we're short on men and anyone with your expertise and your deputy sheriff's knowledge of the law would be welcome."

"What do you say, Jackson?" Hatfield grinned at him. "It looks like we can't escape crime after all, eh?"

"We came to help, sir, in any way we could." Jackson put on his hat.

"And so will we," Adele said, rising.

"I beg your pardon, Miss Gossling?" Edwards glanced at her.

"Didn't my brother tell you?" she asked. "Nin and I regularly help the police in Arrojo solve crimes."

"And so do I," Missy said firmly. "Keeping my newspaper clear of any evidence the police don't give me permission to print, of course." She gave a respectful nod toward Hatfield.

"Women solving crimes!" Edwards' mouth fell open. "Jackson, you shouldn't allow your sister to —"

"I stopped having any say in what Del does or doesn't do a long time ago," remarked Jackson. "It only makes her more determined and ornery."

"I'm neither and you know it, dear brother," Adele snapped.

"You're the stubborn mule in the family, not her," Nin retorted.

"May we accompany you, Sheriff?" Adele turned to Hatfield.

"It's not up to me, Adele," he said. "This isn't my jurisdiction. Sergeant Walker will have to decide that."

They all turned to the sergeant. The man played with the edge of his mustache as he glanced from one woman to another. Then, he looked at Hatfield. "You trust Miss Gossling and Miss Branch, Horatio?"

"Implicitly," said the sheriff.

"Well, then." The man rose. "I can only ask Chief of Police Dinan and see if he gives his permission for me to recruit some deputies on behalf of the police. As we are very short-handed, I don't see any reason for him to refuse."

"Unless you tell him those deputies will be women." Nin eyed him.

"I'm sure the San Francisco police are more progressive in their practices than the Arrojo police, Nin." Adele took her arm.

"Nevertheless, I plan on leaving out that little detail," Walker said with a half-smile.

"And I will come too, Sergeant?" Missy held on anxiously to her pad and pencil.

"I can vouch for Miss Grace that she won't print anything until she gets permission, just as she said," Hatfield said.

"As long as you make it clear she doesn't have permission," Jackson mumbled. Missy glared at him.

"I can't stop the reporters from doing what they please," Walker said.

They parted ways and met an hour later in front of the police tent. Walker informed them he had spoken to the chief of police who granted him permission to handle the case and recruit whatever deputies or army help he saw fit.

"That gives us free rein, Horatio," the sergeant said.

Edwards and the soldier who had given him the message earlier that morning arrived. "I've let Captain Best know you'll be taking over the investigation into this unfortunate crime," the lieutenant said. "He asks that you keep me informed of your progress and, of course, let me know if you need any military personnel to assist you."

"I'll do that, Lieutenant," Walker said with a bow.

The other solider saluted Walker. "They haven't moved the woman, sir."

"Has she been examined?" Walker asked.

"Not yet, sir," said the young man. "Everyone was waiting for official word."

"Well, we don't exactly have a medical examiner under these circumstances," the sergeant remarked. "Better get who we can."

The young private cleared his throat, speaking with a slight Irish trill. "If you'll pardon, Sergeant, a neighbor of mine — that was — he's here in the camp, and he's a fine doctor. Dr. Fleming."

"He'll do," said Walker. "Good work, Private."

The young man smiled.

They found Dr. Fleming in one of the smaller tents created for bachelors bunking together. The man was in his forties with a ruby face and a jovial manner. He immediately rose and pulled his medical bag from under his cot. With a rueful pat, he said, "About the only thing I was able to save before my house went up in flames."

"I'm sorry to hear that, Doctor," Adele said.

"Why should you be?" he asked in a bold voice. "The city's promising to build new houses, so maybe I'll get polished brass faucets and even a bathtub!" He chuckled as he followed them.

The young private, whose name was Allander, had procured a wagon with two horses, and they all climbed in. The horses were clearly exhausted from being among the few left in the city, and they walked slowly through the brush.

Adele was relieved to see the crime looked as if it had been committed some distance away from the Chinese camp. The forest-like area gave off serene sounds of birds that had dared to come back to the city after the black smoke cleared, and she even heard the chirping of grasshoppers in the distance.

Private Allander led them past several clumps of bushes to a clearing where there were two redwoods standing majestically untouched by the tragedy. Lying on the ground was the body of a woman. The woman was face down with her arms flayed out. She was wearing a plain gingham dress. As a few clouds parted, giving a flash of sunlight on the woman's hair, bringing out the ginger color. Adele gasped as she realized it was the young woman she had seen the night before when they were arguing with Sergeant Kerry. She glanced at Nin, whom she saw also recognized the woman.

"Look familiar?" Sergeant Walker looked around the group. "Anyone? Ladies?" He turned to them. "You're more likely to have seen her than we are since you're in the women's part of the camp."

"There are many other camps here, Sergeant," Missy said. "I've been to several of them to conduct interviews. It doesn't necessarily follow she's from ours."

"I suppose that's true." The lawman sighed.

"Perhaps if we saw her face, the ladies would be able to tell," Hatfield suggested.

Dr. Fleming bent down and gently turned the woman over.

Missy's piercing scream echoed among the quiet shrubbery. Nin closed her eyes, clutching Adele's arm. Adele's stomach turned over. The entire front of the woman's body was bloody and full of slits, as if someone had tried to rip the dress off her.

"My God, what an animal!" Jackson stared at the horror.

Adele felt as if another earthquake were swaying the ground. Nin seemed to know what was happening and pulled her friend away from the horrible sight into another clearing. Adele leaned against a redwood, feeling the sharp tips of bark pierce into her back. The breeze brushed gently against her cheeks and the sun created a warm umbrella over her. Gradually, the sick feeling passed.

"How could he have done that to her?" Adele choked out. "So much stabbing!"

"Some men are savages," Nin snarled. "A wild coyote would have been more civilized."

Adele glanced at her friend and gave a small laugh. "You have a strong stomach, Nin."

"I've seen what humans can do to one another," Nin said, her tone heavy.

Adele steadied herself. "The rage is more honest, anyway."

"It *was* rage that did that," Nin agreed.

"What could she have done that was so terrible, I wonder," Adele murmured.

"She probably didn't do anything but live her own life," Nin said.

"That's what I mean." Adele was beginning to feel stronger. "A woman living her own life is bound to offend someone."

Nin put her hands on her shoulders. "It's coming closer, the time when women will be able to live their own lives without offending anybody."

Adele smiled. "Don't tell me you believe in our cause at last, dear."

"I don't believe in causes and you know it," Nin declared. "I believe in what the Generous Ones tell me."

"And they tell you that?"

"The years tell me that," said Nin. "The years passing by other people's prejudices."

Adele pressed her hand. "We should be getting back. I'm all right now."

"Take some peppermint," her friend advised. "There's plenty of it here and it's very soothing."

Adele bent down and picked some of the spiky, rough leaves. Nin was right. The stinging scent calmed her stomach. As she plucked a bunch from the ground, she caught sight of a golden ring that looked as if it had been carelessly tossed there. Picking it up, she saw it was inscribed *L.S. & G.W.*

"Nin, look at this!"

Her friend peered at the ring. "Do you think it belonged to the dead girl?"

"It might have," Adele said. "Or it might have fallen from the finger of a woman who came out here to meet her solider beau."

"A very married woman," Nin remarked with disapproval.

"It looks fresh to me," Adele said. "I don't think it could have been left here for very long."

"The camp's been open for only a few weeks," her friend pointed out.

"No, I think it was even a shorter time than that." Adele slipped it in the pocket of her jacket. "It hardly has any dirt on it."

"Are you going to tell the police?" Nin took her arm.

"I think we'd better not," said Adele. "We don't know that it has anything to do with the girl."

"And you're not going to tell them we saw the girl last night, are you?" Her friend's eyes were shrewd.

"If we tell Sergeant Walker she was near the Chinese camp, it wouldn't look very good for them," Adele said.

"Maybe a Chinese did kill her," Nin suggested.

"I don't think so," Adele said as they carefully made their way among the shrubs. "It doesn't seem likely someone from the Chinese camp would rip through her clothes like that."

"Who knows what anyone would do under circumstances like these?" Nin sighed. "Some people have their sense of decency knocked out of them when Sister Nature reacts with such violence."

"Violence begets violence," Adele said, feeling her body shake.

CHAPTER 9

Jackson's concern for her touched her as he led her to a rock so she could sit down. Private Allender had given him his canteen, and he urged her to drink, speaking in a soothing tone. Even Nin was impressed.

"You can be a good nurse when you want to be, Mr. Gossling," she remarked.

"Jack was always a mother hen to me after I'd been playing outside with some of the boys," Adele said.

"You mean they hit you?" Nin asked.

"Not exactly," Adele said. "I wanted to be treated like a boy and they obliged."

"Don't forget to tell Miss Branch you gave as good as you got," Jackson said with a grin. He joined the men as Missy put her arm around her shoulders.

"I'm sorry I reacted like that." Adele now felt more embarrassed than anything. "So silly of me."

"I'm sorry I screamed," Missy said. "It was just such a shock —" She glanced toward the body. "They've covered her now, so you needn't worry."

Adele saw that indeed the woman's torso was covered up

entirely with an army blanket. Dr. Fleming smiled at her. "If you need a sedative, my dear, I have one here."

"I don't need anything," Adele said firmly. "It was a moment of weakness."

"Anyone would feel weak at the sight of that," Hatfield said in a warm tone. "Edison would have fainted dead away."

Adele giggled at the thought of the fresh-faced assistant deputy lying on the ground in a swoon.

"Cause of death is rather obvious, isn't it?" The doctor looked at Sergeant Walker as Jackson took out a pad and pencil to make notes. "Multiple stab wounds. No question about it."

"Is this a crime of passion?" Edwards glanced cautiously at the women.

"If you mean was she raped, Lieutenant, say so," Missy snapped. "We're not naive."

"Not that I can see, I'm glad to say." The doctor glanced at Adele. "The ripped clothing is from the viciousness of the stabs, not from a fit of passion."

"He tortured her over and over." Adele started to feel queasy again.

"She didn't suffer, Miss Gossling, if that's any comfort to you," said the doctor in a reassuring tone. "She was dead from the first few stabs."

"Someone knew what they were doing," Hatfield suggested.

"You know many times those things are more a matter of luck than skill, Horatio," his friend pointed out.

"I agree," said Dr. Fleming. "I think it's highly unlikely a skilled man, whatever his profession, would have done that to her."

"Blind rage," Nin murmured, getting a distant look. "The hand with the blade, piercing and piercing and piercing —"

"That's quite enough, Miss Branch," Jackson said. "We know how vivid your visions can be."

"Visions?" Edwards raised an eyebrow.

"Miss Branch has some strange gifts," Jackson supplied. "She sees things."

Nin stiffened. "I don't *see* things, Mr. Gossling. I feel them."

"Oh, I see." The lieutenant nodded with some doubt.

"No, you don't," Nin snapped. "I'm not a mesmerizer, if that's what you're thinking."

"Nin's gifts are genuine," Adele defended. "And you needn't sound so apologetic about them, Jack." She glared at her brother.

"Any guess as to what kind of knife was used, Doctor?" Sergeant Walker asked.

"Well, Sergeant, it wasn't a bread knife," said the doctor with a chuckle. "That I can say."

"What do you mean?" Hatfield asked.

"It must have been something rather slim, or it wouldn't have made so many cuts so easily," said Dr. Fleming. "And, I gather, it was unique."

"Unique?" Jackson stopped scribbling. "In what way?"

"The blade was curved a little like a hook," said Dr. Fleming. "The wounds show that."

"How very odd," Adele murmured.

"Could it have been a sickle?" Jackson asked.

The doctor laughed. "I hardly think so, young man. Such a weapon wouldn't be found around here."

"But some kind of curved knife?" Walker questioned.

"As near as I can make out," he said. "Time is not on our side, I'm afraid."

"Eh?" Hatfield glanced at him.

"I can only estimate the time of death, you understand," he said. "With no proper tools and no real way of doing an autopsy."

"What is your estimate, Doctor?" Edwards asked.

"I'd say between Tuesday afternoon and early this morning."

"Good God, man!" Hatfield shot out. "Can't you get any nearer than that?"

"Even Dr. Rhodes could do better in his usual annoyed state," Nin remarked.

"Who is Dr. Rhodes?" Dr. Fleming eyed her.

"The Arrojo County medical examiner," Adele supplied.

"I'm sure he can, given the right tools and time," said Dr. Fleming. "The body is too stiff for me to give less than a thirty-six-hour window."

Adele and Nin exchanged glances. Taking her friend's hand, Adele stepped forward. "Maybe we can give you a closer time than that, Sheriff."

"Indeed?" Both Hatfield and the sergeant looked at them.

"We saw the woman," Nin said.

"Why didn't you speak up before?" Jackson snapped.

"We weren't sure," Adele snapped back.

"It's best not to play games with a murder investigation, Miss Gossling," Edwards said in a lecturing tone.

Adele stiffened. "We're more than aware of that, Lieutenant."

"We've been on murder cases before," Missy said.

"You should have spoken up even if you weren't sure," the lieutenant continued.

"We didn't say we *knew* her," Adele said. "We said we *saw* her."

"When?" asked the sergeant.

"Last evening before dinner, when we were at the Chinese camp."

"It's just as you said, sir!" Edwards looked at the sergeant. "The Chinese are responsible."

"Wait a minute, Lieutenant." Hatfield held up his hand. "That's not what Adele said."

"Stop talking in circles, Del," her brother snarled.

"She didn't come from the camp," said Nin. "She was only passing by it to meet a fellow in the woods."

"We think she was meeting someone," Adele corrected. "We were arguing with a rather stubborn army soldier —" she glanced meaningfully at Edwards, "— when we saw her."

"If it was so close to dinnertime, how did you see her in the darkness?" Edwards asked.

"There was still enough light," Nin said. "Her face was livelier then, of course." She shuddered, glancing at the covered body.

"I think we can assume this is the same woman unless we learn otherwise," Hatfield said.

"Yesterday evening, you say?" Walker asked.

Adele nodded. "I would say it was between six and six-thirty. It was just before we were herded out of there and walked back to camp in time for the dinner bell."

"That does narrow it down considerably," Edwards admitted.

"Here's something to narrow it down even more," said Missy. "One of the more talkative soldiers I interviewed told me they go over the list of who is in the dining tents before they serve the food to make sure everyone is sitting at the table and no one misses a meal since food is so scarce."

"So, if she was killed before dinner, they would have noticed her absence," Adele said. "Good observation, Missy." She smiled at her reporter friend, who grinned and moved some strands of hair off her face.

"We'll check on that," said Sergeant Walker and Jackson wrote it down on his pad. "For right now, we'll assume she was killed between six in the evening and five o'clock this morning."

"Still a large window of time," Hatfield mumbled.

"We do what we can with what we have to work with, Horatio." His friend chuckled. "Anything else of note, Doctor?"

"Well, there are some bruises on her arms." Dr. Fleming rolled up her sleeves to show them. "Very faint, like someone grabbed her through her blouse. No jacket."

"She was wearing a jacket when we saw her," Adele said. "No hat, though. She must have been in a great hurry if she left without one."

"That's all I can tell you." Dr. Fleming rose, brushing the dirt from his knees. "I suggest she be buried immediately since there's nowhere to keep the body."

"We have to identify her first," Sergeant Walker said. "I wish we had one of our police photographers here." He sighed. "The two we had lost their cameras in the fires."

"Would a drawing help?" Missy asked. They all stared at her.

"It would indeed," the sergeant said.

Missy flipped over a page in her notepad to a clean one and scribbled for five minutes with her pencil. She ripped the page off and handed it to Walker. "Will that do or would you like me to make another?"

Walker stared at it, bewildered. "Why, that's a very good likeness, Miss Grace."

"I never knew you could draw, dear," Adele said with her hand on her arm. "Can you draw another for us?"

Missy obliged, now clearly a little self-conscious. "When I was twelve, Papa started taking me to watch court proceedings in Rosa Gris. He taught me how to draw faces of people in the courtroom." She handed the picture to Adele.

"There were no Kodaks then to do the job for you." Adele smiled.

"These are better than Kodaks," Nin insisted. "They're real."

"We can circulate this around the camp." Walker put the picture in his pocket. "I wonder if there's something on her clothes that could tell us more about her, like a name tag or laundry mark."

"I wouldn't trust any name that was," Nin said. "Most people are wearing donated clothes. The name probably wouldn't be the right one."

"Nin's right," said Adele. "Elsie told me most of the women she's seen had next to nothing with them."

"She may have taken some clothes with her," Edwards objected. "A lot of the people who have very little stuffed everything they had into their suitcases or bags before they evacuated."

"I don't know, Lieutenant," Adele said. "I don't think this one is a working girl."

"And how do you know that, dear sister?" Jackson eyed her.

"Because of her hands." Adele bent down and pointed to the palms. "The skin is well cared for and the nails are a little longer than they ought to be." She also noted the left hand had a faint pale ring on the third finger where, she assumed, the wedding ring had been.

"Not the hands of a working woman," Nin agreed.

"I wouldn't say she's been an idle rich girl either," Adele continued. "The combs in her hair are the sort you would buy in a department store, not Kelly & King Fine Jewelers. I'd say she did some work but not for a living. And from the looks of her, it might have been with women's organizations or even reform work."

"It's a mistake to make such assumptions about the girl, Miss Gossling," Edwards said.

"If Adele says she was a reformer, then she was a reformer," Hatfield said stiffly.

"The sheriff is right, Monte," said Jackson. "Del's worked with such ladies many times. She knows them when she sees them."

"Thank you, Jack." She pinched his cheek.

"We might find more when we search around here," Hatfield suggested.

"I'll take my leave, if you don't need me for anything else." The doctor closed his bag. "I'll ask one of the hospital tents to send a wagon and a stretcher for the girl." He gave the sergeant a knowing look. "And I'll make sure they know to be discreet since I doubt the army wants a riot on their hands if word gets out a girl was killed under their watch."

"Good thinking, Doctor." The sergeant nodded.

"Ah, a fine morning for a stroll," Dr. Fleming remarked, looking up at the sky. "Shouldn't take me long to get back to camp."

"I'll come with you, if you don't mind," Edwards said with a glance at the sergeant. "Whatever you need, Sergeant, don't hesitate to ask."

"Thank you, young man." Walker saluted him.

"Fine fellow, that doctor," Hatfield remarked as the two men disappeared from the clearing. "Too bad we can't entice him to join us in Arrojo."

"Not unless you want Dr. Rhodes to have a fit," Nin snorted and Missy laughed.

"I think the first order of business is to search the grounds for anything we can find," Walker said.

"The killer could have been careless if he was so haphazard with the murder," Jackson agreed.

"And we need to find out her identity." The sergeant turned to the women. "Are you sure you didn't see her before the other night, even if just a glimpse in the women's part of the camp?"

Adele and Nin exchanged glances once more. "We haven't, Sergeant," Adele said. "But I found something while I was recovering from the horrible spectacle that might belong to her." She took the wedding ring out of her pocket.

"Any other evidence you've been hiding from us, Del?" her brother demanded.

"We're not hiding anything, Mr. Gossling," Nin snapped.

"Adele only said she *thinks* it might have belonged to the murdered woman," Missy pointed out. "With all the people at the camp, there's no way of knowing for sure. So technically, that's not hiding evidence."

"Just the same, I think you'd better tell us if you have anything else," Hatfield said in a firm tone.

"That's all we found, Sheriff," Adele insisted. "You can take a look over there yourself."

Sergeant Walker examined the ring. "'L.S. & G. W.' Well, well."

"There's a mark on the third finger of her left hand," Adele supplied. "That might have been a wedding ring."

The sergeant bent down and compared the width of the ring to the mark on the woman's finger. "It very well might, Miss Gossling."

"That could be important, Harry," Hatfield said.

"It could give us a suspect, anyway." The man put the ring in his pocket. "If we can find out who L.S. and G.W. are, we can perhaps piece together some kind of motive."

"It doesn't necessarily follow that the husband is guilty," Adele pointed out.

"No, but it gives us a starting place," said Walker. "Miss Gossling, it's clear to me you and Miss Branch have been of some use to Horatio in his work."

"Some use!" Nin snorted. "We practically solve the crimes for him."

Hatfield raised an eyebrow.

"I wouldn't say that exactly." Adele hid a smile. "But we've tried to help, Sergeant."

"Perhaps you can do the same for me," he said. "Since we don't know who the woman is, it might be in order to, erm, search her clothes and person." He looked uncomfortable.

"Do you think you could stand it with her like that?" Hatfield asked.

"Don't worry, Sheriff," Adele said. "I can stomach it now that I know what to expect."

"Funny how you were never squeamish about my frog experiments," Jackson said.

"Frogs are not people, Mr. Gossling," Nin said.

"I don't think it's that," said Missy. "If I know Adele, she doesn't like to see women hurt in any way."

"Indeed." Adele smiled her gratitude at her friend.

"I think we ought to start with the clearing where the ring was found," said Walker. "She might have been killed there and then brought here. Then we can follow the circumference of the area and take it from there."

"Whatever you say, Harry." Hatfield saluted him.

"Just don't be here when we undress her." Nin smirked as Jackson looked mortified.

Once the men had disappeared, Missy asked, "Can I help? I'm not bothered by it anymore." Her eyes became wide with curiosity. "I've never been this close to a dead body."

"You were there when we found Arabella Parnell a few months ago," Nin reminded her.

"Yes, but Jackson refused to let me near her," Missy said with a little pout.

"Jack and his procedures." Adele rolled her eyes. "We could use your help.

They checked the dress and shoes, being careful not to touch the front with all the bloody slits. Adele remarked, "I think I was wrong about the dress."

"How so?" Nin asked.

"It's made of good material and sewn well," Adele said. "Made by a dressmaker, not store-bought."

"But the hands —" Missy pointed out.

"I didn't say I change my mind about her being a reformer," said Adele. "I think she was of a higher status than most of the working women I've seen, though."

"A poor relation," Nin murmured. "I feel there is some conflict there."

"That would make sense," Missy agreed.

"It looks as if she's wearing a necklace." Adele saw both Nin and Missy were hesitating about touching the front of the dress so she unbuttoned the top few buttons, careful to dodge the stained rips. She gently undid a thin gold chain and produced a necklace that looked like a gold coin with a braided border.

"Pretty thing," Missy said. "I wonder how it missed —" She glanced at the bloody dress.

"It was too deeply hidden underneath her clothes to be splattered," Adele said, shuddering at the thought.

"It needs polishing," Nin observed.

"Perhaps it wasn't important enough for her to keep polished," Missy suggested.

"Then it couldn't have been a gift from her husband," Adele said.

"That depends on how she felt about the husband," Nin snorted.

Adele turned the pendant around and noticed hinges on the side. "I think it's a locket." And indeed, it opened slowly to reveal a lock of fine chestnut hair.

"You were wrong, Miss Branch," Missy said. "It looks like her husband gave her a token after all."

"I don't think so," Adele murmured. "It's too silky and fine for a man's hair."

"A woman's hair?" Nin asked.

"A relative, probably," Missy said.

"It might be her mother's," Adele said. "I noticed the woman's hair before they covered her up. It has the same silkiness."

"A pity there's no picture inside," said Missy.

"We can't have every clue be a big one," Nin remarked.

"I think there was a picture," Adele said. "See the edge of black paper here? It might have been a photograph of some kind."

"I wonder why she took it out," Missy said. Adele could see her reporter mind already working on a romantic story.

"It's a shame she removed it," Adele said with a sigh. "It might have helped us identify her."

"With all the city records burned in the fires?" Nin asked. "Not likely."

"We might be able to use the locket to find out who she was," Missy argued. "Someone might have seen her wearing it. Or she might have come with her husband or other relatives who would recognize it."

"Good thinking, Missy." Adele smiled.

"I might try my hand at being a woman detective like you." Missy chuckled.

Adele laughed. "I think Hatfield would find three women detectives a little too much for him."

"Not the sheriff," Nin said. "Your brother."

"Oh, we've gotten Jack used to it by now." Adele buttoned up the woman's dress. "No tags of any kind on the clothes. Pity."

"As Miss Branch pointed out, we can't have every clue be a big one." Missy grinned.

The men returned, with Hatfield puffing a little from the excursion. "I'm used to sending my assistant deputies to do this sort of work," he said apologetically to Sergeant Walker.

The man laughed. "Horatio, you were always more brain than legs." He looked at the women. "Anything?"

"No tags or identifying papers," Adele said. "But we did find this." She gave him the locket.

Walker was clearly disappointed. "She must have left everything back at camp when she went to meet whoever she was meeting."

"How do you know she was meeting anyone?" Nin asked. "When we saw her, she was just taking a walk."

"She was meeting someone all right," Jackson said. "We found footprints in the clearing where you found the ring."

"That's something, isn't it?" Adele brightened.

"I'm afraid not," Walker said. "They belong to a man, but they're rather what you would expect from a man's boots."

"Isn't there any way to match the footprints to the boots?" Missy asked.

"Not under these circumstances, Miss Grace," Hatfield said. "If we were in Arrojo, I would send Edison or one of the lads to take plaster casts of the prints, but here —" He shook his head.

"It wouldn't do much good if you did, sir," Jackson said. "There are so many people trampling around the camp that those prints would probably fit dozens of boots."

"True, Deputy, true." Hatfield patted him on the back. "This is the man who's been my right hand since I started the job, Harry."

"Good man." The sergeant nodded. Jackson mumbled his thanks.

"Did you find anything else?" Adele asked.

"Only the murder weapon." Jackson smiled at his sister's stunned expression.

"We don't know for sure it's the murder weapon," Sergeant Walker said.

"Everything points toward it, Harry." Sheriff Hatfield unwrapped a large cloth to produce a knife with a curved wooden handle that looked like a half moon.

"A Chinese fisherman's folding knife, you said?" Walker looked at Hatfield.

His friend nodded. "Sailors pick them up in the Orient."

"This one could be from Chinatown," Jackson argued. "I've seen them myself in the shops there."

"All the same, we may be looking for a sailor." Walker nodded to Jackson, who wrote this down. "It's possible the young lady married a sailor."

"Odd little thing," Nin said as she looked over Adele's shoulder.

"Also a lethal little thing," Hatfield flicked the knife open to reveal a slightly curved blade.

"Covered with blood!" Missy breathed. Adele could tell she wished she had her camera with her.

"I see now why you say it's probably the murder weapon," Adele said. "Because of the curved edge the doctor described and the blood."

"A shame we don't have a way to extract fingerprints," Jackson said. "I'm sure the killer left them if he was so hasty as to throw it aside like that."

"All our equipment went up in flames," said Sergeant Walker.

"Anything else you found that might be worthy of examination?" Adele asked.

Jackson held up a cigar stub. "It's dried out and frayed, though. Probably some rebel soldier snuck back here to smoke it a long time ago."

"It's hardly likely a murderer would linger to smoke a cigar," Walker agreed.

"You never can tell," Nin said. "We once caught a killer because he left a cigar stub."

"It wasn't only that, Nin," Adele reminded her. "There were a few other things."

"All the same, it's a popular brand in this city," Walker said. "Like the boots, dozens of men here probably smoke it. Those who were able to grab their humidors before they escaped the fires, that is." He chuckled.

"I was thinking, sir." Jackson turned to his superior. "Do you think maybe the killer stabbed her in a blind drunk state?"

"Eh?" Hatfield glanced at him.

"We found bushes broken and askew," his deputy reminded him. "It seems like it might have been done by someone stumbling about."

"I don't buy that theory, sir," said Walker. "As your friend Edwards will tell you, the mayor closed down all the saloons as one of the first orders of business and the army is ever watchful of anyone with a bottle."

"I'm sure they wouldn't even let a drop of apple juice through their gates," Missy added with a nod. "I interviewed some of the privates, and they grumbled about how they couldn't even get a glass of beer anywhere in the city."

"Good thing the mayor did what he did, or we would have had to deal with the drunks too," Walker said.

"But someone could have gotten hold of a few bottles of whiskey before the shutdown," Hatfield pointed out. "That, or they could have taken what they had in their house with them before fleeing."

"We confiscated what we could, Horatio," his friend argued. "No, I don't think it was a drunken rage that made that poor girl's chest what it was."

"Pure black hate," Nin murmured.

There was a rustling in the leaves and some voices not far away.

"Who the devil —" Sergeant Walker mumbled as he bolted toward the path. "I don't want anyone here!"

But it was only the medical men the doctor had promised to send who had come with a wagon and cot. As they carefully lifted the girl into the wagon bed, Adele couldn't help but feel a strain in her throat.

CHAPTER 10

They returned to the main camp with the flies already buzzing around the cook tent which was showing signs of lunch preparations.

"Well, sir, where do we start?" Jackson parted the canvas flap of his and Hatfield's tent.

Before the lawman had a chance to answer, a call came from within. "Sergeant Walker!"

As Adele went through with Nin at her side, she saw a man with a large face and imposing figure sitting on one of the cots with Edwards beside him. From the man's shiny boots and tight-waisted jacket, Adele guessed it was the infamous Captain Best.

The sergeant took it in stride. "I'm Sergeant Walker."

"Captain Best." The man rose and shook his hand. "I understand from my lieutenant here that you've taken charge of this unfortunate occurrence."

"It's more than an unfortunate occurrence, Captain," Adele said.

"It's a murder," Nin said.

The man looked at them with the eyes of a mosquito. "What are these women doing here?"

"They're my sister and her friend, sir," Jackson said stiffly.

"You're Jackson Gossling?" Jackson nodded. "Lieutenant Edwards told me good things about your work with the Anspatch Agency."

"Can I do anything for you, Captain?" Walker intervened, taking off his hat.

"I want a full report of this — murder." He glanced at Nin with narrow eyes.

"With all due respect, sir, the sergeant reports to the chief of police, not the army," Hatfield said shortly.

"Ah, yes, Sheriff Hatfield." The man eyed him. "The lieutenant told me about you too. You're out of your jurisdiction. You realize that, Sheriff?"

"Certainly," Hatfield mumbled.

"I've no objection giving you my report, sir," said Walker. "The body of a young woman was found in the brush near Fort Point."

"Fort Point, eh?" The captain cocked his head. "Go on, Sergeant."

"The woman was stabbed multiple times in the chest with a knife." He paused. "We're still trying to locate that knife."

Adele glanced at Nin, remembering the way Hatfield had flicked open the knife. They both kept silent.

"Perhaps the culprit took it with him," Captain Best suggested.

"How clever of you to think that," Nin mumbled.

"Nothing was found on the woman to identify her, unfortunately," said Walker. "That's why I asked Miss Gossling and Miss Branch to come with us." He nodded at the women. "We thought they might have seen the young lady in the women's tents or in their work. They've come here to help the ladies of the — what is the name of the organization, Miss Gossling?"

"Destitute Women's Aid Society."

"Oh, yes." Captain Best nodded slowly. "I heard about your little fiasco with my men yesterday."

"It was their fiasco, not ours," Nin snarled.

"A Miss Blessings came to see me this morning," he said. "I assume she's one of your ladies?"

"She created the organization, sir," Adele said. "And a good thing too. Those women need help."

"First it was Mrs. Kelly and her followers, as if that wasn't enough of a burden on our hands," the man snarled. "And now this. I don't approve of women being involved in such sordid matters as crime"

"You're at the end of a very long line, Captain," Adele said dryly as she thought of all the people in Arrojo who had not hesitated to voice their opinion of women involved in crime ever since she set foot in town.

"As I said, Captain, these ladies are here on my authority," the sergeant insisted.

"I don't propose to tell you how to do your job, Sergeant Walker."

"Much appreciated, Captain." The lawman gave a deep bow, and Adele caught the quick smile on Edwards' face.

"Anything else you can tell me?" Captain Best asked. "Fort Point, you know, that's where we put the Chinese camp."

"I'm aware of that, sir."

"Do you think they're responsible?" The man leaned forward.

"I'm not ruling out that possibility," Walker said.

"Well, I suppose the police know how to do their job." He rose and Edwards jumped up. "From what Edwards tells me, you have two good men here at your aid. I understand police personnel right now are scarce."

"We are a little stretched, sir," said Walker. "Much like the army, I imagine."

Captain Best chuckled. "Very true." His eyes fell on Missy who was trying to hide the pad and pencil in her lap. "Surely you didn't need *three* women to identify the girl!"

"Miss Grace is a reporter," Hatfield supplied.

"She's writing a series of articles about the army's heroic efforts toward civilians during the rebuilding," Adele added.

"And heroic they are, Captain," Missy said, taking up the cue.

"We try our best." He waved a finger at her. "It wouldn't do to get any of this dirty business out to the public, though."

"I shall only print what Sergeant Walker allows," Missy promised.

"Miss Grace can be trusted, sir," Hatfield said in a firm tone. "You have my word on that." Missy gave him a gracious smile.

The captain grunted. "Sergeant, I expect you to keep Edwards informed of any new developments. He'll be reporting to me daily of your progress. And, of course, you have only to ask and I'll provide any of my men to help you solve this crime quickly and quietly."

"Thank you, sir," said Walker.

Edwards saluted him and Captain Best strode out of the tent.

"The devil!" Hatfield growled and Walker burst out laughing, clamping him on the back.

"Don't let it get to you, Horatio," he said. "It's not the first time we've had the army watching our every move."

"Captain Best can be a little much, sir," Edwards apologized. "He knows you'll solve this case to his satisfaction."

"To *his* satisfaction!" Hatfield growled.

"Perhaps it was best you didn't tell him everything." Edwards gave Jackson a sly look. "Am I right?'

"There are some things best kept secret in an investigation, Monte," said Jackson. "You know that."

"Can you at least enlighten *me*?" Edwards sat down on the cot. "I'll only reveal to Captain Best what you allow, like Miss Grace here." He grinned at Missy.

"We found the murder weapon," said Walker. With a nod toward Hatfield, he pulled it out of his pocket and unwrapped the cloth. "Have you ever seen anything like this around the camp?"

Edwards stared at it. "Why, it's Chinese, isn't it?"

"A Chinese fisherman's knife." The sergeant eyed the young man. "But don't jump to conclusions."

"But, sir, wouldn't this mean we should be looking at their camp?" he asked. "Given where the body was found —"

"I'm not ready to take that leap yet, Lieutenant," said Sergeant Walker. "There are dozens of seamen here. Any one of them could have been in the Orient and procured a knife like this."

"They often do," Hatfield supplied. "They're cheap and they can show them off to their families."

"Anything else of importance you discovered after I left?" Edwards asked.

Jackson filled him in on the clues they had found, including the footprints and the jewelry on the young woman.

When he finished, Edwards looked a little defeated. "How are we to find out who this woman was if there is nothing to identify her?"

"We'll certainly take up Miss Grace's point and inquire within the dining room tents to find out if anyone was missing from dinner last night," Hatfield said.

"And if they don't recall?" Edwards asked. "What then?"

"We keep our eyes and ears open," Jackson said. "Just as we found a thug in the old days."

"I think we can find a better solution to the problem than that, Jack," said Adele. "Missy also suggested we use the locket."

"But there's no photograph or name of any kind here." Edwards held up the chain that Jackson had given him to inspect.

"Miss Grace has kindly provided us with an illustration of the young lady's face." Sergeant Walker produced the drawing. "It's an accurate likeness."

"Well done, Miss Grace." Missy smiled but said nothing. "Then all we have to do is print more of these and —"

"It's not going to be that easy, Monte," Jackson interrupted. "If we start to show the drawing to people, they'll ask questions about why we're looking for her."

"Which is why we ought to start with the locket," Adele said. "No one will think much of people searching for the owner of a lost locket. Once someone gives us a name, then we can show them the illustration and get confirmation."

"Very clever indeed." Walker nodded his approval.

"I told you Adele has a first-rate policewoman's mind," Hatfield said, not without a little pride. Nin snorted behind her.

"What makes you think people will recognize the locket?" the lieutenant asked.

"It's not a very common one," Adele said. "Ladies notice one another's jewelry, especially in circumstances such as these."

"Most women couldn't save much, if any, of their jewelry," Missy added. "Those I've interviewed regret it."

"Any jewelry is going to stand out," Nin said.

"It's worth a try, eh, Horatio?" Walker glanced at his friend.

"When there's a blank slate, everything is worth a try," echoed Sheriff Hatfield.

"May I suggest, Sergeant," Adele turned to him, "that Nin and I take the locket and go around the women's tents?"

"Preposterous!" Edwards boomed. "You've nothing to do with police business."

"Lieutenant, we've had to do with police business for the last three years," Nin said with amusement.

"I don't think it's a good idea, Del," said her brother.

"Why not?"

"Because this isn't Arrojo," he said. "Two women going around with a gold locket might — well, give some people ideas."

"Women don't steal other women's jewelry, Mr. Gossling," Nin snapped. "Not when they've lost their own."

"I think you're a little optimistic, Miss Branch," Jackson said with a smile.

"It's true, Jack," said Adele. "Taking someone else's property is the last thing on their minds. They're just trying to hold on to what little they have."

Hatfield looked at his friend. "I think you should allow it, Harry. Adele and Miss Branch have done a great deal of good in this investigation so far."

"It's preposterous," Edwards mumbled.

"You said that before." Nin glared at him.

"Consider this, Lieutenant," Adele said. "If men like yourselves, in uniform and with badges, start asking questions about a locket, the women are going to get suspicious that something is up, and it will spread like wildfire around the camp. If Nin and I go, we're merely looking for the owner of a valuable item we happened to pick up in the dirt that some poor soul dropped in the chaos."

The lieutenant was taken aback. "I never thought of it that way."

"Neither did I," Sergeant Walker said. "I see your point, Horatio."

"Just make sure to report what you find immediately," said Jackson. "*All* of it." He looked meaningfully at his sister. She returned his look with an exaggerated curtsy.

They both left the tent with Missy at their heels, asking, "Do you really think we can find out who it belonged to, Adele?"

"You know Adele can find out anything," Nin said with confidence, taking her friend's arm.

"We'll start with Elsie and Valda," said Adele. "They've seen countless women over the past few weeks. Maybe they'll save us a lot of trouble."

There was again a long line outside the Destitute Women's Aid Society tent and the ladies standing there looked more harried than the ones the day before. Adele found Elsie raking through boxes of supplies while Valda tended to the women.

"Where the demon have you been?" Elsie asked in an irritated tone.

"Your temper, dear," Adele said mildly.

"That's why I said demon and not the other decidedly male figure," Elsie said.

"We had some business to take care of." Adele pulled her friend aside. "Elsie, we need your help."

"Don't tell me — Good Lord, a crime?" Her friend's tired eyes opened wide.

"A young woman was murdered." Adele spoke in a low tone. "The sergeant who's handling the case doesn't want it to get out."

"Who is she?"

"That's what we don't know," Adele said. "She had no identification of any kind. The only thing we found on her was this." She showed her friend the locket. "Recognize it?"

Elsie turned the delicate gold over in her hands. "Not the sort of thing our ladies would own, even as a heirloom."

"So you think it's upper class?" Adele asked.

"It's certainly not working class," Elsie said.

"It's not from Kelly & King either." Adele remembered the elegant jewelry shop she and Nin had visited when they were tracking down the murderer of Arabella Parnell.

"No, no," said her friend. "I mean it looks like it was hand-crafted. See how rough the gold is here? Like someone took it to a goldsmith and had it made especially."

"Then maybe the girl is an aristocrat after all," Adele said.

"Not necessarily," said Elsie. "Back when the Forty-Niners were here, there were plenty of goldsmiths in the city to help them decide what to do with their claims." She chuckled. "Remember Katie Martin? That lovely necklace with the twin elephants? That was made from what little was left of her grandmother's claim during the forty-niner period."

"Her grandmother went digging for gold?" Nin stared.

"She came from a very progressive family." Elsie sniffed.

Adele laughed. "Then all we have to do is to find a few descendants of the forty-niners, and we'll find the girl's identity."

"Or those who made a profit from the forty-niners," Elsie said. "They kept more of the gold than the finders." She put her chin in her hand. "I'm willing to bet this came from a pretentious family looking to get in with Nob Hill society but only had a few nuggets to show for it."

"Then we'll more likely find out who it belonged to among the refined ladies in the camp," Adele said.

"There's a place near the dining tent that's filled with descendants of the forty-niners," Elsie offered.

"How do you know, dear?"

"Valda and I went scouting around when we first came, hoping to find a little charity among the wealthier ladies. You can imagine our success." She said the last with a snort.

"Perhaps we'll find more success, then," Adele said.

She asked Valda if she had seen the necklace but received an answer in the negative.

Outside the tent, Adele told her friends what Elsie had suggested. "I guess we go call on the aristocracy," Adele said.

"After Mrs. Faderman's tea parties, we ought to be experts at wrenching out information from them," Nin said. "We've had to often enough."

"I've been trying to get an interview with them since we got here." Missy flipped a page back in her notebook. "Now they can't avoid me."

Adele recognized the tents Elsie had referred to right away by their exclusivity. They were larger tents set off to the side over grass rather than dirt. There were even a few flower pots outside and some rickety old chairs. The entrance to the tent was tightly shut.

"I suppose they don't want anyone to even think about bothering them," Adele remarked.

"They must have grabbed their flower pots from the window

sills as they ran." Nin examined them. "Not much use from a medicinal perspective."

"I suspect those were 'donated' by some of the army wives," Adele said.

"How do we get in?" Missy asked.

Before Adele could answer, Nin bent backward and let out a shrill whistle. It was so perfectly pitched that it made Missy jump. She let out a few more. The flap tore open and a woman poked her head outside the tent. She regarded them with loathing.

"Will you please stop making that ghastly noise?" she snarled.

"We had to get your attention so we could come in, didn't we?" Before the woman could open her mouth, Nin yanked the flap aside and pushed past her. Adele winked at Missy and they both followed.

There were about five women in the tent. Their clothes and straight figures told her they had come from the outskirts of Nob Hill. Yet, they had cots with scratchy army blankets and makeshift nightstands from orange crates just like everyone else. However, someone had created a table with crates and a board where there lay a lovely gilded vanity set. There was even a mirror propped up against one of the poles that held up the tent.

"You ought to hide those away." Nin eyed the vanity set. "Someone might steal them."

"What do you want?" demanded the woman who had spoken to them. "You're trespassing."

"Unless the army says so, we're not trespassing," Nin snapped. "We have just as much right to go wherever we like in this camp as you have."

"We'll call someone for help!" another woman shrieked.

"Who, for instance?" Nin looked squarely at her. "One of your maids, perhaps?"

"Oh, the riffraff here!"

"I'll have you know, ma'am, my friend and I come from

respectable people." Adele felt her temper rise. "My friend is the daughter of Atha Branch of the Branches in Sacramento."

One of the other ladies stared down Nin's wild hair and loose dress. "Never heard of them."

"I'm sure they never heard of you either." Nin returned the stare.

"Dorothy, go and fetch John," said the woman who had opened the flap. "He'll know what to do with these infidels."

"And my father was Otis Gossling," Adele said. "I'm sure you know his name."

All at once, the attitude in the tent softened. While the ladies were still not entirely convinced, their tight faces relaxed a little and the woman who had stared Nin down said, "Naturally we know who he was."

"And I'm a reporter from Arrojo," said Missy. "I'm doing a series of articles on the resilience of San Francisco citizens in the wake of the earthquake and fires."

"Oh, indeed?" Now even the woman who had opened the flap for them became interested. "You'll find no better people than in our city!"

"Are you a prime example?" Nin eyed her.

"As a matter of fact —"

"Adele!"

The cry came from behind and Adele whirled around. Looking a little ragged and poorly shaven was the grinning face of John Bellows.

Adele suddenly felt a warmth wash over her. Although she had rejected John's proposals several times, and although he liked to joke about her decision to move to "the sticks," she was never so glad to see anyone in her life. She rushed to him and grabbed his hands.

"Don't tell me you were in the city when all this happened?" He kissed the back of both her hands and nodded at Nin, who looked less than happy to see him.

"We just came a few days ago to help," she said. "I can't say —
I'm so glad —" She suddenly found tears in her eyes.

He put his arms around her. "Did you think I went down with
the buildings?"

"It crossed my mind." She could barely speak.

"You must think I'm a yellow-belly if you thought that," he
said softly.

"Not quite, but almost," Nin mumbled.

"I'm sorry I'm acting so silly." She drew away from him and
wiped her face with her handkerchief. "It's just such a relief to see
friends who are alive after this horrible event."

"John, you know this woman?" one of the ladies spoke.

"Yes, Mrs. Bridges," he said. "She's an old friend." He winked.
"Let's go outside, eh?" He motioned for Nin and Missy to
follow.

The sunshine felt good on Adele's face. "Jack is here too," she
said. "Helping with law and order."

"We need it." He sighed. "I'm afraid things went rather badly
at first, what with the city in such chaos and no one knowing
what to do. Thank goodness General Funston had the sound
mind to take over when he did."

"Without authority," Missy reminded him, scratching on
her pad.

"It was necessary, Miss —"

"Grace." She held out her hand. "*Arrojo Courier*."

"Oh, a reporter." He looked her up and down.

"And editor," Adele said. "She won't print anything you tell
her not to, John."

"Well, you can print what you like," he said. "Is that why
you've accosted Mrs. Bridges and the rest of the ladies?" He was
amused. "They are —were — neighbors of mine, so I've been sort
of their watchdog."

"We came for a good reason," Adele said.

"Adele, maybe you shouldn't." Nin's voice was cautious.

"John's a lawyer, dear," she said. "He knows these matters are discreet."

"What matters?" He put his hands on his hips. "You're not playing lady detective *now*, are you? Under these circumstances?"

"We don't have a choice," Adele said. "Someone's been murdered." She quickly told him about the young woman.

"That is tragic," he said when she finished. "With everyone waiting to get their homes and jobs back, to think a poor young woman could be robbed of her life —" He shook his head. "Let me see the locket." He examined it carefully. "I can't place it, but then, I've been mostly with the men. I wonder if Ginny would know it."

Adele stared. "Your sister?"

He smiled. "I thought Elsie or someone would have told you."

"She's in the city?"

"She's been here for three months," he said.

"They've moved here?" In spite of the grave circumstances, Adele was delighted. She and John's older sister had always been friends.

"She's here without her husband," he said. "Or her children." There was something strained in his voice that made Adele ask nothing further. "She'll be happy to see you."

The women followed John as he led them back to the main tents. Adele recognized Ginny right away. She had the same crane-like figure and face as her brother. Adele's heart went out to her shabby appearance and sagging shoulders. Something told her they didn't come from the tragedy that had just befallen the city.

Ginny greeted Adele and her friends warmly. Adele could see that, while Nin had no love for John, her sympathy was aroused by his sister. She laid her hands on her shoulders and said in a wistful tone, "Great strife is behind you and ahead of you."

Ginny gave a little cry of alarm.

"Nin has a gift for seeing things," Adele said quickly. "She speaks when it comes, sometimes without thinking."

"I doubt a soothsayer would solve any of our problems," John said dryly.

"You sound as doubtful as Mr. Gossling," Nin growled.

"Perhaps that's because Jackson and I both prefer tangible evidence." To his sister, he said, "Adele has a problem, Ginny. Maybe you can help."

His sister examined the locket. "It does look vaguely familiar."

"You know the girl who wore it?" Adele was immediately all attention.

"I didn't say that," said the woman. "It just looks familiar. It might be —"

"Yes?" Nin prompted.

"I had a conversation yesterday at dinner with a group of older women — you know the type, Adele — boasted about their grandfathers coming with the gold rush, could have been millionaires, all that —"

"I know." Adele rolled her eyes.

"It might belong to one of them," she said.

Adele put her arm around Ginny's shoulder. "Will you take us there?"

"Of course." The woman smiled. "It's not as if I have much else to do." A sad look came on her face. "My children are back in Iowa. For now."

"How old are they?" Nin asked in a soft tone.

"Joe is nine and Alison is five." Her voice turned wistful. "I'm glad they're not here now. Perhaps in the future — perhaps."

Adele understood right away what she meant. She had only met Ginny's husband once but he struck her instantly as a self-absorbed man whose desire for ownership bordered on the excessive. She had no doubt he considered his wife and children in the same light.

"There are people who can help you," she said in a low tone.

"Elsie and another friend of mine are in the Destitute Women's Aid Society tent. Go see them, dear. They have resources for anything you need."

"Thank you, Adele." She hugged her. "John always said anyone could count on you to offer a hand in need."

"It will be all right," Nin said in a reassuring tone. "It's a long road ahead, but it will turn out right in the end."

Adele was glad to see Ginny seemed to believe her.

CHAPTER 11

They found the two tents near the creek. These women were even haughtier than the aristocrats though their surroundings made it obvious they came from humble origins. But their conversation with Ginny was clearly friendly, and she was able to coax them with a story of how they had found the locket and were anxious to return it to its owner. One woman was sure the locket belonged to the niece of the two ladies in the tent next to theirs.

The second tent was small and leaned a little so that John had to bend his head as they entered. Two women who looked to be in their seventies were sitting on wooden chairs. One was reading with spectacles perched on her nose and the other was knitting. They had identical white hair and strained faces, but one was thin as a twig and sat taller than the other, who was portly and kept a sweet little smile on her face.

Ginny approached them. "Miss Miriam? Miss Addie?"

The one with the twig figure looked up from her book. "Yes? Who are you?" She took off the glasses and regarded Ginny with suspicion.

Her sister leaned over. "The young lady with the flogging husband, Miriam dear."

Ginny's face turned a little red.

"Oh, yes," said Miss Miriam. "And the lawyer brother." She glanced at John. "I'm assuming you're helping your sister get out of that abominable situation, sir?"

"Indeed, ma'am," John mumbled.

"How good of you to come and see us." Miss Addie spoke through her smile.

"We think we have something that might belong to you." Ginny glanced at Adele.

"I'm a friend of Ginny's, ma'am," Adele began. "Adele Gossling's my name. This is Miss Branch and Miss Grace." Both women nodded.

"Pleased to make your acquaintance." Miss Addie put her knitting in her bag. "It's always delightful to have guests."

"Yes, well, my friends and I were taking a walk around the camp —"

"You shouldn't do that, my dear." Miss Miriam threw out her words like a child threw stones in a river. "There's no telling what trouble a lady might get into in this sort of situation."

"There are soldiers with bayonets at every corner," Nin reminded her.

"All the same, it isn't safe." The woman held up a finger.

Adele glanced sideways at Nin as she continued, "We found this lovely necklace on the ground, and we think it might belong to you." She took out the locket.

"What use would we have with such trinkets?" Miss Miriam shrugged and went back to her book.

Miss Addie, however, took it in her shaking hands, her eyes wide. "Why, it's Lillie's!"

"What?" Miss Miriam ripped off her glasses. "Let me see that!"

After looking at it carefully, she said in an angry tone, "You say you found this in the dirt?"

"Yes," Adele said.

"Careless girl!" snarled the woman. "She's always losing things. And this — her mother should never have given it to her."

"Well, Miriam dear, it *was* hers to give," Miss Addie reminded her. "We couldn't very well —"

"She had no right," Miss Miriam insisted.

"Mother gave it to her," said her sister in a soft tone. "Before she —"

"Yes, I know," said Miss Miriam. "Before Danielle ran off with that blackguard husband of hers."

"Mama always said she wanted to make sure it would go down in the family." Miss Addie's voice was almost dreamy. "And as Miriam and I weren't likely to get married —"

"Never mind that," Miss Miriam nodded at Adele, "Thank you for bringing it back. We'll give it to Lillie when she comes in."

"She's —" Nin began but Adele grabbed her wrist.

"We'd like to give it to her ourselves, if you don't mind," Adele said in a cordial tone. "Do you know where she is?"

"Only heaven can tell." Miss Miriam rolled her eyes. "That girl goes all over the place. You young ladies are far too independent these days." She gave Adele an arched look.

"I expect so, ma'am." Adele tried to keep the annoyance out of her voice. "We'll be happy to find her for you. Can you tell us what she looks like?"

"Well, she's about as tall as you are with red hair and blue eyes." Miss Addie smiled. "Cornflower blue eyes, they used to call it. Her mother had those eyes too. And she has a birthmark on the left side of her neck."

"What was she wearing?" Missy asked.

"A plain cotton dress," said Miss Addie. "Far too plain, but what can one do under these circumstances?"

"Such clothes are fitting for her station in life, Addie," Miss Miriam said in a stern tone.

"She wasn't at breakfast this morning?" Adele exchanged a look with Nin.

"Probably got to wandering about and forgot," Miss Miriam said. "She often does that. Just goes for a morning walk and forgets all about breakfast. Waste of food!"

Adele took out the drawing Missy had made and held it up. "Does your niece look like this woman?"

"Why, yes, that's Lillie!" Miss Addie stared at the picture. "Fancy, what a likeness. Isn't it, Miriam?"

"You draw tolerably well, Miss Gossling," the stoic sister admitted.

"She didn't draw it," Nin said. "Miss Grace did."

"How would Miss Grace know Lillie?" Miss Miriam glared at Missy. "Don't tell me she's been speaking to you about those nonsense reforms and that wicked woman."

"Miss McLeod," Miss Addie said softly.

"Wicked!" Miss Miriam spat.

Missy glanced at Adele and said nothing.

Adele felt a cold sinking in her stomach as she realized they had found their murdered woman. In the silence that followed, both her friends were looking at her, clearly expecting her to make the next move.

John had been listening at the doorway and said in a calm voice, "I think you ought to go with Miss Gossling, Miss Miriam and Miss Addie. There are some things you should know."

"Things we should know?" Miss Miriam eyed him. "What are you trying to say, young man?"

"I think you should go with her."

"Has something happened? Is something wrong?" Miss Addie's voice drew in a little as she clutched the knitting bag in her lap.

Miss Miriam, with all her grouchiness, seemed to sense John meant what he said and, with a sensible expression, set her book down on the cot. "Come, Addie. I think we should follow the man's advice."

"Where are we going?" Miss Addie jumped up, her knitting bag spilling on the ground. Nin quickly picked it up, shaking the dirt out of it and putting it gently on the cot.

"It will be all right, Miss Addie," Adele said gently as she took her arm.

This seemed to satisfy the childlike woman. "It will be good to see other people," she said. "We've been keeping to our tent except at mealtimes."

"Obviously, Addie," her sister said, "one doesn't want to expose oneself in the worst light if one can help it."

"We're all in the same situation," Nin reminded her.

"Young lady, we are *not* all in the same situation." Miss Miriam's lip was tight. "Decidedly not. When we get home —"

"There is no home anymore," Miss Addie said in a small voice.

"There will be one, Addie," her sister assured her. "And it will be much better than the old one."

Adele had no doubt someone like Miss Miriam would make sure the new home was as fine as she could manage it without being on Nob Hill.

John accompanied them to the police tent, making sure the elderly ladies were seated and comfortable. Jackson and Hatfield were there, but Walker had gone to see to police business outside the camp. Jackson was clearly as glad to see John as Adele. His controlled features collapsed as he clasped John on the back.

Adele introduced John to Hatfield. "I don't know what Arrojo would be like without Sheriff Hatfield protecting us." She smiled kindly at him.

Red flags appeared on the man's cheeks. "I only do my duty, Adele."

"And a much-needed duty it is, Sheriff," said John. "There seem to be quite a lot of dead bodies in your county."

"I wouldn't say that, sir." Sheriff Hatfield remained steady. "I worked a number of years in San Francisco, and there were certainly more casualties on a daily basis than one would care to count."

"Ah, but this is a big city," John pointed out. "One would think small towns like Arrojo would be clean of crime."

"Crime is everywhere, John," Adele said. "It takes decent and persistent lawmen to fight them. You must admit, San Francisco doesn't exactly have a reputation for a pristine police force."

John went rigid. "When you see them in the courtroom, they're pristine enough."

"I agree, sir," Hatfield said. "There are many fine lawmen in this city."

"Those who aren't corrupt," Nin remarked.

"Soon there will be no corrupt lawmen," Adele declared. "Roosevelt has reforms in place already."

John leaned against the back of Jackson's chair. "I will say, Sheriff, I'm surprised you would allow ladies like Adele and Miss Branch to help with your investigations."

"He doesn't have a choice," Nin said bluntly.

"Ladies can do anything men can do," Missy insisted. "Even solve crimes."

"I welcome help from all who show an intelligent mind and a keen observation, Mr. Bellows." The sheriff leaned his head back just a little in the intimidating way Adele had observed in him when he was interviewing suspects. "I don't allow someone's sex or social standing to determine who can or should help me."

"I see." From the whiteness of John's face, Adele could tell he was annoyed. "My concern is for Adele's welfare. And Miss Branch's too, of course."

"Mighty grateful," Nin mumbled.

"My concern for Adele's welfare is as great as yours, sir," Hatfield said.

"Crime is dangerous business —"

"I'm just as aware of that as you are," Hatfield interrupted. "I'll remind you, sir, I fight crime on the streets, not in the courtroom."

"Any man can find himself in a lethal situation, and for a woman —"

Adele's temper got the better of her and crossing her arms, she looked from one to the other. "Before you two great, big, strong men come to blows over my welfare, perhaps I'll remind you I've been taught by some pretty nasty women how to shoot a gun and deliver a blow to a man where it hurts the most better than either of you."

A gasp came from the two aunts and Nin giggled.

"Will you see me out, Adele?" John asked.

Adele followed him outside. He took both her hands, his face tender. "I'm sorry. Every time we meet, I always seem to say something to annoy you."

"We've all been under a great strain," Adele said.

"That sheriff is certainly protective of you," he remarked. "I'd go further, but it would probably only anger you more."

Adele looked away. "I think you're exaggerating, John."

"Still determined to avoid matrimony at any cost, eh?" He eyed her with a smile. "Well, now is no time to talk about it. Still, it's been wonderful seeing you." He squeezed her hands. "Only it would be nice to have a conversation without people looking over our shoulders."

"I didn't notice anyone in particular," she said in an innocent tone.

He snorted. "Well, anyway, I can invite you to come for coffee after dinner one evening, can't I? I managed to fit the coffee pot and some grounds in my suitcase before we left. Silly, wasn't it?"

"Very silly," she said with a smile. "I'm surprised the army didn't confiscate it."

"They know who I am," John said. "I suppose they decided a lawyer needs his coffee." He chuckled. "Will you come sometime?"

The last thing she wanted to do was to pay John Bellows a social call, but she couldn't deny that, if it wasn't for him, they might not have found the identity of Lillie Sweenie so quickly.

"If you want me to," she said.

"Alone?" He arched his eyebrows.

"That I can't promise," she said. "But I'll do my best."

He kissed the back of one hand and then the other. She watched as he went down the pathway between the tents.

CHAPTER 12

*J*ust as John left, Walker came up the path.

"You're just in time, Sergeant."

"I just spoke with the soldiers from the dining room tents. They told me no one was missing from the dinner lists on Tuesday evening."

"Then what we discovered will be of great help to you." Adele explained to him what they had found.

He sighed. "We know who our Jane Doe is now."

"And those two sweet biddies inside have no idea their niece's chest was used as a pin cushion." Adele shuddered.

"It's a hard deed, Miss Gossling." He shook his head. "One I don't relish."

"If you'd like, Nin and I could break it to them," Adele said. "We've done it before."

He patted her on the shoulder. "No, no, that's a policeman's job."

"I'm sure you'll do it with kindness and sensitivity, just like Sheriff Hatfield." She smiled. "And I would like it if you would call me Adele. I feel we're friends now."

He bowed and opened the flap of the tent to let her enter.

The two elderly women looked expectantly at Walker, whose police badge shone with an impressive silver glare as he stepped inside. Miss Miriam began right away in an almost accusatory voice, "What is this all about?"

"Something's happened to Lillie, I know it has!" Miss Addie clutched a handkerchief.

"Is that who this belongs to?" Sergeant Walker picked up the locket lying on the table.

Miss Miriam nodded. "Our niece Lillie."

"May I have her full name, please?"

"Lillie Ann Sweenie," said the woman.

"It's really Lillian, but we call her Lillie," said Miss Addie.

"And she's your niece?" Walker glanced at the notes Jackson had already taken.

"Yes," Miss Miriam said. "She is. Is she in some kind of trouble?"

"Can you describe what she was wearing the last time you saw her?"

Miss Miriam repeated the description her sister had given to Adele, her tone growing a little more alarmed. "Now, I grant you, Sergeant, Lillie can be a little thoughtless, and I know she was out past curfew last night —"

"You know that?" Hatfield asked.

"Well, her bed — or cot, as they call them here — didn't look like it had been slept in this morning." She paused. "Lillie has a strange habit of sleeping on the grass when the weather is fine."

"But it was sprinkling last night!" Miss Addie's eyes were wide.

Sergeant Walker pulled his chair closer to them. "I must inform you that we think we found your niece."

"Found her?" Miss Miriam eyed him. "Is she in a jail cell with that McLeod woman?"

"Not a jail cell, ma'am," he said in a quiet tone. "She's in the morgue — or what we've made a morgue under these circumstances."

"Morgue!" Miss Addie began to sob. "I knew it! Oh, I knew it!"

In a slightly trembling voice, Miss Miriam asked, "Are you trying to tell us our niece is dead?"

"There was a woman found this morning," he said. "We believe it's your niece."

"Believe?" A look of indignation crossed the woman's face.

"The woman had no identification on her," Jackson said. "But your description of Miss Sweenie and her manner of dress match the woman we found."

"And you identified her from this drawing my friend made," Adele added.

Miss Addie let out a screech. Nin's compassion took over and she bent down, looking up at the woman. "Don't worry, Miss Addie. She's in a peaceful place now."

"Is she?" The woman's voice, covered by tears, sounded vague.

"I know," said Nin with authority.

"I refuse to believe any of this!" scoffed Miss Miriam. "It's all a mistake. How do you know the girl is Lillie? There are hundreds of girls her age and with her features around this camp, and many are wearing cotton dresses!"

"Hundreds is a bit of an exaggeration, ma'am," Jackson said.

"Well, all the same, it could be someone else." She rose. "I want to look at her."

"Miriam!" Miss Addie grew pale.

"I'm not afraid of dead bodies," the woman declared in a grated tone. "If it is Lillie, I want to know."

"It would help us to make a positive identification," Sergeant Walker admitted. "Especially with our limited resources at the moment."

"Oh no!" Miss Addie shook with sobs.

"Perhaps there's a friend or family member who could go instead." He glanced at Hatfield.

"I'm quite capable of knowing my own niece, Sergeant," Miss Miriam's tone was icy.

"Ma'am." Walker pressed his hand down on the tabletop as if trying to get a good grip. "It's not a pretty sight. She was stabbed several times in the chest."

Miss Addie let out a cry.

"That makes no difference to me," Miss Miriam insisted.

"Really, ma'am, it might be better if someone else —"

She looked at him squarely. "I've been the head of the household since I was nineteen, Sergeant. I don't intend to stop now." She laid her hand on her sister's arm. Adele was touched by the delicate way she spoke. "Addie, you stay here."

"I couldn't go! I just couldn't!"

"There's no need, dear," soothed her sister. "You just stay here and rest."

Missy, whose sympathy had trumped her reporter instincts, said, "I'll get you a cup of tea, Miss Addie."

"Ask Elsie, dear." Adele pressed her friend's hand. Missy nodded and left the tent.

"Well, Sergeant, shall we go?" Miss Miriam adjusted her hat.

"I think we ought to let my deputy take Miss Miriam, Harry," Sheriff Hatfield said. Adele heard him say to her brother in a low voice, "Make sure the body is covered before she sees it."

Jackson nodded and led the woman out of the tent.

Sergeant Walker spoke in an apologetic tone once Miss Miriam was gone. "Miss Addie, I'm afraid I'll need to ask a few questions."

"It's all so distressing!" the woman said. But the tears were slower now, and she seemed more subdued.

"I'd still like someone else to identify Lillie," he said. "In cases like these, when we don't have any records to check the identification, we like to have it confirmed by at least two people."

"Everyone is dead," the woman said. "Mama, Papa, everyone."

"I'm sorry to hear that," said the sergeant. "Any friends?"

"Well, you understand, Lillie wasn't — well, she wasn't our kind." The woman said the last with a touch of haughtiness. "She was a good girl, mind you, but her mother went off and married a seaman or captain or someone like that. They were poor."

"I see." Sergeant Walker glanced at Hatfield.

"You don't exactly look rich," Nin said.

"Oh, we're not, but you see, well, it's different with us," she said. "Wait! Wait!" The woman caught her breath. "There is someone you can ask who would know her well. Clarence!"

"Who is Clarence?" Adele asked.

"He is — was, I suppose now — our boarder. He lived in the room at the top of the stairs. Such a nice young man."

"Clarence what?" Hatfield asked.

"Ross," the woman replied.

"People are scattered all over the city," lamented Sergeant Walker. "I suppose we can find him, but it won't be easy." He looked at Miss Addie. "Do you happen to know where he is, ma'am?"

"Of course I know where he is!" the woman said. "He's right here."

"Eh?" Hatfield glanced at her.

"He's here. In the camp."

"He's in the tent with you?" Adele asked.

"Oh, naturally not," said the woman. "Miriam said we ought to let Lillie into our tent, as she is — was—family. But he's not family."

"Then he's somewhere else in the camp," Walker concluded. The woman nodded. "Well, then, it should be easier to find him."

"Such a polite young man," sighed Miss Addie. "Mind you, he's not the brightest of people, but his heart is in the right place."

"That's the most important thing," Adele said in a reassuring voice.

"Miriam was just saying this morning how much of a shame it

was that we've lost such a good boarder," sighed Miss Addie. "But our house burned down."

"So did everyone else's," Nin remarked.

"Perhaps when we get a new house, he can come again." She looked at Adele with bright eyes. "Do you think he'll come again?"

"I'm sure he will," Adele said kindly.

Miss Addie seemed fully comforted now. "Lillie wasn't a bad girl, really, she wasn't. She just had funny ideas, like her mother."

"Why sort of funny ideas?" Adele asked.

"Oh, she had some such notion we ought to spend money helping people who didn't have much," Miss Addie said. "Miriam always says, 'Charity begins in the home.'"

"I'm sure she quotes it daily," Nin mumbled.

"Is it her mother's lock of hair in the locket?" Missy asked.

"Why, yes." The woman glanced at her. "How did you know?"

"The dead woman had curly red hair, and the hair in the locket is chestnut," Nin said.

"Oh!" Miss Addie's face grew pale.

"She was a lovely young woman, wasn't she?" Adele said with a smile.

"Pretty like her mother, though she had her father's coloring," Miss Addie said.

Hatfield leaned forward. "If you had a picture you could give us, it would help very much."

"Oh, yes, certainly." Miss Addie reached into the bag she had brought with her and came up with a small wooden box. Inside were what Adele guessed were the few mementoes she had managed to gather before she and her sister were evacuated from their home. Miss Addie brushed off a tattered photograph and gave it to Adele.

Adele studied it, marveling at how accurate Missy's drawing had been. The woman in the photograph was young and had an almost reticent look. Her face was more defined than the lifeless corpse they had seen lying on the ground. Here, she was pretty, though not a great beauty, with smooth skin and a pleasant smile. The hair curled like that on the dead woman. The dress Lillie wore was as modest as the gingham though a little more stylish. The background looked like the wooded areas of the Presidio, and Lillie stood leaning one hand against a redwood.

"You were right in every detail, Missy," Nin whispered.

A breath of air entered the tent as Miss Miriam came in followed by Jackson. Adele saw her brother give Hatfield a quick nod, and her stomach tightened. Miss Miriam looked a little gray but otherwise, she remained composed.

"Well?" Her sister looked at her with the eyes of a hunted animal.

Miss Miriam laid her hand on her sister's shoulder. "There's no doubt, dear."

Miss Addie burst into tears, her small shoulders bouncing up and down with sobs. Her sister sat down beside her and spoke tender words in her ear. Adele was touched to see how the elder sibling who, she imagined, had grown crusty and inflexible from years of being the head of the family, found such compassion for her grieving sister.

Miss Addie's sobs eventually quieted, and Miss Miriam looked expectedly at Sergeant Walker. "We must get her buried as soon as possible."

"I agree," said the sergeant. "But we'd like one more person to identify her."

"Whatever for?" The woman looked annoyed. "I know what my niece looked like well enough."

"Under these circumstances, ma'am, it's necessary." He stood firm.

"What about Clarence, Miriam?" Miss Addie dabbed her eyes.

"He'll do," Miss Miriam agreed. "He saw Lillie enough to know what she looks like, and he'll do as he's told." She eyed Walker. "I know what you're thinking, Sergeant."

"I'm not thinking anything except finding the person who did this," said Walker with respect.

"Not so," she said. "You're thinking Lillie was one of those loose ladies you find plenty of in your work on the streets."

Walker half-smiled, and Adele imagined his work consisted more of giving orders than patrolling.

"No one thinks that, Miss Miriam," Jackson insisted. "The police never make assumptions about any victim."

"Victim," Miss Addie echoed in a soft tone. "Yes, she's a victim now, isn't she?"

"Mind you, I won't say Lillie had the sort of breeding we would have wished," Miss Miriam continued.

"Lillie was always good to us," Miss Addie said in what sounded to Adele almost like a defense. "She paid for her food and lodgings and helped us when we had unexpected expenses."

Adele's eyes slid toward Nin. "It sounds like she didn't want to be a financial burden to you."

"My point, Addie, is that Lillie had her ideas even if she wasn't a bad girl," Miss Miriam said impatiently. "But that's hardly her fault, given who her mother was."

"We were just talking about Lillie's mother," Adele said.

"We were born of fine stock, Miss Gossling," Miss Miriam said in a rigorous tone. "Father did well with his general store during the forty-niner period."

"Your family came during the Gold Rush, didn't they?" Adele asked.

"That's right, and the merchants built this city!" Her voice echoed through the small tent.

"They were also the only ones who got rich from the Gold Rush," Nin murmured.

"Our grandfather was honored by Mayor Geary himself," Miss Miriam continued as if she hadn't heard her. "The mayor consulted him about everything."

"Indeed," Hatfield said in a dry tone.

The woman cast a dubious eye on him. "I see you don't believe me."

"I don't doubt your word, miss," he assured her.

"Father had great expectations of us girls," Miss Miriam said. "And when Addie and I turned out not as they would have wished — we hold no claims to beauty or wit — and Danielle was born with all any prosperous young man could ever want — well, Mother and Father made plans for her."

"Danielle?" Walker asked.

"Lillie's mother, poor soul." Miss Addie sighed.

Her sister patted her hand. "Don't upset yourself, dear."

"I take it Lillie's mother didn't quite fulfill your parents' wishes," Adele prompted.

"She was so much younger than Addie and I." Miss Miriam's face was set. "She had no responsibilities other than to marry well. And she couldn't even do *that*." Bitterness grated her voice.

"One can't help who they fall in love with," Miss Addie murmured.

"So your parents chose a husband for her but she refused to marry him," Jackson said. "Is that it?"

"That's it exactly!" Miss Miriam said. "We could have gotten into society if she had married Adrian Runyon. But she had to go and run off with Eric Bowen. He was a third mate on a ship or some such thing, and poor as a —"

"Church mouse?" Nin finished dryly.

"If you wish to put it that way." Miss Miriam gave her a withering look.

"His boat was going to Spain and she went with it," Addie said.

"Ran off and left all of us so ashamed we couldn't show our faces in the neighborhood," Miss Miriam said in a brutal tone. "Father died a year later —"

"But that couldn't have had anything to do with Danielle," Miss Addie objected. "His heart was never good, dear."

"It had everything to do with it!" her sister insisted. "And then Mother followed eighteen months after that."

"But Danielle came back when she heard about Mother," Miss Addie pointed out.

"She came back all right," her sister said grimly. "Alone and with a child. He was the 'woman in every port' sort of man." She looked self-serving. "At least we persuaded her to change her name back to Sweenie."

"She was destitute?" Adele guessed.

"Why else would she have come back?" Miss Miriam snapped. "What little money she had she couldn't save. She spent it all on other people. Always insisting this or that neighbor had it worse than we did. Poo!"

"She had a good heart," Adele said softly.

"She ought to have thought of her family first!" Miss Miriam declared. "She came back only to die three years later."

"How very inconsiderate of her," Nin snarled.

"She ruined our family and then left us to take care of a child when we could hardly feed ourselves." Miss Miriam's hands tightened into fists. "But they say you can't choose your family, don't they?"

"Danielle couldn't choose her family either." Nin said softly.

The two women looked at her as if they didn't understand.

CHAPTER 13

"So you took Lillie in after her mother died?" Sergeant Walker questioned.

"Naturally, we couldn't turn the child away," said Miss Miriam.

"That's why we had to take in a boarder," Miss Addie chimed in. "We had another mouth to feed."

"Clarence was a godsend to us," Miss Miriam said. "Always paid his rent on time and helped us with the chores."

"I don't know what we would have done without him," Miss Addie agreed.

"We sacrificed a lot for Lillie," Miss Miriam insisted. "When we saw she was going to be pretty like her mother, we were determined to raise her the proper way."

"Proper way?" Sheriff Hatfield asked.

"We may have lost our money, Sheriff, but we still had our pride." Miss Miriam struck an aristocratic pose. "We still had friends who were well-to-do. And they had sons who had prospects."

"It was more than Lillie could have hoped for in her situation," Miss Addie added.

"Sadly the case," said Miss Miriam with a sigh. "And, too, Lillie was — well, she was like her mother. She wanted to change the world." This was followed by a sniff.

"Perhaps she could have, had she lived" Nin murmured. Adele looked at her surprised. Nin had never thought much of her work with women and progressive reforms.

Miss Miriam's mouth was so tight that a line appeared above the upper lip. "We took pains to introduce her to the right young men. Spent money on tea things so they could come and see us. All Lillie did was scoff at them."

"Why did she do that?" Missy asked.

"She didn't like them!" Miss Addie said.

"It wasn't that, Addie," her sister said knowingly. "She thought she was too good for them. She called them petty and — what was the word she used? — materialistic. Just because they were more concerned about making their way in this world than they were about the plight of the Mexicans or the Chinese!"

"Lillie was a reformer, then," Adele said. Missy gave her a nod of acknowledgment as if she remembered what Adele said when they examined Lillie's clothes.

"*You* may call it that, Miss Gossling." Miss Miriam set narrow eyes on her. "I don't."

"What do you call it then?" Nin asked.

"Troublemakers!" the woman spat. "No business trying to change the laws."

"That's what we have politicians for," Miss Addie chimed in.

"What sort of reform work did she do?" Jackson asked. "You see, my sister might know some of her friends, and that would help us."

Miss Miriam looked at Adele in horror. "Don't tell me a fine young lady like you would get mixed up with people like that Miss McLeod!"

"I never worked with Karen McLeod," Adele assured her.

"But you know who she is," the woman insisted.

"I've heard her name," Adele said.

"You said before your niece had ideas," Hatfield said. "Is that where she got her ideas?"

"I expect so," said Miss Miriam. "She never took us into her confidence. Just went out in the morning and didn't come back until dinnertime without saying a word about where she'd been or who she'd been with."

"Did you ask her?" Nin asked.

The woman stiffened. "It wasn't our business to ask, Miss Branch. It was *her* business to tell."

Nin gave her an arch look and said nothing.

"It wasn't as if we didn't worry about her," Addie said in a shaky tone. "What with all her notions."

"What notions?" Jackson asked.

"She had a notion there were people one should give a leg up to in this world," said Miss Miriam. "Now *I* say it's every man for himself."

"And every woman for a man?" Nin asked.

"Well, some of us can't be that lucky." Miss Miriam ogled her.

"And some of us choose to be luckier," Adele mumbled. "You think Miss McLeod was the one behind this notion?"

"Knowing her as you do, Miss Gossling —"

"I know *of* her," Adele corrected.

"Knowing *of* her as you do," Miss Miriam continued, "do you doubt it?"

Adele couldn't help but nod. Karen McLeod's name had turned up here and there in her years with the settlement houses, usually associated with reform work related to those on the outskirts of the city's social circles such as the Mexicans of the Mission and people in Chinatown.

"You know what tomfoolery these young women get to these days," sighed Miss Miriam. "Perfectly respectable ladies go into places like Chinatown or even Morton Street with high-minded ideas of turning the filth into human beings."

"They *are* human beings!" Adele could not keep the growl out of her voice.

"They tend to those loose women in the Barbary Coast." Miss Addie shuddered.

"They need to eat too." Missy's face was red. "And they need shelter and clothing, just like any of us."

"Adele's helped many of them," Nin said with some pride.

Miss Miriam looked at Adele now as if she were a bee that had gotten into the honey pot. "I should have thought you had more sense, Miss Gossling."

"We're all one world, Miss Miriam," Adele said. "We all suffer in our own way. Where would we be if there weren't people to hold out their hand to us?"

"I can see you have the same notion as Lillie had." Miss Miriam glanced at Jackson. "And you, young man, I assume you're head of the household?"

"On the contrary," Jackson said with some amusement. "My sister owns the house we live in." Adele couldn't help but smile.

"Nevertheless, as the man of the house, you ought to have a say in it."

"Ma'am, what I say has no bearing on what my sister does," Jackson said dryly.

Sergeant Walker cleared his throat. "If your niece was involved with some of the seedier sides of town, she might have made enemies."

"Why would she?" Miss Addie asked with wide eyes. "She was there to help them!"

"Remember what Ben told us," Miss Miriam pointed out.

"What did Ben tell you?" Hatfield asked.

The woman pursed her lips. "I think you'd better ask him. It's not something I care to speak of."

"We will when we know who Ben is," Jackson mumbled.

"Ben Horne," said Miss Miriam. "He was a young man we hoped Lillie would marry."

The atmosphere changed to intense interest as the lawmen exchanged looks.

"They weren't married?" the sergeant asked.

"Of course not." Miss Addie wrinkled her nose. "She wouldn't have married anybody without our consent."

"They were engaged?" Hatfield suggested.

"Not quite that either," Miss Miriam said. "We could never get a straight answer out of her when we asked about Ben."

"But he was courting her?" Jackson inquired.

"Yes, I suppose you could say that," Miss Miriam said. "They would spend Sundays walking or picnicking in the woods. At least, that's what she told us."

"But you don't believe her?" Adele asked.

"I had no cause not to believe her, Miss Gossling," said the woman stiffly.

"So this picture came from one of these Sunday outings?" Adele took out the photograph of Lillie that Miss Addie had given her.

"I suppose so." Miss Miriam shrugged.

"Can you tell us more about him?" Sergeant Walker asked as Jackson's pencil poised to write it down.

"He's a laborer, of course," said Miss Miriam.

"So not a friend of the sons of friends?" Nin asked.

"Oh, we gave up hope on that a long time ago," Miss Addie said.

"I don't know where she met him," Miss Miriam said.

"But he wasn't the kind of man you would wish Lillie to marry," Adele reasoned.

"At this point we were happy she showed an interest in anybody respectable." Miss Miriam sniffed.

"In other words, you just wanted to get her off of your shoulders and on to someone else's," Nin said.

For all her sharp-wittedness, Miss Miriam seemed oblivious

to the implications of this statement. "It was time she married," she said. "She was already twenty."

"An old maid," Adele mumbled. Jackson chuckled.

"Do you know where we can find this Ben Horne?" Sergeant Walker asked.

"We wouldn't have any idea, Sergeant," Miss Miriam said. "You appreciate we don't associate with that kind of person."

"You would have had to if he had married your niece," Nin said.

Both women raised their eyebrows and said nothing.

"Now, when was the last time you saw Miss Sweenie?" the sergeant asked.

"Yesterday," Miss Miriam related.

"She was with us all day," Miss Addie chimed in.

"Well, except for a little before dinner," said her sister. "She took a walk around the camp."

"Did she do that often since you came here?" Adele asked.

"Oh, every night after dinner," Miss Addie said.

"But you said yesterday she took a walk *before* dinner," Nin pointed out.

"Why would she change her routine suddenly?" Missy asked.

The two women shrugged, saying nothing.

"So she was out before dinner," Sergeant Walker related. "Did she come back in time for dinner?"

"Certainly she did," said Miss Miriam.

"And after dinner?" inquired Hatfield. "She took another walk?"

"Why would she take two walks in one day?" Miss Addie blinked.

"She didn't take a walk," Miss Miriam said. "She stayed and read to us until nine o'clock. Then we all went to bed."

"Including your niece?" Jackson asked.

"Naturally."

"But you said her cot hadn't been slept in," Walker pointed out.

"She must have gone out after we were in bed," Miss Miriam said.

"What was her mood during the evening?" Hatfield asked.

"What do you mean, mood?" Miss Miriam looked at him.

"Was she happy, sad, nervous?"

"She was snappish," Miss Miriam declared. "But that wasn't unusual. She could get quite impertinent with me. I've always looked out for her own good." She sighed.

Adele noticed Miss Addie blinking as if trying to recall something. She gently asked, "Was that how it was, Miss Addie?"

"Well, yes, she did seem rather agitated," said the woman.

"More so than usual?" Sergeant Walker asked.

"I thought so," she said.

"Oh, come, dear, she was always like that," said Miss Miriam. "Well, lately, anyway."

"How lately?" Jackson asked.

"Weeks, months even," said the woman. "Heavens, I don't keep a calendar!"

"Any idea why she may have been agitated?" Adele asked Miss Addie. She sensed the woman had a little more feeling for her niece than her sister.

"I'm sure I don't know." The woman shrugged. "It was —" She paused, looking perplexed. "She seemed preoccupied with something, as if something was worrying her."

"Something was always worrying her," Miss Miriam snarled. "Only it was usually the wrong thing!"

"Have you any idea why she might have gone out later?" Jackson asked.

"She didn't go out," Miss Miriam snarled. "She snuck out."

"Any idea why?" Jackson repeated.

"Who knows?" Miss Miriam shrugged. "She might have

arranged to meet some of those people who work with Miss McLeod."

"Oh, I'm sure she wouldn't have done that, dear," Miss Addie said. "She was probably restless and just decided to take another walk."

"And not come back?" her sister challenged.

Sergeant Walker took from his pocket the wedding ring she and Nin had found and put it on the table. "Could this have anything to do with why she went out that night?"

"What is that?" Miss Miriam stared at it.

"It's your niece's wedding ring," Nin said.

"Nonsense!" The woman glared at her. "You've been reading too many romance novels, my dear."

Nin gave her a sweet smile.

"We can't be sure, of course," said Walker. "But we found the ring not far from where your niece was."

"You mean where her body was." Miss Addie's voice broke.

"What of it?" Miss Miriam demanded. "It could have been lost by anybody! There are hundreds of people here."

"That's true, Sergeant," Jackson pointed out.

"But this one has initials on it," said Walker. "Perhaps you should take a look at it."

Miss Miriam frowned as she examined the ring. She handed it to her sister who looked inside the band.

"L.S.!" Miss Addie dropped the ring on the floor and started to sob. "Oh, Miriam, maybe they're right!"

Miss Miriam picked up the ring, brushed it off, and gave it to the sergeant. "They have no proof, dear."

"All the same, did your niece have anyone in her acquaintance with the initials G.W.?" he asked.

"There's Geoffrey Baum, dear — oh, but that's G.B., isn't it?" Miss Addie looked confused.

"We know of no one, Sergeant." Miss Miriam's voice was firm.

Walker put the ring back in his pocket. Adele could see he was more convinced than before that the ring had belonged to Lillie. "We're much obliged to you for taking the time to answer our questions, ladies. It was a great help."

"We always do our civic duty, Sergeant," Miss Miriam said.

"We have just one more request, ma'am," said Sergeant Walker. "We'd like to look through your niece's things. We might find something that could point us in the direction of the culprit who did this horrible deed."

"Go through her things?" Both ladies were horrified.

"It's necessary, Miss Miriam," Adele said. "The police wouldn't ask if it weren't."

"But it seems such an intrusion!" Miss Addie buried her face in her handkerchief.

"They won't go through her undergarments," Nin said. "We'll do that."

"Miss Branch, please," Jackson murmured.

"My friend is right, Miss Addie." Adele put a hand on her shoulder. "If the sergeant will permit us. We've done it on several occassions back in Arrojo, and we're always very respectful and very careful."

Miss Miriam seemed to be considering this. "Well, I suppose if you'll be there, Miss Gossling, it's alright."

"You did say you always do your civic duty," Nin reminded her. "This is part of your civic duty too."

The tight wad that made up Miss Miriam's face showed she clearly did not feel that having the police rifle through her niece's belongings constituted a "civic duty." "I expect you'll show the men the way?" She turned to Adele, who nodded.

"Miss Grace, will you please take Miss Miriam and Miss Addie to lunch?" Sergeant Walker directed.

Adele could see Missy was debating whether to protest because she wanted to see what they found in the murder victim's belongings or to comply to get the human angle on the murder victim from the family. Thankfully, she chose the latter as she nodded and helped the ladies out of their chairs.

Adele leaned toward her and whispered, "Don't worry, dear. I remember our bargain, and I'll tell you everything I can when we get back."

As they filed out of the tent, Adele felt a light brush on her arm. She turned and saw it was Miss Addie.

"Maybe the woman they found isn't Lillie after all," she said in a weak voice.

"Maybe," Adele said, fighting back tears at the woman's helplessness.

CHAPTER 14

Though the bell for lunch had not yet rung, people were preparing for it. Men stood outside smoking the last of their cigarettes or cigars. Women were washing their faces and those of their children's. Adele was comforted by the cheerful air as they called out to their neighbors, chatting about the latest news they had seen in the morning papers.

"Perhaps San Francisco needed such a tragedy to bring people together," she murmured.

"It won't last," her friend predicted. "The city will go back to the way it was."

"The buildings won't," Adele insisted. "The city authorities have learned their lesson, graft or no graft."

"Mother Nature will always triumph over money, eh, Miss Branch?" Jackson asked.

"I couldn't have said it better, Mr. Gossling."

Adele laughed. "Man over beast is a myth, Jack."

"We have to try, Del," he said. "Especially when the beast is a criminal."

"I wonder why Lillie changed her routine last night." Adele

looked at the hills above the Presidio. "Walking before dinner instead of after."

"And why she was preoccupied," Nin added. "Miss Addie was very definite about that."

"Perhaps her husband, if she really had one, was still making his way among the rubble," Jackson suggested.

"Everyone has been evacuated and accounted for, Jackson," Walker said.

"He may have been lost in another way," Adele said, her voice quiet.

"You mean dead?" asked Walker. "It's possible."

"But then she would have been preoccupied, as her aunts said, for much longer than one night," Hatfield said.

"Maybe she didn't know until yesterday, sir," Jackson said. "The bulletin boards are still filled with casualties."

"But the Sweenies have been here two weeks," Adele pointed out. "Lillie had all that time to find out what had happened to him."

"Nothing happened to him," Nin said with the authority of her gift. "He's not dead."

Walker looked at her. "You know, Miss Branch, I'm beginning to believe these feelings of yours, as you call them."

Nin smiled in a shy way as she did whenever someone showed faith in her gifts.

"If he is still alive, she may have had a rendezvous with him last night before dinner," Jackson said. "That would account for the change in her routine."

"She may have, Jackson," Hatfield answered.

"It wouldn't have been easy, getting away from those two aunts," Nin said.

"I wouldn't be so harsh on them, Miss Branch," Walker smiled. "They did care for her after her mother died."

"I suspect Miss Miriam sees family duty as she sees civic

duty," said Adele. "A necessary evil and one best to remain under her control as much as possible."

"What on earth do you mean, Del?" Her brother stared at her.

"They made her pay for her food and board, Jack," said Adele. "They expected her to report to them."

"That's only natural," Jackson argued. "I don't exactly approve of you going off and doing as you please without at least letting me know where you are."

"Yes, but you don't *expect* it," Adele argued.

"Perhaps this Karen McLeod did lead her astray," Walker suggested. "Some of these reformers are more anarchists than anything else."

"What do you know about her, Del?" her brother asked.

"Nothing really," Adele admitted. "But Elsie and Valda might." She turned to the sergeant. "I can ask them if you like."

"Do that," he said. "She might help us know Miss Sweenie's intentions and relationships."

"It was the aunts who had intentions for her," Adele said. "Intentions for which she was clearly ill-suited."

"They saw her as a burden," Nin agreed. "And they couldn't wait to get rid of that burden as quickly as possible."

"Well, they're rid of it now," Hatfield said dryly.

"Whatever family feeling they had, that would scarcely make them capable of killing," Walker said. "I don't think either of them could have even gotten to the place where we found Lillie."

"I wasn't implying that," Adele insisted. "But I can see why Lillie married."

"And why she kept it a secret," Nin chimed in.

"She kept it a secret, I suspect, because she knew her husband wouldn't meet with their approval," Walker said.

"Then it couldn't have been Ben Horne," Jackson said.

"It wouldn't be anyway, Jack," Adele said. "The ring we found said 'G.W.,' not 'B.H.'"

"We still don't know if that was her ring, Del," he reminded her.

"I'm inclined to think that it was," Walker said.

"So am I," Hatfield agreed. "I think we ought to find Ben Horne and speak to him as soon as we can."

"She may not even be married," Jackson argued. "We're simply going on the assumption that she is."

"She's married," Nin insisted. "I felt it when I touched her hand. It was a hand that held another." Her tone was misty.

"If she broke off their engagement —" Jackson began

"The aunts never said she was engaged to him," Adele said.

"Do *you* tell Aunt Belle everything?" He eyed her and Adele smiled a little, as he knew full well she did not. "If she broke off her engagement or threw him over for this G.W., he might not have been very happy about it."

"But would he kill because of that?" Walker shrugged. "It seems unlikely."

"As we both know, Harry, everything seems unlikely until some criminal does it," Hatfield said.

"I think we should speak with this boarder Clarence Ross as well," Walker said. "He may have known Miss Sweenie better than her aunts believe, and he might be able to tell us something."

"He'll confirm the identity of the body at any rate," Hatfield said as they approached the cluster of tents. There were no men smoking or women washing their faces here and Adele imagined they were all sitting with their hands folded waiting for the lunch bell to ring just as their aristocratic counterparts were doing.

However, she was surprised to see John sitting outside the aunts' tent. He greeted her with a smile. She noted he had shaved since she had last seen him, and his face looked more scrubbed. He had even found some pomade and arranged his hair in a more flattering manner. A twinge of warmth went through her as she recalled how handsome and charming he could be.

"I knew you would come here at some point." He kissed her hand and greeted the lawmen.

"Did you?" Hatfield's boyish eyes narrowed a little.

"It was logical," John said. "After speaking with Miss Miriam and Miss Addie you would want to search the dead woman's belongings."

"We don't search, John," Jackson said. "We look for anything that can help us solve the case."

John nodded. "I've kept guard to make sure no one entered."

"That was thoughtful of you, John," Adele said with a kind smile.

"We appreciate that, Mr. Bellows." Sergeant Walker shook his hand.

"Can't have people tampering with what might be evidence, can we?" John grinned. "I've seen more than one case where tampering cost a well-deserved criminal the noose."

"I was made to understand you're an estate lawyer, sir," the sheriff mumbled.

"I've always had a hankering for criminal law," John admitted. "I've sat in on many trials."

"It's one thing to sit in but quite another to be part of the circus," Hatfield said sharply.

John studied him. "I hardly consider justice a circus, Sheriff. But then, Adele's told me you have some rather unconventional ideas about the law."

"He's a good sheriff," Nin said bluntly. "The best the county ever had. Who cares how he does things?"

"Thank you, Miss Branch." Hatfield bowed.

"I imagine a compliment from you is a rare treat, Miss Branch." John eyed her.

"I don't believe in lavish praise, Mr. Bellows," Nin said with a glare. "Especially for men. It tends to go to their heads."

"That explains a lot," Jackson mumbled and Adele hid a smile. Though Nin and her brother had developed a mutual respect for one another's strengths, Jackson still felt the blow of Nin's sharp tongue from time to time.

John continued to stand guard as some of the women came out of the tent nearby, striking up a conversation with him. The lawmen began to look at one side of the Sweenie tent while Adele and Nin found a small suitcase with the initials *D.S.* shoved in a corner.

"It must have belonged to her mother," Adele guessed. "Danielle Sweenie."

"It's made of fine leather," Nin observed.

"Probably why it has her maiden name initial on it instead of her married name," Adele said. "I wonder if it's the suitcase she used to run away with her sailor."

"It has the feel of the sea." Nin ran her hand over the top. "Rough, thick waves."

They opened it and carefully took out all the garments except for the underclothes one at a time, laying them carefully on the cot.

"Very plain," Adele observed. "Calico mostly. And clearly hand-sewn. No millinery fineries for Lillie."

"The aunts were wearing silk and brocade," Nin pointed out.

"They let their niece wear calico while they wore silk." Adele's contempt for the two elderly women grew. She peered at the more substantial items spread around the frame of the suitcase. "She wasn't an avid reader." She took out a few books with leather bindings. "Adventure stories. How odd."

Hatfield threw out, "Her father's, most likely. Sailors love adventure stories." He grinned.

"She seems to have also saved his lighter and pen set," Adele said. "Her mother must have told her fine stories about her father for her to honor his things like that" Her tone grew wistful as she recalled her affection for her own dead father. The small ache was followed by relief he had not lived to witness the ruin of the city he had loved so dearly.

She discovered several pamphlets, most of them related to education reform for Mexicans and Chinese and volunteer medical services in Chinatown.

"One can't say Miss Sweenie wasn't dedicated to her reforms." Hatfield remarked.

"From what I heard about Miss McLeod, I'm not surprised," Adele said. "She's one of the more ardent ones in the movement, and ardent reformers expect their followers to show the same level of enthusiasm."

"There's something in the pouch here." Nin undid the buckle and out fell a bundle of green silk cut from a bolt of fabric.

"Elsie said people were going down the streets after the quake with the oddest things," Adele mused. "I wonder what I would have taken with me if my house was burning down, and I only had two hands to carry them."

"There's something in it." In her determined way, Nin shook the bolt and out fell two wooden boxes. Adele could see the lids were delicately carved with trees and leaves. The larger box showed a man and woman looking toward one another as if trying to reach each other across a long distance.

The lawmen finished their search and joined them.

"They look Chinese," Nin said.

Adele picked up the larger box. "I've seen similar things in Chinatown."

"So have I," Sergeant Walker said. "Odd Miss Sweenie should take those things out of everything else she could have taken."

"Perhaps they had special meaning for her," Adele said. "May I open the boxes?"

The sergeant nodded, and she unclasped the larger one first. She carefully extracted a paper fan and unfolded it, gazing at the brilliant red color with the delicate web of lotus blossoms painted on it.

"A lovely thing," she murmured.

"And quite vain," Jackson remarked.

"No vainer than your gold cufflinks, Mr. Gossling," Nin snapped.

"But I wouldn't fill precious space in my suitcase with cufflinks if I were escaping a fire, Miss Branch," he said with no small irritation.

"Neither would a woman who wore simple cotton dresses and had only one rusty comb for her hair," Adele observed. She handed it to Sergeant Walker.

"It looks quite old," Walker said. "The last century or even before that, wouldn't you say, Horatio?" He handed it to the sheriff.

"That at least," his friend agreed.

Adele was now anxious to see what was in the smaller box. She lifted the lid, feeling the roughness of the carved wood against her fingers. Lying in a bed of velvet was a jade pendant. Its green color was like murky seawater, but the carved figure of a man beside an altar was clear. His smile was brilliant as his hands held a ribbon.

"How odd!" Adele said. "I wonder what it is."

"A Buddha," Jackson said. "They're always finding interesting things to do with the poor fellow for the tourists."

"No." Nin reached for the pendant and held it tightly in hand. "No, it means something."

"He's a rather happy little man," Adele chuckled. "Perhaps it's some sort of good luck charm."

"It could have been a gift from her husband," Jackson pointed out.

"So could the fan," Nin said.

"We'll have to ask Miss Miriam and Miss Addie." Sergeant Walker held out his hand for the pendant.

"I don't think they know about these," said Adele. "Otherwise, why would she have hidden them?"

Walker took the items and wrapped them in the cloth with a sigh. "Were these normal times, we could have tracked down where they were bought in Chinatown. But there's very little left there now and certainly no record books in all the rubble."

"Don't worry, Harry." Hatfield patted the man's shoulder. "We'll get to the bottom of it nonetheless."

"You found nothing?" Adele inquired.

"No luck," said the sheriff. "But we didn't expect to, did we?" He glanced at his deputy.

"It was a slim chance, Del," he said. "Depending on how important the fan and pendant are, though, you might have had better luck." He smiled ruefully. "You and Miss Branch always do."

"Maybe because we come with no expectations of finding anything," Nin said as she shook out a robe. Adele noticed a slip of paper on the ground.

She reached it before her brother and unfolded it. She read it out loud:

After curfew. The tree bent like an old man. News that will solve all our problems.

George

"George!" Hatfield said. "G.W! He *is* here, then."

"We don't know that G.W. and George are one and the same person," said Jackson in a cautious tone.

"Until we find out otherwise, I think we can assume they are," said Walker. A piercing whistle echoed through the camp. "We'd better go to lunch and discuss this later."

John rose as they emerged. "I must say, Sheriff Hatfield, you certainly seem to allow the ladies liberties."

"Eh?"

"I couldn't help but overhear what went on in there." He motioned to the tent. "It seems as if they were doing the work for you."

"You're overstepping, John," Jackson said in an angry tone. "I've worked with the sheriff for four years now and I can assure you —"

"It's all right, Deputy." Hatfield's tone was calm and placid. "I believe I can answer that allegation on my own."

"It was hardly an allegation, sir," John mumbled. "It was only an observation. From a lawyer's standpoint, it's a little unconventional."

"You yourself admitted the sheriff worked in unconventional ways," Nin pointed out.

"I don't deny I conduct my investigations in a different manner than what you might be used to with the city police," Hatfield said to the young lawyer. "But the ladies have been helping me from the beginning. Some of our toughest cases have been enlightened by their astuteness and intelligence. I would even —" he seemed to be struggling to keep his emotion intact, "I would even gladly hand over my badge and gun to them if my deputy and I were totally incapacitated!"

"Let's not exaggerate, sir," Jackson mumbled.

Adele felt a lump in her throat as she took the sheriff's arm. "I'm deeply touched, Sheriff. Truly I am."

"So am I," Nin said, and in a rare moment of affection, took his other arm.

"I don't know as I would choose to go *that* far," Sergeant Walker admitted, "but I certainly can attest to some of the women who are working for the police, even in an unofficial capacity. They've provided us with information we might never have gotten otherwise."

"And as a lawyer, John, you ought to know how to look at the facts," Adele said. "Nin and I just happened to find some things that might help with this investigation. It could have easily been Jack, or the sheriff, or the sergeant."

John bowed his head. "I stand corrected, Adele. I apologize, Sheriff."

"Yes, well," Sheriff Hatfield mumbled. Adele could see he wasn't quite ready to forgive John.

CHAPTER 15

Lunch was a slow affair between the number of people and the general lax feeling permeating the camp. They were at the end of the long table, so conversations around them were somewhat muffed, giving them time to talk.

"Maybe Lillie received the fan and pendant from someone she worked with at the settlement houses," Jackson now offered. "People were always giving you gifts when you worked there, weren't they, Del?"

Adele nodded but picked at the wilted green beans on her plate. "It doesn't seem likely she would keep those particular gifts and not others that were given to her."

"Maybe that was all she could find in the rush to evacuate," Nin said.

"I never kept the things that were given to me," Adele said. "I gave them away to others. Most of the women I worked with did the same. We preferred to give what we were given to someone else."

"I think, Jackson, your first idea was right," Sergeant Walker said. "Those were gifts given to her by her husband, or maybe some other beau."

"From what her two aunts described of Ben Horne, it seems unlikely it would be him," Hatfield said. "A man working hard just to keep his head above water would scarcely have the desire to spend his pennies on things like that, even if he loved the girl."

"You have a rather cynical view of courtship, Sheriff," Adele said with a smile.

The sheriff blushed. "I only meant a man would save his hard-earned pennies for something grander, like marriage."

"The fan and pendant are decorative but not grand," Nin agreed.

"Not to mention Del thinks that pendant has special meaning." Jackson eyed his sister. "If I know her, she's going to find out what it is, by hook or by crook."

"Hopefully not by crook," Sergeant Walker said with a laugh.

"Nothing like that, Sergeant," Adele promised. "But I'd like to keep the fan and pendant for a time if you don't mind. There are some people I know who might recognize them and give you a lead."

The sergeant clearly looked uncomfortable, but Hatfield pressed his arm. "We can't get fingerprints on them anyway and it probably wouldn't do us much good if we could. I can assure you, Harry, Adele will take great care of them."

"She's had a lot of experience with borrowing evidence," Nin added.

Adele's cheeks flared as she thought of all the times she had sweet-talked Assistant Deputy Edison into letting her take evidence out of the station to follow an idea.

"Very well," said Sergeant Walker as he handed her the boxes. "You'll of course let us know immediately if you find out anything."

"Naturally," Adele promised.

"Maybe your friends could give us a lead on this George as well," the sergeant said with a chuckle. "I suppose that's too much to hope for."

"If Dr. Blessings were here, he might tell us something about the man's handwriting," Nin said.

"He's Elsie's father," Adele supplied to the sergeant. "You met her at the train station."

"Oh, yes, the rather forceful young lady." Walker grinned.

"He's a handwriting expert," Hatfield said. "But he evacuated to Los Angeles."

"I might be able to help too, sir," Jackson said. "I'm sure I could get Monte to give us a list of people staying at the camp who go by the name of George."

"George might not be here, Jack," Adele reminded him.

"If he arranged a meeting with Miss Sweenie, he likely is," Jackson argued.

"That might have come from the outside," Nin said.

"Considering we have no leads right now, it's worth a try." Sergeant Walker settled the argument. "We'd be much obliged to you, Deputy, if you would get that list from your friend. Tell him we need all the men whose first or middle name is George and with a last name that begins with a W, since we're going on the assumption right now that George and G.W. are one and the same person."

"That's clever," Nin said with a nod of approval.

"Perhaps it might be worthwhile if he also added to the list men whose initials are G.W., even if their first name isn't George," Hatfield added. "In case George and G.W. are not one and the same person."

Jackson pushed his empty plate away and rose. "I'll go do that right now, sir, with your permission."

"Thank you, Deputy." Sergeant Walker said. "I can see your sheriff was right about you being a fine lawman."

Jackson smiled gracefully and left the half-empty tent.

"And you and I?" Hatfield looked at his friend.

Walker pushed his chair back. "We have a call to pay to Mr. Ross."

"And Mr. Horne," Adele reminded him.

"I have a feeling Mr. Horne is going to be more complicated to locate," said the sergeant, putting his hat on. "Mr. Ross is already here. I think I know where he is too. There's an entire section of bachelor tents beyond the hospital tent."

Adele exchanged glances with her friend and rose. "May we come too, Sergeant?"

Walker grinned. "After the extraordinary work you and Miss Branch have done so far, I would almost swear you both in as assistant deputies."

"Heaven help us," Nin mumbled.

The bachelor section had about four or five tents with unmarried men who were clearly delighted to see pretty ladies in their midst. Their reactions grated on Adele's nerves as she tried to ignore their whistles and calls as they went from tent to tent with Walker asking for a man named Clarence Ross. Hatfield tried to quiet them, but as he was not in his capacity as sheriff, they only scoffed. Nin had no qualms about growling at every man who approached her and there were many, as her exquisite dark beauty and cat-like eyes always drew the opposite sex to her like bees to honey.

They finally found Clarence Ross. As they entered the tent, the smoke from cigars made the air gray. There were four other men, all of them looking as if they had just survived a year of camping in the mountains. Three pairs of eyes immediately feasted on Adele and Nin.

Walker did not miss a beat. "Finley!" His tone lost its pleasant pitch and he became at once the high-level lawman. "Put out that cigar! You know you're not supposed to smoke inside the tents."

"Aw, Sergeant, I was just finishing up," said Finley, puffing on the cigar in question.

"You heard the man." Hatfield's quiet voice grew threatening and his size and stature obviously impressed Finley more than the medium-height sergeant, as he stubbed the cigar out on the ground.

"Meyers!" Sergeant Walker glanced sideways at another man whose beard hung like a bib down to his shoulders. "Where did he get that cigar?"

"I'm sure I don't know, Sergeant."

"I'm sure you do," said the sergeant. "Mack's Cigar Store *after* the earthquake, maybe?"

"Are you implying —" Finley began.

"I don't have to imply anything," Sergeant Walker said. "I've got a file on you with a list a mile long of your liberties with the city shops."

"Don't got no list now," Finley mumbled. "Everything's all burned up."

"I've got the list right up here, Finley." The sergeant tapped his forehead. "Once the police stations are up and running again, we'll be bringing you in for fingerprinting and all the rest so you'll have a nice, fresh file with us."

Finely growled. "Sergeant, it ain't right for you to give these ladies the wrong impression of me." He grinned at Adele, surveying her with feasting eyes. "It's a shame there ain't nothing going on, darling, or I would take you out for a good time. A very good time indeed." He winked.

Hatfield's reacted like a bull, grabbing the man by the collar. "You better watch yourself, Finley, or I might be inclined to knock a few teeth loose so you won't talk at all!"

"Is that right?" The man surveyed him. "And who might you be?"

"A lawman," Hatfield said in a hard tone. "That's all you need to know."

"Not in this city," Meyers said. "We never seen you."

"And you've seen them all, haven't you, Meyers?" Sergeant Walker glared at him.

"This lady happens to be a friend of mine and my deputy

sheriff's sister," Hatfield continued. "I imagine between the Sergeant and me, you'd be a mighty fine sight for that hospital tent."

Finley straightened his collar. "I'm sorry if I offended you, miss," he said to Adele with a quick bow.

"I was more disgusted than offended," Adele said and the other men laughed as Finley's face turned red.

"Is there a Clarence Ross here?" Sergeant Walker called.

Another man, who looked a little less grubby, pointed to the corner of the tent. Set a little apart from the rest of the cots was a young man who sat playing with a shiny object. His stringy hair tumbled forward over his forehead as he played with the thing, and Adele wondered if he had heard them come in.

"All right, all of you, out!" Sergeant Walker growled. "This is official police business. We need to speak with Mr. Ross."

"What's he done?" asked Meyers.

"That's for us to know and you to find out, Meyers." The sergeant tore back the flap of the tent. "Out!"

The men grumbled but left, and Finley had the audacity to give Adele another wink as he stepped out of the tent. Nin spit after him.

"I'm sorry you had to endure that, Miss Gossling," said the sergeant. "They're petty thieves, the lot of them, but they would never harm a woman."

"We're used to it, Sergeant," Adele said. "In spite of the sheriff's gallant if rather bearish reaction, we can take care of ourselves." She glanced at Hatfield.

Mr. Ross sat up and gave them a cautious look. He was a small man and Adele guessed when he stood up he would be only a little taller than her and Nin.

Sergeant Walker approached him with a smile. "How do you do, son? I'm Sergeant Walker of the San Francisco police."

"I didn't do nothing, honest!"

"Nobody said you did," Hatfield said.

"Them officers in San Jose said so." The young man's voice was high-pitched. "I was just walking out of the drugstore, and they hit me on my head."

"I'm sorry that happened to you," Walker said with genuine regret.

"We're here to get some information, son," Hatfield said. "Nobody's going to hurt you."

Mr. Ross's frightened look returned as he stared at the imposing sheriff. "I ain't got no information."

"You used to board with Miss Miriam Sweenie and Miss Addie Sweenie. Is that correct?" Sergeant Walker asked.

The young man relaxed slightly. "They give me olives sometimes. I like olives."

Adele and Nin exchanged a sharp look. Hatfield raised his eyebrows.

"That was kind of them," Adele ventured.

"They were kind," he said with a wide grin. "Like Ma, only Ma ain't around no more."

"Mr. Ross," the sergeant said, "I'm sorry to inform you Miss Lillie Sweenie has been killed."

"Who?"

"The Misses Sweenie's niece." Hatfield gave him an odd look. "Didn't she live in the same house where you boarded?"

The young man looked from one lawman to another, his eyes widening with each gaze. The shiny object in his hand fell on the cot, a silver shaving brush. "I saw her sometimes, but I didn't know her. What do you want with me?"

"We're just looking for information," Sergeant Walker said.

"Dead." The young man blinked. "You mean she went away?"

"Yes, Mr. Ross," Adele said. "She went away."

"But she's coming back, isn't she?" he asked. "She goes away sometimes. But she always comes back."

"She won't come back," Nin said. "Not this time."

"You mean like Ma?" He peered at her.

"Yes," Adele said. "Like your mother." She wondered when the young man's mother had died.

"Grandma said she took a walk too," said Mr. Ross. "To Heaven. Is that where Lillie is?"

"Let's hope so," Nin said.

The young man relaxed a little more. "Heaven's a nice place, Granny said."

"Son." Walker gripped his shoulder. "We need your help to find out who killed her. Can you understand that?"

"She was killed?" the young man asked. "Like in a gunfight? I seen gunfights." He picked up the silver brush and held it in his palm.

"Not a gunfight," said Hatfield. "But we don't know what happened so we want your help. It's your duty to help the police when there's a crime, you know." Hatfield's rigid tone seemed to unnerve Mr. Ross.

"I don't got no duty to the police!" Mr. Ross threw his hair back from his forehead. "They ain't nice to me. They give me this." He lifted his sleeve to show a thick bruise that had clearly not completely healed. "Why should I help you?"

"She was Miss Miriam's and Miss Addie's niece," Adele said. "Don't you want to help them?"

"I'd do anything for them!" He turned to Adele. "They get me a place with Mr. Hoff and a feather bed and real lace curtains!"

"All right, then," Walker said. "The first thing we need you to do is to help us identify Lillie's body."

"No!" The young man folded up in a corner with his arms across his chest.

"It's not scary," Adele soothed. "She looks like she's asleep."

"See Lillie — like that?"

"You said you wanted to help her aunts," Nin pointed out.

The young man remained cowered, staring at her with vacant eyes.

CHAPTER 16

Adele gave Sergeant Walker a quick look and he nodded. She sat down beside the young man. "That's a fine shaving brush, Clarence. May I call you Clarence?"

"What's your name?" he asked.

"Miss Adele," she said. "And this is Miss Branch." Nin gave him a dead look. "May I see it?"

"See what?" Mr. Ross blinked.

"What you have in your hand," Nin snapped.

The young man looked at her as if he were in a dream. Then, he handed the brush to Adele.

It was rather majestic. About six or seven inches in length, the barrel hid the brush itself, which had fine hairs and felt like cat's fur against Adele's palm. The silver barrel had a simple monogram and a crown engraved above it.

"You keep it nice and polished." Adele smiled.

"Soap ain't as good as the polish Miss Miriam gave me," he said. "She said I had to leave it when we ran from the fire."

Adele handed it to Nin, whose face grew soft as she examined it.

"Miss Miriam and Miss Addie said it belonged to a Russian nobleman." The young man's voice became boisterous.

"Did they give it to you, son?" Sergeant Walker asked in a congenial tone.

"Yes, sir," said the young man. "Give it to me last birthday."

"A fine gift," Hatfield said warmly and the young man smiled.

"Clarence," Adele ventured. "You could really help Miss Miriam and Miss Addie by telling the police if the girl they found is really Lillie. You understand what I mean, don't you?"

He blinked. "They won't beat me?"

"Of course not." Nin's compassion for the young man rose a little. "They just want you to look at her and tell them if it's Lillie."

"That's all?" He peered at Adele.

"That's all."

He glanced at Sergeant Walker and slowly nodded.

There was a slight commotion outside with men's voices rising, and Adele could hear her brother's steely tone. He entered the tent.

"I have the list, sir." He handed Sergeant Walker a piece of paper.

"I'm sure you would be happy with *this*, wouldn't you, Mr. Gossling?" Nin said slyly as she held up the silver brush. "You like such fineries, don't you?"

"Don't touch it!" Clarence shrieked, glaring at Jackson.

"I wasn't going to give it to him," Nin assured the young man as she put the brush back in his hands.

His breath relaxed as he put it in his shirt pocket. "You're nice too. And real pretty."

"Mr. Ross," said the sergeant, "I'd like you to take a look at these names and tell me if you recognize anyone."

"Recognize?" Clarence blinked.

"If you've seen any of the men listed here," Hatfield explained.

"I stay in the tent, except for meals," said the young man. "I don't talk to anyone."

"They might be people you knew before the quake," Jackson said with a little annoyance. "Will you please just look at the list, sir?"

The young man's eyes ran up and down the names. "Don't know any of them."

"Will you please read each name carefully?" Jackson asked in a sharp tone.

"Clarence," said Adele. "It's very important for the police to know if any of the names look familiar to you. Please."

The young man started reading in earnest, his finger following along with each line.

Adele crossed the tent to the sergeant and sheriff. "Will you let Nin and I ask the questions, Sergeant?" she asked in a low tone.

"You think you can get farther than we can?" Walker asked.

"He seems — I don't know. He seems to be missing a mother."

Hatfield grimaced. "And you think you and Miss Branch can play that role for him."

"I think we'll get more out of him than you will," said Adele.

"That's possible," the sergeant agreed.

"He seems to resent the police," Sheriff Hatfield added.

"Well, who doesn't, Horatio?" asked his friend with a chuckle. "And if the San Jose police crossed the line —"

"We only have his word for it," Hatfield pointed out.

"He has that bruise, Sheriff," Adele said.

"It's not pleasant to be dealing with the police at a time like this," Walker said. "Since you and Miss Branch are appointed deputies, I have no objection to your asking questions as long as you let Horatio and I guide you."

"They always take their cues from the police, Harry," Sheriff Hatfield promised.

Adele returned to the cot. Nin had already found a place on the ground in her usual cross-legged position in front of them.

The young man finished the list and held it out to Jackson. "Don't see anyone I know."

"No one that Lillie might have known?" asked Adele.

"Oh, well, I didn't know her friends," he said.

"You must have known a few," Nin insisted. "You said Miss Miriam was like your mother."

"They were both like Ma," said Clarence with a little vague smile. "Fussing and doing for me."

"And Lillie," Adele asked. "Was she like a sister to you?"

"They helped me find work," he continued. "I came here and had nothing."

"Where did you work?" asked Sergeant Walker.

"Hoff's Grocery." The young man looked cagey. "I never stole nothing from him!"

"No one said you did," Jackson said. "No one mentioned stealing."

"He rents the store from Miss Miriam," Clarence said. "She tell him to give me a job and he done it."

"Did it," Nin corrected. "There's no store left now."

He gave her a vacant look.

"How long did you live with the Sweenies?" Adele asked.

"I come when the president come."

"That was about three years, then." Adele smiled. "And they treated you like family."

"Family." He murmured. "Sounds nice the way you say it, Miss Adele."

"Did Lillie treat you like family too?" Nin asked.

"You've been asked the question twice, sir," Jackson said in a firm tone. "You'd better answer."

"Lillie don't like me much," said the young man. "She say once my head's like molasses. The thoughts come slow."

"I shouldn't wonder," Jackson mumbled.

"She thought she was too good for them!" Clarence said in a loud tone.

"Too good for whom?" Adele asked.

"Their granddaddy was a forty-niner, come here with all the gold diggers," the young man said with a note of pride. "They got class, Miss Miriam and Miss Addie. Lillie's daddy was a sailor!" He spat the word out.

"Sounds like Miss Miriam talking," Nin observed with a shrewd glance.

"They're better than her anytime!" the young man declared. "She didn't do nothing around the house, just cost them money. She ought to have married a long time ago!"

Adele realized Nin was right. It was clear the young man had heard the exact words coming out of Miss Miriam's mouth, probably many times. He even mimicked the high-minded tone the elderly woman had taken when she spoke to them.

"Lillie did good work, Clarence," she said in a gentle tone. "She helped people."

"A lot of riffraff!" the young man snarled. "She should have been looking for a husband."

"Are those your words or Miss Miriam's?" Adele asked.

"Well, it's true." He sniffed. "She was ungrateful for all they done for her."

"I see," she said in a soft tone. "Clarence, you can help us a great deal. I'm sure, being part of the family, you saw the young men Lillie stepped out with."

He was clearly flattered by the assumption he knew about the family, as he sat a little straighter and his shoulders were less hunched. "I seen a lot."

"Do you know if she had a beau?"

"A what?"

"A young man she saw a lot of," said Jackson. It was clear his patience had run out.

"You mean like Ben Horne?" he asked.

"Yes, like Ben Horne," Adele said. "Miss Miriam and Miss Addie said something about him."

"I liked Ben," said the young man. "He told me once he's going to marry her if she'll have him."

"But she wouldn't have him?" Nin inquired.

"She said he wasn't very smart," said Clarence. "But that ain't true. Ben's a good fellow. He's helping with the rocks now."

"What do you mean, son?" Walker asked.

"I saw him couple of days ago," said the young man. "He says he's down where the streetcar lines are, getting them out with that big machine they brung from Oakland."

"Where?" Hatfield asked.

"Down South of the Slot somewhere." The young man shrugged.

"Might be the streetcar lines on Brannon," Walker said to his friend. The sheriff nodded.

"She had no other young man who came to call?" Adele asked. "Nobody by the name of George?" She looked at him hopefully.

"I don't think she ever wanted to get married," the young man declared. "She'd have stayed with Miss Miriam and Miss Addie forever."

"You don't think she wanted to get married, eh?" Jackson's exasperation got the better of him.

Sergeant Walker laid the wedding ring on the cot next to Clarence. "We found this near where Miss Sweenie was killed."

The young man turned it around and around in his hand, handling it as a child would handle a pretty stone. His eyes were almost jewel-like. "Ain't it pretty?"

"It's more than pretty," Jackson snapped. "We think it's Miss Sweenie's wedding ring."

"But Lillie ain't married," the young man objected.

"Wasn't married," Nin corrected. "She's dead, remember?"

"It's not true, not true!" Clarence's voice rose to a screech. "Lillie wasn't married."

"Then why are her initials on the ring?" Jackson snatched the ring from the young man's hand and shook it in his face. "It says L.S. for Lillie Sweenie."

"No, no!" the young man screamed. "It's all a lie!"

"That's enough, Deputy!" Hatfield's voice came loud and clear. One of the men outside poked his head in, and the sergeant waved him away.

Adele glared at her brother. He retreated to the other end of the tent.

Adele patted the young man's hand. She felt it was hot and trembling. "My brother shouldn't have said that."

"It's a lie, Miss Adele." His voice squeaked. "It's a lie, lie, lie!"

She let Clarence calm down a little. "Clarence, do you know where Lillie got these?" She unwrapped the silk and showed him the pendant and the fan.

He squinted. "Those people in Chinatown, maybe."

"You mean the Chinese," Nin said.

"What Chinese do you mean, Clarence?" Adele asked carefully.

"She said they were nice people who needed food and jobs." He shrugged. "Everybody needs food and jobs, don't they?"

"But some people more than others," Adele said. "They gave her presents?"

"They were always giving her things," he said. "She went to Hayward 'cause they needed help with some barn they were building."

"She built a barn?" Nin inquired.

"She brought food and coffee," he said. "She and another person. They gave her a chicken!" He burst out laughing. "Ran around the house with Miss Addie screaming until we caught him!"

"So you think these were a presents from the people she helped," Adele surmised.

"Miss Addie sure didn't like that chicken," he said. "She was screaming and crying." His voice became indignant. "Lillie gave it to Mr. Hoff. Said he could do what he wanted with it." He looked at Adele with tight eyes. "It ain't right giving away a present someone gave you."

There was silence for a moment and then Walker cleared his throat. "Thank you for your help, Mr. Ross."

"That's all?" The young man looked hopeful.

"We need you to come to the morgue and identify Lillie," said the sergeant. "You promised us, remember."

"Morgue?"

"It's only a tent we placed out of the way so people wouldn't see her," Walker assured him.

"No other dead people?" asked Clarence.

"Only Lillie," Nin said.

The young man wavered and Adele said kindly, "Remember, you're helping Miss Miriam and Miss Addie."

Clarence rose. "Well, I suppose so. If it will help Miss Miriam and Miss Addie."

The activity outside was a little chaotic with people heading toward the dining room tents for lunch. Clarence looked from left to right as if afraid of them.

The tent where they had placed Lillie was small and surrounded by bushes, well out of the way. As they entered, a police officer saluted Sergeant Walker and the sheriff.

"The doctor has been giving the body ice baths, sir," said the young man in a hushed tone. "The family has been by to ask when they can bury her."

"This won't take long, Deputy, and then we'll send someone to let the family know they can take her," Sergeant Walker answered.

Adele saw Lillie's body was swathed with cloth inside a bathtub filled with water. The doctor nodded at the sergeant, and after a few whispers, uncovered Lillie's face.

Adele gripped Nin's arm, anticipating the young man's reaction. But he seemed almost calm looking at Lillie's face, which had now been cleaned of wounds.

"Why, she looks like she's sleeping!" he whispered.

"She's not so you don't have to whisper," Nin said in her blunt way.

"Do you think she's in Heaven, Miss Adele?" Clarence peered at her.

"I'm sure she is," Adele said in a soft voice.

"She was a bad girl, but she oughtn't to be in hell," he said.

"I'm sure she isn't, Clarence," Adele assured him.

"We need you to sign some papers declaring the person you're seeing is Miss Lillie Sweenie," said Sergeant Walker, nodding to the deputy.

"It's her," said Clarence shortly. "It's Lillie."

"I think we're done here." To Hatfield, he said, "We ought to send a man to let the aunts know they can bury her as soon as possible."

"I'll do it after lunch," Jackson said.

As they filed out of the tent, Clarence grabbed Adele's hand. "Do *they* know?"

"You mean do her aunts know about her being dead?" Nin asked.

Clarence nodded.

"Yes, we told them," Adele said.

"How did they — were they sad?"

"Very sad." Adele glanced at Nin.

"Did Miss Addie scream and cry?" He seemed anxious.

"She cried a little," Adele admitted. "But she's alright, Clarence." She patted his hand. "We'll let you know if anything happens to them."

"Wish I could see them," he said with a sigh.

"Maybe you can," Adele said kindly. "I'm sure they'll want you at the funeral."

"Oh, no!" He looked at her in horror. "That wouldn't be right."

"Why not?" Nin asked.

"They're fine and good and I ain't nobody."

"You're just as fine and good as they are," Nin said in a savage tone.

"No, no," he said, and before they could say anymore, he rushed toward the camp.

CHAPTER 17

"Good Lord!" The exclamation came out of Jackson's mouth the moment they returned to the police tent. "The man is a half-wit!"

"You didn't have much patience with him, Jack." Adele removed her hat and fluffing out her front bangs.

"You practically hounded him about the ring," Nin said.

"I don't think I've ever had such a frustrating interview," Jackson grumbled.

"He's likely confused by the earthquake," Sergeant Walker said. "I've seen it all around the city. People bewildered, walking to nowhere, clutching things that don't matter. It's bound to happen in a case like this where so many people are homeless."

"But it's been over a week," Hatfield pointed out. "The army has done its best to give people shelter."

"There are still people who haven't gotten their bearings, Horatio," Walker argued.

"I don't think it's that, Sergeant," Adele said. "Miss Addie said he's not a very bright young men."

"Bright or not, he seemed positive he didn't know any of the names on the list," Hatfield said.

"I wouldn't trust that," Jackson said. "He barely looked at them."

"Maybe he can't read," Nin offered. "Did you ever think of that, Mr. Gossling?"

The anger left Jackson's face. "No, Miss Branch, I didn't."

"I think he was telling the truth about George," Adele said. "Even if he and Lillie weren't friends, he would have known if she were stepping out with anyone but Ben Horne."

"Speaking of Horne." Sergeant Walker turned to Jackson. "Do you think Lieutenant Edwards could discover Horne's whereabouts in the city now that we know he might be clearing tracks down South of the Slot?"

Jackson nodded. "He told me the army is keeping track of people working to rebuild the city. Private companies are required to report names of anyone working for them to the Presidio."

"Good idea centralizing everything in one place even when the army isn't involved." Walker nodded his approval.

"There are a few things the mayor did right," Adele said dryly.

"Horne is our next stop?" Hatfield asked.

His friend nodded. "He might be able to shed some light on Miss Sweenie's state of mind."

"Or he might reveal himself a prime suspect if he was none too happy about the wedding ring," Nin pointed out.

Walker grinned. "I'm not discounting anything at this point, Miss Branch. We have so little to go on and in all this chaos—"

"Don't worry, Harry." The sheriff clasped him on the back. "They've got the best man for the job right here."

"Sergeant," Adele asked, "may Nin and I come with you to see Mr. Horne?" She glanced at her friend. "We've been curious to see what they're doing with the rebuilding."

"I don't see any harm in it." The sergeant nodded.

"You don't yet." Jackson rolled his eyes, "Just wait until she comes to you with her wild theories."

"I don't have theories, dear brother," Adele said airily. "I have ideas."

"And they usually prove useful, Mr. Gossling," said Nin. "I'll thank you to remember that."

He made a face and Hatfield chuckled.

Later that evening, Valda came to their tent and shared a few stories from a convention she had attended right before the earthquake. Her chirpy tone and manner made the stories amusing, and Adele felt the heaviness of the day's events lift from her breast. Nin seemed to enjoy them as well. Only Elsie frowned, and Adele knew what she was thinking — all the convention talk was worthless without the sort of radical action she had once favored before her father had grown ill and she had vowed to give up such things.

Soon after Valda left, Missy came in, her usual breathless self. She pulled a crate from under the table and plopped down in front of Adele. "Well?"

"You needn't look like an expectant father," Nin mumbled.

"I want to know all about that search you made of Lillie's things," Missy insisted. "And that strange young man you saw."

"How did you know about Clarence?"

"You know I have my sources, Adele." She gave her a sly look.

"Is your source a certain deputy sheriff who has the heart of a gossip?" Nin eyed her.

"Jack wouldn't gossip," Adele objected. "He'd complain, but he wouldn't gossip."

"Come on, Adele." Missy took out her pad and pencil.

Adele related their findings in Lillie's tent and the interview with Clarence Ross. Missy seemed especially interested in the Chinese artifacts.

"It's intriguing, you must admit," she said.

"I'm sure there's a very simple explanation," Adele insisted.

"If there's a simple explanation, why did she hide them?" her friend challenged.

"Because her aunts fancy they're fine ladies, and fine ladies don't touch anything from Chinatown with a ten-foot pole," Nin said.

"Maybe they didn't come from Chinatown," Missy argued.

"Where else would they have come from?" Elsie glanced at her.

Adele took out the fan and pendant. "I thought you might tell us."

"Chinatown isn't really my territory, you know," Elsie reminded her. "I believe Valda and her people have more of an interest in helping the underprivileged."

"We're all underprivileged," Adele said. "The Chinese are treated abominably, Elsie."

"I never said they weren't," Elsie retorted. "I managed to get them some clothes and supplies in spite of Captain Best's efforts to stop me, didn't I?"

"Of course you did, and I'm sure they were very grateful," Adele said. "Will you look at these anyway and tell us what you think? I promised the sergeant we would try to find out where they came from."

"So now you're on the San Francisco police force?" Elsie eyed her.

"She ought to do better work than they do," Nin snapped. "She's had more practice with murder!"

"You and I both, dear." Adele said. Nin smiled.

Her friend inspected the artifacts with Missy sketching them on her pad. She became a little more interested in the fan. "I don't think this is from one of those cheap shops. The material is too fine."

"Maybe someone brought it over from the Orient," Missy suggested. "Something valuable they smuggled in."

"I doubt the story behind it is that romantic." Elsie rolled her eyes.

"How would you know since you haven't a romantic bone in your body?" Adele asked in a teasing tone, winning a self-satisfied look from her friend.

"I think this is valuable too." Elsie fingered the pendant. "I've seen dozens of this sort of thing in Chinatown shops. Dragons mostly, but there were some little Buddhas like that."

"It doesn't look like a Buddha," Nin said.

"She may have stolen the things for all we know," Elsie said. "You didn't see what pandemonium there was here in the city after the fire, Adele. People were digging in the rubble before the military could restore order."

"Even from Chinatown?" Nin asked.

"Even from Chinatown."

"I don't think that's likely," Missy said. "I had a conversation with those aunts of hers during lunch and from what they told me, they kept close to one another their entire journey here. I doubt Lillie would have been out of their guard for even a minute."

"I agree," Adele said. "If she had stolen them, she wouldn't have wrapped them up so carefully. And the boxes would have been bruised from the crumbled buildings. She put a lot of effort into taking care of these." She wrapped the boxes in the silk, thinking of how lovingly they found them embedded in the suitcase.

Missy rose and put on her hat. "I'm off now."

"Off?" Adele looked at her with alarm. "But curfew is in another half hour."

"I'll be back by then," Missy insisted. "I've got half a dozen stories I need to get out to Carla."

"Your friend Adam?" Nin eyed her.

Missy smiled. "He's been very obliging."

"I'm sure he has." Adele gave her a look.

Her friend laughed. "I didn't have to sweet-talk him, you know."

"More than likely, he sweet-talked you," Elsie snorted.

"I ought to get there as soon as possible." Missy adjusted the pins on her hat. "There will be a storm of reporters there on the telegraph line. It seems they've opened it up for nearly every small newspaper down the coast."

"They shouldn't be doing that," Nin said.

"Why not, Miss Branch?" Missy asked. "They have to get their stories out." She snapped the last button on her jacket in place. "I'm meeting him outside the gate."

"A very obliging fellow, this Adam," Elsie said in a teasing tone.

"And what does that mean?" Missy glared at her.

"You tell me, dear," the woman said with fluttering eyelashes.

"Oh, for heaven's sake —" Missy growled.

"How will you get back in if you're late?" Adele asked.

"I expect I'll find a way." Missy waved at them. "You and Miss Branch aren't the only resourceful ones!"

"I must say, she's quite determined at her job," Elsie remarked after Missy had gone.

"The *Arrojo Courier* may not be the *Chronicle* or the *Sun*," Adele said, "But she's made it into something the town can be proud of."

"She's been leaning toward yellow journalism too much in the last year," Nin said in a disapproving tone.

"They're all doing it, Miss Branch." Elsie lounged on her cot.

"I only hope she keeps quiet about George," Adele said. "I don't think the sergeant wants it known we're looking for him."

"We don't even know who we're looking for," Nin pointed out.

"But we do," Adele said. "George W. We just don't know what the "W" stands for." She said to Elsie, "You don't happen to remember if you ever ran into a George whose last name began with a 'W,' do you, dear?"

"No." Elsie was quiet for a moment. "Have you a picture of Lillie, Adele?"

"We have a drawing, compliments of Missy's unusual skill," Adele said.

Elsie's face changed instantly as she sat up, looking at the picture. "Why, I knew her!"

"Now you tell us?" Adele was annoyed.

"Well, I didn't know what she looked like before, did I?" Elsie asked. "I didn't know her well, but I've seen her face before."

"Where?" Adele leaned forward.

"A few years ago when we collaborated with a few organizations in the city for that fair in the Mission," Elsie said. "We were trying to raise money for poor migrant women who got caught without jobs during the drought." She sniffed. "Karen McLeod and her City Dwellers League made a stink about everyone sharing the profits for a general fund that would go to all workers. We couldn't move her to see it was the women who needed it the most."

"And Lillie was there with Miss McLeod's group?" Adele asked.

Elsie nodded. "She had the lace booth." When Adele looked blank, she laughed. "The booth where they sell lace, silly. Tablecloths and things."

Adele put her chin in her hand. "What can you tell me about Karen McLeod?"

"What do you know about her already?" Elsie countered.

Adele chuckled. "Not much except she's staunch in her belief of equal rights for all and wary of those who fight for one particular group."

"That's about it," Elsie agreed. "She's one of those reformers with myopic vision."

"How do you mean?" Nin asked.

"We call them 'bee reformers.'" Elsie grinned. "Not that they like it much."

"Their first interest is recruiting people to their organizations," Adele explained. "They woo and win anybody who looks promising, and once they get them into their group, they fly to the next person."

"Like a bee spreads its pollen." Nin nodded.

"Their loyalty is to the cause, not the people in it," Elsie said sourly.

"Have you heard through your sources where Miss McLeod is now?" Adele asked.

"Her group fled to the southern part of the state. Cowards!" She grunted.

"The police may want to talk to Miss McLeod," Nin said.

"Why should they want to do that?"

"From what the aunts claim, Lillie was quite devoted to Miss McLeod and her cause," Adele said. "She might know more about Lillie, and she might know something about this George person."

"Karen will have nothing to tell the police," Elsie declared. "She would have sweet-talked Lillie into joining and then moved on to the next victim when she had her signed on. She wasn't the kind to get intimate with the people who worked with her."

"Still, the police will want to know about her, Elsie," Adele said.

"I've nothing to tell them either," Elsie snapped. "I'm not as partial to them as you and Miss Branch seem to be."

"Because they've bound your wrists with handcuffs when you deserved it?" Nin snickered.

"I did *not* deserve it!" Elsie objected. "We had a right to picket the civic center. If we had been men picketing about unfair wages, they wouldn't have batted an eye."

"Probably not," Adele agreed.

"I hardly know Miss McLeod, and I didn't know Lillie," said Elsie emphatically. "Actually, I thought her rather trite at the fair."

"Why was that?"

"She seemed more interested in flirting with a young Mexican fellow than selling lace."

"Was the young man's name George by chance?" Adele perked up.

"His name was Pablo," said Elsie. "He helped us take down the booths later that day."

"Not our man, then." Nin shook her head.

"Still," Adele said thoughtfully, "if Lillie was flirting with a Mexican man, she might have been flirting with others at that fair."

"You mean others who aren't white men," Nin said in her blunt way.

"Which would mean what exactly?" Elsie eyed her.

"Which would mean that maybe the police ought to cast a wider net when looking for George," Adele said.

CHAPTER 18

The next morning, they were at breakfast when Lieutenant Edwards came in. He saluted Sergeant Walker and nodded to the others. "I tracked down Ben Horne, sir."

The sergeant wiped his mouth with his napkin and looked at him expectantly.

"Your Mr. Ross was right, and he was wrong," said Edwards.

"Meaning?" Hatfield inquired.

"Mr. Horne is helping clear streetcar tracks, but he's not South of the Slot." He took a map out of his pocket and unfolded it. "He's on Divisadero in the Haight Street area. Tough work I'm told, sir. One of our men was down there the other day, and they broke a tractor on the tracks."

"Not a pleasant task they assigned Mr. Horne, is it?" Hatfield remarked.

"Oh, he wasn't assigned, sir," said the lieutenant. "He volunteered."

"Mr. Horne sounds like a decent man," Adele remarked, taking full advantage of the strawberries on the table, wondering where the army had procured such a gem.

"Very noble of him." Jackson nodded with approval. "Where would San Francisco be if every man shirked his responsibility toward the rebuilding?"

"No one is shirking anything, Jackson," Edwards promised. "We're not even pushing anyone. We all have a stake in seeing San Francisco become the shining jewel of the West that it was before this tragedy."

"More like a diamond in the rough," Nin sneered.

"But a diamond nonetheless, Miss Branch," Jackson reminded her.

"I've General Best's automobile waiting outside for you," said Edwards.

"I don't think the general need be involved in this," Sergeant Walker said.

"Not the general, sir." The lieutenant grinned. "Just his car. With me as driver, of course."

"That was very kind of him." The sergeant drank the last of his coffee.

"Well, sir, when he heard the women were going with you," he glanced at Adele and Nin, "he couldn't very well let you walk, could he?"

"Your general underestimates our resilience, Lieutenant," Adele said sharply. "I used to walk down to the Slot many times when we lived in the city, and usually in the early hours of the morning. I assure you I could find my way through its back alleys blindfolded."

"*Could*, Del," her brother reminded her. "We haven't lived here for some time."

"And I've walked miles and miles in the woods and found my way without running into any wild animals," Nin said. "I'm not afraid of a few alleyways."

"Perhaps not, Miss Branch," Lieutenant Edwards said, "but these are not ordinary circumstances. The gridline streets have all disappeared. There's rubble everywhere and one must know where to go so one doesn't end up falling through one of the cracks in the road left open by the earthquake. That's why the general sent me as your driver." He tipped his hat to the sergeant. "If that meets with your approval, sir."

"Naturally," said Sergeant Walker.

The moment they left the Presidio and headed down Divisadero Street, Adele saw what Edwards meant. Her fingers tightened on the back of the seat as she saw what remained of buildings on either side, the still-smokey air sending a gray mist that made her cough. They passed Eddy Street, and she drew in a breath at the sight of church towers with only an iron frame to show their former magnificence. Rocks and wood were cleared from the road but not from the sidewalk, and people stepped around them.

As they reached Divisadero and Hayes, she was relieved to see most of the houses looked untouched. There was a crowd outside a store in the corner.

"Someone doing business already?" Nin frowned.

"That's the army, Miss Branch," Edwards threw over his shoulder. "Giving out food to people."

"They're waiting for food?" Adele murmured.

"They're the lucky ones," Jackson said. "They have a home to go back to." He glanced behind him at the row of houses.

They reached Haight and Adele again drew in a breath. She could see bricks overturned and large gaps in the road where the streetcar lines had already been removed. A large tractor stood a little way down the street.

Edwards pulled the car to the side. "Perhaps I'd better stay here, sir. Vehicles are still precious in the city."

"You don't really think someone would try to steal an army car, do you, Lieutenant?" Adele asked.

"I must protect our property, Miss Gossling." He glanced at her and Nin. "It might be a good idea if the ladies stayed too, if you'll pardon my saying so, Sergeant."

"*He* may pardon you but *we* don't," Nin snapped.

"I only mean it might be dangerous to walk around here," he said. "We still don't know if the ground might give way."

"We'll be very careful, Lieutenant." Adele lifted her skirt a little and took Hatfield's hand as he helped her out of the automobile.

Nin rejected the sheriff's help and made her way out of the car. Just as she stepped down, a brick on the road slid and she almost lost her balance. Jackson, who was behind the sheriff, quickly caught her. She blushed and thanked him.

Men were standing around in overalls. The tractor had a crane and the driver was hauling up one of the streetcar rails.

A slim man with a cap pulled over his forehead hurried to them. "What are these women doing here?" he demanded. "You folks ain't supposed to be here. This is a restricted area. Don't ya know it's dangerous?"

"I hardly think that's a secret, sir," Sergeant Walker said dryly as he pulled out his badge. Hatfield nodded at Jackson, and they both pulled out theirs too. Adele hid a smile, as she realized they were counting on the fact that the irate man would not read the badges too closely and think they were from the San Francisco police.

The man's voice became more professional. "What can I do for you, Sergeant?"

"Are you the foreman here?"

"That's right?"

"We need to talk to one of your men." The sergeant pointed to the large tractor. "I think he's up there? Ben Horne?"

"That's Ben all right." The man put his hands on his hips. "He done something?"

"We just want to talk to him," Walker assured him.

The man gave him a suspicious look but retreated to speak with the man in the tractor. A young man with springy dark hair and a round face descended carefully. The foreman tossed him a old rag, which he used to wipe his hands and face as he made his way toward them.

"You want to see me, sir?" The voice was pleasant and low.

"That's a mighty big vehicle you're driving there, son." Sergeant Walker stared at the massive tractor with its crane folded like the arm of a giant.

"I'm used to it, sir," said the young man. "Been driving them since I was eighteen."

"It must be a difficult task," Jackson remarked. "Getting those rails out of the ground."

"You don't know the half of it." Mr. Horne waved his hand. "Some of them melted right into the bricks from the fire. It's a devil of a —" He glanced at the ladies. "Sorry."

"We don't shrink from strong masculine language, Mr. Horne," Adele said with a smile. "It's very decent of you to volunteer to do such hard labor."

"As I said, miss, I'm used to it." Mr. Horne glanced at the sergeant, waiting.

"I'm afraid we have some bad news for you, son." The man glanced at Hatfield.

"Bad news?" The young man straightened up "Well, let's hear it."

"You're acquainted with a Miss Lillie Sweenie?" Hatfield asked.

"Yes, sir," he said.

"I'm afraid we must inform you that Miss Sweenie is dead." Sergeant Walker peered at the young man's face.

Mr. Horne turned white and clutched the rag still in his hand. He collapsed on the sidewalk.

"So it was her," he murmured.

"Eh?" Hatfield glanced at him.

"There was talk last night of a young woman found dead in the camp," he said. "But I never dreamed — never imagined —" He covered his face with his hand.

"You were her intended?" the sergeant asked.

"I'm afraid I don't understand fancy language, Sergeant. I ain't got much education."

"You were engaged to marry her," Nin said.

"No, miss." He shook his head. "Oh, we were courting for a while."

"How did you meet her?" asked Sheriff Hatfield.

"I was helping a friend do handy work for some organization Lillie was with." He paused with a slight smile. "One of those groups that waves signs around and makes Sunday speeches in Golden Gate Park."

"Was it, by chance, the City Dweller's League?" Adele asked.

"I can't say, miss, but it might have been."

Adele glanced at her friend. "Karen McLeod's people."

"There was a Miss McLeod, as I recall." The young man cocked his head. "Gave me some story about my duty to the city and the bartenders working down in the Barbary Coast." He grimaced. "Wanted me to hand out some fliers to the men I was working with on a site at the time."

"But you didn't," Nin guessed.

"No, miss," he said. "Oh, I ain't got anything against the bartenders or the Mexicans or Chinese. But when a man's got to earn a living, his mind is on earning a living."

"He doesn't always have the luxury of thinking of others struggling like him," Jackson agreed.

"Lillie tried to get me to go with them sometimes," he said. "I did my best but Sundays, honestly, I just want to find a hammock somewhere and sleep, not go out pushing pamphlets to people who don't want them."

"So you stopped courting?" Sergeant Walker asked.

The man nodded. "I ain't seen her in six months or so."

"That's not what her aunts think," Adele said.

Mr. Horne gave a little smile. "Lillie didn't tell her aunts everything."

Adele sat next to him on the sideway, ignoring her brother's look of disapproval. Nin dropped down as well. "Mr. Horne, how did Lillie feel about her aunts?"

The young man stared into the distance at the building across the street which looked like the haunches of a horse without the horse's body or head. "I'm not sure what you mean, miss."

"Do you think she liked them? Hated them?" Adele persevered.

"I don't have to think, miss," he said. "I know. She didn't hate them but well, I can't say she liked them either." He faced her. "She said once that she felt like a burden to them."

"Was she a burden to them?" asked Jackson.

"She paid her way as much as she could, sir," said the young man. "Oh, they meant no harm. But they're spinsters, you see, and not used to taking care of children."

"And they hadn't planned on taking in a niece," Adele finished. "Especially one who had no money and no prospects for the future."

He shrugged. "I guess they wanted her to marry a finer man than me."

Adele pressed his hand. "I'm sure Lillie couldn't have found a better person than you, Mr. Horne."

"I guess she did in the end," he mumbled. "The last time we met she told me she was in love with someone else."

"You don't sound very brokenhearted about it," Nin said.

"It ain't that, miss," he said. "But when a lady says she's got another fella she likes more than you, not much you can do about it, is there?"

"Not much," Jackson agreed.

Sergeant Walker propped his foot up on the curb and leaned against his knee. "Did you ever meet this man?"

The young man shook his head. "His name's George. That's all I know."

Walker glanced at Hatfield.

"Do you know his last name?" asked the sheriff, though Adele could see he wasn't holding out much hope.

And, indeed, Mr. Horne shook his head. "No idea, sir."

"Could he have been someone in your circle of friends?" Jackson suggested. "Perhaps even a friend of a friend?"

"Her only friends were the people in that organization," said the young man. "She met some of my friends but she wasn't interested in them." He made the rag into a ball. "They're not educated, and they don't think much of the bartenders or the Mexicans or Chinese, and they don't read. So I guess they didn't have much in common with her."

"I didn't think Lillie was educated," Adele said.

"Oh, not proper, miss," he said. "But she did lots of book learning. She took books from the Mechanics Library and read them. Even about things like the stars and physists."

"Physics," Nin corrected.

"She wanted to know a little bit about everything," he said. "She said a well-rounded education was better than a narrow one."

"And there was no one you know who could have encouraged her to do this?" Sergeant Walker asked.

"Those people in the organization, probably," said Mr. Horne.

"Miss McLeod, perhaps?" Sergeant Walker suggested.

"I don't think so," Adele cut in. "Elsie told me she is the sort of reformer who is only interested in recruiting."

The young man grinned vaguely. "I'm not surprised you know about her, miss. You look like one of them."

"One of who?" Nin's eyes narrowed.

"The good Samaritans, naturally," Jackson chuckled. His sister threw him a look.

"I mean the women who help the Mexicans and Chinese and all of them," said Mr. Horne.

"You mean a reformer," Adele said.

He nodded. "I used to come to see her after work in the organization — kind of a dirty, run-down place, if you ask me — and there were a bunch of ladies dressed like you."

Adele glanced down at her pale blue jacket, and matching skirt and the high-collared linen waistcoat shirt. She had been vain enough to think she had looked smart that morning in Elsie's tiny square mirror. But now she felt a little self-conscious.

"Where else did you visit her?" asked Jackson. "We're trying to locate people who might have known her."

"The Good Samaritan Center," he said. "That wasn't such a bad place. And she sometimes did work with the Occidental House in Chinatown." Mr. Horne shuddered.

"The Occidental Board Presbyterian Mission House," Adele prompted.

"I guess so." He shrugged. "I didn't like her going down there, but she felt so sorry for those Chinese girls and the way they were being treated."

"I did some work there as well," Adele said.

"I also saw some men when I went down to see her," the young man said. "The shabby type that always has his nose in a book. Some of them were Mexican and some were even Chinese. That's why I didn't like her going down there."

"That's understandable." Jackson nodded. "I didn't like my sister going into Chinatown either."

"Did she seem to take a liking to anyone in particular?" asked Hatfield.

"Well, no, sir, not that I could tell," he said. "But I wasn't there all the time. And none of them looked like they had two nickels to rub between their fingers, if you know what I mean."

"Was Miss Sweenie looking for a rich man?" Jackson asked.

"Oh, it ain't that," said the young man quickly. "Lillie wasn't that kind. But this George gave her a present and it looked expensive to me."

"What kind of a present?" Sergeant Walker asked.

"Some jewelry," he said. "A necklace, I think."

"You mean a pendant?" Jackson asked.

"I guess that's it," said Mr. Horne with a grin. "I reckon you've given a few to your lady friends, sir."

Jackson sniffed and Adele burst out laughing, thinking of her kind but frugal brother losing his head over a woman enough to buy her jewelry.

She slipped out of her pocket the small wooden box with the pendant, "Mr. Horne, is this the necklace Lillie showed you?"

"That's it," he said. "I remember because the little man with the round face looked strange to me. But she said it came from George's family."

"Why do you think George's family might have owned this sort of thing?"

"I couldn't say, miss," he said. "Those shabby men go all over the place, don't they?"

"And what about this?" Adele slipped the fan out of her purse which she had wrapped carefully in a handkerchief. "Did George gave her this too?"

"I ain't never seen that before, miss," said Mr. Horne. "Don't look like something Lillie would like, though. She didn't go for ladylike fineries."

"Maybe it's another heirloom," Adele said quietly.

"I beg your pardon, miss?"

"Nothing important." Adele put the necklace and fan back in her purse.

Walker brushed the dust from his shoes. "Where were you last night, son?" He added quickly, "As a matter of record, of course."

"I was in my tent." Mr. Horne's pleasant features became anxious. "You think I killed Lillie because she threw me over?"

"No one thinks anything of the kind," Hatfield insisted. "As the sergeant said, the police must know the whereabouts of people who knew the victim on the night in question. It's a matter of routine. Nothing more, Mr. Horne."

The young man nodded. "I was in my tent, as I said. I share it with three others, and we were playing cards until curfew. Not for money," he added. "None of us have much right now, what with the banks all burned down."

"They'll pay everyone back," Jackson assured him. "It will just take time."

"They say that Italian, Giannini, he was the smart one," said Mr. Horne. "Got all the money from his bank out of town before the fires."

"These tentmates of yours can vouch for you?" Sergeant Walker asked.

"I'm sure they will," he said. "We've all become pretty friendly."

"I'm sorry I had to ask, son." Walker clasped him on the back. "This must be distressing for you."

"Even though I hadn't seen Lillie for six months," he said, rising, "I still cared for her. I'd like to help any way I can."

"You've helped, son," the sergeant said.

"Wouldn't surprise me if one of those shabby bohemians did it," he said in a harsh tone. "They looked none too gentlemanly to me. Maybe I don't got an education but I know what a gentleman looks like." He glanced at Jackson as if to prove his point.

"We won't discount that possibility," Hatfield assured him.

"Lillie was too good a person." He picked up the rag he had dropped on the sidewalk. "She'd go anywhere and help anybody. Even when it was dangerous."

"My sister is the same," said Jackson, his voice a little tender as he looked at her.

"Is that all, Sergeant?" Mr. Horne asked. "I must get back to work, you know."

"That's all for now," said the lawman.

"Mr. Horne, were Lillie friends with any of the Mexican people in the Mission?" Adele inquired.

"Friends?" The idea seemed to appall him. "Certainly not!"

"And the Chinese?" Adele asked. "Any friends among the people in Chinatown?"

"Lillie was kind, to be sure, miss," said the young man. "But she never would have made friends with any of *them*."

"*They* are people just like us, Mr. Horne," Adele said stiffly.

"It's only stupid people who refer to others as if they were animals," Nin snapped.

The young man slunk away and climbed back on the massive tractor. In a moment, the cranes were moving like the legs of a spider.

CHAPTER 19

They drove back slowly through the street. The smoke had cleared a little, and there was a pleasant breeze. The tractor noise behind them soon died away, and the car's crawling speed made it possible for them to talk. Jackson filled his friend in on their interview with Mr. Horne.

"It doesn't sound as if he had anything to do with Miss Sweenie's death," Edwards said when Jackson finished. "A man who volunteers to put his life at stake to clean up the city would hardly kill a woman in cold blood."

"The timing wouldn't make sense," Jackson agreed. "Mr. Horne said he and Miss Sweenie broke off their courtship six months ago. Why would he wait six months to do her in, if that was his intention?"

"It might have been a crime of passion," Adele offered. "You saw the stab wounds, Jack."

"It's true it wasn't a planned crime," Sergeant Walker agreed. "But I'm inclined to agree with Deputy Gossling. What do you think, Horatio?" He turned to his friend.

"I think when we get back to camp, and you have a talk with

the other young men in Mr. Horne's tent, you'll find he was where he said he was," the sheriff said.

"So we're back where we started." Sergeant Walker sighed. "Well, at least we know one man is innocent."

"Once we find this husband of hers, I'm sure things will become clearer," Jackson insisted.

"And we might talk to Miss McLeod and some of her people," Sergeant Walker added. "Though I don't relish the task. Some of those staunch reformers can get rather nasty with the police."

"According to what my friend said, Sergeant, you might have a time locating them," Adele said. "They fled to Southern California after the earthquake."

"Typical," the lieutenant mumbled.

"My friend didn't think too highly of their actions either," said Adele dryly.

"And they probably wouldn't have much to say about Lillie anyway," Nin said.

"I'm inclined to agree with you, Miss Branch," said the sergeant. "It would be difficult to locate refugees in other cities right now. I prefer not to do it unless absolutely necessary."

"We know the pendant was a gift from this George fellow, anyway," Hatfield said.

"Seems an odd gift for a husband to give his wife." Edwards shrugged.

"Maybe George lived or worked in the Orient," Jackson offered. "Or maybe his family did. They might have been in the naval service."

"It's possible." Walker nodded. "Not that we would have any way of finding out. There would have been records but they're all burned now." He shook his head.

"I don't think George was a navel man or a sailor." Adele looked into the distance where rocks piled on rocks.

"And what makes you draw that conclusion, Del?" Her brother looked at her.

"The well-rounded education," she said. "She put a lot of effort into educating herself."

"She might have been motivated by her settlement work," Nin offered.

"More likely someone like Lillie would have been motivated by love," Adele said. "I didn't get the impression she was — well, devoted through her heart, if you know what I mean. She wanted to help unfortunate people, but it was more because she had been unfortunate herself."

"You mean her reasons were more personal than altruistic," Jackson said.

"It just happened she was doing good for others at the same time." Hatfield nodded.

"So she wouldn't take the trouble to read many books unless she wanted to impress someone," Nin remarked.

"And I don't think George was one of those 'shabby young men' Mr. Horne described," Adele added. "I've met some of those shabby young men."

"Their talk is inflated but their ideas are shriveled," Nin agreed.

"I think he was a respectable young man, though most people wouldn't think it to look at him," Adele said.

"That sounds like circle talk, Del," her brother said.

"She means he might be Mexican or Chinese," her friend said bluntly. "People don't think Mexicans or Chinese are respectable even though respectability has nothing to do with either."

Adele smiled. "I knew you would know what I was driving at."

"Heaven forbid!" the lieutenant snarled as he turned a corner.

"Really, Del," Jackson sniffed. "There was nothing anyone said about Miss Sweenie to suggest such a thing."

"I think it's highly unlikely," Sergeant Walker agreed.

"So do I," Hatfield chimed in. "With her upbringing, I doubt her aunts would have even allowed the idea to enter her head."

"Well, Sheriff," Adele said in a sly tone, "as Mr. Horne pointed out, Lillie didn't tell her aunts everything."

"If she was flirting with a Mexican man, she wouldn't think it beneath her to marry one," Nin pointed out.

"That was Elsie's impression of what Miss Sweenie was doing," Jackson said. "Elsie can be a bit fanciful."

"You know the last thing someone would say about Elsie is that she's fanciful, Jack," his sister protested. "But Valda worked with Miss McLeod and her people more than Elsie, and she might know something about this George."

"We ought to talk to her, then," Nin said.

Adele patted her hand. "We will, dear."

After dinner that evening, Adele put on the most decorative suit she had brought with her and brushed off her fanciest hat. Nin watched her with a shrewd eye.

"What's all the dressing up about?" Elsie asked in an offhand manner.

"I'm going visiting," Adele said with a smile.

"Who on earth would you need to dress up for?" Elsie asked. "Valda wouldn't care if you came dressed in a flour sack."

"It's not Valda she's going to visit," Nin said slowly. "It's that detestable John Bellows."

Elsie sat up. "You're dressing up for *him*?"

"It's not 'dressing up' to put on a more refined suit and hat," Adele argued.

"You're not thinking of letting him court you again, are you, Adele?"

"Detestable!" Nin growled.

Adele laughed, pressing her friend's hand. "I've no intention of doing anything of the kind. But I promised him a visit, and I'd rather get it over with so we can concentrate on more important things."

"You didn't promise him a visit," Nin insisted. "He made you promise to visit him." She jumped up and pulled a clean dress out of her bag. "But you didn't promise to visit him alone."

Missy, who had been typing up notes from her notepad with a charred typewriter her friend Adam gave her, looked up. "May I come?"

"Don't tell me you're going to write a story on *him,*" Nin said.

"I have no interest in writing a story on a well-to-do lawyer," Missy said in a haughty tone. "I've been sitting at this thing all day and my back is killing me. I need a little air." She rose and went to her bag looking for a more presentable suit.

Adele was amused at her friends. "I hardly think John is going to be happy when I bring a whole party to his little tent."

"If he's staying with a few other men, I'm sure they'll be thrilled to see some skirts," Elsie said with a yawn. "I, for one, don't intend to give them that satisfaction."

John was happy to see her, though visibly disappointed at seeing the other women. The other two bachelors in the tent were all smiles. John, however, was shrewd enough to see Nin was uncomfortable as the men swooped over her, trying to start a flirtation.

"Gentlemen, this tent is too small for all of us. I suggest you do the ladies the honor of leaving." His tone was polite but final.

"You take my seat, my dear," said one with slick blond hair as he pushed a worn chair at Nin. "I insist upon it."

"I insist upon sitting on the floor." In her usual manner, Nin sat cross-legged on the ground. "It's much cleaner."

After the men had left, John burst out laughing. "An admirable retort, Miss Branch."

"It was the truth," Nin insisted.

"Nin likes to be as near to Mother Earth as she can." Adele sat on the chair the man had offered her friend.

"I'm afraid I don't see the point." John blinked.

"You wouldn't," Nin said.

He seemed a little put out as he reached inside a wooden box that contained coffee and sugar. "I'm afraid there are only three cups here. I didn't expect so many visitors." He looked pointedly at Adele.

"You needn't make any for me," Adele said.

"Invite a lady for coffee and then not make her coffee?" John asked with a frown. "That wouldn't be very cordial of me, would it?"

"I'll skip the coffee," Missy volunteered. "I've had too much today anyway."

"Getting your stories off about this murder?" John asked with a smile. "I heard you're a rather persistent newspaper woman."

"You don't approve?"

"Oh, it's fine when in the right place," he said.

"But San Francisco's greatest disaster isn't the right place?"

"I meant the courtroom," he said. "I still have scars from reports made by women reporters."

"You're an estate lawyer," Nin declared. "It's not as if you defend people who have killed someone."

"Families have their secrets too, Miss Branch." He turned to Adele. "And how is the case for the poor murdered woman going?"

"In the usual way," Nin said.

He still addressed Adele. "And what would the 'usual way' be?"

"The police think they've eliminated two suspects." She took the hot cup between her hands. The evening was a little chilly.

"The two aunts?" John suggested. "Surely they don't think those two old biddies —"

"Naturally not," Adele said quickly. "It would hardly be likely they would risk their social status — whatever little of it there is — by becoming involved in a murder plot."

"Still, those same old biddies aren't exactly kind and loving,"

Missy pointed out. "I had a long chat with them, and they certainly showed no real affection for their niece."

"They showed more affection for Mr. Ross than they did Lillie," Nin agreed.

"Who's Mr. Ross?" John asked.

"A former boarder," said Adele.

"And what did Mr. Ross have to say for himself?"

"Not much," Nin said. "His level of intelligence borders on the idiotic."

"That's not a very kind thing to say, Miss Branch," the lawyer said in a judicial tone. "I've seen dull-witted men accused of crimes they didn't commit."

"He was rather like a child," Adele admitted. "I suppose that's why it's unlikely he did it."

"Anyone else you think couldn't have done it?" John inquired.

"Mr. Horne — Ben Horne, Lillie's former beau."

"That sounds a little more plausible." John leaned back.

"Plausible or not, he has an alibi." Adele told him about their interview with Mr. Horne, though, aware of Missy's presence, she was brief.

When she was finished, John said, "Well, you must admit, this Horne man had the best motive for murdering Miss Sweenie if she rejected him for this George person."

"I don't think he's the type to murder a woman," Adele objected. "Especially not in that gruesome way. He has too good a heart."

"So a dull-witted man and a kind-hearted one," John mused. "Is that how you go about solving crimes? Deciding if a man is capable of committing a crime based on his character?"

"The police ruled them out, not us." Nin took a sip of the coffee, frowned, and pushed the cup away.

"You can't say character doesn't enter into the equation, Mr. Bellows," Missy pointed out.

"Of course it does," John argued. "I may only make wills and manage estates, but even my work requires a certain judgment of character." He was thoughtful for a moment. "I wonder what this George person is like."

"He has connections to the Orient." Adele's mind wandered again.

"Yes," murmured Nin. "Foreign fingers on the jade."

"Eh?" John stared at her.

"I saw it," said Nin with finality.

"You mean it's one of those otherworldly visions of yours?" John looked amused.

"I don't have otherworldly visions, Mr. Bellows," Nin said. "I see truths others don't see."

Adele felt her anger rise. "I think you owe Miss Branch an apology, John."

The lawyer bowed. "My abject apologies, Miss Branch."

Adele poured the last of the sludge-like coffee in her cup. "If what Mr. Horne said is true, and George gave Lillie the pendant, then he probably also gave her the fan. And they both came from the same place."

"Which is?" Missy asked. "The Orient?"

"Perhaps," Adele said vaguely.

"The police are going to have a hard time finding the fellow," John said. "No records left at city hall nor any of the government offices here."

"Mayor Schmitz will be happy of that, from what I hear," Missy said.

"I don't think they would have helped anyway," Adele said. "I've a feeling George is someone she knew through her work."

"Why do you say that?" John asked.

"Her aunts clearly kept a tight leash on her acquaintances," Adele said.

"They wanted her to marry some fussy young man with a good education and position," Nin agreed.

"I think Mr. Ross and Mr. Horne painted a picture of a young woman who wasn't going to follow that prescription." Adele nodded. "Not that I blame her one bit. I know what those young sons of the rich are like."

"Thankfully, I don't fall under that category," said John in a dry tone.

"She could only have met George during the work she did when she was away from them," Adele concluded.

"What about Elsie?" John inquired. "She has a fairly wide net when it comes to good works."

"We do get ideas of our own now and then, John," Adele said archly. "We asked her and she doesn't remember encountering a George in her work."

"Well, her circle includes lots of other young ladies," John argued. "I'm sure several of them ended up here, or Elsie knows where they are. Why not ask them?"

"The reform organization Lillie worked with fled to Southern California," Adele said. "No one knows just where."

"George might have worked with other organizations," he pointed out.

Adele smiled. "You might have something there, John."

"Lawyers get ideas once in a blue moon too," he said ruefully.

"Perhaps you'll get an idea about these." Adele showed him the fan and necklace. When she saw he was squinting, she handed him the magnifying glass her father gave her, which she always wore on a chain around her neck.

"You certainly come prepared with the tools of your trade," he remarked as he scrutinized the items.

"Papa gave that to me," she said in a quiet voice. There was silence for a moment. "Well?"

"I don't think these are from the Orient," he said. "I think they were bought right here in Chinatown."

"Elsie said she's only seen dragons and Buddhas," Nin said.

John chuckled. "Elsie's only worked with the poor, Miss

Branch. What she saw were likely cheap souvenirs in the windows of curioso shops."

"I thought this was more expensive." Adele nodded.

"The necklace is a fine piece of jewelry," John said. "And the fan is exquisite. These are the sort of things a fine jeweler or an antique shop would carry."

"I've never seen a fine jeweler carry Chinese artifacts," Missy observed.

"They do in Chinatown." He leaned back. "We had a case once, a dispute between two merchants, one a jeweler and one an antique dealer. The jeweler had a shop in Chinatown. I went down there to give them some papers, and there were pendants displayed in the window similar to this one. The owner told me only the most expensive jade can be used for their deities. No jewelry maker would dare use the cheap jade you find in the curioso shops for such distinguished figures."

Missy's eyes were shining. "That would mean this George person might be wealthy."

"Not wealthy, perhaps," said Adele. "But well-off. And cultured."

"Not one of the shaggy young men from the league," Nin scoffed.

"No," Adele murmured. "An educated man who knows about Chinese culture." She felt Nin's cat-like eyes on her. She rose. "We ought to get back, John."

He took her hands. "Come anytime, Adele." He lowered his voice. "After all this is over, perhaps you'll spend the day with me in the city. Alone."

Adele tried not to smile. "I consider you a friend, John. You know that."

"Friend!" Nin snorted as they made their way back to their tent. "You can bet his life will get back to normal in no time once the city gets on its feet while everyone else will still be struggling."

"I daresay Mr. Bellows is one of those sharks who is prepared for anything," Missy agreed. "He probably has most of his assets in a bank outside the city."

Adele laughed. "I don't think John is that devious." She pulled her jacket closer around her. "He gave me an idea, though."

"An idea about George?" Nin's gaze was shrewd. "You think you know who he is?"

"No," Adele said. "But I'm beginning to get a picture of him in my mind."

"When you have the picture, will you let me know?" Missy asked. "I promised Adam an exclusive on all of this."

"An exchange of favors?" Nin eyed her.

"Don't be vulgar, Miss Branch," the reporter snapped.

In their tent, Valda was just getting ready to leave. She greeted the ladies warmly. "We missed you at the women's aid tent today."

"We were going to come in the morning," Adele said.

The woman's face grew worn. "Those poor ladies!"

"Dragging their offspring by the hand with nothing but the clothes on their backs," Elsie agreed with a sigh. "They didn't have much to begin with but now they have nothing."

"We're almost out of supplies again," Valda said. "The Sacramento women won't get the boxes on the train until the day after tomorrow."

"You can offer them comfort and hope." Adele pressed her hand. "That means something, dear."

"Comfort and hope won't feed their children, Adele," she said.

"They came to Angel Island fleeing Russia," Elsie supplied. "Not a very warm welcome for their squalid homes to be ruined with Mother Nature's rage, is it?"

"Mother Nature builds as easily as she destroys," Nin said. "She brings them into your hands."

"What a lovely thing to say, Miss Branch." Valda gave her a sweet smile. Nin smiled back.

"Before you go, you might be able to give us some information." Adele took off the visiting gloves and hat.

"Elsie's been telling me about this young lady found dead in the brush." She shook her head. "It's tragic to have a murder amidst all this pandemonium."

"Maybe that was the idea," Missy suggested. "Maybe whoever killed Lillie saw his opportunity with all the chaos."

"With her chest full of holes?" Nin shuddered.

"Jack told me when a killer uses that much violence, it's like he swallowed a match that's lit him on fire on the inside," Adele said. "It's a sudden wave of rage that comes on and then is gone."

"What could she have done to ignite such a rage?" Valda murmured.

"Nothing," Elsie said with a tight lip. "Women only have to breathe the wrong way for some man to attack them."

"Oh, Elsie, not all men are like that," Valda chided. Her fellow suffragist sniffed and turned over on the cot.

The woman took Adele's arm. "What information do you need from me, dear?"

Adele told her what they had learned so far.

"Lillie Sweenie." Valda repeated. "I think I remember her. Red hair, oval face, medium height?"

"That sounds right." Adele looked at Nin, who nodded in agreement.

"She worked with Karen's group?" Valda glanced at Elsie. "The City Dwellers League, wasn't it?" Elsie nodded. "I remember them all right." Her tone was not exactly warm.

"Could any of them could have befriended Lillie?" Adele asked.

"I doubt it," said Valda. "They're strictly for the cause. They have that hypocritical approach of fighting for humanity when they have little affection for it."

"That's what I told her," Elsie said.

"Do you remember a George among them?" Adele asked. "Or have you ever worked with a George?"

Valda laughed. "We must have a dozen Georges working with us. As for the league, I really can't say." She blinked. "Why George and not Tim or Tom?"

"Because the police believe a George gave Lillie these." Adele took out the pendant and fan.

Valda touched the fan, unfolding it carefully so it looked as grand as the open feathers of a peacock. "Rather stunning, isn't it?"

"John's theory is that it comes from a jewelry shop, not one of those shops pouring out their wares into the streets of China-town," Adele said.

"You talked to him about the case?" Elsie looked surprised.

"He dragged it out of her," Nin grumbled.

"I think he was just looking to practice his lawyer skills," Missy said with a giggle. "Lawyers love to act like lawyers even when it isn't their case."

"He might be right." There was silence in the tent as Valda inspected the jade. She was almost as thorough as John.

Elsie watched her. "A rather strange Buddha, don't you think?"

"That's because it's not a Buddha," Valda said. "It's Yue Lao."

"Who?" Elsie sat up and Missy had her pencil poised over her pad.

"Yue Lao," the woman repeated. "The god of marriage and love."

"And just how do you know that?" Nin challenged.

"The ribbon he's holding," said the woman. "It's a symbol of the cord that ties the marriage bond." Her voice lowered as she handed it back to Adele. "It's a very lovely thing and must have been given with the utmost affection."

"By her husband!" Adele grasped the pendant. "Who else would give Lillie a symbol of love and marriage?"

"But who would know this Yue Lao was the god of love and marriage?" Elsie asked. "It may all be a coincidence."

"I think not." Adele's eyes grew misty as she now had an outline of the man named George. "I think not."

As she put the pendant away, she caught Nin's intense gaze. She wondered if her friend sensed what was on her mind.

CHAPTER 20

$\mathcal{A}$dele slept restlessly and woke up early the next morning, her eyes as wide as if it were midday. She quietly dressed so as not to wake up the others. She took the pendant and fan out of their boxes and tucked each carefully in the pockets of her skirt. As she stepped out of the tent into the early morning fog, she felt a tug on her arm. She knew who it was even before she turned around.

"You're not going to the Chinese camp alone," whispered Nin. Her friend was also dressed with her hair gathered on top of her head in combs, an uncommon look for Nin.

"How do you know where I'm going?" Adele asked.

"I knew what you were thinking last night," said her friend.

"If John and Valda are right and those artifacts came from a lucrative shop, someone there might know where they would sell such things." Adele pulled her jacket around her to block out the chilly morning air.

"You can't hide things from me, Adele." Nin looked hurt. "It's not the shops you're looking for. It's George Wu."

Adele was silent for a moment. "I didn't think you'd remember his name."

"I remember him all right," she said. "G.W. It fits, doesn't it?"

"We have no proof."

"Well, then, let's get some." Her friend took her arm.

Adele lingered near a tree. "It might not be pleasant, dear. We'll have to dodge the diligent Sergeant Kerry."

"They have their breakfast before the rest of us," Nin said simply. "There ought to be only a few of the lower-ranking soldiers on guard, and they'll be half asleep at this hour."

Adele grinned. "And just how do you know that?"

"Because yesterday morning I took a walk before the sun was up and peeked into the dining room tents, and there they were," Nin said with a sly smile. "Sergeant Kerry and Private Dobson in all their military glory with their heads down on the table, snoring away."

Adele laughed and pressed her friend's hand.

They made their way along the gritty paths near the brush, stepping carefully so as not to make too much noise with broken twigs and moving branches. It seemed like hours before Adele could at last see the paltry candles around the small tents that made up the Chinese camp. By then the sky had more of a gray pallor and she could see outlines of the landscape. She saw Nin was right. There seemed to be only two soldiers, and they both had their heads lolled forward, their bayonets shrugged over their shoulders as they sat in front of the entrance to the camp.

Treading carefully, she and Nin crept along the outside of the camp and entered from the back. Many of the Chinese people were already up, moving slowly and silently. They noted the newcomers but seemed neither alarmed nor surprised. They only stared as she and Nin passed.

Adele approached an elderly woman, her face wrinkled but her eyes alert. "We'd like to see George Wu." She kept her voice low.

The woman looked at her and suddenly began to speak in Chinese in a loud voice. Adele tried to explain their purpose but the woman seemed not to understand. Her loud talk made a little girl of about eight or nine pop her head out of the tent, her eyes still half closed. Her thick black hair hung around her face like a shell.

The girl said something to the woman in Chinese with a yawn. The woman turned to her and unleashed a string of Chinese words, occasionally pointing to Adele and Nin. The girl was wide awake now and stepped out of the tent. Adele's heart went out to her as she saw the child wore a dress obviously made of flimsy material and no shoes.

"You're looking for someone?" the child asked in perfect English.

"George Wu," Nin said.

"I can show you."

Adele took her hand, and the girl turned around, looking surprised, but then relaxed and smiled. Nin took her other hand.

She led them through a maze of tents, and Adele saw many of the people were already starting fires and making tea. She hadn't realized there was no dining room tent for them, and her anger swelled at the injustice.

They turned a corner and came upon one tiny tent with leaves and roots hanging on a cord like laundry. Nin stopped, her eyes wide as she touched a branch with flat leaves and a root that looked like a beige carrot with fringes at the end of it.

"Ginseng," Nin breathed. "So hard to find."

"Jun Shu is a medicine woman," said the child. "When I have a cold, she gives me a terrible-tasting medicine."

Adele laughed. "But it makes you feel better, doesn't it?"

"I suppose so," grumbled the girl.

A woman came out and rushed toward Nin, growling in Chinese and waving her arms. Nin backed away, clasping her hands together.

"Tell her my friend knows about herbs," Adele said.

The girl spoke to the woman in Chinese. The woman smiled

and pointed to some of the herbs. When she saw Nin didn't understand her, she plucked them from the cord, pushing them into Nin's hands. Adele could see her friend was touched, and, after putting them in her pocket, Nin kissed the woman's hands. Contented, she returned to her tent.

"Why do you want to see George Wu?" the girl suddenly asked.

"We have some questions we'd like to ask him," Adele explained.

"He knows us," Nin added.

"Oh, everybody knows you," said the girl in an offhand manner. "You're the ladies who give us things."

Adele smiled. "Then we should introduce ourselves. I'm Adele and this is Miss Branch. And who are you, young lady?"

"Lei Chang." The girl put out her hand. "I spell it like L-E-E because it's more American."

Adele shook her hand and Nin, although it wasn't her practice to touch strangers, shook it also.

"George is over there." Lee pointed toward a larger tent with a few chairs outside. "I have to get back to Grandma. She's not very well." Her little face darkened.

"You tell Grandma we'll send some food and clothes for you and her." Adele petted the girl's head.

"You're good ladies." Lee smiled. "Everybody says so." She trotted off in the direction of her tent.

"That's why no one is bothering us," Nin said as they passed a tent with a family bending over a fire. "They think we're good."

"They *know* we're good," Adele said in a firm tone. "Elsie isn't the only one who has connections. I'll tell Missy to send a telegram to Oda in Sacramento. I'm sure she can get some things for them."

They reached the tent just as two Chinese men were coming out. They were well-dressed with severe expressions as if they had just been debating some serious issue. They did not ogle them as the young men in Mr. Ross' tent had. They gave the women a bow without looking at them and retreated to another part of the camp.

Adele could barely see inside the tent as the light was dim, but she caught sight of George Wu sitting at a broken table in the corner. He was leaning forward with his face in his hands. Her heart went out to the clearly distraught young man.

"Mr. Wu?" she ventured.

He jumped up. "Miss Gossling! Miss Branch!"

"You remember us." Adele smiled at him as she advanced.

"You shouldn't be here." He glanced toward the front of the camp. "If the patrol sees you —"

"We're not afraid of them," Nin said.

"We must speak with you, Mr. Wu," Adele said. "It's urgent."

"You shouldn't be here," he said again. "It isn't fitting for —"

Adele smiled. "Mr. Wu, my friend and I have been in many places not fitting for a woman."

"We've been in bars and lion's cages," Nin declared.

The young man's lips curved into a little smile. "Perhaps that's why you're not afraid of the patrol."

"Is there somewhere else you prefer we talk?" Adele suddenly noticed there were faces peering in with open curiosity. Nin jumped with alarm as two children reached out a tentative hand to touch her long dark hair.

Mr. Wu took command. "They won't hurt you, Miss Branch. They haven't seen many white women since the quake."

Nin's cat-like eyes lost some of their suspicion.

"I think we'd better go someplace else." Mr. Wu put on his coat. "We'll have a crowd here soon, and the patrol will wonder what's going on."

Adele saw immediately how people respected the young man. As he guided them, they spoke to him in Chinese, men nodding with smiles, women bowing, and children dodging his playful pats on their heads.

They made their way outside the camp with Mr. Wu glancing carefully around. He guided them into the wooded area. Adele realized with a little cold running in her blood the place was not far from where they had found Lillie.

They reached a cluster of redwoods. He took off his jacket, laying it like a blanket on the ground and motioned for them to sit.

"Is this about aid?" he asked. "We received a few boxes of clothes and food yesterday from your forceful friend, but we wouldn't refuse more."

Adele smiled, realizing the "forceful friend" was Elsie. "We'll send over as much as we can, Mr. Wu. But we've come to see you about something entirely different."

"Oh?"

"Murder," Nin said with finality.

"I beg your pardon?" He flinched.

"I'm sure you've heard a Caucasian woman was found dead in this area." Adele watched the young man's face. Although the sun was weak, she could see the delicate features bend.

"We don't hear anything about the main camp here," he said shortly. "I don't think I can help you."

"But you've heard it, haven't you?" Nin eyed him.

"I'm like everyone else here, Miss Branch," he said. "No better and no worse."

"I imagine you work with the army to procure supplies and food for your camp," Adele said. "Camps are much like neighborhoods, Mr. Wu. When people are bored, they turn to gossiping about what's going on inside their own little worlds."

There was silence for a moment as Mr. Wu played with a piece of dry brush. "You ought to be a detective or a policewoman, Miss Gossling."

"She practically is," said Nin.

"My friend and I are helping the sergeant in charge of this murder investigation," Adele said.

"How intriguing," he mumbled.

"It's necessary, Mr. Wu," said Adele firmly. "The police are stretched thin with this tragedy, and Sergeant Walker needs all the help he can get."

"I still don't see what I can do," he said. "Naturally, it's a terrible thing, but it has nothing to do with us."

"Her name was Lillie Sweenie," Adele said.

"I'm not familiar with that name." He broke a leg from the branch.

Nin whispered in Adele's ear, "He's lying!" Her friend always seemed to know when people weren't telling the truth.

Adele took the drawing Missy had done of Lillie and held it out to him. "This is what she looked like."

For a moment, the young man seemed to be losing the well-designed look of indifference as his face became even more distorted. But he quickly caught himself and handed it back to her. "As I said, we have little to do here with the other side of the camp."

"She wasn't found on the other side of the camp," Nin said. "She was found here."

"And the police suspect a Chinese killed her, is that it?" His tone was grim.

"The police are considering all possibilities, Mr. Wu," Adele said.

"All possibilities that lead to our camp," he said warily. "If the girl was found near here, they'll hardly look elsewhere." He rose. "Thank you for the warning. We'll deal with the police when they come."

"We found some interesting things in Lillie's suitcase," Adele said as she took out the fan and pendant. "Perhaps you can help us identify them."

Only then did his plaster countenance break down. He stared at them and suddenly crumpled to his knees, burying his face in his hands as he let out shaking sobs. She and Nin sat silent while the young man cried.

Strains of high-pitched voices from the Chinese camp could be heard from a distance. In a soft tone, Adele said, "She was your wife, wasn't she?"

The young man did not look at her. "Yes. She was my wife." He raised his head. "May I see that picture again?"

Adele pressed it in his hand. "Keep it."

He clutched at it. "Who drew it?"

"A friend of ours," said Nin.

"How did you know we were married?"

"Her wedding ring," Adele said. "G.W."

"You told the police?" His eyes widened with terror.

"We haven't told them anything," Nin assured him.

"I didn't kill her!" Mr. Wu looked from one to the other. In spite of the dimming light, Adele could see he was really frightened.

"We haven't come here to accuse you, Mr. Wu," she said.

His voice softened. "I know. You've come as friends. Call me George, please."

"You call me Adele." She smiled. "Miss Branch is Miss Branch."

"Adele." He leaned a little toward her and then, as if remembering his place, jerked back. "Believe me, I want to find who did this to my poor Lillie as much as you do. I loved her."

"We don't doubt that, George," she said kindly. "And you can help us by answering our questions openly and honestly."

"I'll try," he promised.

Adele wrapped her arms around her knees. "Tell us about you and Lillie."

He was silent for a moment, as if gathering his thoughts. "Lillie was — I don't know if I can describe it."

"Color-blind?" Nin asked, then blushed. "I'm sorry. That was an awful thing to say."

"But it's what most people would say," he said ruefully. "But it wasn't that, Miss Branch. It was everything. She didn't care how someone looked or where they came from. She cared what sort of person they were. She used to say people were like the lion in winter. Strip him of his roar and you have a cat looking for affection, just like any other cat."

Adele's heart pinched to see the tender look in his eyes as he spoke of his wife. "It's no wonder she became interested in settlement house work." He glanced at her in surprise. "I've done such work too, George. I have friends who remember Lillie."

He gave a small smile. "I'm glad they remember her that way."

"How did you meet her?" Nin asked.

"Lillie did a lot for our community," he said. "She never saw us as pariahs like everyone else. She won our trust, and that's not an easy thing to do."

"I can imagine," Adele said with sympathy.

"She worked with the Six Companies during the plague," he said. "When it was all over, they invited her to the Chinese New Year parade."

"That is an honor indeed," Adele complimented.

"It seems odd you and she would meet at a parade with hundreds of people," Nin mused.

He smiled. "It wasn't quite like that, Miss Branch. She was standing outside a shop right next to my father's and some boys were setting off fireworks. The noise made her jump, and she ran right into our place, thinking it was another Chinese rebellion." He chuckled.

"And she ran right into your arms?" Nin asked, a little incredulously.

"It wasn't quite that romantic," he said. "I was tending my father's shop at the time. I offered her some tea and we talked. She was interested in some of the artifacts we had from the Qing Dynasty." He paused and explained, "My father owned an antique shop and was a dealer until the quake."

"Is that where these came from?" Adele nodded toward the fan and pendant.

The young man nodded. "My father gave them to her."

"What lovely gifts," Adele said softly.

"Lillie started coming by after that whenever she was in Chinatown," he continued. "We would have tea and chat, or my father and I would invite her upstairs to our flat for a meal." He added, "My mother was a Southern belle from Mississippi and taught me how to fry catfish and make hush puppies."

Adele laughed. "You had a very adventurous childhood indeed!"

"I suppose it's what happens when you're a child of a miscegenational marriage."

"When did you ask Lillie to marry you?"

"About a year after the Chinese New Year," he said. "On the day of the parade, in fact."

"Rather a bold move," Nin remarked. She blushed again.

He smiled a little. "If you had known Lillie and what she was like, Miss Branch, you would know it was more like a confirmation of what we both knew in our hearts."

"And she accepted right away," Adele said with a smile.

"She accepted, but we didn't get married right away," he said.

"Because her aunts knew nothing about you?" Nin guessed. "We've spoken to them. They think she should have married Ben Horne."

"Ben Horne?"

"A young man she knew," Adele said quietly.

"The way her aunts treated her —" He sighed.

"Like she was a burden," Nin said.

"She didn't want to hurt them," he said. "She never wanted anybody hurt."

"But you did eventually get married," Adele prompted.

"We had to go to Washington to do it," he said "They don't allow miscegenation in California."

"When did you marry?"

"April of last year." His voice caught, trying to hold back tears. "Just a year ago."

"And you kept the marriage secret for a year?" Adele stared at him.

"When you're in love but there are obstacles, Miss Gossling, you do what you have to." He stiffened. "I've been looking for work in Hawaii where there are more opportunities for Chinese men like myself."

"But you're only half-Chinese," Nin objected.

He glared at her. "My heritage is as important to me as yours is to you, Miss Branch."

"I don't give a hang about my heritage," she retorted. Adele knew she was thinking of her mother and how she had turned away from the rigid social obligations of her wealthy family to live her life as a healer.

"Well, I do," he said with a half-smile. "And Lillie agreed with me."

"You lived apart for a year," Adele said softly.

"We saw one another as often as we could," he said. "We met on Sundays."

"The aunts told us she was meeting Ben Horne," Nin said with a sly look.

"I suppose she had to give them some excuse." He looked down at the ground. "I'm sorry for the fellow, but love is love."

"Sundays were your meeting days, then," Adele said.

"It was the only time she could really get away from her aunts, as they usually went visiting after church services on that day."

"You must have been frustrated she didn't tell them," Adele said.

"I understood, Miss Gossling," he said. "If we had plans for the future, it would have been different. But we didn't, other than knowing we couldn't live together in this state." His voice was firmer. "It's against the law in California for a Chinese man and a Caucasian woman to marry."

"You were both taking a risk," Nin said.

"Only a slight one," he insisted. "She was working with Miss McLeod's group so people were used to seeing her in Chinatown. Now I wish I hadn't insisted on staying here. I wish we had found passage to Hawaii or anywhere but here after the fires burned out. This might not have happened if I had." He bit his lip and bent his head so his face was invisible.

"You couldn't have done anything." Adele laid a hand on the young man's shoulder.

"Your father approved of your marriage, didn't he?" Nin asked. "He gave her gifts, after all."

The young man smiled. "The fan was my grandmother's. My great-grandfather made it for her."

"And the pendant?" Adele asked. "It's Yue Lao, isn't it?"

"How did you know?" He stared.

"A friend told us," Adele said. "The god of love and marriage."

"Father gave it to her after we told him we were engaged," he said. "He said it would ensure a happy union."

"And he was right," Adele said. "It was a happy union for a year, in spite of all the obstacles, wasn't it?"

He gave her a hard look. "It would have been a happy union for fifty years if Lillie hadn't been —"

"Of course it would have been," Nin said in a fierce tone.

Adele gripped the young man's hand. "George, you realize you need to tell the police all of this."

"If I did, they would arrest me," he said.

"They're looking for a George now," Nin said. "They found your note to Lillie."

The young man was silent for a moment. "I see."

"You must go to them and tell them what you've just told us," Adele said firmly.

"They'll be looking for a Caucasian George, not a Chinese George," he pointed out.

"There's no way your name can be kept out of this," Adele insisted. "They'll have to know about your marriage. We also found her ring, remember."

"You don't know what it's like, Miss Gossling," he said. "You don't know how they treat us. We're not just inferior in their eyes. We're infidels, no better than the rats that roam this city."

"All the more reason you should come with us," Adele said. "An honorable man would do that. And you're an honorable man, George."

"Yes," he said quietly. "I'm an honorable man. But will they let me be honorable?"

"We'll see to it that they do," Adele promised and Nin squared her shoulders in agreement.

CHAPTER 21

By this time the sun shone a brilliant yellow against the blue sky, and the morning was in its full glory. The three of them walked to the main camp, keeping to the edge of the wooded area so the patrolling soldiers wouldn't stop them. The young man looked nervous, his eyes darting around and his shoulders flinching at every noise.

"If anyone should see me with two white women —" he started.

"What will they think?" Adele asked. "That you're kidnapping us?"

"You don't know how imaginative bigoted people can be, Miss Gossling," he insisted.

"Then we'll beat them with this to knock some sense into them," Nin snarled as she snatched a thick branch from the ground, holding it like a club. This made George laugh.

It was past the breakfast hour, and people had returned to their tents or were lingering outside chatting. Several turned to look at them, a few surprised, several sneering, but most curious.

They made it to the police tent and when Adele peered in, she saw the lawmen along with Edwards. They were all sitting at the small wooden table hunched over papers.

"We might divide the list into the refugee camps —" The lieutenant stopped as they entered. His eyes fell immediately on the young man behind them.

"Good morning!" Adele said in a cheerful tone. She could already see the thundering look on her brother's face.

"Where the devil have you been, Del?" he roared.

"Really, Mr. Gossling, such language in front of ladies." Nin sniffed.

"I know it's impossible to regulate your comings and goings when we're in Arrojo," he said. "But I was hoping you would be a little more disciplined here with all this chaos."

"We're not prisoners, Mr. Gossling," Nin said archly. "We can go where we please whenever we please."

"That's just what you can't do," Edwards said. "The army has strict rules about where civilians can and cannot go, Miss Branch." He glared at George. "They have even stricter rules for the Chinese."

"I'm well aware of that, sir," George said in a quiet tone.

"You'll want to speak to this man." Adele took his arm and brought him forward so all the men could see him.

"You'll want to hear what he has to tell you," Nin added.

"This is George Wu," Adele announced. "Lillie's husband."

"G.W!" Sergeant Walker sprang up. "Good Lord!"

"A Chinaman!" the lieutenant exclaimed. "I don't believe it!"

"You mean you don't believe Miss Sweenie — or should I say Mrs. Wu — married this man?" Hatfield asked with a little smile. "And why not? He looks like an upstanding and bright young man."

George bowed in gratitude.

"Upstanding and bright!" Edwards growled.

"I think we ought to hear what Mr. Wu has to say, Monte,"

Jackson said in a quiet tone. He produced a plate covered with a napkin, pushing it at his sister. "We saved you some toast."

"I am a little hungry," Adele admitted as she accepted the chair the sheriff offered her.

"I'm starving!" Nin plucked the toast from the plate.

"Didn't we see you with my sister a few days ago?" Jackson studied him. "The night before Miss Sweenie was murdered, in fact."

"I came to thank her and Miss Branch for helping us." George's tone was soft but dignified.

"Has Miss Gossling explained to you what this is all about, Mr. Wu?" Walker moved his chair to let the young man sit down. Edwards, who had been sitting next to Jackson, immediately moved his chair a little away from the young man.

"Yes." He hesitated for a moment, before adding, "You're trying to find my wife's murderer."

"Then she really was your wife?" Walker asked.

"Can you prove it?" Edwards challenged.

George took a ring out of his pocket and handed it to the sergeant. Sergeant Walker examined it, then handed it to Hatfield. "The same inscription as the one we found near Mrs. Wu's body."

"You can also contact the county auditor in King County in Washington for a copy of our marriage license," George said. "I suppose that would be proof enough."

Seeing the gray look on George's face, the sergeant put his hand on his shoulder. "I'm sorry, son."

"We'll do all we can to find who did it," Hatfield promised as he handed him back the ring. "Maybe you'd better tell us all about it, Mr. Wu."

George briefly related the same story he had told Adele and Nin. As he spoke, Edwards circled the tent, his arms crossed, and his gaze never wavering in its suspicion toward the young man. Despite the fact that he was her brother's friend, Adele felt her anger rise. She could tell Jackson was none too happy about the lieutenant's attitude.

"So your wife never got a chance to tell her aunts she was married," Sergeant Walker concluded after George finished. "That much is evident from what they told us."

"She was going to that night." George swallowed. "The night she was killed, that is."

"You met with her then?" Walker glanced at him.

"I believe you found the note I wrote," said the young man. "That's what I've been told, anyway."

The sergeant produced a tin box and unlocked it. "Miss Gossling, if I may have that fan and pendant now. I don't believe you'll need them anymore." Adele dutifully gave them to him, and he put them in the box. He then took out an envelope where he had put the note they found in Lillie's dressing gown. George didn't even glance at it as he nodded.

"Weren't you taking a chance getting a note to her?" Jackson eyed him.

"I sent it with one of the children," he said. "The soldiers are more favorable toward Chinese children than they are adults."

"So you used a child as your liaison?" Edwards narrowed his eyes. "That's a low thing to do."

"It's a smart thing to do," Adele said. "As Jack will tell you, we use young ladies from a local school in Arrojo to get information for us. No one minds a child being where she oughtn't to be, and they don't assume she has enough intelligence to understand what they're saying. Especially girls." She met his gaze with equal vigor.

"Lee's a spirited sort," said George. "She wants to be a spy someday."

"She'll be a very successful one," Nin said dryly. "We've met her."

"When did you send this note with the child?" the sergeant asked.

"Early morning when the soldiers are at breakfast," he said. "I told her to wait until Lillie stepped out of the tent to wash her face. She always rose earlier than her aunts." He smiled ruefully. "Lee told me she put it in the pocket of a dressing gown lying over the end of Lillie's cot to make sure she would find it discreetly. I told you the girl is spirited."

"No wonder Lillie was excited and agitated all day," Adele said. When George gave her a questioning look, she added, "Miss Addie told us."

"Miss Addie," the young man murmured. "One of the aunts."

"Why did you want to meet her after curfew?" asked Jackson.

"Isn't it rather obvious?" asked George. "The soldiers take their dinner late, and the ones on guard are more interested in their food than in us. I knew it would be easier for me to get away from the camp."

"And put your wife at risk for an attack or worse," the lieutenant snarled. "And the worst happened." He eyed him. "Or did you know that was going to happen, Mr. Wu?"

"I had nothing to do with my wife's death," the young man declared in a jagged tone. "When I left her, she was alive and well." He paused a moment. "She was happy. Very happy." The muscles of his neck strained.

"And why was she happy, sir?" Sergeant Walker asked.

"Because we were going away together. We were going to leave this place." He pressed his hands together.

"You were going to Oakland?" the sergeant prompted. "I realize that's where most of your people went after the fires ceased."

"Not to Oakland," said George. "Hawaii." Walker stared at him. "I found employment there with a man who owns several antique shops and wanted someone who knows Chinese artifacts to manage them."

"And the Hawaiian people are much more tolerant than we

are," Adele said softly, remembering the young man's words. He glanced at her and she gave him a smile of encouragement.

This seemed to calm him. "It's what we've been waiting for, Sergeant. She was going to tell her aunts about it in the morning." A small gasp came from his throat. "But she never got the chance, did she?"

"You mean you never gave her the chance!" Edwards said. "You were going to Hawaii alright but without the burden of a wife on your hands!"

George gave him an ironic look. "If you had any knowledge of miscegenation, Lieutenant, you would know such marriages can be quite advantageous."

"For your side," the man snapped.

"For both sides," George corrected. "I should know. I'm the child of one."

"You had no business —"

"Lieutenant." Walker's voice was sharp and resonant. "Mr. and Mrs. Wu's marriage is not in question here. So I would greatly appreciate it if you would keep your mouth shut!"

"I'm sorry, sir." The lieutenant retreated to the corner.

"He sounds anything but sorry," Nin mumbled.

When was all this to take place?" Sergeant Walker continued. "Your leaving, that is?"

"As soon as my father could get us passage on a ship," said George. "He has some connections in that area. He thought it could take him three days, perhaps a week."

"That soon?" Hatfield asked. "Your father must be a very important person indeed."

"Only in our community, sir," said George. "To the outside world, he's just another Oriental."

"What time did you meet and for how long?" asked Walker.

"I can't say for sure, Sergeant," said George. "I didn't look at my watch."

"To the best of your knowledge," Sheriff Hatfield said, a little impatient.

"I knew it would take Lillie at least forty minutes to reach the meeting place," he said. "And I knew she would need to wait a little bit until her aunts were asleep. She was a very cautious person."

"Go on." Walker leaned back.

"After the curfew bell rang at ten o'clock, I deduced she would wait about twenty minutes, a half hour at the most," he said slowly. "And it would take her at least forty minutes to walk, so I arrived at our meeting place at —"

"Eleven forty-five," Edwards finished. "We can count just as well as you can."

George glared at him. "As this is a crime, sir, I imagine the sergeant will want the information to be as accurate as possible."

"I appreciate that, son," said Sergeant Walker.

"Lillie came about five minutes later," he said. "It might have been ten. Again, I didn't look at my watch so I can't be sure."

"How long did you stay?"

"No more than twenty minutes, a half hour," said the young man. "I told her about my job offer. She was a little hesitant about going to Hawaii, mostly because she wasn't sure whether people would look upon our union in a favorable light." He smiled a little. "Lillie was always game for anything but I suppose the earthquake and fires unhinged her a little."

"Just as it has everyone else," Jackson remarked.

"But you convinced her?" Hatfield prompted.

"I showed her an article a friend of mine had written in a Hawaiian newspaper," he said. "A Caucasian friend." He looked meaningfully at Edwards. "It was all about how we're treated here and how Hawaiians consider the Chinese to be decent people and contributing citizens to their communities."

"And that convinced her," Adele guessed.

"She wanted both of us to be happy," he said in a soft tone.

"She would have gone to China with me if I had asked her." He added in a rueful tone, "China is as foreign to me as it is to her. We're Americans and we intended to stay in America." This last earned a growl from the lieutenant.

"I imagine she was excited about leaving," Adele murmured.

"Leaving pain behind and looking forward to happiness," Nin added in a vague tone.

"She agreed to be ready to leave when my father arranged for passage," said George.

"Then what happened?" Walker asked.

"It must have been midnight when I left," he began.

"You saw her back to her tent?" Jackson asked.

"No, sir," said the man. "I left first to go back to my camp alone."

"Left first!" Edwards pounced on him. "You mean you let a woman walk across this camp at that hour alone?"

George stiffened. "Lillie insisted. She knew the army was stricter with curfew for our camp than for other camps, and she didn't want to risk my being caught.

"I imagine she could take care of herself," Adele added.

George nodded. "She spent many hours in areas of the city I'm sure the fine lieutenant would never dare to approach."

"It might have been risky for you to have accompanied her at that," Walker agreed. "A Chinese man with a white woman — and with 'shoot to kill' orders all over the place —" He shook his head.

"So you didn't see Mrs. Wu leave," Hatfield surmised.

"She told me she would wait a few minutes and then go back to her camp," he said.

"Did you now?" Edwards studied him. "Or maybe the story is quite a different one, Mr. Wu."

"What do you mean?" George stared at him.

"Maybe Mrs. Wu wasn't so keen on moving to the other side of the world," the lieutenant began.

"I would hardly call Hawaii the other side of the world," the sergeant remarked.

"Maybe she wasn't keen on being married to a Chinaman anymore," Edwards continued. "And maybe that didn't sit quite well with you."

"Monte —" Jackson began in a warning tone.

"So you took a knife and stabbed her in the chest!" the lieutenant said.

"And where would I get a knife?" George growled.

"You said your father owned an antique shop." Edwards reached into the box and took out the knife. "You could have gotten this very easily."

The Chinese man stared in horror at the weapon. "Is that what killed my wife?"

"We're told it's a Chinese fisherman's knife," Edwards said. "That's true, isn't it?"

"Well, yes, but —"

"Your father has such a knife in his shop?" the lieutenant darted out.

George seemed to collect himself a little. "My father no longer has a shop, sir."

"I asked if he had a knife like this," Edwards snapped. "One you might have taken with you for sentimental reasons before you fled."

George's lip tightened. "No, Lieutenant. My father dealt with high-quality artifacts, not peasant tools."

"And he just told you Lillie agreed to go with him to Hawaii," Nin said. "You're talking through your soldier's cap, Lieutenant."

"You always were a little too bulldog in your ways, Monte," Jackson snapped.

"Perhaps if you would open your blind eyes, Lieutenant, you would see George has helped us," Adele said.

"And at the risk of incriminating himself," Nin added.

All the men turned to them.

"Dr. Fleming gave us a window of time for Lillie's death," Adele reminded them. "Thirty-six hours, he said."

"Tuesday afternoon to Wednesday early morning," Nin repeated.

"George just reduced it to a few hours within that window of time," Adele said.

Walker drummed the table. "I hadn't thought of that."

"If you left Lillie at around midnight, she must have been killed early Wednesday morning," Nin said.

"You were probably the last to see your wife alive." Jackson's voice was quiet.

This seemed too much for George as his calm countenance broke. He bent his head down on the table and sobbed.

CHAPTER 22

A shout came from outside the tent. Hatfield rose and stuck his head out. Adele could see through the parting of the flaps that someone had gotten hold of a ball and some of the men had shed their coats and rolled up their shirtsleeves to play a game with it in the space that separated the tents.

The noise seemed to bring Lieutenant Edwards to life. "Of course he was the last to see her alive. The killer always is!"

"Don't jump to conclusions, Monte," Jackson said sharply. "I know the Anspatches teach us to shoot first and ask questions later —"

"It's obvious, isn't it?" the soldier looked from one lawman to another. "He saw her after curfew. No one saw her until we found her that morning."

"That doesn't mean Mr. Wu killed his wife," Sheriff Hatfield said in a gruff tone. "I think you should listen to my deputy and start thinking with your head instead of your prejudices!"

Edwards leaned over the young man's chair. "I suppose you're going to tell us you have no excuse for those early morning hours!" He looked at Walker. "Sergeant, why don't you ask him about that?"

Walker said in a polite tone, "Mr. Wu, I assume you share a tent with others like the rest of us."

"I've a very small tent, like the rest of *us*," George said sharply. "The Chinese people respect me and gave me one to myself."

"Then you don't even have tentmates to corroborate your whereabouts!" The lieutenant's eyes were shining.

"If he had, you wouldn't have believed them anyway," Nin snapped.

"Understand we're not making any accusations, sir," Walker began.

"You're only doing your duty," George finished in a tight voice. "I'm sorry to disappointed the lieutenant, but I was not in bed during the early morning hours when the doctor says my wife was killed. I didn't go to bed at all."

"Eh?" Sheriff Hatfield raised his eyebrows.

"And I'm sorry to further disappoint the lieutenant, but I have what you police call an alibi for those hours," George continued.

Walker leaned forward. "I think you'd better explain yourself, sir."

"The Six Companies appointed four men to help re-establish our community once all this is over," George began. "We're ensuring they get the services they need and have a future ahead of them."

"Very kind of you," Adele said with a smile.

"I'm sure you would do the same for your neighbors, wouldn't you, Miss Gossling?" asked the young man and she nodded. "We must see to it everyone gets what they need."

"You say four men." Sergeant Walker took the pencil and pad from Jackson. "You and who else?"

"You wouldn't know their names, Sergeant," said George.

The lawman's eyes were almost amused. "I've done a great deal of work in this city, Mr. Wu, including Chinatown. Don't underestimate my knowledge of your community."

The young man bowed. "My apologies, sir. Fen Young, Larry

Quan, and Yu Shun." He added, "All men, like myself, from respectable Chinese families who have lived in Chinatown all their lives. None of us got to bed that night — or early morning, I should say."

"Naturally, they'll vouch for you," the lieutenant said. "Never let it be said a Chinaman doesn't protect his own."

"As a soldier protects his own," George threw back.

"What were you doing during those early morning hours, Mr. Wu?" Hatfield asked.

"I was helping to obtain medical aid for several of our elders." He gave a grim smile. "The army neglected to set up adequate care for us so far away from the main camp."

"You've a hospital tent six feet away from you!" Edwards snarled.

"George said *adequate* care," Adele snapped back. "One small tent that probably has no doctor attending it and no real medical supplies at its disposal."

"The army is doing the best it can, Miss Gossling," the lieutenant defended.

"They're doing the best they can for whom they choose," Nin said.

"Many of our elders are still suffering the effects of the fires," said George. "They're seventy, even eighty years old, Lieutenant."

"Go on," Waker said.

"I was informed of six elders who were ill before I left to meet Lillie," he said. "When I came back to camp, the other men told me there were now ten coughing and wheezing so badly they feared they wouldn't make it through the night."

"Don't tell us you went in search of a doctor!" Lieutenant Edwards stared at him.

"Of course they went in search of a doctor," Adele growled.

"We — I and the three others — went to the main hospital tent and asked them for help."

"And help wasn't forthcoming," Jackson guessed, a tone of anger in his voice.

"Not at first, Deputy," the young man admitted. "It took some doing. We went from hospital tent to hospital tent trying to get a doctor to agree to look at these elderly women and men. We finally found someone who would see them — a Dr. Barr."

Hatfield glanced at Walker. The latter nodded. "I've met Dr. Barr," he said. "Good man. And not one to reject treating anybody, no matter who they are."

"But on his terms." George's tone was bitter. "He refused to come to our camp."

"He knew he wouldn't have the right equipment," Nin said with a nod.

"He said if we wanted his help, we would have to bring them to him."

"You mean he wanted elderly, sick people to walk all the way from the Chinese camp to the main camp?" Adele asked.

"I don't think he was concerned with how we would get them there, Adele," said the young man. "The Chinese are used to restrictions and rules. We're resourceful people."

"Yes, yes," Edwards sneered. "We're all very well aware of your staying power."

"Lieutenant!" Sergeant Walker had clearly had enough. " I realize you've been sent by your superior to help with the investigation but antagonizing a witness —"

"A suspect!" the young man growled.

"A witness," said the sergeant emphatically, "is of no help to us." He turned once more to George. "Go on, son."

"The doctor allowed us to take two of the stretchers they used in the fires," said the young man. "We used those to carry the elders from the Chinese camp."

"That must have taken some time," Hatfield remarked.

"It was nearly morning by the time we brought in the last ones," George said. "They were frightened, of course." His face was grave. "They'd never been beyond the gates of Chinatown. So we stayed with them." He glanced at Edwards. "I've no doubt you don't believe me."

"It's a convenient story, to say the least," the young lieutenant said. But his tone was less assured.

"Then maybe you'll believe your own people," George said. "Dr. Barr was there. And there was a young man helping him. I don't know his name."

"Which hospital tent?" asked Walker.

"The one at the edge of this camp," said George. "Just before you turn off to the army barracks."

The sergeant turned to his friend. "Shall we go and see Dr. Barr and this orderly? Eh, Horatio?"

Sheriff Hatfield nodded. Adele could see his face had the mild-mannered ease she knew well. He patted George's shoulder, a little too hard. "I believe you, Mr. Wu."

"Thank you, sir." The young man bowed his head.

"We'll see," Edwards said in a doubtful tone.

The party left the tent, and George led them through the camp to the hospital tent. Eyes narrowed at them as they passed with the same looks Adele had seen only a little while ago. This time, the looks were accompanied by whispers.

She realized many people in camp knew who Sergeant Walker was and about the dead girl found near the Chinese camp. She wondered if the whisperers were putting two and two together, thinking the police had found a suspect among the refugees from Chinatown and were now taking him away. Some had satisfied looks on their faces, others doubt, and some looked sympathetic.

The hospital tent was one of the smaller ones, and the scent of cleaning fluid permeated its doorway. Inside was crowded with people lying on the ground, bedded down with blankets. Their faces were wrinkled with distress and age, and some let out soft cries from gaping mouths.

"They're sleeping on the floor!" Nin cried and held her friend's arm.

Even Jackson, whose police experience had made him more tolerant of unfair treatment, looked angry. "You could have at least found these people cots, Doctor," he said in a harsh tone to a man with his back to them, bending over a wash basin filled with instruments.

"That's not the doctor," George said in a low tone.

The man who turned around looked barely eighteen. Her brother's height and muscular build made an impression on him, and he shrank back a little.

"Who are you, young man?" Sergeant Walker flashed his badge at him.

"Joseph Nixon, sir," he said.

"You're an orderly?" asked the sergeant.

The young man grimaced. "I was at Saint Mary's Hospital before all this happened."

Walker pointed to George. "Mr. Nixon, was this man in your tent on Wednesday in the early morning hours?"

Mr. Nixon studied George, and Adele could tell by the slight leer of his lips he didn't think much of the Chinese man. "Well, Sergeant, I can't say he was."

"That's not true!" George shrieked. "He was here the entire time helping the doctor."

At the same time, Nin whispered to her, "He's lying!"

Adele leaned against her parasol. "Mr. Nixon, you were here on Wednesday, weren't you?"

The young man stiffened, the same leer on his lips. Adele imagined he thought as much of women as he did the Chinese. "I wouldn't be anywhere else after the uniformed men forced me here, would I?"

"You speak respectfully in the presence of ladies, sir." Hatfield took a step forward.

"I didn't mean any harm, miss," said Mr. Nixon in a more even tone.

"You did see four Chinese men bring these people here on Wednesday in the early morning, didn't you?" she asked.

The young man looked again at George. "What would Orientals be doing here, miss?"

"Bringing these poor people for the medical attention they should have gotten as soon as the fires were out," Adele snapped.

"Oh, them." The young man cast a distasteful eye. "Well, they were here when I came on duty. Don't know anything about them."

"He's lying!" Now Nin said it aloud with gritted teeth. "How else did they get here if they weren't carried by this man and his friends?"

"They could've walked here." Mr. Nixon sulked.

Nin snatched up a well-worn cane lying next to the nearest Chinese woman and held it up to the young man's face. "It's a forty-minute walk from their camp to here for someone with two strong legs. You think this woman could have walked that distance with this?" She shook the cane menacingly in his face.

Mr. Nixon flinched. "I didn't say there weren't any Chinese men here!"

Sergeant Walter glanced at Sheriff Hatfield. Hatfield grabbed the orderly's arm. His commanding face gathered like an angry bear caused the young man to pale. "I didn't do anything!" he screeched.

"You didn't tell the truth," said Hatfield. "You will now, won't you, Mr. Nixon?"

"Sure, sure." When Hatfield let go of his arm, the young man rubbed it with a resentful look. "Is he in trouble?"

"Who?" Jackson asked.

"Him." He flicked his head toward George.

"Answer the question, Mr. Nixon," Edwards said.

"Sure there were Chinese here that night," he said.

"Night?" Sergeant Walker asked. "Or early morning?"

Mr. Nixon shrugged and started to wipe the instruments lying in the clean water with a starched towel "Both, I guess."

"Son, we need you to be more accurate than that." By this time, Walker was also losing his temper.

"Guess it was early morning," said the young man. "I don't have a watch, but the doctor was saying something about it already being almost midnight and getting no sleep." He glared at George.

"How many Chinese men came to the tent?" asked Hatfield. "The truth now!"

"Four of 'em," said Mr. Nixon. "I remember him." He pointed to George. "Thought it was odd because he didn't look as Oriental as the rest of them."

George's eyes narrowed but he said nothing.

"What were they doing here?" Jackson asked.

"They wanted the doctor to treat some of those people, I guess." The young man nodded at the patients lying on the ground. "They wanted him to go all the way to their camp, but the doctor wouldn't." His face looked self-satisfied. "Doc's got to stay around here in case anyone needs him."

"At midnight?" Adele eyed him.

"Lots of things can happen at that time, miss," he said. "I seen 'em coming in when I was working at St. Mary's." He continued, "They argued with the doctor for a long time."

"Then what happened?" Walker asked.

"Doc just kept saying they had to bring the people here if they wanted them treated," he said. "So they did."

"How did they bring them here?" Jackson asked.

"Two at a time." The young man chuckled. "They were mighty determined."

"Thank you for that acknowledgment," George muttered.

"Doc lent them two stretchers," said Mr. Nixon. "They brought their people in, and the doctor took care of 'em." He glanced at the elderly women and men with a blank look. "They didn't kick up any fuss, but he and his friends sure did. We had them on our backs all day."

"What day?" asked Adele.

"That day," he snapped.

"What day?" Hatfield thundered.

"Wednesday, sir," said the young man. "Especially this one." He flicked his head at George. "He acted like we were going to stab one of 'em in the chest when he wasn't looking."

"I wonder why," Nin snarled with narrow eyes.

"So you can attest Mr. Wu wasn't out of your sight all day on Wednesday?" Sheriff Walker asked. Adele could see George was fairly holding his breath.

"He wasn't in my sight when he and his buddies went to their camp to bring those people over here," Mr. Nixon pointed out.

"But before and after?" Edwards asked.

"Sure, I guess so," he said. "Except for meal times, of course."

"And the doctor?" Adele asked. "Where was he?"

"Oh, he was here the whole time," said Mr. Nixon. "Guess he felt sorry for the old people."

"Fat lot you care about them," Nin snapped.

The young man looked at her for the first time with a little dignity. "I may not look like more than a bedpan cleaner to you, miss, but I got a duty to take care of whoever comes in here just like any doctor or nurse."

"Of course you do," Adele said kindly. The young man's words clearly showed he took his work seriously.

"Where is the doctor now?" Sheriff Walker asked.

"He went to get some mustard plasters from the main hospital tent for them." He jerked his head toward the patients. "He'll be back soon."

George turned to Edwards. "Satisfied now, Lieutenant?"

Edwards gave him a wry look. "You forget, Mr. Wu, there are gaps of time unaccounted for when you weren't in this tent."

"I'm sure Mr. Wu's friends will fill those in," Hatfield said.

"Mr. Wu's *friends*." Edwards glanced at the sergeant.

Adele had been holding back her temper as much as she could, but it finally got the best of her. "Did you ever consider George and his friends must have made quite a ruckus here that night?"

"I'm not sure I see what you're getting at, Miss Gossling," he said.

"The tents are very close together," she said. "Tents have no walls."

"Everyone would have seen them," Nin supplied. "George and his friends probably have at least twenty witnesses who could vouch for them."

Before Edwards could answer, the flap parted and a man in a white coat carrying a large bottle of yellow powder entered. He stopped, glancing at the people. His eyes rested on George.

"Well, you again, young man," he said in a good-natured tone. "Come to look in on your people, eh?"

"You know this man, Dr. Barr?" Sergeant Walker asked, showing him his badge.

"Certainly." The doctor set the bottle down on the small table. "A very persistent and stubborn young man, but very dedicated to his people."

"Your orderly has just been telling us Mr. Wu and his friends brought these people here on Wednesday in the early morning." Hatfield nodded toward the patients.

"That's right," he said. "Smoke inhalation can be dangerous to older people."

"So can delays in treatment," Adele snapped. "You could have gone to their camp."

"The army gave us strict orders to remain within the confines of the main camp, miss," Dr. Barr said simply. "I'm already disobeying their orders by letting Mr. Wu's patients stay here. They really ought to be on the other side of the camp."

"We appreciate all you're doing, Doctor," George said.

"Now, perhaps you'll tell me what this is all about?" He eyed the sergeant. "Is this young man being arrested for anything?"

"We're making some inquiries into the death of a young woman that occurred on Wednesday in the early morning hours," said Sergeant Walker. In a lower tone, he added, "That's not to go beyond this tent, of course."

The doctor nodded. "I heard about that tragic incident. I don't know the details, of course, but I don't think Mr. Wu had anything to do with it. As I said, he was very stubborn and persistent." He chuckled at the last.

Lieutenant Edwards stepped forward. "Doctor, would you say the time it took for the men to go to the Chinese camp and bring back the patients is consistent?"

"I'm not sure I know what you mean, Lieutenant," said Dr. Barr.

"Were there any lapses in time or any delays bringing in the patients?"

Adele raised her eyebrows as she realized exactly what Edwards was asking.

Her friend realized it too, as she said, "He wants to know if you think there would have been time for George to steal away, find the girl among all the people here in pitch darkness, kill her, and then drag her body all the way to the other end of the camp."

Dr. Barr hid a smile. "Well, if that's the question, I would say there was no way he could have done that, nor any of the other three men, for that matter. The time it took to get to their camp, put the patients on the stretchers, and carry them back here was consistent with my expectations." He nodded at George. "This young man was far too concerned with his people's care to think about killing some young woman, whoever she was."

"She was my wife," said George with a woeful tone.

The doctor's eyes showed compassion. "I'm sorry to hear that, son."

George turned to Edwards. "Well, Lieutenant?"

"It's not my place to say anything," Edwards said. "I'm not in charge of this investigation."

"That's right, Lieutenant, you're not." Walker glared at him. "We'll want to speak to the other men to confirm what you and the doctor said for the record, Mr. Wu. But there will be no arrest for now."

George's entire figure deflated. Adele felt a pull at her heart as she thought of how many innocent Chinese had not been so lucky with the police.

"Sergeant, am I free to go now?" asked George. When Walker nodded, he turned to the doctor. "I'd like to stay here for a while, if you don't mind."

"If *you* don't mind helping me with these mustard plasters." Dr. Barr tapped the bottle. "This should do a lot to speed up their recovery."

"Mind you, don't go jumping on any boats to Shanghai," Edwards said with a meaningful look.

Adele had had enough. She slammed the edge of her parasol into the dirt like a stake in the ground. "Lieutenant, I've been holding my tongue until now because you're my brother's friend. But you're the coarsest bigot I've ever met!"

"Del," Jackson causioned.

"You think those stripes on your arm make you better than anyone who isn't like you," Adele stormed.

"You're nothing but a military pig," Nin added with a growl.

Edwards stood very still. "May I say, Miss Gossling, all of us at the Anspatch Agency suspected your father was too lenient with your position in life, and I see Jackson hasn't been able to do much better!"

"My place!" Adele's temper lit like a flame. "Women should be seen and not heard, is that it?"

"The world would be much better off if that were the case!"

The young man gave Sergeant Walker a jerky salute and stormed out of the tent.

"You certainly told him off," Mr. Nixon, who had been watching from the corner, said in an almost admiring tone.

"No less than he deserved," Hatfield said sharply. He patted Jackson on the back. "I appreciate he's your friend, Deputy, but I don't like it that he's tried to push this investigation in one direction since we started."

"I can't deny that, sir," Jackson said in a tight voice.

Walker said in a stern tone, "No one is going to push this investigation anywhere but where the facts lead."

Adele turned to her brother, who had been silent, and put her arms around his neck. "I'm sorry, Jack. I shouldn't have lost my temper that way."

He gave her a half smile. "I was waiting for it to happen. I commend you for holding it in this long."

"The lieutenant's views are no less than those of most people," George said. "I never held it against him."

"After what you've been subjected to, sir," Walker tipped his hat. "I think many of us could learn from your tolerance. We'll leave you to your work here and hope for the patients' speedy recovery."

As they filed out of the tent one at a time, George held Adele back a little with Nin hanging on her arm. "Thank you for standing up for us, Miss Gossling. And you too, Miss Branch." He grinned. "I don't think I've ever seen a military man told off so well."

"It should happen more often," Nin said.

"George," Adele lowered her voice, "is there anything you can tell us about the night you met Lillie? You were the last to see her. Anything could help us."

The young man was quiet for a moment. "I didn't want to say anything to the sergeant. It might have been someone from our camp, and we've had enough trouble."

"You saw someone?" Nin's eyes widened.

"Not exactly," he said. "It was only a shadow. When I was going through the brush, I thought I saw a dark figure skulking away as I passed. I also saw a flash of light."

"Can you describe anything about the figure?" Adele asked.

"It was very dark," he said. "But it was either short in stature or bending down. I tend to think the former."

"Why is that?" Nin asked.

"Just the shape of it," he said. "You see a lot of people stealing through the shadows in Chinatown at night, Miss Branch."

"Saw a lot of figures," she murmured.

"Saw a lot of figures," he answered in a quiet voice.

Adele pressed his hand. "Chinatown will be rebuilt just like the rest of the city."

"I think it was a man, judging from the outline." He lowered his voice. "Chinese men tend to be on the short side which is why I didn't want to alert the sergeant. But now —"

"Now?"

"Given the circumstances," he said, "I want to help find out who killed my wife, whoever he is."

"We'll find out, George," Adele promised.

CHAPTER 23

At lunch, Adele ate very little, as the heaviness of the morning's events weighed on her. The lawmen talked about what their next move would be in the investigation, and her heart sagged at the realization that they were stumped. She knew Nin noticed her mood but her friend said nothing.

After lunch, they went to the women's aid tent. Neither Elsie nor Missy had been in the dining room for lunch, and as they approached the tent, Adele could see why. There was a crowd of women and children clutching at whatever they could get into their hands, their faces slacked with weariness. Inside was bustling. Elsie and Valda were tending to the women while Missy was with the supplies replenished just that morning, jotting down notes in between handing out clothes, cans of food, and toiletries.

"Where have you been?" Elsie asked in an agitated tone.

"Trying to solve a murder," Adele said simply.

"What happened?" Missy was now all ears.

Adele related the story of George Wu. Missy's eyes remained wide as she scribbled every word on her pad. "I must get this off to Carla right away."

"Don't sensationalize it," Nin warned her.

Missy looked at her indignant. "I've no intention of sensationalizing anything. On the contrary, I'm glad the husband was cleared. Just because he's Chinese doesn't mean he's a killer. I do have some discretion, Miss Branch, even if you don't believe it." She stomped out of the tent.

"That wasn't very kind, dear," Adele said gently. "You know how she's tried to make the *Arrojo Courier* the exact opposite of what her brothers made of it."

"She's fallen into the trap a few times," Nin insisted. "You're too determined to see her as one of your women warriors for justice to recognize it."

"I agree with Miss Branch," Elsie said. "Do you think it was wise to tell a reporter all that?"

"Missy and I have an agreement," Adele insisted. "As George has been cleared, there's nothing to hide. And it might do the Chinese community some good if people hear a Chinese man was cleared of murder, and the police are looking elsewhere."

"Exactly," Elsie said. "The *police* are looking elsewhere. You didn't come down here for that."

"We didn't plan for a poor girl to be killed," Nin insisted.

"Well, now you can do what you came here for." Elsie moved aside to make room at the table, bringing two crates for them to sit. She made a point of pulling Nin onto one of them. "The army finally let us into their offices. We've mimeographed these checklists. Each woman is supposed to checkmark what she really needs here." She tapped the checkboxes on the front of the sheet. "Then here," she turned a sheet over, "she checkmarks what she'll need once the rebuilding is finished. Then she's to take one of our cards," she pointed to a stack on the table, "and come back here in another five or six weeks to see if we have any news about temporary shelter."

"Five or six weeks?" Adele felt her stomach churn. "Surely, you don't think you'll be here all that time."

"I haven't the faintest idea how long it takes to rebuild a city," Elise said in a bothered tone.

"You don't intend to join your father in Los Angeles?" Nin inquired.

"There's too much work to be done," said Elise. "I miss Papa, but he understands." Adele could tell she was trying not to break with tears.

She held her hand. "Why don't you both come and stay with us? You can coordinate things from Arrojo which is what you do best, dear."

"Coordinate from the sticks?" Elsie snorted. "No thank you. It's very sweet of you, Adele, but you know as well as anyone our work's got to be done here in the field."

"In the field," Adele murmured. "I suppose San Francisco is sort of like a battlefield after the war is over, isn't it?"

Valda caught the tone of her voice. "Don't worry, Adele. It will be better than ever. You'll see."

Adele knew from her experience with settlement house work that the best way to forget her burdens was to get involved in helping others lift theirs. She threw herself into the task Elsie had given them. Nin also proved herself a most efficient ally to the poor women who came in. Her usual misanthropic wariness disappeared, and she listened to the women's stories of woe with patience and sympathy.

But as much as Adele was glad to be helping these destitute women, her mind kept going back to another young woman whose body had been demolished by stabbings and whose crime seemed to be nothing more than her desire for an independent life. The smiling picture of Lillie haunted her mind, and she saw Lillie in each sagging face. She bit her lip, thinking, if only Lillie were still alive, she would surely have joined them and relished the work they were doing.

"Are you sad, lady?" a small voice asked beside her. She turned to see a little boy of about seven or eight looking at her with large blue eyes. A wooden figure was tied around his neck, and his arm was curled protectively around a little girl who looked to be about four or five years old. She had a doll tied around her waist.

Adele's heart went out to the bewildered faces. "I suppose I am a little sad," she admitted.

"We're sad too," the little girl said in a solemn voice. "Mama says we got no house anymore."

"Lots of people got no house," her brother scolded. "We're no different."

"But their house wasn't swallowed up!" the girl insisted. "The sidewalk just opened up and swallowed it. We saw it!"

Adele held back tears.

"Bea! Artie!" a warm voice sounded above them, and a woman with the same blue eyes approached Adele with an apologetic smile. "You mustn't mind what they say, miss. Times like these, you got to let children just talk."

"Talking is good," Adele said kindly as she pushed a pencil and form toward the woman. "If you'll fill in your name, last address, how many in the family, and anything you need, we'll do our best to get it to you."

"Just me and the kids," said the woman as she bent over. A tightness came to her throat. "My husband — we can't find him!"

"Maybe he's in one of the other camps," Nin offered.

"No, we've searched them all," she said. "My husband and his brother went to help the neighbors down the street when the fires came. And we haven't seen them since." Tears filled her eyes.

Elsie took charge. "The army is keeping a list, Mrs. —"

"Andrews," said the woman. "Kate Andrews."

"They're keeping a list of people, Mrs. Andrews," Elsie rose. "Since they're clearing the city, they might have found your husband and brother-in-law already." She pressed the woman's hand as Mrs. Edwards looked away, knowing full well what Elsie meant. "Then again, they might not have," Elsie added quickly. "Shall we go and see?"

"The children —" She glanced down at them. "If their father's name is on the list, I don't want them to find out that way."

"You can leave them here and we'll watch them," Adele promised, glancing at Nin. Her friend wrinkled her nose. Adele believed she was a little frightened of children because so many in Arrojo teased her about being a witch.

As if recognizing Nin's wariness, Mrs. Andrews said, "They won't be any trouble to you. Will you, darlings?" Both children shook their heads vigorously.

Elsie and the woman left the tent, and the children turned to Adele with big eyes as if awaiting instructions. Adele smiled at the little boy. "You watch over your sister, don't you?"

"He's a dragon!" Bea said.

Adele laughed. "I thought my brother was a dragon too when I was your age."

"He still is," Nin mumbled.

"I got to watch over her, miss," said Artie. "Ain't got Papa or Uncle Neil here to watch over us, so I'm the man of the family."

A snort escaped Nin.

"Is that why you carry your soldier with you?" Adele nodded at the toy.

"He helps me stay on guard," said the boy.

"May I see it?"

"You'll give it back?" he asked in a hesitant tone.

"Of course she'll give it back," Nin said with impatience.

"The lieutenant said we couldn't take it so Mama tied it around my neck," he said. "You'll be careful with it, won't you?"

"I promise." Adele held up her hand in oath.

Artie slipped the twine from his neck and gave her the toy. The soldier was like none she had ever seen. It was carved of a rough wood and painted with a blue shirt and brown pants. The hands were covered with gloves and the boots went up to the knee. The soldier wore a hat with flaps at the side pinned up like the ears of a cat ready for battle, and a handkerchief was tied around his neck. The face was carved crudely with two uneven eyes and a mustache.

"It looks like the President," Nin remarked. Bea, Adele noticed, had advanced a little toward her friend, staring at the hair that hung around her shoulders.

"It is!" Artie said with delight. "People don't know who it is because he ain't got any glasses."

"It's hard to put glasses on a soldier," Adele remarked with a smile. "Did your father make it for you?"

"Uncle Neil did," said the boy. "He was with the President when he was in Cuba!"

"You mean he was a Rough Rider," Adele said.

"He helped the president capture San Juan," Artie boasted.

"You couldn't have even been born yet," Nin mumbled.

But Adele was touched by the boy's obvious pride and showed the kind of awe she knew he was expecting.

"He didn't get killed," said Bea in a tiny voice. She was now near Nin, her eyes still on her hair.

"No, but he was wounded," said Artie. "He got a bullet in his shoulder. He had to keep it in a sling for a month."

"How very brave of him," Adele said.

"Can I touch your hair?" Bea suddenly asked.

"No," Nin said promptly.

"Oh, let her touch it, dear," Adele said. "She's probably never seen any woman with her hair loose except her mother."

Nin's face was set in a grim expression, but the girl's pleading face seemed to change her mind. "Well, all right. But don't pull it!"

The little girl reached her hand out and petted Nin's hair as if she were petting a rabbit.

"Don't do that, Bea," her brother hissed. "Your hands are dirty."

"I don't mind that." Nin had clearly calmed down now that she saw the girl was gentle. "I sit on the floor all the time."

"Sit on the floor!" Artie's eyes opened wide. "Mama doesn't let us do that."

"When you're a grown-up, you can do whatever you want," Nin said in an assured tone.

"Can I see your doll, sweetie?" Adele smiled at the little girl.

Bea hesitated. Her brother hissed, "Let her see it, Bea. She's a nice lady, and she won't hurt her."

This seemed to decide his sister, as she stopped petting Nin's hair. "Mama tied the string with a big knot."

"I'll get it out," Nin said briskly, her deft fingers working the twine until the knot was untied in minutes.

Adele was even more careful with the doll than she had been with the soldier as it was clear by the worn and fringed fabric that the girl played with it constantly. It was homemade, like the soldier, fashioned out of bits and pieces of rags. The doll had very long curly hair made out of yarn and a cloth face with features painted on. It was unusual, as it did not have the fancy pink outfits she had seen on many dolls of its kind. This one wore a button-up shirt and skirt made of rough material, painted on boots, and a wide-brim hat.

"Is it a cowgirl?" Adele asked.

"It's Annie," said the girl.

"Annie Oakley?"

Bea nodded. "Papa saw her with Buffalo Bill."

"She's not with Buffalo Bill anymore," Nin said.

"I know that!" said the child. Adele could see she was getting agitated, staring at the doll and hopping a little on her small legs. She handed the doll back to Nin, who tied it to Bea's waist.

Elsie came in with Mrs. Andrews behind her. Adele could tell by the woman's face her husband and brother-in-law were not among the names of those found dead under the rubble. Her mood had changed considerably, and her face showed only a little tiredness now.

"Miss Blessings has found us a better place, darlings," she said as she squeezed each child to her. "It's much bigger and there are two other women who have children your age. You'll have someone to play with."

The children were all smiles. Elsie leaned toward Adele and snarled, "Those army maggots put her in a tent with two women who can't be less than sixty. Needless to say, they were happy to hear the children were moving!"

"I daresay they don't like children," Adele agreed.

"You've been good, haven't you, darlings?" Mrs. Andrews asked and the children gave a vigorous nod.

"Miss Gossling wanted to see Teddy and Annie," said Artie.

"And Miss Branch let me pet her hair!" The little girl grinned. "She has such pretty hair."

Nin's face turned a little red as she mumbled, "Thank you."

"They were telling me all about their toys," Adele said with a smile.

"I'm grateful they have them," said the woman. "The soldiers were herding us away and wouldn't let us take anything we couldn't carry."

"That's why you tied the toys to the children that way." Adele guessed.

The woman nodded. "They couldn't very well say the children couldn't carry them then."

"Very clever," Elsie mumbled.

"It's been hard on them." Mrs. Andrews bit her lip. "All this and their father and uncle missing. Every child needs a comforting toy."

"Indeed every child does," Adele agreed. "I had a rag doll of my own when I was a child. My brother had a toy horse my father gave him one Christmas. Not that he would ever admit to needing it." She chuckled.

The woman smiled. "When Artie and Bea go to bed at night with their toys, the situation doesn't seem so grim to them."

"It won't be soon," Nin said in a determined tone.

"I don't know, Miss Branch." The woman sighed. "They say it will take years to rebuild this city."

"But surely we won't have to stay in these tens for years," Elsie insisted.

Mrs. Andrews shrugged. "Who knows? It took Chicago two years to rebuild after the Great Fire, and I read that was only three miles of destruction."

"We're made of tougher stuff here than they are in the Middle West," Elsie said in a stubborn tone. "I wouldn't count on it taking us even that long to get people into their homes again."

Mrs. Andrews gave her a wan smile and hurried her children out of the tent with repeated thanks.

"Toys!" Elsie snorted. "She might have saved more clothes for the children instead of useless toys."

"They're not useless to them," Nin pointed out.

"I've no patience for mothers who indulge their children with such fancies!"

"You're being very cold-hearted, Elsie, dear," said Valda with more annoyance in her voice than Adele had heard in a long time. "It's just as Mrs. Andrews said. Children need their comfort. Especially in times like these."

"It's times like these we must teach children to look at the way things really are," Elsie argued. "They see how we're coping, and they learn from us, so when they grow up, they can cope too. What would happen if all of us went around clutching our dolls and toy soldiers?"

It was as if a tremor left from the earthquake shook Adele, and she grabbed the edge of the table. "That's true, isn't it? Clutching dolls and toy soldiers —"

"Adele, are you all right?" Valda peered at her.

"Or things that shine in the moonlight," she murmured. *A flash of light.*

"Zounds, she's gone batty." Elsie stared at her.

"No, she hasn't," Nin said. "She just has an idea."

Adele pressed her friend's hand. "When we went to see Mr. Horne. We saw it all over the streets."

"Saw what?" Elsie asked.

"People clutching things," said Adele. "The man holding that bottle of brandy as if it were a baby, for instance."

"Must have been a very expensive brandy," Elsie mumbled.

"And that old woman who was pushing the baby carriage," Nin recalled. "There was nothing in it. No baby, nothing. Just empty." Her eyes dimmed with sadness. "She lost her grandchild in the fires."

"I forgot you know things like that, Miss Branch." Else looked at her with a little alarm.

"It's true," Valda agreed. "I was walking the streets just after the fires were out. All the smoke still filled the air. People were carrying the oddest things. A woman carried a knitted cap, nearly torn in half."

"She wouldn't have worn it anyway," Elsie said. "It was hot as blazes after the fires."

"It must have had meaning to her." Adele sat down slowly. "People clutch to things that have meaning for them. What might look absurd or silly to us is precious to them."

"I suppose when you've lost everything, you grasp at what you have," Elsie sighed.

"A woman with a broken pitcher refused to give it up when the soldiers tried to take it away from her," Valda mused. "They were only trying to help her. The handle was broken and it was scratching her hands. She fought like a wildcat."

"Well, now with what Lloyds of London is giving people, she'll be able to buy five unbroken pitchers." Elsie resumed her seat in front of the stack of forms. "We've got another hour or so before dinner, and the line's only half down out there."

"Silver," Adele mumbled. "Silver in the moonlight can cause a flash of light. Small in stature." She jumped up and grabbed Nin's hand. "Elsie, dear, we have something we must do before dinner."

"Oh, for the love of Heaven." Elsie did not hide her exasperation.

CHAPTER 24

"Well," Nin asked after they left the tent. "What is so urgent that we have to do it now?"

Adele pressed her hand. "Nin, I think I know who killed Lillie."

"Ben Horne?" Nin asked. "Men are animals when they're jealous."

"Not Ben Horne," Adele said. "It was Clarence."

"The imbecile?" Nin stared at her.

"He's not an imbecile," Adele insisted. "He lacks intelligence, but you don't need intelligence to be a killer."

"But he loved the aunts," Nin objected.

"Exactly!" Adele pulled her to a corner where there were fewer people going in and out of their tents as they were getting ready for dinner. "He loved the aunts. And the aunts didn't love Lillie."

"He killed her to get her out of the way?" Nin shook her head. "If you say so, but I can't see it."

"You know as well as I that murder is always complicated," Adele said. "We know Lillie was a burden in her aunts' eyes. We know it and so did she. And so did Clarence."

"Go on." Her friend was listening with attention.

"They're like mothers to him. He said so himself." Adele continued, "A son would do anything to protect his mother."

"You're not making any sense," Nin said. "How would killing Lillie protect them? Lillie wasn't doing them any harm. She was even paying her own way."

"I told you murder is more complicated," Adele insisted. "The aunts wouldn't balk at a financial burden, even if it were true. They would grumble and sniff, but not balk."

Nin's eyes dimmed. "But a marriage like Lillie's would bring ruin on their delusional ideas about their social standing. That's what you mean, isn't it?"

"A marriage to a Chinese man would be the ruin of them," Adele said. "At least in their tiny social circle, which is everything to them. If word got out their niece had married George Wu —"

"It would be like Danielle all over again," Nin murmured.

"Worse than Danielle, in their eyes," she said.

"But how would Clarence have known?' Nin questioned. "George said they were keeping it very secret."

"It's hard to keep a secret under these circumstances." Adele threw a glance at the tents. "Canvas is the thinnest of walls, and you can hear everything everyone says. You can see what everyone is doing when they're outside their tent. There is nowhere to run. And even if someone did run, where would they go? Hide in the rubble?"

"I see what you mean." Nin's face grew sharp. "He was following Lillie!"

"He may have been keeping an eye on her," Adele said. "He probably thought he was doing the aunts a favor."

"He followed her that night." Nin said. "It makes sense."

"If he saw her go out after curfew, he might have wanted to know what she was doing."

"He found out what she was doing all right," Nin growled. "Meeting her husband! But where would he get that dagger?"

"People were running through the streets during the tragedy," Adele said. "He may have gone through Chinatown and picked it up in the rubble. He wouldn't have even seen it as looting. It would be like a child finding a shiny object on the floor and picking it up with fascination." She was quiet for a moment. "Shiny object."

Nin eyed her. "I saw the look on your face when George mentioned the flash of light." She took a deep breath. "So he intended to kill her all along if he brought the knife with him and was just waiting for his chance."

"I don't think the flash of light was the knife," Adele said.

"Well, what could it have been?"

"The shaving brush that so captivated him," Adele said.

Nin stared at her. "Good God! Now I see!"

"His comfort." Adele took her arm. "Grown-up people have their toys too."

"A grown-up person who has the mind of a child," Nin snorted. "Well, what do we do now? Tell all to Sergeant Walker?"

"Based on an idea?" Adele grimaced. "You know how the police work as well as I do."

"Well, then?"

"I think we can get Clarence to confess," she said. "I don't think he realized what he did until we took him to see Lillie. There's a barrier between his child mind and adult mind. If we could permeate that barrier, I think he would realize what a horrible thing he'd done and would give himself up."

"We go and talk to him," Nin concluded.

"He liked us," Adele said. "He was like a child with us."

"Remember, a child never confesses," Nin warned her.

"I think he will," Adele said with assurance.

On their way to the tents, they ran into Miriam and Addie Sweenie who were waiting with a few other women for the dinner hour to strike.

"Miss Gossling!" Miss Addie fluttered her arms like a bird.

"Hello, Miss Addie." Adele was wary of seeing the aunts again. She could tell Nin was also far from sympathetic from the way she glared at Miss Miriam.

"Why haven't the police been keeping us informed of their progress?" The latter demanded.

"Because they've been busy trying to find a killer," Nin snapped.

"That's precisely it, Miss Branch," the woman snapped back. "You perhaps forgot the victim *was* our niece."

"I haven't forgotten." Nin gave her an intent look. "Have you?"

"I believe I was speaking to Miss Gossling." Miss Miriam turned to Adele with an expectant look. "Well?"

Adele said coldly, "Sergeant Walker will be glad to tell you anything you want to know."

"I'm not asking him," Miss Miriam grunted. "I'm asking you."

"Miriam, don't be so mean," Miss Addie smiled patiently at Adele. "We've been so worried since the funeral." Her eyes filled with tears.

Adele's heart softened a little toward the woman. She had met many such elderly ladies whose plain countenance kept them tied to an elder sibling who bullied them and treated them like they were nothing.

"The police are doing all they can," she said. "These are unusual circumstances so it was difficult for them to locate people."

"Who did they need to locate?" Miss Miriam demanded.

"Mr. Horne for one." Adele paused. "And Mr. Ross. People who knew Lillie and worked with her."

"Nonsense," the woman snorted. "There are hoodlums all around here who may have done it. I've seen them."

"Why would they want to kill a woman they didn't know?" Nin asked.

"Men are beasts, Miss Branch," Miss Miriam declared. "Who knows why they do anything."

Adele knew her friend, whose opinion of the male sex was as low as Miss Miriam's, would not argue with this.

"What about this Chinese man?" Miss Miriam continued. "There's been talk around the camp."

"What about him?" Adele gave her a pointed look.

"Then it's true!" Miss Addie's eyes widened. "The police think some Chinese man did it."

"Not exactly." Adele gave Nin a sharp look, warning her not to say anything about George and his relationship with their niece. Her friend flicked her head in understanding.

"Well, then?"

"They had a suspect," she admitted. "A very educated and refined young man. Lillie worked with him in Chinatown."

"He must have done it, then," Miss Miriam said. "You just said the police were looking for the killer in someone Lillie knew, didn't you?"

"She did *not* say that!" Nin objected. "You're twisting her words around."

"Lillie knew this Oriental," Miss Miriam continued, ignoring her. "They're dangerous people."

Adele raised her eyebrows. "Are they?"

"You haven't been reading the San Francisco newspapers, I see." Miss Miriam folded her arms. "There was trouble in Chinatown all the time."

"Maybe there won't be once the city moves them to Hunter's Point," Miss Addie suggested. "It's not entirely their fault, after all."

"Of course it's their fault!" Miss Miriam declared. "And moving them won't make it any better." She turned to Adele again. "Why haven't the police arrested this man?"

"To make an arrest, the police have to have evidence," Nin said dryly.

"Evidence!" the woman growled. "He knew her. Isn't that enough?"

"Luckily, the police are a little more broad-minded than you are, Miss Miriam," Adele snapped. "Now, if you'll excuse us, you're keeping us from very important business." She grabbed Nin's hand and pulled her away as fast as she could.

"The ogre!" Nin snarled. "It would serve her right if she were knifed in the street one night — by a white man!"

Adele frowned. "That wouldn't do Miss Addie much good, would it?"

"Why not?" Nin asked. "She might finally be able to live."

"Not Miss Addie," Adele said with a sigh. "She's probably never had to do any living on her own her whole life."

Nin's hard lines softened a little. "I can't say Miss Miriam doesn't take care of her sister. She might even love her."

"As far as Miss Miriam is capable of love," Adele agreed.

They reached the bachelor section of camp just as the dinner bell started to ring. They endured the catcalls and whistles from men coming out of their tents. Adele held her friend's hand and they pressed on, ignoring the men.

Unfortunately, those in Clarence's tent had not yet gone to dinner. Finley and Meyers were putting on the last finishing touches of their pomade, and a third man was combing his walrus-like mustache and making offhand conversation with Clarence, who was washing his hands in a small bowl of water. But he stopped talking when they came in and, with a nod to the other two, the three men immediately descended upon them with too-friendly greetings and offers to escort them to the dining room tent. Adele lamented to herself how it was clear that, if Mr. Ross had forgotten who they were, his tent mates certainly had not.

The man with the walrus mustache was clearly taken with

Nin as he pressed her arm. "Now, don't you tell the ol' sergeant this, but I hear tell there's a place way at the other end of the camp where some of the boys get together every night with their harmonica and guitar and play some music for a dance. How about it, sweetheart?"

"How about you taking your hand away from my arm before I break your fingers?" Nin answered in a sweet tone.

Finley, with another cigar in his mouth, burst out laughing. "I wouldn't toy with the lady, Sheppard. She means it."

The man gave her a rueful look but removed his hand and bowed in apology.

"You gentlemen can go to dinner. Don't mind us," said Adele in an airy tone. "We'd just like to have a few words with Mr. Ross."

"Clarence, old boy, ain't you the lucky one!" whistled Meyers.

The young man suddenly leapt from the corner and, with his hands still wet, held them in fists up to the man's face. "You leave them alone! They're fine ladies!"

"We were just trying to be friendly, boy," Finely mumbled.

"I'll kill you if you —" He stopped. "Miss Adele, you come to see me?" Then, with a little more suspicion, he added, "Why?"

"Maybe they think you're a right nice-looking fellow," Finley said and the other men laughed.

"Why don't you all go crawl back into the hole you came out of?" Nin snarled. "I'm sure they've cleared the rubble from it by now."

Sheppard threw back his head with a laugh. "Land, she's a spicy one! Sure you won't come to the dance with me, precious?"

"I'd rather dance with an anteater," she snarled.

Amidst the laughter, Meyers slapped both men on the back. "Well, gents, I think we ought to leave Clarence with his lady friends. Ain't right to muscle in on a man when he's got company." He said "company" with a leer that made Adele's stomach turn. But the rest of the men followed him out.

Clarence said, "Don't you worry, Miss Adele, ain't none of 'em gonna hurt you. I'll see to it."

"You're very protective of people you like and respect, aren't you?" Adele asked.

The young man peered at them. "The police sent you?"

"Of course not," Nin insisted. "They don't know we're here."

The young man's face relaxed. "That's all right then."

"Why is it all right, Clarence?" Adele asked.

"I don't like the police," he said. "I don't want to think they got you doing their dirty work."

"The police aren't dirty," said Nin. "They're trying to find out who killed Lillie so her aunts can have some peace."

"We have some news about Miss Addie and Miss Miriam." Adele pulled a chair from underneath a small table and sat down. "We said we would let you know about them, remember?"

His eyes immediately became anxious. "They ain't sick or hurt or nothing, are they?"

"They're doing just fine," Adele assured him. "They send you their love."

"They told us they mean to take boarders into their new house and would like to have you come back," Nin added. Adele thought this might be taking her white lie a little too far.

"I'm sure they would be happy to see you," Adele said. "Especially now with Lillie gone."

"But I couldn't!" The young man said. "I ain't good enough for them. Not to see them in public, that is."

"That sounds like something someone told you." Nin looked at him with shrewd eyes.

"They told me," he said.

"That wasn't very considerate since you're like a son to them," Adele said.

"They been nice to me," he insisted. "But Miss Miriam said, 'You stay in your place and we stay in ours.' I reckon she's right."

"You know, Clarence," Adele said in a thoughtful tone, "this earthquake and the fires put everyone in the same place. Even wealthy ladies like Mrs. Hopkins and Mrs. Crocker lost their homes just like Miss Addie and Miss Miriam lost theirs."

"But they're rich!" he declared.

"What's the good of being rich if you have no home?" Nin pointed out.

"Miss Miriam and Miss Addie are better than those rich old ladies," Clarence declared. "They're fine and kind and decent."

"They certainly are," Adele agreed with enthusiasm. "They must think an awful lot of you to have given you that silver brush." She held out her hand. "May I see it again?"

He was a little less flinching than the first time. He used the woolen blanket to polish the silver casing and even examined it with narrow eyes before handing it to her. Adele made sure to be very careful, admiring the etching and the soft bristles on the brush.

"Did Lillie ever resent the affection her aunts showed you, Clarence?" she asked with her eyes on the brush.

"Re-send?" he repeated.

"Re-zent," Nin pronounced the word slowly. "Was she ever mad the aunts liked you better than her?"

"I ain't hardly talked to her," he said. "I had nothing to do with her."

"You must have had something to do with her," Adele said. "You lived in the same house, didn't you?"

"My room was way at the top," he said. "I hardly ever saw her." His voice was even. "I said so to the police, didn't I?"

"What about mealtimes?" Nin inquired. "Didn't she eat with you?"

"Only Sunday breakfast before church." He hunched his shoulders a little. "She was always going off with those dirty people."

"What dirty people?" Adele asked.

"You know them," he said. "They ain't got faces like us."

"We're all different, Clarence," Adele said in a soft tone.

"Oh, different," he said with a grin. "I know different. But Miss Miriam says they're bad people."

"Who are bad?" asked Nin.

"You know, the Mexicans and the Chinese," he said. "Come in and take jobs from people and spread all kinds of diseases around. Why, they don't even go to church!"

"They have their own religion, Clarence," Adele said.

"They do?" The young man was clearly surprised.

"Sure they do," Nin said.

"Well, they take jobs from people," he said firmly.

"They do the jobs no one else wants to do," Adele said. "And many of the Chinese are educated." She cupped the brush in her hand. "Why, we met a young man named George Wu who's been to college."

"George?"

"He was the George the police were looking for, Clarence," she said. "You were wrong, you know."

"Wrong?"

"You said Lillie couldn't have been married and the ring we found couldn't have been hers. But it was hers." She looked at him. "She and George Wu were married."

"No, no!"

"They got married in Washington," Nin said. "I'm sure the police already sent a telegram to the Washington police to get a copy of the marriage certificate."

In a barely whispering voice, he asked, "Do Miss Miriam and Miss Addie know?"

"We haven't told them, and I'm sure the police haven't," Adele said.

He grabbed her arm with both hands. "Please don't tell them, Miss Adele. It would kill them."

Adele felt a little sorry for the young man who had taken the two women's regard for him, which was no more than appreciation of an obedient boarder, as mother love. "I imagine it would," she said in a soft voice.

At that moment, the tent flap opened. A young man with his shirttails hanging out of his pants came in, a tin cup in his hand. "I lost my shaving brush, and Finley says you got a brand-new one. Can I borrow it for two minutes?" He blinked. "I'm meeting my girl and her mama later on, and her mama don't like me looking like this." He brushed his hand on his stubbled face.

Without a word, Adele held it out to him. With a bow of thanks, he rushed out.

Clarence shrank to the corner of the cot. "You shouldn't have done that, Miss Gossling."

"Don't you want him looking fine for his girl?" Adele smiled.

"You shouldn't have done that."

"Why not?" Nin demanded. "We're all in need of a little help right now. What harm could it do for him to borrow it for two minutes?"

"Because it's all I got left."

"All you have left from the aunts?" Adele pressed her hands together.

"I ain't got nothing from my ma, you see," he said. "Man came and took it all away. Ma owed a lot of money." His tone became resentful. "He even said I couldn't have the picture because it was in a silver frame and people paid money for pictures in frames." His eyes flashing, he added, "Why would anyone want a picture of a woman they didn't know?"

"Why indeed?" Adele asked. "Clarence, that man won't take your brush. He's just using it for now."

"It's all I got left," he repeated in a quivering voice.

"Now you're all they have left," Adele said. "They don't have Lillie anymore."

"Lillie wasn't anything," he insisted. "Miss Miriam told me. She wouldn't marry Ben and she wanted to be with those Chinese and Mexicans."

"And if she would have married Ben or one of their friends' sons like they wanted?" Nin asked in a hard voice. "What kind of life would that have been for her?"

"A nice, quiet life!" he insisted.

"Some people don't want a nice, quiet life, Clarence," Adele said. "They want to do something in this world."

"Miss Miriam said Lillie was going to turn out just like her mama." He paused.

"Marrying a man who would bring disgrace on them," Adele said in a steady voice. "You didn't like Lillie, did you, Clarence?"

He seemed stunned for a moment, his eyes and mouth open. "I never said —"

"You didn't have to say it," Nin said. "You talk as if you could spit in her eye just as soon as look at her."

"I never spit in her eye!" the young man thundered.

"Of course you didn't," Adele said. "You're a gentleman."

"Miss Miriam and Miss Addie teach me that," he said with pride. "They say it don't matter if a man don't got money. He can still be a gentleman!"

"Usually, it's the men who don't have money who are more gentlemanly than the men who do," Nin said dryly.

"Miss Miriam and Miss Addie were so kind to Lillie," his voice began to rise. "They took her in when her ma died. Her daddy, he was a bad one. She wasn't grateful." In a stronger tone, he repeated, "No, she wasn't grateful!"

"You think people should be grateful for what other people give them even when it's their duty to give it?" Adele asked.

"All they wanted was for her to marry right," he said.

Adele's glance slid toward Nin. "Did you think she would be better off dead?"

"Yes, yes!" The screeching tone filled the entire tent.

The rising agitation in the young man's voice alarmed her. She suddenly realized he had been staring beyond her shoulder, his eyes wide. She slowly turned and saw flashes of light in the parted canvas doorway. Although it was darker by this time, she realized the young man who had borrowed the shaving brush was just outside, shaving his stubbled face and the flashes of light were coming from the silver brush as it hit the candle glow just outside the tent. Flashes of light…

In a soft tone, she said, "You killed Lillie, Clarence."

He stared at her in terror.

Adele said. "You wanted to save Miss Miriam and Miss Addie from being disgraced all over again. She told you in the brush that night the Chinese man she met — George Wu — was her husband and they were going away together." A cry escaped his lips, but she continued, "You did a terrible thing but your intentions were honorable."

A sob came from the young man. He grabbed her hands. "She was just there. With the trees and that Chinese man. She was going away with him and leaving Miss Miriam and Miss Addie to suffer."

"And you couldn't let that happen," Adele said.

He broke down, sobbing with his face in the pillow, pounding his fists into the cot.

The young man came back in with the brush. "I cleaned it all good for you, Clarence. Thanks a million."

Without a word, Adele took the brush as Clarence continued to sob and laid it down on the cot next to him.

CHAPTER 25

It wasn't difficult for Adele and Nin to convince Clarence to come with them to the police tent and have Sergeant Walker take down his confession. The young man was in shambles as the full realization of what he had done took over like an invisible demon. He stumbled as he walked, wailing "I won't go to Heaven, I won't go to Heaven, I won't go to Heaven."

By the time they got to the police tent, he was a little calmer but his speech was even more childlike and chaotic than usual. They spent several hours getting the entire story from him. Adele relayed the confession to Missy later in the following way:

Clarence knew there was "something fishy" going on with Lillie even before they came to the camp. On Easter Sunday, he came home from church with the aunts, and Miss Miriam found a note from Lillie saying she would not be in for dinner and not to wait for her. Miss Miriam had been annoyed and grumbled about it all through the meal.

Later, the aunts sat in the parlor with their needlework, expecting Lillie to walk in the door at any moment. But Lillie did not appear. Miss Addie started to worry, but Miss Miriam assured her Lillie was being "thoughtless as usual," and no harm had come to her—she would certainly be in by bedtime. Clarence knew Lillie had gone out plenty of times and even stayed away late into the night, but he didn't like to see Miss Addie worried and Miss Miriam upset. So while they were in the parlor, he stole away to Lillie's room to search it.

"What was he looking for?" Missy asked.

"I scarcely think even he knew," Adele said.

Though Clarence's limited intelligence did not take him as far as knowing why he was looking through Lillie's things, he felt he had to look for *something* — something that would explain where she was going and why she stayed out so late. And he found it — two boxes with "some Chinese things."

"The fan and the pendant?" Missy guessed.

Adele nodded. "He didn't know they were heirlooms, of course, but he knew they 'cost lots of money.'"

He put the boxes away and went back to the parlor. Miss Miriam read to him and Miss Addie while Miss Addie continued her needlework until bedtime. Lillie was not back, and Miss Addie started to fret. Miss Miriam reassured her Lillie was probably staying the night with a friend. But Clarence could see Miss Miriam was getting worried too. After they had gone to bed, he sat at the top of the stairs, waiting. Lillie came "not too long afterward."

"He confronted her with what he found," Adele said. "She said they were things the Chinese people had given her in gratitude."

"Lying through her teeth," Missy said with a spark in her eye.

"What else could she do?" Adele defended. "She wasn't ready for her aunts to know about George — George told us that — and she knew anything she told Clarence would go straight to them."

He knew "she was fibbing," but he was too sleepy by that time to argue with her, so he went to bed. He then forgot about everything until the day of the earthquake. They all fled the house, taking with them only what they could carry as the military men herded them out with the fires coming their way. They fled through the downtown with the others, passing through China-town. That was when he saw, amid the dirt and rubble, the fisherman's knife.

"He just picked it up?" Missy's eyes were wide as she scribbled on her pad.

"The military was too busy trying to get people evacuated from the fires," Adele said. "He said he didn't mean to steal it. He just saw something 'pretty' in the dirt, picked it up, and put it in his pocket without thinking about it."

"He knew what it was, Adele," Missy insisted. "He may be slow-witted but he knew."

He and the Sweenies reached the Presidio where they were at first assigned the same tent. But Miss Miriam told Clarence it wouldn't be fitting for him to stay in the tent with them and he must go find a tent with the other bachelors.

"That was rather cruel of the old bird." Missy said.

"For Miss Miriam, it wasn't a matter of cruelty but social status," Adele reminded her. "He knew that more than anyone."

Clarence was determined to keep the aunts safe, and even though he wasn't with them, he watched Lillie whenever he could.

"Why Lillie in particular?" Missy asked.

"He said he didn't want her upsetting them more than they were already upset," said Adele. "He thought if he knew what she was doing, he could warn them ahead of time."

"Maybe you're right about him not being as slow-witted as we thought," Missy mumbled.

He knew Lillie took walks after dinner but he didn't know she was meeting her husband on the other side of the camp. He never took the trouble to follow her until that last night.

"Now, how much sense does that make?" Missy asked with

annoyance. "He makes a vow to protect them by knowing Lillie's whereabouts but he doesn't follow her."

"His mind didn't make that connection," Adele said.

"I take back my previous remark about him not being as slow-witted as we thought," Missy said dryly.

On the day of the murder —

"You mean the day he killed her," Missy corrected.

Clarence told the police he was up very early as he always was because he liked to see Miss Miriam and Miss Addie get to the dining room tent all right for breakfast. So he hid himself among the shrubs where he could see their tent. That was when he saw Lee Chang —

"Who?" Missy's pencil froze.

"A very bright and friendly little girl who helped us find George." Adele smiled.

As George had told them, he sent Lee with the note for Lillie to meet him after curfew, as he had something important to tell her. Lee, being the fearless child she was, slipped right into the tent to put the note in the pocket of Lillie's dressing gown.

"And Clarence saw her." Missy nodded.

"He knew 'something wasn't right,' as he put it," Adele said. "And he knew it had to do with Lillie because why would the aunts have anything to do with the Chinese?"

Clarence observed Lillie with the dressing gown later that morning when she went to the washrooms with the other women. He also saw her reading something after the aunts went back to the tent.

"Don't tell me he put two and two together!" Missy stared.

"He was so proud when he described it," Adele said with a grimace. "He didn't know who wrote the note, of course, but he figured it was a note to meet someone."

"Maybe he is cleverer than we thought," Missy mumbled.

Clarence devoted the entire day to following Lillie. He

confirmed Miss Addie's observation that Lillie was agitated and her mind was preoccupied. Just before dinner, she stole away from the tent, and this time he followed her. She "walked so long" and when he saw the other camp, he was at first in awe that the military had put a camp on the other side of the Presidio. But then he saw the Chinese and realized what it was. He followed Lillie around the edge of the camp where she had her eye on a few white ladies arguing with some soldiers.

"He didn't even realize those ladies were Nin and I," Adele remarked.

Then Lillie looked at the Chinese camp and her face became "scrunched up with worry." She slipped into the wooded area behind the camp and he followed her a little ways to a clearing. He was proud of how he kept so silent and out of sight that she never saw him. She waited there a little while, then walked back to the main camp.

"What do you think she was doing, Adele?" Missy asked.

"I imagine she was anxious to meet George and couldn't stand the wait any longer," Adele surmised. "So she went to the Chinese camp to see if she could catch his eye but didn't find him. Then she went to their meeting place, thinking he might come anyway."

"Why would he come earlier?" Missy blinked.

"I suppose George knew she was taking walks around the camp so he might have thought she would come early and intended to meet her." She felt a sadness in her chest. "Maybe it would have been better if they had met earlier."

Clarence stayed watching Lillie the rest of the evening. He only went back to his tent to get the fisherman's knife he had found in the rubble.

Missy jumped up. "He intended to kill her all along!"

"That's what Jack said," Adele noted. "But Clarence said he only took it for protection since he concluded she would be meeting the person who wrote the note later on. If she was attacked by a Chinese person, he wanted to defend her for the aunts' sake. I believe him and so did the sergeant."

Missy sank back down on the cot and took up her pencil again.

Not long after the curfew bell rang, Lillie emerged from the tent. Clarence followed closely behind her as she went to the same place she had been earlier in the evening. This time there was a man there — "one of them." Clarence was hidden too far away to hear what they were saying, but he could tell from the way she smiled, the glow on her face, and the way she held his hands that "there was something bad between them."

"Bad!" Missy snorted. "They were married, for heaven's sake!"

"Yes, but he didn't know that," Adele pointed out. "Not yet, anyway."

At that point, Clarence knew he had to have it out with Lillie to learn what was going on. But he didn't want "the bad Oriental" there. So he waited until George left. He was afraid just once when George came in his direction and Clarence thought he might see him. But he just "folded himself into the brush" and George passed without seeing him.

"That was what George described to you," Missy concluded. "The stubby figure in the dark."

Adele nodded. "Clarence was playing with the silver shaving brush Miss Miriam had given him. That was the flash of light George saw."

Lillie had taken only a few steps when Clarence emerged from his hiding place. She was "surprised and alarmed" to see him and tried to order him to go back to the main camp and stay out of things that were none of his business. When he pressed to know who was the man she had just met, she blurted out, "My husband!"

He, of course, didn't believe "she could have done such a wicked thing." She took out the wedding ring with the engraved initials, saying how she had been carrying it with her since they were married on April first, and now she would be able to wear it with pride and love and not have to hide it anymore. He was so enraged, he grabbed the ring and threw it in the dirt. She got very angry at him and said she had someone to love her at last, and now they would be going away so she would never have to see her hateful aunts again. She said, "I'm married to George and there's nothing they can do about it."

It was then that everything for Clarence became a gray light. He remembered scratching at her arms as she fought him. He remembered the feel of the knife's thick wooden handle in his hand and a choking sound. He remembered the cutting, like when he had watched his mother cut up a chicken for Christmas dinner. The cutting sound was soothing to him, with the glow of light around her like a halo, the scents of apples and cinnamon rising from the kitchen.

"Was that why there were so many cuts in her?" Missy asked, her face pale.

"I imagine so," Adele said.

But then his strength gave out and through the gray light was black and then red. He smelled the blood, and he thought at first he had stumbled upon a bird someone had killed in the woods. Then he saw Lillie lying on the ground and the knife in his hand, sticky with blood.

His mind was still hazy but he remembered Meyers telling them of a man he knew who killed his "lying and cheating" wife and threw the gun in the river. Clarence had asked why he did that and Meyers had answered, "'Cause if the police couldn't find the weapon, they wouldn't know she'd been shot by his gun and trace it back to him. They can do that with fingerprints now." Clarence asked what those were, and Meyers explained it to him.

He realized if they found the knife, they could take finger-prints — Meyers had said the police had them for everyone who had gotten arrested, and Clarence had that one time in San Jose — and know he was the one to stab Lillie.

He threw the knife as far as he could. Then he ran farther into the woods, far away from any light from the camps until it was pitch-black. He took off his coat, which also had blood, and threw it in the bushes.

"He was hiding evidence of his guilt." Missy nodded as she wrote it down.

"You should have heard how he told the police about the coat," Adele said. "He was so proud he'd 'thought it all up himself.'"

"I suppose they won't find it now." Missy sighed.

"They don't need to," Adele said. "He not only confessed but there was a witness."

"A witness to the crime?" Missy's figure was pointed like an arrow.

"Not quite," Adele said with a smile.

On his way back to camp, he ran into a soldier with hair so blond that it was glossy under the soldier's lantern. The man demanded to know what he was doing out after curfew. Clarence made an excuse about hearing a noise outside his tent. The soldier was dubious but escorted him back to the main camp. He grumbled how the civilians needed to let the soldiers do their job and left Clarence where he quickly fell asleep.

"My God!" Missy gasped. "Fell asleep after he'd just killed a woman."

"A child's mind forgets," Adele said.

"I hope the police find this soldier," Missy declared. "It would seal his fate for sure."

"They already did," Adele said. "With the help of the very effi- cient Lieutenant Edwards. The soldier's name is Private Hanson, and he admits although he was groggy that night, he remembers seeing Clarence and escorting him back to camp. He took Jack to the place he met Clarence and the route they took to his tent. There's no mistake about it."

"So that's that, then?" Missy leaned back and rubbed her wrist as she laid down her pencil. "All because he wanted to protect Miss Miriam and Miss Addie from disgrace."

"They were like his own mother," Adele said, then added in a sorrowful tone, "A boy who loves his mother will fight the most vicious monsters to protect her. Even those that don't exist."

CHAPTER 26

It was a week or so later when they decided they had done all they could for San Francisco and it was time to go home. They collected themselves near the entrance to the camp where Edwards had promised to bring the wagon to take them to the ferry.

Adele surveyed the camp as they walked to the gate. She felt less of the fear and hopelessness that had plagued her when they first came. People had now gotten to know their faces from the dining room tent and the washrooms, and many women smiled at them while some men came to talk to Jackson, telling a joke and laughing with him. Sheriff Hatfield had encountered a few old friends from his days on the San Francisco police force and they came, pumping his arm and thanking him for his help.

Elsie, who had gotten a few more recruits to help with the destitute women's aid, accompanied them while Valda stayed in the tent to supervise. Adele had seen the exhaustion leave Elsie's face in the last week as the recruits took over much of the brunt work and now she was enthusiastic. Several women's organizations from Nevada had written and promised to send supplies.

"Miss Grace is writing a whole series of stories about our

work," Elsie said. "She thinks she can get them into the national newspapers." She held tight to Adele's arm. "If she succeeds, we might be able to get aid from all over the country."

"I'm sure Missy will do her best," Adele said. When they reached the gate, she grasped both her friend's hands. "I only hope we did our part."

"You and Miss Branch did all right for yourselves," Elsie said with a sly look. "You helped bring a killer to justice."

"He's not brought to justice yet," Nin reminded her.

"He will be," said Elsie. "I suppose that was more important than handing out clothes to destitute women."

"Elsie!"

She laughed. "I meant it, dear. I wouldn't be surprised if that Sergeant Walker recommends you and Miss Branch for the San Francisco police force once it gets its bearings."

"How loathsome." Nin made a face.

"You know my offer still stands." Adele looked hard at Elsie. "It won't be easy doing your work from the camp if this keeps up much longer."

"I might consider it," her friend said. "For Papa's sake." She sighed, as she had received a letter from him just that morning. "I do miss the odd duck."

"He's not an odd duck," Nin said. "He's a very distinguished professor."

Elsie looked at her with amusement. "From what Adele told me, I didn't think you were such an enthusiastic supporter of the male sex, Miss Branch."

"Some of them are all right," Nin mumbled.

She laughed and gave Adele a warm embrace. "I'll expect, you and Miss Branch and Miss Grace over for tea once we have our new home."

"We'll be there," Adele promised. As she watched her friend trot back toward the tents, she felt a heavy heart.

Among the bobbing heads of the people walking in and out of the gate, she saw John.

"So you caught your culprit," he said as he took her hand. "Not that I had any doubt you would."

"We didn't do it alone," Adele reminded him. "We had the police behind us."

"Nevertheless, from what Jackson told me, you and Miss Branch are the ones who got Mr. Ross to confess."

"I'm sure he told you with much disapproval." Adele raised an eyebrow.

"And you agreed with him," Nin added.

"I don't think it was wise of you to go see him on your own," he admitted. "If a man's killed once, he can kill again."

"When a lawyer is standing up in court next to a murderer, does he think that if he killed one person, he'll kill him too?" Adele challenged. "Justice demands we disregard such things."

"Lawyers are trained to look for signs of criminality," he argued. "I wouldn't have wanted anything to happen to you." He said the last in a warm tone that touched Adele.

"You forgot I was with her," Nin said. "I wouldn't have let Clarence do anything."

Adele took her friend's arm. "Nin's as good as ten policemen."

John laughed. "From what Jackson told me, I'd say a roaring lion would be less dangerous when provoked."

Nin sniffed, showing she didn't think much of Jackson's analogy.

John looked at Adele with soft eyes. "Promise me you won't be a stranger."

"You keep trying to force her to make you promises," Nin barked.

"Promise you'll come to the city once it's been rebuilt and see what we've done with it."

Adele smiled. "Elsie has already invited us to tea once she and her father establish residence again."

"Then you'll come see me too," he insisted. "Alone." His eyes slid toward Nin. She raised her eyebrows but said nothing.

The smoke of dust flew around them and when it settled, Adele was face to face with George Wu. The young man was out of breath from having run so fast and his suit and shoes were covered with dust. "I was afraid I would miss you!"

"You shouldn't be on this side of camp, Mr. Wu," said John in a stern tone.

"I wanted to say goodbye to Adele and Miss Branch." Pausing as if to gather his courage, he added, "And to thank you for all you did to catch the man who killed my wife."

"Did you ever suspect Mr. Ross?" John asked, clearly curious.

The young man shook his head. "Lillie spoke of him only as a boarder. I don't think she even noticed him beyond another chair at the dinner table."

"That's why he almost got away with it," Nin said.

"I'm glad you and Adele didn't let that happen," George said.

"What are your plans now?" Adele asked.

"My father has secured passage for us for Hawaii on a boat sailing in a few weeks." Blinking, he added, "There are too many memories for us here."

"It's best to make a fresh start," Nin agreed.

"We might be able to buy a small shop there and he wants me to run it," said the young man. With a chuckle, he added, "He claims he's getting too old to stand on his feet all day long."

"Your plans have changed a little, then," Adele said.

"Sometimes one's plans change when one has lost everything." George gave a deep sigh.

There was silence for a moment and then John patted the man on the back. "I'll come with you back to camp. The soldiers won't bother you if I tell them you're a client of mine."

"Poor man," Adele said as she watched them disappear in the crowd. "He and Lillie were just starting their married life."

"I wouldn't have thought you that sentimental, Adele." Her

friend eyed her. "Don't tell me John Bellows has put the same idea into your head."

Adele grinned. "Not a chance, dear. I'm anxious to get back to my shop and see what Beatrice has done with it."

"Nothing good, I'm sure." Nin rolled her eyes.

The creaking sound of wheels and neighing horses brought Edwards with the wagon. As he jumped down, Adele stiffened a little. They had not spoken since the outburst in the hospital tent.

But it was clear the man intended to be amiable as he took his hat off and bowed. "Miss Gossling. I'd like to apologize."

"You should," Nin snarled.

"I apologize too," she said. "As Jack will tell you, my temper sometimes gets the better of my words."

"And as Jackson will tell *you*, I have a habit of jumping to conclusions based on what's in front of me instead of digging deeper," he said. "You were right about Mr. Wu having nothing to do with his wife's murder."

"Of course he had nothing to do with it," Nin said. "He loved her!"

"I wasn't seeing beyond his race," the man continued. "It was wrong and I won't repeat that mistake again."

"I'm pleased to hear it," Adele said. "If you don't, then maybe others working with you won't either."

"We part as friends then?" He held out his hand.

She took it. "There was never any question of that, Lieutenant. You're invited to our house in Arrojo whenever you wish."

"Thank you, Miss Gossling," he said with a bow. He repeated the gesture with Nin, who only sniffed.

Within a few days of their return to Arrojo, the Gosslings and Nin were invited to the Hatfields' for a welcome home feast.

The end of May hit Arrojo with the edge of spring as the blossoms in Lady Augusta's garden stretched their faces to the sun and seemed to resist the withering afternoon heat. The wave of sweet scents filled the air as they entered the gate.

"Isn't it lovely?" Adele closed her eyes and took a deep breath. "Mother Earth really does give her blessings after a tragedy."

"The flowers in Twin Peaks probably still smell of smoke and cinders," Jackson observed.

"Surely not." Adele stared. "The fires didn't even reach Twin Peaks."

"But the smoke may have," her brother said.

"Sister Sun will work her magic on them soon enough," Nin assured her.

"I'm sure you're right, Miss Branch." Jackson squeezed his sister's hand. "It's good to be home, isn't it?"

"Only three days," she reminded him. "I haven't even gone over the sales receipts to see what chaos Bea has made of them."

"You're lucky she didn't sell off the entire store for a song," Nin remarked. "She practically gave those ink wells away!"

"I'd have a sharp word with her, Del," Jackson said.

"I mean to," Adele said. "I suppose she thought with the check from the council we could easily get new ones."

"I have to hand it to Mrs. Faderman," Jackson said. "I thought her promise to see to it Arrojo businesses received compensation for damages was all talk."

"The shrew does a lot of talking but she never makes promises she can't keep," Nin pointed out.

"I can buy some new typewriters now and maybe even set up a corner for ladies writing desks," Adele said.

"Maybe if ladies here had more options for a writing desk, they would write more and talk less," Nin agreed.

"And what will you do with your check, Miss Branch?" Jackson asked as he stopped short of the door. "Will you also be expanding your shop?"

Nin smiled sweetly. "No, Mr. Gossling. I'll be doing what I've always done."

He laughed and knocked on the door.

Lady Augusta did not disappoint. When they went into the dining room, the table was so crowded with Rowena's delectable dishes that Adele could hardly find room to put a plate down once she had lifted it up.

"You've outdone yourself, dear." Lady Augusta patted Rowena's arm.

"After those army rations, this is a feast." Jackson helped himself generously from every dish.

"Don't let Ruth hear you say that." Adele laughed. "She might get offended and think her cooking isn't good enough for you."

"It's not Ruth who gets offended," said Nin. "It's her husband. Funny how men get offended about things they know nothing about." She cast a glare at Jackson.

"I adore Ruth's cooking and she knows it," Jackson said.

"When did the Cordobas get back?" Hatfield asked.

"Only the day after we did," said Adele. "Jack's been helping to restore order there. It's almost as if Tomas forgot everything when they were away."

"I'm glad they were able to help their people," Lady Augusta said with a nod of approval. "That's as it should be. When tragedy happens, everyone helps."

Jackson looked at his superior. "How did things go at the station, sir?"

"You mean did Edison let crime run rampant in the county while we were gone?" Sheriff Hatfield chuckled. "The lad did better than I expected."

"I'm sure he didn't do better than *I* expected," Jackson grumbled. "Eugene Gardner stopped me at the post office this morning. It seems some of the boys down on Quarry Lane have been stealing food from the restaurant's kitchen. He said he told Edison about it a week ago."

"And Edison told me he spoke to the kitchen staff and found one of their busboys has a few friends down there who have been left with short supplies from the earthquake," the sheriff said. "The entire staff agreed to turn a blind eye to their taking food."

"Pringle can afford it," Nin said.

"Eugene is the one who's been getting Pringle's wrath," Jackson argued. "He wants to be a partner next year but Pringle's been on him about it."

"Mr. Pringle will find any excuse not to give his son-in-law a piece of his business," Adele said. "You know that, Jack."

"I think Edison was right not to get involved," Hatfield said. "I also think he did a fine job while we were away." He looked at the centerpiece on the table for a moment, lost in thought.

"Anything wrong, Horatio?" his mother asked.

He took her hand and kissed it. "Nothing at all, Ma. I was just thinking. Edison's a hard-working lad and while he may not be as bright as I would wish him, he's got the compassion necessary to make a good lawman."

"I think you give him too much credit, sir," Jackson said.

"I agree with the sheriff," Adele said. "He has a good heart and a policeman's way of thinking about the law. Perhaps he lacks a little common sense —"

"A little!" Nin snorted.

"But if you're thinking of promoting him, it might be just the thing he needs," Adele finished.

"Promoting him!" Jackson dropped his fork. "Surely not, sir."

"Well, we'll see," said Sheriff Hatfield with a chuckle.

"We were rather lonely here without you all, weren't we, Rowena?" Lady Augusta's grated tone tossed over her shoulder as she glanced at her companion.

"Like flies dead in the lime," Rowena replied with her usual strange associations.

"We weren't dead," Nin insisted. "Only one of us."

"Not even us," Hatfield added.

"The poor girl." Lady Augusta sighed. "To think of her the way Horatio said you found her —" She bit her lip. "No one ought to do that to any human, not even an animal."

"I imagine the prosecution will try to make Mr. Ross out to be just that," Jackson said.

"Has he a good lawyer?" Adele put down her fork.

"He's not exactly rich, Del," said her brother.

"I'm sure Sergeant Walker will do the best he can to help him find one," said Hatfield.

"I think those scarecrow aunts of Lillie's ought to pay for it," Nin said. "He did it for them, after all."

"If they're as socially conscious as Adele says, I doubt they would dare help the young man who killed their niece." Lady Augusta plucked a slice of bread from the basket. "And I daresay I wouldn't blame them."

"They haven't got much to be socially conscious about now," Adele said. "Missy wrote me all the women who were friendly with them at the camp now avoid them. They even insisted the army move Miss Miriam and Miss Addie's tent."

"At least they see the aunts as we do," Nin said with satisfaction.

"I don't think so, dear," Adele said. "Missy says they told her they can't abide by ladies taking in a boarder who is a killer."

"But that's not fair!" Nin said. "They didn't know he was going to kill their niece."

"Ladies of society are rarely fair, dear," Lady Augusta said with a chuckle. "You know that better than anybody.

Nin grimaced and Adele thought of the way Mrs. Faderman and the ladies had treated Nin, keeping alive the rumor that she was a witch not to be tampered with.

"In spite of everything, I feel sorry for them," Adele said. "They have only each other now and neither of them are young. I've asked Elsie and Valda to help them get settled once more shacks are built. They might even find some work doing needlepoint. Missy says Miss Addie has a wonderful hand with lace." In a softer tone, she added, "They're going to need all the help they can get."

"Everybody will be starting from scratch," Hatfield agreed, taking a large chunk of corned beef, one of his favorites. "I'm sure in six months, those ladies who shunned them will be seeking their friendship again."

"In six months, hopefully Mr. Ross will be in jail where he belongs," Jackson said in a harsh tone. "I don't like the idea of that jail tent. But Monte told me they have it well guarded."

"Horatio feels rather sorry for the boy. Horatio!" His mother tapped the side of his shoe with her cane. "Don't you feel sorry for the boy?"

"In a way, Ma," he said.

"But, sir, he's a killer," Jackson said. "He admitted to killing Miss Sweenie —"

"Mrs. Wu," Adele reminded him.

"He admitted to killing Mrs. Wu and then trying to hide the fact," her brother continued with a meaningful glance at her. "He had no remorse whatsoever when he told us about it. He went to sleep the same night he knifed her." This earned a shudder from Lady Augusta, for which Jackson bowed in apology.

Hatfield leaned back, his linen napkin hanging over his lap like a bib. "I had a lad working on my ship one time who was about as lacking in intelligence as Mr. Ross," he said. "He adored animals. Tried to bring a cat on board, but my first mate caught him before we left the dock." He chuckled. "It turns out we had a rat in the cargo and he caught it and kept it as a pet until we were halfway at sea." His face darkened a little. "When the doctor saw it, he was horrified."

"It was diseased?" Adele nearly dropped her spoon.

Hatfield nodded. "Two of our men died before we could get them to shore to a hospital."

"I hope you dealt severely with him, sir," Jackson said in a rough tone.

"I didn't. The authorities did," he said. "Clarence reminded me of that young man. The way he completely broke down once he realized what he'd done, even though he didn't realize at the time what he was doing was harming others."

"Just like a child," Adele observed.

"I'm sure the lawyer Sergeant Walker finds for Mr. Ross will make the case for his mental incompetence," Jackson said. "Can't say I approve of such a defense."

"You're not a lawyer, Mr. Gossling," Nin pointed out.

"That's right," he said. "I'm not a criminal lawyer." His face set with a crustiness that Adele knew came from thinking about their father.

They retired to the parlor with the coffee just as Rowena brought in the evening paper. Jackson picked it up and sat back on the chair opposite Hatfield.

"Mr Gossling!" Nin growled. "It's very rude to read the paper when you're a guest in someone's house."

"Force of habit, I suppose," Jackson said as he set it down. "I'm sorry, Lady Augusta."

"Not at all, not at all." She waved him away. "I like to see a man enjoy his paper."

Adele glanced at the page and saw the byline with Missy's name on it. She couldn't resist and picked it up, reading it quickly. Missy told of the interview she had with Mr. Ross, who was being moved to San Quentin State Prison the next day. She couldn't help but feel warmed by the sentiment Missy showed toward Clarence. Her last line was "With the light falling over the buzzing camp as everyone prepares for dinner, Mr. Clarence Ross sits, his head bent, clutching at the silver gift the aunts of the dead woman gave him.'"

"You can't hold on to the rubble," she murmured. "You have to clear it and build something new and better."

"Did you say something, Del?" Jackson blinked.

"Nothing." She folded the paper neatly and put it back on the table.

~~~~~

Author's Note

Hello reader!

You're getting this second author's note as a big THANK YOU for reading Book 7 of the Adele Gossling Mysteries. If you've made it this far in the series, I can only assume you love the sassy and sensitive Adele Gossling and her clairvoyant friend, Nin Branch, as much as I do!

This book is a very special one for me because, as someone who used to live in San Francisco (and would live there still if it weren't for the prohibitive cost of living in the city), its history has always intrigued me. The Great San Francisco Earthquake of 1906 was a chance to make the city better than it was and shrug off the unsavory reputation that it had acquired since the days of the Forty-Niners. The notorious reforms of the Progressive Era also came in and created a better city by throwing corrupt city officials out of office and cleaning up places like Maiden Lane and the Barbary Coast. While San Francisco didn't become a completely pristine town, it became a place that offered much more than vice and sin.

I had no idea when I was writing this book that its publication would be so timely. As I was putting on the last finishing touches to the final proofread, elsewhere in the United States, natural disasters were happening. Not earthquakes and fires this time,
~~~~~

but hurricanes, tornadoes, and floods. On September 26, 2024, Hurricane Helene hit Florida, learning 250 people dead. Then, on October 9, 2024, scarcely two weeks after, Hurricane Milton hit roughly the same area, taking at least 130 lives. The damage to homes and buildings was, like in the 1906 earthquake and fires, enormous.

But the 21st century is now a global world, unlike in the early 20th century, and these types of disasters touch all of us. As an adult ESL teacher of mainly Spanish students, I was deeply touched by the stories I heard from them about the flash floods that hit the eastern region of Valencia on October 29, 2024. As I write this, the death toll is still being tallied, with more than 200 people killed. Many of my students have family and friends or coworkers in that region.

We are all one world. What happens in one part of it affects us all in any era, past or present.

What's next? Well, a lot of things. Book 8 of the Adele Gossling Mysteries won't be out for a while, but you can catch a preview of it in the next pages. And in 2025, I'll be launching a whole new series! You can read all about the Grave Sisters Mysteries (more about the series here: https://tammayauthor.com/about-pages/about-the-grave-sisters-mysteries-series) and an excerpt from the first book, *The Case of the Washed-Up Corpse* (which you can find on preorder at all online bookstores here: https://tammayau thor.com/the-case-of-the-washed-up-corpse-grave-sisters-mysteries-book-1) when you turn the page!

. . .

Happy reading!
Tam

BOOK 8 INFORMATION

The publication date for this book is yet unknown, but here's a sneak peek at the cover and blurb!

Literature and culture come to Arrojo in the wake of the Great San Francisco Earthquake of 1906—but at what price?

Now that the 1906 San Francisco Earthquake and Fires are but a distant memory, things are back to normal in Arrojo. Adele

Gossling is even expanding her shop to sell women's writing desks and convincing her friend Nin Branch to act more like a businesswoman than a wild mountain woman.

Her timing could be better, as a trainload of literary enthusiasts arrive in Arrojo looking for a place to set up shop away from the city that is still being rebuilt. Encouraged by the town council, they form the Calliope Society and draw people to their inaugural soiree.

The spectators get more than they bargained for when one of the society's leading poets keels over on stage, pronounced dead on the spot.

The police are at a loss about where to start, as the man has a long list of enemies, including his own wife and his best friend.

It's a mess that only Adele and her spiritualist friend Nin can get them out of!

Want to stay updated on when this book comes out? Consider joining my mailing list! Details to come in later pages of this book about that, but in the meantime, turn the page for information about my new upcoming series!

GRAVE SISTERS MYSTERIES BOOK 1 INFORMATION

Introducing… The Grave Sisters Mysteries!

Coming in 2025

Three sisters couldn't be more different but share one thing in common — a taste for solving crimes!

. . .

It's 1921 and Americans are still reeling from the effects of World War I. In a small town on the California/Nevada border, three sisters own the only mortuary in town. The eldest, Eve, clings to values from the past and takes care of the administrative and accounting tasks of the business. Middle sister Helena uses her scientific and medical knowledge for the more hands-on side of the business. Eighteen-year-old Violet, the youngest, skirts the edge of a flapper's life, preferring parties and bootleg liquor over funeral services and burials.

Then the new district attorney of Gyver County asks them for assistance in identifying the body of a young woman found to have committed suicide in a remote part of the river. Only it isn't suicide — it's murder!

As far as the sisters are concerned, murder is police business. Their business is to see the dead are at peace, body and soul. But District Attorney Oliver Clarke needs their knowledge of the town and its people to help him and they can't say no.

What follows is a twisted tale with few clues to untangle it: a missing engagement ring, a piece of rope, and a torn lapel.

For more information about this new series, check out this page: https://tammayauthor.com/about-pages/about-the-grave-sisters-mysteries-series.

Read on for an excerpt from this book!

"What gives?" the sheriff repeated, glaring at the two women.

"I want Miss Grave and Mrs. Wright to see the body," said Oliver.

The sheriff's cigar almost fell out of his mouth. "This ain't no place for women!"

"You forget, Sheriff, we're no strangers to corpses," Eve said.

"We know them better than you do," Helena added with an even look.

"I got the coroner on my hands and Parks with his damn Kodak and now women!" the man grumbled.

"Parks is here because I called him," Oliver said in a gruff tone. "Maybe you haven't heard, Warner, but police take photographs of the crime scene these days."

"Maybe they do in the city where you was, but not here."

"As long as I'm district attorney, we'll do things right," Oliver said. "Tell your men this isn't a peep show! Get out of there!" His roaring voice made the men scatter like deer fleeing a hungry tiger.

Sheriff Warner bit down on his cigar. "I spoke to Peterson on the phone. He'll be down soon."

"Good," Oliver said. "We don't want the papers speculating before the coroner has made his ruling."

"He thinks we ought to get Dan Frazier here." The sheriff led them carefully down the slippery incline that separated the road from the river bed. "Might turn out to be his case."

"The girl's on our side of the river," Oliver insisted.

"That don't mean she didn't get killed on the Nevada side," Sheriff Warner insisted.

Oliver helped Helena down the last muddy piece of the incline. Eve could see the overgrowth had been stripped away, probably by the police. Now that the officers had cleared the way, the figure of a girl was in plain sight.

"Poor thing," she murmured.

"I told you this ain't no place for women," The sheriff growled.

"Better our sympathy eyes than the gawking ones of your men," Helena snapped, taking her sister's arm. "Come on, Eve."

They stepped carefully along to the edge of the river, as the chalky dirt had turned into mud. Oliver hurried around them, flicking on his flashlight.

"Evening, Parks." He nodded at the wiry young man with the camera as he crouched at the feet of the body lying on the ground "Getting much?"

"How can I when the sheriff won't keep the flashlight here?" He grumbled. "Only so much I can do with the flash lamp." He greeted the sisters with a smile. "Giving the corpse the full treatment, eh?"

"Eve and Helena are here is see if they know who the girl is," said Oliver.

He nodded with approval. "These ladies even know the new additions before they're born."

"I assume that's a compliment?" Helena eyed him. He tipped his hat in response.

"With all due respect, Mr. Clarke, I can't see why Miss Grave and Mrs. Wright would know who the girl is if I don't," said Sheriff Warner. "Warners have been 'round here at least as long as the Graves have."

"People ain't afraid of Miss Grave like they are of you, Sheriff," Parks said with a chuckle. "Well, and I guess Miss Grave has a way with her so people tell her things."

"Yes, I noticed that," Oliver said, smiling.

Is Sheriff Warner right? Is a river bed with a dead body lying beside it no place for women? Or is he just afraid the Grave sisters will show him up by solving the case before he does? Find out by preordering your copy of *The Case of the Washed-Up Corpse* from your favorite online bookstore <u>here</u>: https:// tammayauthor.com/the-case-of-the-washed-up-corpse-grave-sisters-mysteries-book-1

How about a little more of the Adele Gossling Mysteries, right here, right now? Read on for how to get hold of my free novella, *The Missing Ruby Necklace*.

"Coffee!" Miss McCarthy laughed. "Heavens, no! I haven't had my first taste of champagne yet." She flung her hand out to her brother. "Bring me a bottle of champagne, my good man."

"I don't mind," he said.

Before he could saunter out the door, Mrs. Abberton jumped up. "I'll get it."

"I really think we ought to get coffee," Mr. Abberton mumbled.

"She wants champagne," Mrs. Abberton was almost stern. "It's a celebration, after all!" She practically fled from the room.

Adele followed her and caught her arm. She spoke in a soft tone. "Mrs. Abberton, why did Miss McCarthy faint?"

"She just told you, didn't she?" The woman gave a shrill laugh. "Albert said we ought to open some windows, but it was such a windy night, I —"

"It wasn't the windows," said Adele. "Or the corset."

"Of course it was!" The woman examined some bottles on the floor. "I never could read these labels."

"You were staring at Miss McCarthy as if something more was wrong."

"What an imagination you have, dear," the woman said.

"Miss McCarthy had her hands on her throat when she fell," Adele continued. "You were looking at her throat."

"Nonsense," the woman hissed.

"I noticed she wasn't wearing her ruby necklace," Adele declared.

Mrs. Abberton tore through a row of bottles lying on a table. One rolled onto the floor with a crack and the bubbly drink spilled across the marble. She sunk into one of the chairs. "You've always been very observant, Miss Gossling."

"You saw it too."

"Just before the lights went out," she said. "But Eleanor is one of those girls who gets easily flustered with her jewelry. She says it weighs her down."

"If that's true, why were you so alarmed?" Adele asked.

"I wasn't," the woman insisted. "She has a locked box for that necklace. Albert tried to persuade her to put it in our safe, but she refused."

"That's rather unusual," Adele said.

"Eleanor's a lovely girl, but rather flighty," the woman said in a harsh tone. "I expect Celestine spoils her."

"If the necklace is missing, there might be a theft involved," Adele suggested.

Jewelry goes missing all the time. But does that mean theft? And why is Mrs. Abberton so nervous?

How can you get your hands on a copy of *The Missing Ruby Necklace*, not available in any bookstore? Simple. Go to this link: https://landing.mailerlite.com/webforms/landing/ l2u0c3. What else will you get when you get this novella? How about fun facts about women in history and true crime classic mysteries, which are just as fascinating, if not more so, as contemporary true crimes?

ABOUT THE AUTHOR

Writing has been Tam's voice since the age of fourteen. She writes stories set in the past that feature sassy and sensitive women characters. Her fiction gives readers the experience of women struggling to carve out an identity for themselves during eras when their options were limited. Her stories are set mostly around the Bay Area because she adores sourdough bread, Ghirardelli chocolate, and San Francisco history.

Tam is the author of the Adele Gossling Mysteries which takes place in the early 20th century and features suffragist and epistolary expert Adele Gossling whose talent for solving crimes doesn't sit well with her town's conventional ideas about women and their place.

Tam is also working on a new series, the Grave Sisters Mysteries about three sisters who own a funeral home and help the county

D.A. solve crimes in a 1920s small California town. The first book of the series is up for preorder now and will be coming out in 2025.

In addition, Tam writes historical fiction about women breaking loose from the social and psychological expectations of their time. She has a 4-book series set in the 1890s titled the Waxwood Series and a post-World War II short story collection available.

Although Tam left her heart in San Francisco, she lives in the Midwest because it's cheaper. When she's not writing, she's devouring everything classic (books, films, art, music), concocting yummy plant-based dishes, and exploring her new riverside town.

Tam May can be reached at:
WEBSITE: http://tammayauthor.com/
EMAIL: tammay70@tammayauthor.com
FACEBOOK: https://www.facebook.com/tammayauthor
INSTAGRAM: https://www.instagram.com/tammayauthor/
PINTEREST: https://www.pinterest.com/tammayauthor/